ANTHROPOCOSMIC THEATRE

THEATRE, RITUAL, CONSCIOUSNESS

NICOLÁS NÚÑEZ

TRANSLATED
BY RONAN J. FITZSIMONS AND HELENA GUARDIA

REVISED AND EXPANDED EDITION
EDITED BY
DEBORAH MIDDLETON AND FRANC CHAMBERLAIN

Published by University of Huddersfield Press

University of Huddersfield Press
The University of Huddersfield
Queensgate
Huddersfield HD1 3DH
Email enquiries university.press@hud.ac.uk

Text © 2019
2nd Edition first published 2019

1st Edition published by Harwood Academic Publishers GmbH 1996 as *Anthropocosmic Theatre: Rite in the Dynamics of Theatre*

'At Play in the Cosmos' originally published in *The Drama Review* in 2001.

'Secular Sacredness' originally published in *Performance Research* in 2008.

'High Risk Theatre' originally published in Spanish in Núñez, N. *Teatro de alto riesgo* by Consejo Editorial de TIT de UNAM in 2007.

This work is licensed under a Creative Commons Attribution 4.0 International License

Images © as attributed

Every effort has been made to locate copyright holders of materials included and to obtain permission for their publication.

The publisher is not responsible for the continued existence and accuracy of websites referenced in the text.

A CIP catalogue record for this book is available from the British Library.

ISBN: 978-1-86218-160-1

Designed by Dawn Cockcroft

Cover illustration © Emigdio Guevara

For María, Miranda, Jimena, Grizelda and Helena.
And for Roberta, Nicolás and Alexia.
To all the members of the gang, wherever they may be.

CONTENTS

ACKNOWLEDGEMENTS · I

PART ONE:
ANTHROPOCOSMIC THEATRE (1975 - 1990) · 1
Nicolás Núñez

FOREWORD TO THE FIRST EDITION · 3
Deborah Middleton

INTRODUCTION · 7

1 TIBETAN THEATRE · 11

2 NAHUATLAN THEATRE · 33

3 WESTERN THEATRE · 53

4 ANTHROPOCOSMIC THEATRE · 89

PART TWO:
BEYOND ANTHROPOCOSMIC THEATRE (1990 - 2018) · 147
Edited By Deborah Middleton & Franc Chamberlain

INTRODUCTION TO PART TWO
Deborah Middleton · 149

AT PLAY IN THE COSMOS: THE THEATRE AND RITUAL OF NICOLÁS NÚÑEZ
Deborah Middleton · 153

SNAPSHOT 1: THE COMMUNAL SELF
John Britton · 183

SNAPSHOT 2: SWIMMING IN THE INNER SOURCE: A WORKSHOP WITH NICOLÁS NÚÑEZ
Cassiano Sydow Quilici · 187

'SECULAR SACREDNESS' IN THE RITUAL THEATRE OF
NICOLÁS NÚÑEZ
Deborah Middleton — 189

SNAPSHOT 3: WHAT THE *TALLER DE INVESTIGACIÓN
TEATRAL* REVEALED TO ME
Etzel Cardeña — 215

SNAPSHOT 4: AND I SANG
Edward McGurn — 219

DEFINING THE DYNAMICS
Deborah Middleton — 223

SNAPSHOT 5: CONTEMPLATIVE RUNNING
Daniel Plá — 241

SNAPSHOT 6: *CITLALMINA* AND *NANAHUATZIN*
MEXICO (2010 - 2016)
Karoliina Sandström — 243

SNAPSHOT 7: BEING THE SUN - *NANAHUATZIN*
Tray Wilson — 247

PLOTTING A PATH FOR LATER STEPS: TUNING IN
WITH NÚÑEZ, RANCIÈRE, AND SOLOGUB
Franc Chamberlain — 251

CASE STUDY: THE FLIGHT OF QUETZALCOATL –
TEOTIHUACAN, MEXICO (2000)
Deborah Middleton — 263

HIGH RISK THEATRE
Nicolás Núñez — 267

CASE STUDY: CONSPIRACIÓN HAMLET -
CASA DEL LAGO, CHAPULTEPEC,
MEXICO CITY (2012)
Karoliina Sandström   289

MANDALA: THE SACRED ART OF ACTING -
A PLAY IN ONE ACT
Nicolás Núñez   293

THEATRE AS A SECRET SOURCE
Nicolás Núñez   311

CASE STUDY: PUENTES INVISIBLES –
CHAPULTEPEC FOREST, MEXICO (2016)
Cash Clay   321

SNAPSHOT: EL ENSUEÑO DE LOS ÁRBOLES
- A REFLECTION
Ana Luisa Solís   325

COSMIC MANNERS
Nicolás Núñez   327

APPENDIX I   **335**

A SUMMARY OF MY LEARNING
Alí Ehécatl   335

APPENDIX II   **353**

SPEECHES   353

CONTRIBUTORS   **377**

INDEX   **381**

ACKNOWLEDGEMENTS

We are grateful for the generosity we have received from the Dalai Lama and from all the sentient beings who, consciously or unconsciously, have helped us in the development of our work.

We thank the National Autonomous University of Mexico, alma mater of our country, which has lovingly sustained our research for almost fifty years, and the University of Huddersfield, our 'alma mater' in the UK.

We are grateful to all the members of the gang, past, present and future, especially to Dr. Deborah Middleton and Helena Guardia for their unconditional support of the *Taller de Investigación Teatral* UNAM.

Nicolás Núñez (April 2018)

PART ONE
ANTHROPOCOSMIC THEATRE

Nicolás Núñez

Translated by Ronan J. Fitzsimons

FOREWORD TO THE FIRST EDITION

Anthropocosmic theatre is the term given by Nicolás Núñez to the participatory theatre form developed by himself and his 'gang', as he refers to the *Taller de Investigación Teatral* (Theatre Research Workshop). Based in Mexico City, under the auspices of the National Autonomous University, Nuñez has been working on his project for the past twenty years. This book, first published in Spanish in 1987, is both a dossier of Núñez's researches in pre-Hispanic Mexican, Tibetan, and Western theatre, and also an exposition of the consequent theatrical form, anthropocosmic theatre.

My intention in writing this foreword is to offer the reader some guides to and perspectives on Núñez's work, in order that the early chapters may be contextualised, and that the direction of Núñez's development may be clear from the outset. These comments are based upon my experiences of Núñez's work both in the workshop which he ran at a Centre for Performance Research conference in Cardiff in January 1993, and during my time spent working and talking with Nicolás and colleagues in Mexico City in November 1993. The points which I touch on here will, on the whole, be expanded upon within Núñez's text in the final section of Part One.

An essential feature of anthropocosmic theatre is its participatory quality. All of Núñez's work involves audience participation although this occurs to differing degrees. A 'dynamic' or 'action' such as *Citlalmina* activates all participants equally; the actors serve as guides in what is, essentially, a ritual dance. *Los Cenci*, premiered in 1993, uses a more conventional actor-audience relationship where the spectators' participation is more subtle and encourages self-speculation rather than physical involvement. Between these two extremes lie various experiments with formal relationships; the objective is always the same - whether by physical or emotional means to involve the spectator in the raising and focusing of energy, and in a journey of self-knowledge.

The journey to self-knowledge is a theme inherent in many kinds of theatrical activity, and, in a heightened form, in paratheatrical activity in particular. 'Paratheatre' involves the use of dramatic structures and psychophysical exercises to reawaken the participant's sensitivity to the self, to others, and to nature. For Núñez, working within a culture still fascinated by the Aztec cosmology of its ancestors, paratheatre becomes 'anthropocosmic theatre' - a theatre concerned with 'man' in the cosmos; the human sense of our place in the Universe. The dance-ritual, *Citlalmina*, developed by the *Taller*, contains within it 'mandalas in movement'; representations of the patterns of the universe transformed into physical actions. The language of the body-code, whilst being iconic to a degree, is designed to raise and focus mental and physical energies (which are 'offered', not withheld). Other dynamics involve the principle of meditation through movement, the intensifying of visceral sensitivity and physical awareness. A central principle within each action is the requirement to focus oneself upon the here-and-now. This demands a great mental effort - a continual drawing together of mind and body - and results in an intensified sense of experience and a peace of mind which would seem to arise from one's centrality within the present moment (thoughts of past and future are dispelled). This raising and consolidating of energy is both a key to the fullest experience of the work, and also an important end in itself - the fight against mental and energetic dispersal; the attempt to inhabit one's own experience.

Clearly this activity has similarities with ancient systems such as Yoga or Tai Chi, and, indeed, many of the actions were generated from research into, and experience of, pre-Hispanic dance forms. *Citlalmina* is itself, as you will read, a blend of Nahuatlan and early Tibetan dance.

The dramatic substance of Núñez's participatory theatre revolves around myth and archetype, and this factor is significant to the anthropocosmic character of the work. Núñez seeks to establish a contact with the mythic past through the archetypes and emblems of the collective unconscious. In this, he feels, there lies a key to existential security, to a sense of one's place in history and a connectedness to the world and to the past. The performance events and 'actions' which Núñez describes in this book draw most frequently upon the imagery of Nahuatlan religio-philosophy. Whilst physically the actions bring participants to a state of holistic balance and well-being, the mythological content offers what many mythologists would see as ballast for the soul. For Núñez, these ciphers from the past may provide answers to ontological insecurity and a sense of continuity with history.

This aspect of anthropocosmic theatre gives it a special place in contemporary Mexico since it encourages a redressing of the imbalance between the Nahuatlan and Hispanic cultures and thereby makes possible a fuller personal cultural identity for the participants. In this respect, Núñez's participatory theatre form could provide a significant model for those working within multicultural or segregated communities in other parts of the world.

Núñez believes the work has further significance in the modern world of enforced leisure time. As an alternative to the numerous secular activities - many of them technological - with which we fill our time, Núñez suggests a form of play with more holistic rewards; 'games' in which all aspects of the human body, mind and spirit are engaged and refreshed. For Núñez, theatre has the potential to offer the structured dramatic situations which, involving human contact and in the context of the natural world, might become new 'rites' for personal development. These would be games which would enhance real life; which would not kill time, but 'enlighten' it; in which the players would not lose themselves, but would find themselves.

Deborah Middleton (1996)

NOTE ON THE SECOND EDITION (2019)

Originally published by Harwood Academic Publishers in 1996, **Part One** was translated by Ronan J. Fitzsimons. The sections of **Part Two** originally written in Spanish were translated by Helena Guardia (with the exception of *Mandala* which was translated by Karoliina Sandström and Helena Guardia); these texts are indicated in footnotes.

In places, minor amendments to the 1996 translation have been made, in order to reflect a more nuanced understanding of the author's original intentions. Additional footnotes and citations have been added.

In the foreword above, and in the republished articles that constitute chapters five and six, the English translation of *Taller de Investigación Teatral* was used, abbreviated to TRW, but since Núñez's group is known everywhere as the *Taller*, in this volume, where possible, we have retained the Spanish title in its short form.

Deborah Middleton (2019)

INTRODUCTION

Faced with the need to find dramatic forms which allow us to investigate actively our body and mind, we have undertaken searches in the theatrical rite area with the purpose of developing devices of 'participatory theatre' which give back to our organism its capacity to be the echo box of the cosmos.

The text we are introducing now does not claim to be a highbrow study of the dramatic trends or sources with which we deal. As modest investigators, we simply want to make an account of our influences, so as to share our point of view and to make our vision of an anthropocosmic theatre understandable to those who may be interested. Having been fortunate enough, on the one hand, to study Tibetan theatrical rite both at the Tibetan Institute of Performing Arts, and in various monasteries in India and, on the other hand, to research Nahuatlan ritual theatre at the Autonomous National University of Mexico, as well as in the indigenous communities, we decided to summarise briefly these two dramatic sources and link them with the studies we have done on western theatre.

So as not to lead scholars astray, we would emphasise that both Tibetan and Nahuatlan theatre, and the trends in western theatre set out in this text, are treated synthetically and exclusively from the point of view of our particular interest.

We share the concern of those who see the possibility of developing a new art involving contemporary scientific skill and archaic instruments of ritual, the religiousness of the East, the scientific skill of the West, and whatever Central America may offer for this new construction.

It must be said that the research into theatrical rite which we carry out in our workshop is very close, in its focus, to quantum thought: science of the future - bearing Capra in mind - which allows us to imagine dramatic designs as complicated machines of concentration and direction of energy; theatrical spaces and atmospheres as vehicles of cosmic conciliation; play structures of revision and transformation of our condition, and not only of information and entertainment.

The final part of this text sets out our workshop's principles and ways of working. Here we share some schemes of participatory theatre which are based on the idea of an anthropocosmic theatre.

When I entitle a chapter 'Tibetan Theatre', 'Nahuatlan Theatre', or use names such as Stanislavski, Brecht, Strasberg and Grotowski, my intention is not to make an analysis of their work, but rather to mention some aspects which are of interest in relation to our work.

When we study our body, we are also studying part of the cosmos. Not all behaviour systems understand this truth. Our research stems from this thought to draw us closer to theatre in an anthropocosmic way.

It is not our intention to formulate a theatrical system under the heading of 'Anthropocosmic Theatre'. Anthropocosmic theatre is a research process which recognises that there are as many systems as there are performers in the world.

Nicolás Núñez

The efforts of Nicolás Núñez and his theatre group have a special interest which I would dare to call essential: re-discovering the inspiration and the logic of ancient rituals.

Theatre is literature and spectacle, play and catharsis, but it is also an initiation ceremony. Núñez and his colleagues have striven to re-introduce the sacred dimension into theatre.

Octavio Paz

ANTHROPOCOSMIC THEATRE

1 TIBETAN THEATRE

Walking along a red-stone track dotted with monkeys, exotic birds and cawing crows, we reached the Tibetan Institute of Performing Arts in Dharamsala, in the north of India. This Institute was founded by the Dalai Lama in 1960 to promote and preserve Tibetan culture.

As soon as we arrived, we learned that we would soon be setting out for Bodhgaya, the place where Buddha was enlightened. There, the Institute was to take part, with its theatre and dances, in the Tibetan celebrations of the Kalachakra.

We made use of the few days we had before starting the trip to consult documents in the Tibetan library relating to the history of the country's theatre and dance. The material we found there was enough to keep a reader occupied for several weeks, if not months, mainly due to the fact that there is no precise information concerning this subject - all the information is spread around articles, books full of symbols, and the verbal communications of the Tibetans themselves. We worked discreetly on this material as and when we could, both before and after the trip to Bodhgaya, in the months we spent in Dharamsala.

It can be said that Tibetan theatre originated in the 8th Century AD, when the Tibetan King Chisongdegan (742-797) invited an Indian monk named Padmasambhava to preach his teachings in Tibet.

Padmasambhava arrived in Tibet in approximately 779 AD. He began preaching and came into contact with the regional festivities. Since he was a holy man, (it was he who helped to introduce Buddhism firmly in Tibet, by establishing and consecrating the first Buddhist monastery in Samye), he was asked to bless the spaces, exorcise the demons and summon up good fortune, among many other things. Everything seems to indicate that his work was that of a shaman or magician.

When he had been settled in Tibet for some time, Padmasambhava composed the Dance of the Wizard or the Dance of the Black Hat, taking for the composition local rhythms and elements of Tibet, many of them connected with the Bon tradition.

This shamanic dance which united rhythm and folklore was established in Tibet with the name of Garcham and it survives to this day.

Six hundred years later in 1395 a Tibetan saint, Thangton Gyalpo, took up this dance in the following way:

Myth relates that Thangton Gyalpo noted that two neighbouring villages could benefit from the exchange of their produce, but they were separated by an abyss. He therefore persuaded certain authorities to help him pay for a bridge to join the two villages. He obtained financial help and began to build the bridge. But due to certain unforeseen expenses, the money ran out before the bridge could be finished. Thangton Gyalpo knew that he could not ask his benefactors for more money, so it occurred to him to get together the most beautiful women from his group of workers, and based on the Dance of the Wizard, which by this time was famous, he organised the recital and singing of some local stories and Buddhist sayings. In this way he established a structure which spectacularly combined the telling of mythical stories, song, dance and the preaching of Buddhist sutras. The first play was called *Spun/bdun* (The Seven Relations). Some researchers interpret it as The Seven Brothers and others as The Seven Sisters.

So Thangton Gyalpo was able on the one hand to get together the money he needed and hence finish the bridge, and on the other hand to give rise to the birth of Tibetan opera theatre.

This Tibetan opera theatre is known as *Ache Lhamo*. The structure promoted by Thangton Gyalpo gained momentum as the years went by and became defined as an established cultural form of the Tibetan spirit. It was at the same time a religious and a secular structure.

Between 1617 and 1682, the fifth Dalai Lama decreed that the by now consolidated Tibetan opera should be performed separately from religious services; hence an independent art was created. It became firmly established as a secular art, respectful of religious services. This structure has prevailed to this day.

In ancient times opera festivals were held once a year, on the Tibetan plateau; they were called *Zol-ston*. Nowadays in Dharamsala, there is a festival of Tibetan theatre opera held during the month of April. On this occasion, the Institute offers the public, for a period of two weeks, its entire repertoire of dances and operas.

The libretto of the opera is known as *Khrad-gzun*. Its dramatic structure is based traditionally on three parts: *Doin*, *Xong* and *Zhaxi*.

Doin is the introduction in which the narrator introduces himself and calls the fisherman, the fairies and the woodcutter, characters who appear in almost all the operas, with a greater or lesser degree of importance.

The actors are known as *lha-mo-ba*; first they offer their prayers to the gods and ask for their blessing, requesting permission for the space which they are going to occupy in the performance. Then they discuss the plot and the characters of the opera, accompanied by songs and dances.

From there they proceed to the *Xong*, which forms the main body of the opera. The actors form a circle, the narrator explains the plot in a tone of litany, and at the appropriate moment certain actors separate from the circle and dance, sing and act out their roles, even performing acrobatics on occasions.

The sequence of narration and acting alternated with songs and dances is the basis of Tibetan dramatic structure. The action is accompanied and accentuated from start to finish by a drum and cymbals.

The last part is the epilogue, known as *Zhaxi*, which in Tibetan means blessing or good omen. These blessings are sung and danced by the whole group of actors. The performance is ended by a signal from the leading actor.

In ancient times these performances lasted from 10 to 12 hours, and a single performance occasionally lasted several days. Nowadays shortened performances can be seen, lasting only six hours.

Each opera has its own characteristic musical theme, as well as the inclusion in each one of popular dances from different regions of Tibet. These dances are known as *Ache Lhamo*. The monastic dances performed during the operas are called *Cham*. They are public religious dances.

The main plots of the operas are based on the narration of the lives of characters with surprising ethical behaviour. Some take as their structure previous lives of Buddha, but all include some amusing passages in which, for example, monks and nuns are satirized, to the delight of the audience, without anyone being offended.

Some sources indicate that there are nine operas documented as being classics, and others point to there only being eight. We would certify the existence of the following:

- *Chogyal Norsang*
- *Sugkyi Nyima*
- *Gyasa Bhelsa*
- *Drowa Sangmo*
- *Nangsa Woebum*

and the Indian dramas assimilated by Tibetan theatre opera:

- *Drimeh Kundan*
- *Donyoh Dondruh*

We were able to observe the performance of four of these operas on different occasions, obviously in their shortened version of six hours' duration since nowadays the long versions are not performed anywhere.

We can certify their real popular theatre structure. The contact and feedback with the people can be understood when one sees with one's own eyes the look of an audience open to the wonder of taking part in a moment of shared drama, a drama which helps us to discover the joy of being together, here and now, marvelling at being alive and happy. This audience breaks out in fantastic bursts of raucous laughter, eats, drinks, prays, urinates and defecates in the area around the performance, without losing its enthusiasm and attention.

We were lucky enough to see a moment of Tibetan theatre and its audience, due to being able to go to the festivities of the Kalachakra. There, for one month, about 250,000 Tibetans gathered together. For many of them it was the first time they had been out of Tibet since the Chinese invasion, and they had come to Bodhgaya to receive the blessing and the initiation of the Dalai Lama.

We were lucky, as this celebration only takes place in Bodhgaya once every twelve years. Otherwise, it would have been difficult to evaluate the social phenomenon which Tibetan theatre represents.

Being in the middle of this Tibetan concentration, the largest seen in exile, we were able to see that, even though the Tibetans are temporarily driven out of their external territory (bearing in mind that China invaded Tibet in 1959, obliging the Dalai Lama to set up his government in exile), they nevertheless keep their society very much alive in their internal territory; not only through keeping alive their cultural structures, such as theatre and dance, but also through the active power of their religion.

The dynamism of the country's theatrical structure has a correlation with its religious celebrations. An air of exuberant theatricality can be felt in the Tibetan atmosphere in general: the way in which they ritualise their spaces, both the actors and the monks; their sung prayers; their adornments; monastic debates; the very tasks of everyday life; everything can be seen as a constant fluid of the country's dramatic nature. We see their religious world as a ritual theatre which makes a profound reading of the universe, of the operativeness of its fluids, cycles, rhythms and vibrations: a reading of emotions and human behaviour which teaches us the path we ourselves are taking; a reading, at times surprisingly scientific and always up to date. Its religious constructions and the design of its celebrations are tools of concentration and direction of energy. But we will return to this point later on. What is important to underline now is that in Bodhgaya we discovered Tibet's dramatic nature in its very essence, both on and off the stage.

Part of the spectacle off the stage was, for instance, the striking dignity visible in the behaviour of the Khampas (Tibetan nomads, who formed the main bulk of the Tibetan guerrilla forces), with their muttering as they spat out their mucus, snorting it onto the ground; their phlegm; their farts and noisy defecation, mingling with the continuous hum of their chant *om mani padme hum*. Not to mention the visual effect of their dress: hair, coats, boots and caps which often reminded us of images of snowy landscapes in the Tibetan mountains, and which, in view of the heat in Bodhgaya, seemed bizarre. Their strong appearance of men from the mountains contrasted vividly with the presence, equally strong in its own way, of the occasional Tibetan punk.

In short, we were able to confirm the importance of the dramatising of Tibetan life, through public, political, religious, artistic and domestic acts.

Researchers such as Nicholas and George Roerich, Jacques Bacot, Giuseppe Tucci, John F. Avedon, Marcelle Lalou, among others, helped us with their writings, to acquire a greater vision of Tibetan culture.

Others, such as Samten G. Karmay, showed us areas of folklore and the *Cham* dance, a sacred dance with Bon influence, which in an indirect way is linked to Tibetan theatre. Cynthia Bridgman Josayma and Wang Yao directly analyse Tibetan theatre/opera. Other researchers, such as Ricardo O. Canzio, Barbara Nimri Aziz, Martin Brauem Dolma, Tashi Tsering, Nawang Tsering Shakspo and Amy Hellen, all of whom took part in the seminar run by the International Association of Tibetan Studies at the Colombia University in New York in 1982, have a great deal to say on the subject, without actually investigating theatre directly. The results of this seminar are published in Delhi, under the title of *Soundings in Tibetan Civilization* (Aziz and Kapstein: 1986).

The help and friendly guidance of one of these researchers, Tashi Tsering, whom we met in the Tibetan studies and archives library in Dharamsala, where he works, was invaluable, as through him we gained access to texts which were scarcely divulged and carefully guarded, and which proved important in the course of work.

The most important text about Tibetan theatre, in which we can find the guidelines for the actor, the scenery, costumes, music etc., is the *Rolmoe Tenchoe*, by Sakya Pandita. This text only exists in Tibetan, and its content can only be known, until now at any rate, via the verbal and written interpretations of it passed on by the masters of Tibetan theatre.

In addition, we were able to learn that the *Rolmoe Tenchoe* is inspired by the *Natyasastra*. This Indian text is well known as the bible of fine arts in India, and was originally written in Sanskrit.

To give the reader an idea, here is the basic table of emotions, as they appear in the *Natyasastra*; a table which has its Tibetan equivalents in the *Rolmoe Tenchoe*:

Basic Emotions According To Baharata

1	Rasa	love	Shrigaru	erotic love
2	Hasa	humour	Hasga	comedy
3	Shoka	grief	Karuna	illness
4	Krodha	anger	Raudra	fury
5	Utsala	energy	Vira	heroism
6	Bhaga	fear	Bhaganak	terror
7	Jugapu	disgust	Bibhatsu	unbearableness
8	Vismaga	astonishment	Adbhuta	amazement

Before the Chinese invasion of Tibet, there were two professional theatre/opera schools: the 'white masks' and the 'blue masks'. At the moment, the only professional group is the Tibetan Institute of Performing Arts.

In addition to this, there are also groups of country-folk who do amateur performances of the operas. The way in which these groups follow the performance guidelines is incoherent, and the dancers' movements are nervous, as are the quality of the voices and the performances themselves. Nevertheless, in spite of the precariousness of the wardrobe and the props of these groups, the quality of performance lies in their definite pledge to share with their people the phenomenon of the fantastic 'theatrical' experience.

The quality of the Institute's wardrobe and props is lavish and colourful. Its complicated designs for masks, hairstyles, hats and costumes for each of the performers, reach sophisticated extremes.

The space in which the theatre/opera is performed is a circle approximately 15 metres in diameter, marked out in an open area so that the audience can gather round. In the middle of the circle there is always an image of Thangton Gyalpo, the holy patron of Tibetan theatre, together with a few offerings.

It is interesting to note that the offerings, both those in theatre and those in Tibetan religious ceremonies, always feature a cob. Corn, as we found out, appeared in Tibet as a symbol of worship in the year 600 AD. How did this come to be? What was its origin and how did it spread? We came across an oral tradition which tells us that for the Tibetans, corn is the primary food, a gift from the gods; this is precisely the same context in which it appeared in Central America. This could be a rich source of research.

Returning to theatrical space, the offerings and the altar to Thangton Gyalpo are the only scenery used, except for a few objects placed by the actors themselves to represent woods, rivers, mountains or houses. The circle is connected to the dressing rooms by a narrow passageway which gives the performers access. A round awning serves as an enormous parasol above the circle.

The performance begins at nine o'clock in the morning and ends at four or five in the afternoon. Just before the official opening of the opera two musicians, who accompany the entire performance, take their places outside the circle. As we have already mentioned, one plays the cymbals and the other the drum. The din of these instruments announces the beginning of the performance, and the performance itself develops according to the structure of *Doin*, preamble; *Xong*, main body of the opera; and *Xhaxi*, epilogue.

The Institute's performances in Bodhgaya, both of operas and of their folk dances, brought together hundreds of thousands of Tibetans. The sense of living together around the performances was another spectacle in itself. We have already spoken of the attitude of this spectacular audience who laugh and get excited with childlike innocence, while at the same time, and in the most natural way, they defecate and urinate nearby. They share not only the performances, but also the heat of the sun and the food and drink, all this amid raucous laughter and comments on the performance. Their respect for the dramatic action is startling, as is the fondness they exhibit towards the actors. In spite of the performance's six-hour duration, the audience's attention is always very much alive, perhaps due to the fact that some characters on stage are identical to the audience who are watching them. It is very likely that this game of mirrors stimulates their interest.

The performance ended at twilight, and at dusk at different points in the camp one could pick out the songs and dances of Tibetans moved by their theatre.

Aside from the theatre/opera repertoire, the Institute has a series of Tibetan folk dances called *Ache Lhamo*. This series also features some monastic dances known as *Cham*. This repertoire of dances was performed in Bodhgaya, in a programme which lasted two hours and which took place at nightfall in an improvised Italian-style forum, lit by western-style spotlights, before an audience gathered in a rectangular area enclosed by sheets of material, seated on the earth floor or using stones as seats. The atmosphere it created was fabulous. Amid the green of the palm trees which grew majestically across one corner of the roof of the improvised stage, the dark blue sky laden with stars, the presence of a warm-hearted, vibrant audience and the primitive stage almost cut out of the horizon, full of lively colour, it all seemed like a jack-in-the-box in motion. Add to this in the firmament some crescent moons like in a fairy story and, all around, the curious onlookers who, as they could not afford to attend the performance, were peeping in from outside the rectangle with attitudes reminiscent of Bosco or Van Gogh.

The completeness of the performance, both on and off the stage, allowed us to sense a circulating current of energy which encapsulated the whole thing. We were certain of having viewed for an instant the quality of this enormous cosmic soup in which we were all submerged. These performances, with their magical atmosphere, took place during a two-week period in Bodhgaya, as part of the Kalachakra celebrations in December 1985.

The range of musical instruments used by the Institute is wide and complicated. Suffice it to say that these instruments have been the subject of study for several ethnomusicologists, for instance Terry Jay Ellingson. The most striking Tibetan musical instrument, in our opinion, is the famous Dong Chen trumpet, whose size and vibratory scale are immense. We were lucky enough to witness the quality of its sound in a large number of celebrations. Good fortune brought us the privilege of sharing in an exclusive ceremony during the celebrations of the Tibetan new year, the 'Tiger of Fire' (1986) in Dharamsala. In this ceremony, presided over by the Dalai Lama, we heard music of the highest quality from these trumpets, due perhaps to the fact that on this occasion the enormous trumpets were made of silver. We shall not expand here on the matter of musical instruments, since our research leads us to concentrate on other areas. Those interested could refer to the aforementioned ethnomusicologist, whose work involves extensive coverage of the music and instruments of Tibet.

Now we would like to say something about the training of the Institute's actors. It must be emphasised that their rehearsals, and music, singing and dancing classes fit into a rather strange atmosphere. The entire Institute, actors, teachers, the administrative team - including the director - dressmakers, musicians, cooks, manager, wives and children, and 19 orphans under the age of 14, all live in buildings around the work areas. Being a member of the Institute, therefore, is not merely a job but rather a way of life: they have breakfast and lunch, pray, rehearse and perform in the same place. Although they tend to spend their spare time in the Mcleod Ganj village, their activity essentially centres around the Institute. Given these circumstances, it is not surprising that they consider themselves to be a huge family. Rehearsal, eating and performance times are defined according to a discipline based on the needs of circumstances, that is to say that when there are festivities coming up in which the Institute is going to take part, whether it be with operas, dances or public parades, then that specific material is what is prepared. Away from such obligations, the rehearsals respond to the particular learning needs of the group: if some new members do not know certain dances, or if it is necessary to polish up the work with certain musical instruments, or if an old

Tibetan opera teacher appears in Dharamsala for long enough to teach the group a new dance or an unperformed passage of an opera, and so on, then these factors influence the rehearsals.

Tibetan opera/theatre is a discipline designed by Tibetans for Tibetans. There is, therefore, no system - at least, not yet - whereby outsiders can structure their learning. The only way to learn it is by getting a gradual idea through the rehearsals and performances, and also by getting to know the actors and teachers better, since a large amount of information is based on oral tradition. To learn a few specific areas, the best thing to do is to attend special classes, which is what the Institute management decided we should do.

Our dance, music and singing teachers were generous with their knowledge; they helped us, without doubt, to acquire a greater understanding of the cultural phenomenon which their theatre represents, and they made a great effort during the months we spent with them to share their skills with us.

What definitely gave our learning greater depth was the discreet contact we were able to establish with a few monasteries. When you think of Tibetan monasteries, it is impossible to shake off the fictional image of huge stone buildings, in the peaks of the Himalayas, with their enormous gates covered in cryptic ironwork at which you knock and are granted mysterious access for certain periods of time and to certain spaces according to your level of understanding, and so on.

The reality, as we experienced it, is different. The monasteries we visited are in Dharamsala and its environs, in the same atmosphere as the Institute enjoys, if not in the very peaks, then certainly in the foothills of the Himalayas. The snowy peaks of Dhauladhar can be seen from there. Monasteries are dotted all around. Some are clearly defined and stand out due to their traditional rigid, white construction, with lavish ornaments on the frames of the main door, where occasionally the images of the Yidams - or doormen - turn up their moustaches with an inquisitive stare, scrutinising the visitor. The majority of these well-defined buildings are crowned with golden decorations.

Many other monasteries can be found in the most surprising places, with no hint or sign as to their true identity, like for instance the one which is above the only video-cinema, or another one which is on the top floor of a hotel. They can be found in semi-tumbledown houses, at the bottom of ravines, or by following a small path off the beaten track. The whole village of Mcleod Ganj is littered with monastic activity, and the monasteries' locations are as surprising as the quality of their prayers.

We were admitted to the monasteries we visited strictly as visitors. Although we were eventually afforded some form of privilege, we cannot say that we discovered their secret. We know full well that the secret keeps itself, and that to discover an element of truth - about this or any other teaching - an entire life's dedication is necessary. Nevertheless, the contact with certain sources of vibration (like the strong sessions full of human warmth held by all the monks from the Gyuto Tantric College, who always displayed a Buddhist temperament and patience for our presence in their prayers), afforded us a greater understanding of the use of the voice and vibration as tools for concentration, thanks mainly to the guidance given to us by their abbot Khempo Lungrik Namgyal.

We also received guidance about meditation in motion, through the observation and practice of the dances of the 'Black Hat'. We were illuminated on the one hand by being able to watch these dances of the 'Black Hat' at the Namgyal monastery in Dharamsala, and on the other by attending the dance sessions at the Khampa-Gar monastery in Tashi Jong. In Tashi Jong there are a great number of 'Black Hat' dances which are performed from morning to night throughout the three-day duration of the celebration of the birth of Padmasambhava. There, the reverend Dorzong Rimpoche kindly invited us to build up the necessary contact to go more deeply into the study of the sacred Tibetan dance. This, combined with the practice of one of the dances of the 'Black Hat' which we performed in the Institute, helped us to understand more fully its meaning and content.

We also had the advice of the venerable Khamtul Yeshe Dorje Rimpoche, of the Zilnon Kagyeline monastery, who is also known as 'the man who controls the weather', on account of his facility to hold off or bring on rain. This lama, in a very friendly way, helped us with our research by showing us that both to perform a dance and to play the human bone flute, it is necessary to find the path that will allow us to do it from the heart.

The dance of the 'Black Hat' is meditation in motion. There are eight different forms which are performed in different monasteries, and a large number of variations. Each form or variation is a complete sequence. The structure is that of a warlike dance, or at least that was the case in the version we learned, which was called *Lha-lhung Pay-dor*, and which originated in the Tashi Lhumpo monastery. The warlike dancer frees the village from tyranny, by killing the bad king or the ego, depending on the version.

This war dance is performed according to a specific body code which has the quality of bringing the consciousness up to date, due to the deprogramming structure of its movements. Its sequences are organised such that they flow with the energy of the cosmos. They are really a mandala in motion. This dance uses for its body code the archaic designs of ritual, which are very similar to contemporary scientific diagrams. Its origins seem to be closely related to the Bon part of Tibet, a trend somewhat scorned in the Tibetan structure, but eventually recognised as another religious option within its structures.

As is widely known, the four schools of Tibetan Buddhism are:

- Nyingma
- Sakya
- Kagyu
- Gelug

Now, as an option recognised by the Dalai Lama, Bon Po can be added to this list. Since we are not Tibetologists, let us now leave the Tibetan religious schools and return to the dance of the 'Black Hat'. This dance has only three points of contact worth underlining here:

1. It is a dance, or meditation in motion, performed through a defined body alphabet; a type of mandala in motion which charges the performer with energy.

2. The performer, allegorically, is a warrior fighting his battle, through the dance, to achieve individual and group freedom. The dance is performed in a circle.

3. This battle is essentially internal. The performer is striving to maintain the level of attention in the 'here and now', by offering energy to the essences, with energetic resonance in the external world.

These three points of contact can be applied exactly to the conchero dance of Central America.[1] Its essential similarities are extraordinary. At the same time, we would point out the sacredness of the snail in both areas: Tibet and Central America.

These parallelisms - the snail, dance, corn - may be due to a type of coincidence, as Jung believes. Given the correlations, it is said that some researchers have sought a common source for Tibetan and Central American cosmology. However, so as to keep to the structure of our modest plan and not get too deeply into this, we shall limit ourselves to establishing as a point of contact between Tibetan theatrical rite and Nahuatlan theatrical rite, vibration and body movement used with the same intention, aside from the relationship of the three points of contact in the dance, mentioned above.

As we establish that vibration is a bridge of contact, musical instruments, voices and dances now take on a specific quality for us. What happens if we remove all the paraphernalia of Tibetan dance's wardrobe, and likewise remove the paraphernalia of the feathers in Nahautlan dance? Although it is clear that within its own orthodoxies each detail has its meaning, we wonder whether, if we stripped it down to the essential tool, that is to say the body alphabet (or dance movements) and its internal code (the repetition of a mantra), which contain within them meditation in motion, it would work and resist updating. Our answer, according to the research we have carried out, is affirmative, that is to say yes, it is possible to do

---

[1] The *concheros* are highly organized dance groups, who practise traditional pre-Hispanic Mexican ritual dances.

meditation in motion through these dances in a tracksuit and sports shoes, with no need for all the trimmings.

With regard to the voice and musical instruments, we focused our attention on the quality of vibration and its resonance. We found out, for instance, that the same drum, with the same type of scale, played by somebody who is thinking about crisps, obtains a different resonance from when somebody plays it keeping the beat in his mind, shall we say, at the centre of the sun. Mental polarisation is therefore more important than a certain type of virtuosity. This is specifically true of certain instruments in the field of theatre/ritual, and it should not be thought that it applies in general terms.

The same thing happens with the quality of a voice's vibration. We are more interested in a vibratory register which is well conducted mentally, than in one which is well intoned but which mentally remains on the surface. We are more interested in intention than intonation, whether it be sung in Nahautlan or in Tibetan.

It was gratifying to find out that this vibratory criterion is shared by Tibetan and Nahautlan people. This vibratory bridge which links Tibetan theatrical rite with Nahautlan, features in its possibilities the designs of participatory theatre which we perform in our workshop. In conclusion, we can point out that during our stay in Dharamsala, we were nourished by the vibratory quality of the voice, essentially with the teachers from the Gyuto Tantric College, who gave us a good lesson on what can be achieved by a register which keeps its concentration continually alive.

We took up the body code of the dance of the 'Black Hat' and found out about the structure of Tibet's theatre/opera and its folk dances, both in the Institute and in the monasteries; we also collected a few musical tools, like the human bone trumpet, the 'tingshak', or summoning bells, and some cymbals, to name but a few.

I am sure that the research and participatory theatre schemes which we work on in our workshop will reflect in certain points Tibetan influences, as well as Nahautlan and western ones, defining our work as a transcultural process.

We were fortunate enough to receive an audience with the Dalai Lama, which took place in one of the rooms of his palace, in Dharamsala. As some of his comments are of use in our research, the interview is reproduced below[2]; the *Taller* members present in the conversation were Nicolás Núñez, Helena Guardia, and Ana Luisa Solis Gil.

TALLER: Your Holiness, first of all, we would like to thank you for your hospitality and for everything we have received from Tibetan culture and, of course, to thank you for offering us this audience. We would like to know, how do you think Mexicans interested in Tibet can best help the country?

DALAI LAMA: Well, the best thing you can do to help Tibet is spread the truth about the current situation, in political, cultural and anthropological terms. You can help us by writing articles which talk of Tibet in the contemporary world: articles about painting, philosophy, religion, dance or theatre. The important thing is that you help us to establish Tibet's presence, so that both the culture of the Tibetan world and its present condition become more widespread...

TALLER: What is this?

DALAI LAMA: A Tibetan trumpet made from bone, from our hands.

TALLER: What is it for?

(*The **DALAI LAMA** picks it up and plays with it*)

TALLER: (*making a joke*) If you don't know...

(*The **DALAI LAMA** smiles*)

DALAI LAMA: This is to work the Tantra. It is a very powerful tool and a constant reminder of our temporary nature. It can be used in this sense or to... (he waves it about amusingly like a club. We all laugh). How do you intend to use it?

---

2 The conversation, and the quotation which concludes this chapter, were recorded verbatim by Núñez in Dharamsala in 1986 and reproduced from his notes, with the permission of the Dalai Lama.

TALLER: In our work in the theatre we use vibration to induce states of deep consciousness. We use the conch and we're thinking of using this trumpet, if you will allow us to.

DALAI LAMA: (*He smiles and breathes in silence, looking at the trumpet*). Yes, use it, why not, building bridges hurts nobody. Your work is a bridge between the cultural and the mystic, is that right? Use it. Do you have masks in indigenous theatre in Mexico?

TALLER: Yes, indeed.

DALAI LAMA: Are any of them made of shells?

TALLER: Yes, indeed. Incidentally, the similarities which we have detected between Tibetan and Central American designs are fantastic.

DALAI LAMA: Well, Asians, Eskimos and the Red Indians of North America do have a lot in common.

TALLER: We think the Central and South American Indians are related, as well as the North American ones.

DALAI LAMA: It's quite likely, as we all belong to the same family. In that sense there is a lot still to be confirmed. Research has not really begun yet. It's virgin territory.

TALLER: Do you think it is due to a cultural synchronism, or to the fact that Atlantis really existed as a common origin?

DALAI LAMA: I couldn't explain it exactly; a lot could be said on the matter. The reality is that we need serious research to be done into this point. It could give us a lot of surprises.

TALLER: For instance, corn is the pillar of Mexican culture, and even so, it appears in all the Tibetan ceremonies and offerings.

DALAI LAMA: Corn in Tibet is known as the original food. It is said that it was a gift, at the beginning of time; that it appeared without being sown, so that man could be nourished. Later, man began to grow it and the different types of corn were developed. However, in Tibet it has not been grown for general consumption. It is considered symbolic.

TALLER: It seems that recent research has discovered that corn is a food which does not attract radioactivity.

DALAI LAMA: Oh, I didn't know that, that's something new to me. So, if there is a disaster we'll be able to survive on corn... how marvellous! But there is no corn in Tibet..., all the Tibetans would have to go to Mexico. (He lets out a hearty laugh, and sets us all off). I really don't know very much about Mexico. What I do know about are those enormous hats.

TALLER: Mexican cowboy hats.

DALAI LAMA: Yes, yes, Mexican cowboy hats... Mexico is a Third World country, a country in the process of development, isn't it?

TALLER: Yes.

DALAI LAMA: I think that small or developing countries should bear in mind one very important thing, which is the realisation that it is as important to work hard to achieve their economic development, as it is to work for their spiritual development; the two must go together, with neither the spiritual nor the material aspect being neglected. If they do not work like this, the whole thing turns into a disaster. A while ago, the ex-President of Costa Rica came to see me, a very intelligent man. I was amazed to hear that Costa Rica scarcely has an army, and that they therefore have to defend themselves with other arms, the sort I agree with wholeheartedly: human rights, people's free right to choose, non-intervention, humanism. To defend ourselves with these arms we must be spiritually very strong. That is how small countries or those with hardly any army, or developing countries like Mexico can defend themselves. We must be spiritually strong.

TALLER: Those are the exact principles which govern Mexico's foreign policy and which, in our opinion, date back to pre-Hispanic wisdom.

DALAI LAMA: Another coincidence, don't you think?

TALLER: Your Holiness, you set out these principles in your text, *A Human Approach to World Peace* [1984], and show the urgency of this type of understanding among peoples. It is an important document which could sensitise processes. We want to ask you if you will allow us to translate it into Spanish so that it can reach the leaders of Central and South America; we are sure that some of them will be able to help, just as we are confident it will be of some use to Ronald Reagan, who received it via a friend of yours.

DALAI LAMA: Yes, of course, please do translate it. Why not? Part of the Dharma's work is to help to establish currents of positive energy. How long has the Mexican Society of Friends of Tibet been going?

TALLER: Fifteen or twenty years. The only person who knows exactly is its secretary, Antonio Velasco Piña.

DALAI LAMA: Oh, I see. I remember a Mexican colonel from many years ago, called Osorio. Do you know him?

TALLER: No.

DALAI LAMA: But you've heard of him...?

TALLER: A little.

DALAI LAMA: Well, anyway, what have you learned from the time you've spent among the Tibetan people?

TALLER: We have focused on the monastic dance, *Cham*. We have been to a few monasteries and the Institute. We have also studied the human voice, at the Gyuto Tantric College.

DALAI LAMA: Oh, the *Cham* dances and the tantric registers of Gyuto. Very good. How long have you been studying that?

TALLER: For seven months now.

DALAI LAMA: And how much longer will you be here?

TALLER: Another month and a half or two months.

DALAI LAMA: When was the first time you came into contact with Buddhist teaching in the flesh?

TALLER: During the Kalachakra celebration, in Bodhgaya last December.

DALAI LAMA: What a good thing that you were in Bodhgaya. It was a great concentration, not only of Tibetans, but also of Dharma.

TALLER: It was fabulous to see 250,000 Tibetans from such different regions. We think it was the largest Tibetan concentration in exile, is that right?

DALAI LAMA: (*Nods*) The important thing is to keep the spiritual work going; that is something we must never forget, regardless of the external circumstances in which we may have to live.

TALLER: In that sense, you are a living example of Buddhist teaching (bearing in mind his attitude to the Chinese invasion).

DALAI LAMA: (*Smiles politely*) Is there anything else?

TALLER: If you want to send a message to the Mexican people, we will try to make sure it reaches them.

DALAI LAMA: A message? What message can I send to the Mexicans? They are human beings too, aren't they? Therefore what is good for any other human being is good for them: I would tell them not to forget that working towards peace of mind is the discipline of internal education, together with courtesy, love and compassion; they should be fully aware of that; that only through spiritual growth balanced with technological growth can the possibility emerge of living without anguish; that it is very important for them not to neglect either of these two aspects, the spiritual and the material. Anything else?

We then exchanged with the Dalai Lama a series of personal comments, and finally left his palace convinced of his admirable coherence of action and thought. This 'simple' coherence gives him a superior place in the world. The only policy of the Dalai Lama, the god/king of Tibet, is one of living together in peace, one of good faith, where we can all seek our own happiness, for as he himself says: 'We must understand that when my enemy does something wrong against me, he does not do it to hurt me; he is simply seeking his happiness. We are all seeking happiness and we must help each other to achieve it, without hurting each other'.

ANTHROPOCOSMIC THEATRE

2 NAHUATLAN THEATRE

We arrived at the Faculty of Arts of the Autonomous National University of Mexico (UNAM), seeking refuge for our research needs. Fortunately, we found an excellent old professor of ours: Oscar Zorrilla, who as well as knowing our anxieties in some depth, was also sympathetic to our quest.

Via the seminar which he was leading, we made contact with researchers such as Miguel León Portilla, Alfredo López Austin and Gabriel Weisz, who helped us in our studies and gave us a deeper understanding of Nahuatlan theatre/rite.[3]

For this brief analysis, we have taken as a base the broad study carried out by Professor Fernando Horcasitas, which was published by the National University with the title *Teatro Náhuatl* ([1974] 2004) (Nahuatlan Theatre). We shall also look at our field research into indigenous theatre/rite, undertaken in various parts of the Mexican mountains, as well as our contact with the pre-Hispanic conchero dance, and our own behind-closed-doors quests in our workshop.

Using these foundations as a starting point, we form our way of thinking which, in spite of any faults it may have, allows us to show the ways in which our work in the workshop has been nourished by these sources.

Does or did a Nahuatlan theatre exist? Since when and with what dramatic structure? In his excellent essay, Professor Horcasitas tells us that: 'Our reply to this question will depend on our definition of the word "drama"' (Horcasitas, [1974] 2004: 33). What is drama?

> In the widest sense, the most rudimentary dialogue, or dance, or dialogued singing, can be termed drama. If we were to make a compilation of all the dramatic forms which have existed and which

---

3 Oscar Zorrilla (died 1985) was an academic renowned for his writings on Artaud. Miguel León Portilla is a Mexican anthropologist and historian, as is Alfredo López Austin. Gabriel Weisz is a Mexican theatre director and professor of theatre.

exist now, in all five continents, the variety would amaze us (Horcasitas, [1974] 2004: 34).

After giving various examples, he concludes: 'It is not unlikely that a form of theatre, in the widest sense of the term, has emerged in every culture, and the ancient Mexicans were no exception' (Horcasitas, [1974] 2004: 36).

Assuming the criterion of theatricality to be confirmed, what were the Nahuatlan dramatic forms? Horcasitas replies:

> According to León Portilla, the dramas and their texts can be divided into four categories:
>
> 1. The most ancient forms of performances in the Nahuatlan religious festivals. For example, the author includes a hymn sung on the feast of Tláloc, performed by several characters, among whom are the god himself and the choir.
>
> 2. Several forms of comic acting and entertainment in the Nahuatlan world. León Portilla copies the words of a jester who performs as various birds.
>
> 3. The staging of the great Nahuatlan myths and legends, for instance there appears a dialogue sung about the flight of Quetzalcóatl from Tula.
>
> 4. Performances of subjects relating to problems in social and family life. The aforementioned investigator presents us with the text of a short but important comedy. Six voices are heard in the text: those of two 'gladdeners' or women of pleasure, that of the mother of one of them, those of two repentant 'gladdeners' and that of a young man called Ahuitzotl (Horcasitas, [1974] 2004: 48).

In this way, Miguel León Portilla confirms in Horcasitas' text the existence of four dramatic forms of Nahuatlan theatre before the Spanish Conquest.

It must be noted that the Nahuatlan language, as Horcasitas tells us, 'also known as Mexican or Aztec - is divided into three dialects: náhuatl, náhuat and náhual. Náhuatl is the language of the Mexican plateau' (Horcasitas,

[1974] 2004: 51), and its influence extends - or extended - from the northwest USA to Nicaragua.

With this reference framework, we can imagine the number of ritual, social or entertaining dramas which emerged in the Nahuatlan language. Where are they now? Horcasitas points out: 'Whoever tries to have a general vision of indigenous theatre in the Mexican language, will soon realise that the dispersion of data and texts is frightening' (Horcasitas, [1974] 2004: 11). It seems that a great deal of material is still intermingled with chronicles in Nahuatlan brought out by people like Sahagún and Durán[4] in the Colony, as well as being found in various ancient codices awaiting the hand of a specialist to make a compilation. There have, however, been several advances made in this sense. Those interested can delve into the bibliographies of Angel María Garibay[5], Miguel León Portilla or Alfredo López Austin, as a starting point.

Up to now, we can be quite sure of the deep and vast, ritualistic theatrical sense of Mexican people before the Spanish conquest; from the seriousness of the dramas in which somebody incarnated for forty days, living as a god and dying at the end of these celebrations, to the relaxation of certain dances, like the one which Durán mentions in Horcasitas' text:

> With so many movements and face-pullings and dishonest pranks, which can easily be seen to be the dance of dishonest women and frivolous men. They called it *cuecuechcuicatl*, which means 'ticklish or itchy dance', and it features Indians dressed as women (Horcasitas, [1974] 2004: 41).

Without a shadow of doubt, an atmosphere of vivacious religious theatricality enveloped the pre-Hispanic world. In all these pre-Hispanic Nahuatlan theatre forms, there is no documented register which would allow us to

---

4 Fray Bernardino Sahagún and Fray Diego de Durán were friars during the Conquest of Mexico who defended the Indians against colonisation. Sahagún and Durán recorded hundreds of folios of oral history materials in the Nahuatlan language.

5 Angel María Garibay: scholar of Nahuatlan; paleographer and translator.

rebuild fully the pre-Conquest Nahuatlan dramatic phenomenon. We know for certain that this phenomenon existed and exists today. On the one hand, the documentation is in impatient need of an expert's hand and, on the other, phenomena of Nahuatlan theatre/rite which have survived to the present day need to be restored and borne in mind as, in our opinion, is the case of the conchero dance; we shall explain why later on.

What happened to all this great theatrical rite activity which existed in pre-Hispanic Mexico, when the Spanish arrived? After the Conquest, says Horcasitas,

> [T]here were remains of what had been a society of experts: singers, actors, dancers and jesters; poets and orators, voices trained for recital, memorising experts - as this did not depend on literacy. There were florists and scenery designers, specialist ceremonial dressmakers, craftsmen working with jewels, feathers and fabrics (Horcasitas, [1974] 2004: 82).

All these highly qualified people, on the one hand, and the missionaries' need to convert them to Christianity, on the other, as well as the high-point of religious theatre in Spain at the time of colonisation, stirred up in the minds of the Franciscans the possibility of cementing, through theatre in Nahuatlan, their evangelisation project. It was, in any case, an innovation, as evangelist theatre, Horcasitas tells us, 'had not been part of the missionaries' systems in the Old World', and he adds, 'the drama which existed in Europe in the Middle Ages was not intended to convert pagan tribes, but rather to strengthen the faith of people who had been Christians for many generations' (Horcasitas, [1974] 2004: 18). He also notes,

> [I]n short, by 1524, many professionals connected with dramatic performances were idle, men who had received the acclaim of throngs in public places and had served the ruling class before the cataclysm, and now - in 1524 - the ruling class was the Franciscan order. It would have been very surprising if a theatre had not been born with the arrival of the missionaries (Horcasitas, [1974] 2004: 82).

Horcasitas then goes on to pinpoint the intention of the Franciscans:

> the missionaries proposed, through theatre, to change the mentality of peoples who did not know the religion brought by the Europeans. They expected Mexican aborigines, through audio-visual methods, to abandon their age-old cultural and religious features, some of which dated back to Teotihuacan and Tula. Overnight the indigenous people, who twenty years earlier had adored Huitzilopóchtli and Tezcatlipoca, now had to learn about and believe in Adam and Eve, Abraham and Isaac, redemption, St. James' capture of Jerusalem, and so forth. By means of theatre, they also had to learn a new moral code and accept a whole series of new cultural features (Horcasitas, [1974] 2004: 56-57).

This is how a new Nahuatlan-speaking theatre appeared in Mexico, the famous theatre of evangelisation, run by the Franciscans.

The first play of this type was staged in 1533. Entitled *The Final Judgement*, it caused a great sensation in its day and opened up a new age for theatre in Nahuatlan, which lasted until about 1600.

The number and scale of these evangelist plays were abundant. Only in Professor Horcasitas' text can we find complete versions of thirty-five such plays.

Everything seems to indicate that the adventure of evangelist theatre came to an end due to the problems which the Franciscans had with the authorities of that period, who began to fear that on account of the popularity and strength which the Franciscans developed from 1533 to 1570, they might have been thinking of setting up as a state. These fears emerged because it was clear that the Franciscans were in a privileged position, as they were able to assimilate the ritual structure of the indigenous peoples and promote an exceptional unification with Christianity.

The period of Nahuatlan theatre with a western dramatic structure, known as evangelisation theatre, therefore lasted, essentially, from 1533 to about 1600.

The pre-Hispanic dramatic structures were sifted with the western ones brought by the Franciscans, so what then happened to Nahuatlan theatre?

It seems that the structure conceived and developed by the Franciscans dissolved slowly from 1600 onwards, although in some parts it has survived to this day.

Experts tell us that it is in pastorale, by this time in Spanish, where there are the most reminders of Nahuatlan evangelist theatre.

The pastorale is a dramatic phenomenon which has survived in some parts of Mexico and is performed specifically in the week leading up to Christmas Eve. Its theme is always that of the birth of the infant Jesus and the adoration of the Three Kings.

Apart from the pastorale, we believe there are various phenomena of theatrical rite which were not essentially affected by the Spanish Conquest, since their capacity for unification allowed them to survive as transcultural phenomena awaiting their renewal. Their transcultural condition, in other words the fact that they are not purely indigenous - or purely western - is what gives them mobility and the chance to grow. We are well aware that pure cultures do not exist, that all civilisations have been forged in the pot of crossbreeding. In reference to the crossbreeding of Nahuatlan theatre, Horcasitas tells us:

> It would therefore be wrong to state that drama in Nahuatlan is not indigenous because it deals with matters about which Mexicans knew nothing in the pre-Hispanic period. In that case, we would have to deny the authenticity of the village *talavera*, the hat woven from palm leaves, tequila, mariachis and shawls, as they did not exist in Mexico before the Spanish arrived. Aztec civilisation itself was impregnated with elements from other cultures. The worship of the jaguar came from the tropical region of the south-east, metallurgy probably from the Guerrero-Oaxaca region, polychromatic ceramics from the Puebla-Mixteca area, the Tlazoltéotl cult from Huaxteca (Horcasitas, [1974] 2004: 61).

In contemporary Mexican culture it is difficult to define precisely what is indigenous and what is western; a new vision of the world has developed through our crossbreeding, transformed into a country, and this does not exclude our pre-Hispanic phenomena which have survived to the present day.

We have already spoken of the importance of the Nahuatlan language in Central America. This importance was well evaluated by the missionaries, proof of this being the fact that the first book to be printed on the American continent, the *Breve y más compendiosa doctrina cristiana en lengua mexicana y castellana* (Brief and most condensed Christian doctrine in Mexican and Spanish), published in Mexico in 1539, was in Nahuatlan and Spanish.[6]

An interesting fact about Nahuatlan theatre, promoted by the Franciscans, is that it was presumably the first theatre to be written in prose. Horcasitas says: 'In the western world, since the Greeks and the Romans, writing theatre was synonymous with writing in verse' (Horcasitas, [1974] 2004: 81). If this continued in the west until after the Spanish Golden Age, we realise that, as Horcasitas points out: 'Theatre in the Mexican tongue was probably the first to be conceived and written entirely in prose' (Horcasitas, [1974] 2004: 81).

Another question is: what type of actors performed this Nahuatlan evangelisation theatre?

Here, the Franciscans were successful from the very beginning, as they made indigenous people work as actors. The latter's ability to memorise and understand the dramatic sense of the situation was in their blood. Motolinia[7] comments that such was their aptitude that in two days they learned and performed four sacred acts. Horcasitas says of this: 'We can deduce that the actor-singers in the performances were not amateurish young novices, but mature men with excellent training and experience in the rites, chants and ways of the Franciscan order' (Horcasitas, [1974] 2004: 173). We discovered that Philip II, in the second half of the 16th century, decreed that women should not be allowed to act in theatre. Hence in this evangelist theatre all

---

6 This text is available today only in its original form in the Museum of Anthropology, Mexico City.

7 Motolinia: like Sahagun and Duran, a Franciscan friar and observer of Indian life.

women's roles, such as that of the Virgin Mary, were performed by men. This prohibition was redeemed by Innocent XI a hundred years later.

The fact that women's roles were played by men was not so extraordinary for the indigenous people. They were used to this type of transfer, and the seriousness with which the roles were surely played is confirmed by Horcasitas:

> This psychological condition dates back to the period before Columbus. In pre-Conquest theatre, as we have seen, the characters were so possessive of their roles that not only did they believe they were gods, but the faithful also looked upon them as divine. This identification of the actor with his role seems to have survived strongly through the colonial period. A traveller from the beginning of the 17th century talks of the beliefs of the Chiapas Indians with regard to theatrical performances: it was common for the actor who was going to play St. Peter or John the Baptist to hear confessions first, where people would say that they had to be saintly and pure like the saint they were playing, and equally prepared to die. In the same way, the actor who was playing Herod or Herodias, or one of the soldiers who had to accuse the saints during the scene, went afterwards to confess his sin and ask for pardon, as if he had been guilty of spilling blood (Horcasitas, [1974] 2004: 96).

It would be interesting to discover the exact training procedures for pre-Hispanic actors, although we can guess that most, if not all, of this training was carried out in the Calmecac [Aztec school of religious instruction].

The stages in pre-Hispanic Nahuatlan theatre were basically *mamoztli*.[8] We do not mean that all platforms of this type were strictly stages; they would presumably have other uses unknown to us. Horcasitas tells us that these platforms have the following common features:

> 1) it is stone; 2) it is square; 3) it has one, two or four staircases at the sides; 4) it is isolated, not supported by the building; 5) the building is always of the utmost importance; 6) the height of the platform is

---

8 *Mamotzli*: stone platforms erected opposite pyramids and used for certain celebrations.

little more than the height of a man; 7) its surface varies in size from four hundred to twenty-five square metres; 8) it does not appear to have had a permanent building placed over the top, since its plastered floor, in the cases in which it has survived, seems to be flat (Horcasitas, 1974/2004: 115).

Horcasitas adds:

> Not only were there performances on the platforms I have described, but also during ball games (reference: León Portilla), in the courtyards of palaces (Garibay), in artificial forests (Durán), in markets (León Portilla) and even in the *temalacatl*, or the stone area of gladiatorial sacrifice (Sahagún) (Horcasitas, [1974] 2004: 104).

Performances of colonial Nahuatlan theatre took place in church porches, in pavilions propped up against the walls of churches, or on small wooden platforms built specifically for the occasion.

A typical feature of Nahuatlan theatre is the presence of nature in its plays: trees, fruit, live and dead animals, flowers, feathers, golden and natural birds; all this scenario decked with nature could, we believe, be a type of giant offering in the form of stage decoration. The lavishness of the performances is described in detail by, among others, the chroniclers Sahagún and Durán, and there is no doubt that it represents an inheritance of Nahuatlan theatrical rite which has survived to this day.

There are sixteen musical instruments used in Nahuatlan evangelisation theatre, according to Professor Horcasitas' diligent investigation: eleven woodwind instruments, only three from the string family, the drum and the bells. Musicologists seeking a more detailed description of these instruments should consult Professor Horcasitas' text *Teatro Nahuatl* [Nahuatlan Theatre] ([1974] 2004).

However, in this list of instruments, no mention has been made of one which has discreetly coloured all manner of performance and dance up to the present day, as well as being, we believe, one of the most important: the snail shell.

This organic structure, perhaps due to its isolated elocutions and its purely animal origin, has not been thought of as a musical instrument; yet, given its vibratory quality, it is one of the most important for raising energy. Just like the Tibetan trumpets, the Central American snail shell is an effective instrument to assist in the updating of the consciousness.

In our workshop we have carried out some explorations in this sense, and we have verified the significance of its vibratory quality, due to the fact that its organic spiral structure reflects the rhythm of the cosmos in a synthetic way. When it is made to vibrate with appropriate mental polarisation, contact with deep scales of energy is almost immediate. With good reason the snail shell is looked upon as a sacred instrument, both in Central America and in Tibet.

Our first contacts with festivities of Nahuatlan theatre/rite were in the atmosphere, and formed part, of the reality in which we were living. This has surely been the case with many Mexicans, who without looking for it - even less wishing to study it - have discovered themselves at birth, submerged in an atmosphere of celebrations and festivities which conserve much of their pre-Hispanic origin.

Although these first contacts have not been diligently registered, as research work demands, they nevertheless left a deep impression on us. In my case, I began to feel these impacts when I was five years old. On the ranch of Chimalpa in the State of Hidalgo, where I was born, we celebrated the patron saint's day. The peasants and pulque cultivators would ask for permission to use both the church and the internal courtyard or the interior passageways of the ranch, to celebrate their performance, *The Life of the Glorious Apostle St. James*. So the spaces for our everyday games were transformed as my brothers and sisters and I looked on in awe, into a coming and going of men dressed in loud colours, who burned resin, wore masks and feathers and shouted, danced and drank with gusto. As part of the dance they crossed the blades of their machetes with such intensity that sparks flew up at every strike. There was, nevertheless, a sense of deep security; these men, for all their ferocity, and with the volcanoes - Popocatépetl and Iztaccíhuatl - at the bottom of the garden, were praying to

God. I never felt afraid. The parts of the dances I still remember are the skips and jumps which seemed like explosions of colours, sounds, smells and emotions. They appeared to me to be living offerings of their own energy. Several times, I do not know exactly how many, we experienced this festival of Nahuatlan theatre, spoken in Spanish but dotted with odd phrases in Nahuatlan, which inadvertently came violently into my house.

The fact that the ranch was close to Tlaxcala explains the power this festival always had, bearing in mind that Tlaxcala was one of the most important centres of Nahuatlan theatre.

In later years, we have been to various indigenous performances in different parts of the Republic, sometimes as guests of people such as Rodolfo Valencia,[9] that great figure of indigenous theatre, and other times, pursuing our own research.

This type of dramatised festivity, or theatrical rite, survives in almost all the Central American ethnic groups. In some places it is dotted with Spanish, with the sung voice in Nahuatlan; in other areas, it is the other way round. The performances or celebrations are mobile, and hence not easy to locate. It could be said, as anthropologists confirm, that these ethnic groups, with their rites and celebrations, are tending to die out in a relatively short space of time.

Paradoxically, as recently as 1985, we watched in Mexico City a play directed by Andrés Segura, who is said to be one of the inheritors of Mexican indigenous tradition. This play told the myth of the Sixth Sun with a strictly western dramatic structure. The stage was designed in an Italian style and the play, was, of course, in Spanish with some words in Nahuatlan. There was no sign of the open spaces or the lavish presence of nature, which always characterised pre-Hispanic theatre. This work could be considered an authentic piece of contemporary Nahuatlan theatre. We believe that it

---

9 Rodolfo Valencia was a Mexican theatre practitioner whose Teatro Campesino worked in rural and indigenous communities in Mexico.

is possible that this group, if they work on their theatrical tool and polish it, could be a huge success on the stage. Nevertheless, they could lose a lot, if not all, of the theatre's ritual, festive sense.

The excellent voice and speech-style of Juan Allende vibrated out, in Nahuatlan, the *Plan of Ayala* (the version authorised by Professor Miguel León Portilla for this work), while Helena Guardia translated it simultaneously into Spanish. As far as we know, this was the first time that a speech in Nahuatlan had been heard in Mexican university theatre.

The phenomenon of a recovery of Nahuatlan values through contemporary theatre is growing stronger by the day, essentially in Mexico City. Here, the important thing is that those of us who are working on this recovery should realise that we must be prepared to investigate the most suitable dramatic options for our intentions; there is no reason why we should stick to the structures of a western theatre which could make our content rigid, when the area and time are right to look into theatrical alternatives which allow us to define and mature our own spiritual and cultural concerns. In our workshop, we have been advancing in this sense for more than ten years, developing what we have termed designs for participatory theatre.

Our experience with pastorales, considered the very essence of Nahuatlan theatre, lies in, on the one hand, our role as spectators at a good number of them, and on the other, in our collaboration in directing a few. We had the chance to learn in depth the ins and outs of what is involved in performing a pastorale these days, for instance the one performed at Tepozotlán, possibly the most famous one performed in Mexico at the moment. The spectacular effect of the pastorale lies in the use of part of the convent of Tepozotlán as a stage, its large production, and the completeness of the party when the performance is over: fireworks, jars of sweets, food, drink, mariachis and so on. Without doubt, we could expand on each of these points, as we are fully aware of the richness of theatrical festivity which this pastorale contains, having directed it in 1975.

Elsewhere, the contact we have with a type of Nahuatlan theatre which is still alive, like the conchero dance, has been quite helpful in the development of our schemes for participatory theatre. We were introduced to the conchero dance through people like Gonzalo Alvarado and Armando Alvarez, the latter being a member of our beloved General Teresa's group.[10]

The conchero dance was, and is, an instrument of pre-Hispanic religion. Horcasitas says of pre-Hispanic dance in general:

> Dance was part of the ancient religion, it was still very popular in the period of viceroyalty, and even today it has not died out as a religious demonstration in fiestas. It would have been logical for the missionaries to use it for their missionary theatre, but they did not (Horcasitas, [1974] 2004: 158).

It is clear that the missionaries could not find a way to use the code of the dances to convert people. Nevertheless, as it was a prehispanic religious dance, in order to survive it had to take in images and effects of Catholic orthodoxy, thus creating a religious union which is difficult to define.

In present-day gatherings to perform this dance, Christian and pre-Hispanic elements can be seen to harmonise splendidly, intermingling to such an extent that it has so far been useless, and we would even dare to say hurtful, to attempt a 'purist' recovery. All religions are fusions, amalgamations, melting pots. The phenomenon of union in pre-Hispanic shell conchero dances is a true reflection of how the aspirations of authentic Christianity and pre-Hispanic religion are blended in a single impulse to dance for God. This phenomenon, with this unified structure, is what the Mexicans of today are living through. In this structure we can find Nahuatlan theatrical rite totally alive, together with images and guidelines of Christianity brought to life by this dance. We believe it is a religious phenomenon corresponding to contemporary Mexicans, that is to say racially mixed people. Through this phenomenon it is possible for us to blend and reach a deep understanding of our two basic religious sources, the pre-Hispanic and the Christian one.

---

10   General Teresa is the captain, leader and guide of a conchero group researching and performing ritual dance, working within the Mesa del Santo Niño de Atocha.

Nowadays, contacts are on the increase; cultures and religions are interacting more than ever; the opening up of opinion makes us appreciate on the one hand the humanism and teachings which are so magnificently developed in Nahuatlan philosophy and religion, and on the other hand, their absolute convergence with authentic Christianity. We feel that a contemporary Mexican must try to gain a deeper knowledge of these two sources in order to open himself up to his own evolution.

Returning to the theme of dance, Professor Horcasitas tells us that, 'in fact, on reading the chronicles of the colonial period, it becomes obvious that pre-Christian dance outlived the Conquest' (Horcasitas, [1974] 2004: 156). It can clearly be understood that, since dance was religion in motion, pre-Christian religion outlived the Conquest and instead of adopting a shy attitude towards the conquistador, assimilated Christian values and images into its structure.

At this point we shall leave these matters. We would point out that our commentary on Nahuatlan theatre is brief and schematic. Anybody interested in looking into the area in greater depth would be advised to consult Professor Horcasitas' excellent study *Teatro Nahuatl* ([1974] 2004), the essential source of our quotations. We would also mention that the importance of Professor Horcasitas' text spurred us to try and act as a bridge for the furthering of his work.

We shall now turn our attention to the importance to our workshop of the conchero dance, which is of interest to us from a strictly scientific angle: on the one hand, its great capacity as an instrument for updating the consciousness, and on the other, the help it offers us in working out significant parts of our designs for participatory theatre.

In its internal structure we have discovered:

1. It is a dance - or meditation in motion - performed through a defined body alphabet, a type of mandala in motion, which charges the performer with energy.

2. The performer, allegorically, is a warrior fighting his battle through the dance, to achieve individual and group freedom. The dance is performed in a circle.

3. This battle is essentially internal. The performer is striving to maintain the level of attention in the 'here and now', by offering energy to the essences, with energetic resonance in the external world.

These three points of contact, the reader will remember, are exactly the same as we have shown for the Tibetan 'Black Hat' dance.

It disturbs us that two theatrical rite dances, so far apart from each other, should essentially unite the same intentions. Might it be due to coincidence, as we have mentioned, or to a common ancestral source for the two cultures? The experts are the ones to discover these unknown factors; we simply set out the evidence.

In conclusion, we can say that the conchero dance could possibly be looked upon as the most significant phenomenon and the most convincing proof of the continuity of a type of Nahuatlan theatrical rite which is very likely to survive into the future and play a significant role in Mexican culture.

In addition to the conchero dance, we have also had the chance, up in the Mexican mountains, to come into contact with certain indigenous ceremonies which have given us an insight into another living aspect of the strong pre-Hispanic culture.

These ceremonies are isolated and difficult to get to; distances and discomforts must be overcome, and one has to be lucky enough to arrive at the right time, as it is never known exactly when the celebrations will be held, except in Holy Week, on All Souls' Day, or another day when it is known beforehand more or less when and where they are due to take place. This uncertainty is due to the movable nature of these feasts.

We travelled, during our period of research, to various parts of the mountains in Nayarit, Puebla, Oaxaca, and the Yucatán Peninsula, as well as to certain areas in the centre of the Republic. In our search for ritual sources in Mexico, we invariably found the voice as an instrument of induction and a guide to achieving deep states of consciousness; the quality of the voice's vibration, as used by *mara'akames*, shamans, or pre-Hispanic priests, always has a litany, or a chant structure, designed to summon up energies for different purposes: to cure, celebrate, marry people, punish, give thanks, or help the dying to pass away with dignity and correctness.

Of all these celebrations, perhaps the most suitable to talk about here was the one we attended in San Andrés Coamiata, in the Huicholan mountains.

There, in December one year, in the celebrations for the change of governor, we attended the sacrifice of a bull, which had its throat slit so as to feed the Sun with its blood. The blood fell into a pit which was mythically connected to the centre of the Earth. In this sacred pit, people dipped their fingers respectfully and made the sign of the cross on their foreheads. The first to do this were the local dignitaries, and then gradually all those present went on to splash a bloody blessing onto relatives - present or absent, alive or dead - property, cattle, business possibilities etc. Afterwards they moved on to the communion with the meat of this bull, which was ritually cut up there and then and shared out among the congregation, who numbered about three hundred in total. The performance's archaic sense sent shivers down the spine. After the communion with the meat, a pilgrimage was begun which ended by the temple door, in a rectangular space of about twenty metres deep by seven wide, completely empty apart from a cross, erected a few metres from the back, on which there could clearly be seen the drawing of the 'eye of God', or the Huicholan cross - yet another fact suggesting an exceptional sense of unification. Here people made offerings, lit candles, and left *mauvieris* (little arrows with their tiny bow, which are 'charged' with the wish of the offerer). The action is accompanied throughout by violins, little bells and little drums which emphasise the continual sung prayer. At nightfall, the people get together in various houses around the fire, which is in the middle of the room, to eat and drink *tehuino*, a drink which contains peyote. Sprigs of peyote were offered up by the people in charge who - according to their judgement - offered them to some people and not to others. The main aim of the meeting is to keep the chant alive, which helps them to get through the night and steer clear of all the *chamucos* (demons) released by the darkness.

The imposing austerity of the mountains, protected by a sky full of stars, and the murmur of human warmth giving itself over to the energies of the light, instilled in us a deep sense of brotherhood. There we were, high up in the mountains, gathered in small groups around a fire, provoking a rather extraordinary flow of communicating vessels; seeing and hearing the reflections of our minds. Looking at the spectacle from outside, it seemed like a group which was too exposed, vulnerable, extremely fragile and delicate, and at the same time blessed with unique strength and beauty, like the orchid.

The clarity of dawn slowly uncovered the other reality, the everyday one. Shapes regained their volume and colour, and certainty tentatively built its path back to reason, to common sense. Nevertheless, in our stomachs, there was still a feeling which linked us to emptiness.

As we received the sunrise with songs and offerings, the rhythm and the rite of this interpenetrant fullness and emptiness became clear to us, audibly and visually.

It is a well-known fact that the Huicholans are among the Mexican ethnic groups who most rigorously uphold their traditions. They may well be among the most highly-charged in this sense.

We should make it clear that the appreciation we have set out here is barely the subjective and fragmented vision of an outsider, for we are a long way from finding the internal code of these ceremonies, despite having studied them and even having been lucky enough to share with these people the pilgrimage to Viricota, where we took part and shared in the sublime, luminous flight in the hunt for peyote.

We could also mention how lucky we were to share, up in the Mazatecan mountains, in a ceremony performed by Apolonia, the daughter and heiress of

María Sabina,[11] who by the end of her life was deeply saddened and lamented the publicity prostitution which belittled the strength of the child saints, one of the most striking and revealing rites of pre-Hispanic religion.

So as not to cast our net too widely, we shall simply underline the fact that in this ceremony, as in most of those in which we took part in Mexico, the vibration of the voice synchronised with the mental intention of the performer is, we believe, one of the main tools used; this is not to detract from the musical, odorous and alimentary elements which characterise all these ceremonies.

In our research, we place particular emphasis on vibration since, as is scientifically proven, the solidity of matter does not exist, and in the universe the only things which move are impulses of energy susceptible to change direction, size, intensity and colour, according to their vibration quality. This is why vibration seems to us to be the most suitable reference framework for the cultural proposal and design of mechanisms which speed up and purify our vibration; cultural designs which help us to shake off the sick vision of a staticised universe. We could mention here that quantum theory and contemporary psychology - as we understand them - have helped us to form a much fuller vision of our work in the theatre.

The reader may be wondering why theatrical people should be interested in ceremonies, vibration, psychology and quantum theory.

Investigation is an inherent human impulse. Through investigation we discovered that theatre was breaking down its frontiers. One of our first steps was to study our own body, spirit and origin. Octavio Paz's *El Laberinto de la Soledad* (1950) (*The Labyrinth of Solitude*, 1961) was our starting point for beginning to discover our identity. The stage version of this text was called *Laberinto* (Labyrinth). There it was revealed to us not only that a philosophical essay can be turned into a theatrical performance, but also that it is possible for

---

11 María Sabina was a Mazatec *curandera* (or shaman), brought to international attention in Gordon Wasson's *Maria Sabina and Her Mazatec Mushroom Velada* (1976).

us to delve deeper into our roots. The research and performance of *Laberinto* was authorised by Professor Octavio Paz, who was pleased to see in dramatic images and situations what he had constructed in his words.

The impulse to work through theatre, and the study of ourselves gave us access to Nahuatlan philosophy, pre-Hispanic theatre, ceremonies in Mexico, Turkey, Poland and India, quantum thought and its resonances in contemporary culture. It led us to experience western theatrical trends close-up, like in the Old Vic in England, the Actor's Studio in New York and the Laboratory Theatre in Poland. It also led us to research into Tibetan theatre at the Tibetan Institute of Performing Arts in India. But, essentially, it led us to develop tools for participatory theatre as an alternative option for contemporary theatre. These are designs in which certain tools and the vital impulse of Nahuatlan philosophical thought still survive.

ANTHROPOCOSMIC THEATRE

3 WESTERN THEATRE

Stanislavski

We should, at this point, consider once again what is the essential function of theatre. We must realise that the deep-rooted theatrical rules established by the Greeks have been in a state of crisis for some time, and far from finding contributions which would strengthen them, they have gradually fallen apart.

In spite of the monumental jewels of human inquiry which enriched western theatre, supplied by people like Aeschylus, Shakespeare, Calderón, Molière, Ibsen, Shaw etc., its Italian or Greek-style orthodoxy has always ended up making these people waterproof; the theatre's fantastic contents are alive in each and every one of its lines, but nowadays a new approach is needed. Our stage inheritance, at the turn of the century, was a dying body whose moments of glory were already long gone. As a result of this, some innovators thought it possible to revitalise it, to plot its rebirth. 'Here and now' was wisely formulated by Stanislavski, who in doing so laid the touchstone which brought the essential content back to western theatre. During and after the time of Stanislavski, other renovators appeared such as Craig, Meyerhold, Vakhtangov, Brecht, Artaud, Grotowski, Brook, Barba and Schechner, all of whom were revolutionaries in theatre. Stanislavski stands as a central image of all those who seek through their work to question theatrical orthodoxy, to give back to theatre its original sense of confrontation and movement.

Despite all the innovators, orthodoxy in theatre still exists and will continue to do so, like a bureaucratic consequence of what at one time was a simple act of faith; it will survive particularly in the hands of businessmen, which is also the fate of the orthodoxies of various established religions. In saying this, we do not wish to give the impression of attacking the structures of any particular religion, nor those of theatre in general since, despite the fact that some of these orthodoxies are essentially dislocated from a true rhythm, between them they fulfil a specific function. Arnold Hauser expresses this particularly well when he speaks of conventional means of expression:

> However much conventional means of expression may confine and obstruct the opening up of the inner life, they are the initial means of access to it and there is thus little point in bewailing their insufficiency (1982: 31 - 32).

In declaring the 'here and now' and establishing the idea of 'as if' as a mechanism for action on the stage, Stanislavski was not inventing anything new; the huge significance of these two propositions which revolutionised theatre lies in the fact that they form the cornerstone of the majority of the religious and philosophical conceptions known to us. In the light of this and what Stanislavski himself states in his texts, we can consider it to be no accident that these propositions, as archaic mechanisms of rite, are well known to him and are brought back into a discipline which, having started from these same bases, had forgotten them. Stanislavski did not invent these formulas, but he had the farsightedness to reawaken these principles in theatre; he promoted the spread of this consciousness, and hence has become a kind of prophet in contemporary theatre. Another of Stanislavski's great merits is his putting these formulas into practice and working with them until the very end; remember that in the last years of his life, private rehearsals were far more important to him than public performances.

Nobody nowadays would dare to deny the immense connection which exists between the Stanislavskian propositions of 'here and now' and 'as if', and the same propositions used in rituals as vehicles to arouse another reality.

These formulations can be found in almost all trends sought by human development, from the oldest orthodoxies to the most novel philosophical movements. When Stanislavski brought them into consideration, he left implanted in contemporary theatre a path which will lead us to the heart of the human being. It is part of theatre's arduous task, to keep alive an instrument of work with the flexibility to set up as many techniques as there are performers in the world, aware that as a performer I will establish my own technique which will make me perceive, and launch me into the world from my own essence, when I know how to use the tools properly to discover myself. The touchstone to begin this knowledge process was given to us by Stanislavski when he reminded us of the importance of the 'here and now'.

The 'happening' also owes almost all its structure to these postulates, only that it is like a younger son because as it uses the 'here and now', it does not do so with complete consciousness of integration. On the contrary, it generally delves childishly and furiously into certain areas, to make certain in the first instance that it is alive; this is not essentially bad, it is just that it belongs to an elemental level of dramatic creation. These harsh statements are valid at certain times, as long as there is always the commitment not to find sense in what we do, but rather that if we do it in a more organic way, we will find our capacity for surprise to be alive; that is, we should be prepared for that something which we are essentially incapable of formulating, to become apparent through us. If the 'happening' is good because it celebrates the moment, it is unsuccessful because it lacks the channels which would make it whole; it is an isolated explosion, a disjointed jubilee, which closes in on itself selfishly, will not act as a bridge and wants to be everything, and indeed it is for an instant. As it cannot keep up the rhythm, it switches off, succumbing to the pressure which cannot stand still and which demands that it carry on in the attitude of 'here and now'. This 'here and now', as summoned up by Stanislavski, does not explode fleetingly like the 'happening', but rather opens up slowly and dumbfoundedly and sets itself up on the stage, as the channel of authentic reality. Stanislavski proposed the development of a rigorous mechanism which would allow us to live in an instant. In that sense, we repeat, he took the first steps in contemporary theatre, thus indicating his deep commitment to the true performer.

Nowadays, there are many theatrical trends concerned with the development of the human being. With our work on anthropocosmic theatre, we aim to seek out the game in which we can freely make contact with other human beings. In this we recognise, in true theatre, one of the paths which favour the development of that internal richness in which, by way of a simple act, it is possible to touch in the heart of our being the rhythms which lead us to a more complete understanding of our destiny and our meaning. We would like to quote Mircea Eliade, who clearly defines this possibility:

> With the help of the history of religions (or the study of the dramatic phenomenon), modern man could always rediscover the symbolism of his body, which is an anthropocosmos. What the different techniques of imagination, and especially poetic techniques, have done in this respect, is nothing in comparison with the living promises in the history of religions. All the necessary data still survive, and are included in modern man; it is merely a case of reviving them and bringing them to the threshold of the consciousness. When he is once again aware of his own anthropocosmic symbolism - which is merely a variant of archaic symbolism - modern man will achieve a new existential dimension totally unknown to current existentialism and historicism: a way of being genuine and superior which will defend him from nihilism and historicistic relativism without removing him from history on account of this. For history itself could find its true sense: that of the epiphany of a glorious and absolute human condition (1961: 39).

The significance of Stanislavski, for us, lies therefore in his updating of the formula of the 'here and now'.

Brecht

At the very outset, we would like to emphasise the need to expand certain theatrical concepts used up to now, such as the distancing proposed by Brecht. Brecht worked splendidly in his particular moment of history because the theatrical circumstance of that time needed that focus; that is to say, theatrical illusion needed to be destroyed so that the audience, without compromising themselves emotionally, could have their objective, intelligent point of view about what was being offered in the theatrical performance, always committed to processes of social development.

When Brecht takes certain elements of Noh theatre, such as masks, music and the process of distancing in itself, and transposes them to European theatre, he leaves out the internal plan of Noh theatre. In other words, he leaves out the conception of rite, merely taking certain techniques and socialising them. He is right to do this, as it is what his period needed; but he himself is not unaware of the importance of rite for theatre, and he knows that techniques like those he brought from Noh to European theatre lose part of their original force when they are socialised in this way. Also, if they are used for a time without being returned to their origins, they tend to weaken. He knows, as a good German who knew and studied in depth Nietzsche's *The Birth of Tragedy*, that the pact between the Apollonian and the Dionysian has been in theatre from time immemorial, accentuated sometimes in favour of the former and others in favour of the latter. Now, after more than fifty years, things have changed sufficiently to understand the need to reconsider the mechanisms of action so as to get into theatrical development and its social derivations; in other words, we see the need to propose that Brechtian distancing be expanded, not only because we consider this proposition to be correct, but because, whoever does it, it is fitting for our time.

This expansion must go beyond socio-psychological conflict so as to give us a new distancing which lets us understand our commitment as human beings in relation to ourselves and to the world. This means realising that we are submerged in a movement which transcends our human condition; we see revealed to us the fallacy of many of our mental structures which we treat as material social institutions, and the majority of which are not only disjointed, but also, at times, work actively in the opposite direction to the expansion of the consciousness. This new distancing takes us nearer to an essential reality which has lain in theatre since its origins and which we now need to take up again. It could be said that at this time, a minimal distancing keeps us apart from essential reality, and a greater one draws us closer to it. That is the reality of the times in which we live.

Now we must find our own masks, our signs and our own meaning by supplying ourselves with feedback from other sources, as Brecht did with Noh theatre, but without losing our roots. This is a terrible challenge, but it is one which we must face up to if we want to survive. In other words, we must get closer to other theatrical cultures, but finally prepare ourselves to be qualified to discover universal essences from our particular profile. I am convinced that this path nowadays is one of the few which really offer the promise of a new breath of life for theatre.

Let us now leave Brecht. Another of the concepts which we would like to expand on is that of the technique of the actor (with a small 'a'), compared with the technique of the Actor (with a capital 'A'). We shall see straight away why this proposition has been made:

- Technique of the actor (small 'a'): being masked over being masked.
  Use: exclusively the product of official consumption/advertising.

- Technique of the Actor (capital 'A'): unmasking.
  Use: body and psychological training from various perspectives of the nature of man, without destroying the performer; relation with its anthropological and ethical context, as an apprenticeship. Finally, its professional application.

This means that the technique of the actor (with a small 'a') allows the performer to learn modes of masking which he uses over the masks which he has as a human being, in other words, he does not purge himself, but learns the art of pretending. The technique of the Actor (with a capital 'A') aims to help the performer to unmask himself and discover himself without any fraud; to help him to be real to himself and others. This position is closer to the essences which originated theatrical rite, than those which, with a desire to consume, corrupt the essences and build false realities.

Having stated this, let us now draw up a brief summary so that the reader can follow the coherence of our thought and understand why we have reached the proposition of an anthropocosmic theatre.

The primary function of acting systems is to qualify the human being to master his instrument, which in this case happens to be his own organism, with all its states, internal and external. This, by any reckoning, is a principle of development and knowledge; to get to be self-regulated is to take the appropriate steps towards evolution; to discover that every single part of our body and our emotions is connected to, or rather interplaying with, the cosmos, is to realise that when we study our body we are also studying part of the cosmos. Not all acting systems understand this truth.

At the beginning of theatre, when there were no acting systems, performers handled their instrument in direct relation to the universe, that is they experienced rite, but in order to experience it they developed a special form of learning about their bodies as instruments. We do not intend to go quite so far, although we know that rite was, and still is, the essence of theatre. We merely wish to develop a modest acknowledgement of our possibilities, in keeping with the period and circumstances in which we live.

We have been aided by the discovery, in the studies of Mircea Eliade, of the idea that theatre can well be considered the oldest religious/festive phenomenon in humanity, a phenomenon which appears not only in ancient Egypt, but also in China, Tibet, India and Europe, as well as in Africa and Central America.

In global terms, let us say that we did not realise that to a greater or lesser extent, rite appeared all over the world as the manifestation of an internal need of the human being. We then became fully aware that theatre began as an instrument of magical thought par excellence, giving rise to man's original religious celebration. That is why a type of theatre which we could consider anthropocosmic should aim to investigate the mechanisms which offer the performer-human being the chance to develop his own 'personal' path which will put him in contact with his entire body and its cosmic resonances, so as to work here and now, in our own lifetime.

The Old Vic

Our experience at the Old Vic theatre school in Bristol, England, centred on the chance we were given to work on the staging of the Royal Bristol Old Vic's version of *Plunder*, by Ben Travers, in 1973. Although our participation was like a shadow passing in the depths of darkness (so to speak), it did give us the chance on the one hand to tread the English boards and experience the break-up of the ordinary world and observe the magic of its theatre from inside, and on the other, to see first-hand the technical devices of contemporary English sets; discipline; rehearsals for specific areas; set-building and the acquisition of the wardrobe; what could be done with light and sound; methods used to achieve special effects, etc. Most importantly, we learned how to link the atmospheres in rehearsals so as to build up that unity of actions, reactions, expressions and words which provide the necessary states of animation to produce theatre. We were also there for two more productions of the Old Vic: Chekhov's *Uncle Vania* and Bernard Shaw's *The Apple Cart*.

The experience with these three productions, and the brotherly guidance we always received from the Irish actor Peter O'Toole, who led the cast in these plays, allowed us to widen our acting education and take it directly from the classroom to the stage, and from there to the cafes and bars, where we may well have received our best acting lessons.

Learning from the acting quality of Peter O'Toole in the rehearsals and plays which we have mentioned, was obviously very important to us, but the best part was learning from his acting as a friend and a theatrical guide in the cafes and bars. He would say, for example,

> The most important thing for an actor who is starting out, is to be aware that there is no system or school that is going to make him an actor; he must seek and design his own system. Every great actor has his system, but it is only good for him. Learning to act, therefore, is learning to build our own acting system - the one which suits us best, according to what sort of animal we are. A good acting school is one

which gives us a suitable atmosphere whereby everyone can develop their own system; it gives us information and gives us freedom to investigate, without imposing its method on us[12].

O'Toole generously allowed us to attend private rehearsals where we slowly took note of how he simultaneously formed his points of attention on the stage and his internal register. He clearly did it using his own system. One was constantly aware of the mindfulness with which he performed every detail. He would say, 'The secret is to keep yourself in the here and now with total mindfulness, and do what you have to do, not pretend to be doing it.'

In short, we can say that at the Old Vic, particularly through the teachings of Peter O'Toole, we received some of the best acting lessons we have had.

O'Toole always showed us the path from the internal offering of our being 'here and now' to an energy which lets us float on the platform of the moment.

Strasberg

On 44th Street in New York there is a small Greek-style building, which once served as a church and since 1949 has been the headquarters of the Actor's Studio.

Here Strasberg, together with Elia Kazan, Shelly Winters and Anna Strasberg, among others, taught the mechanism of his famous 'method'. At the time of writing, there are two 'Lee Strasberg Theater Institutes', one in New York and the other in Los Angeles, apart from the headquarters at the Actor's Studio.

Strasberg tells us that the value of his 'method' lies in having taken up Stanislavski's postulates and developed them,

> My discovery is merely that of a method of approach for the actor with his instrument, which in this case is the actor himself. This method of understanding for the actor is based on information given

---

12   All quotations cited here were recorded verbatim by the author in Bristol in 1973 - 1974, and in Mexico in 1975, with the permission of Peter O'Toole.

to us by contemporary psychology, knowledge which has allowed us to ascertain more about the condition and internal structure of the human being; knowledge to which Stanislavski did not have access. The influences begin with Pavlov, Skinner, Jung, Laing and Cooper, Gestalt itself, parts of Reich, and all contemporary thought - influences which give us a greater understanding of our structures. In theatrical terms, Stanislavski and Vakhtangov are the most direct influences on my work, as are certain aspects of Meyerhold and... anyway, a full list would be horrible; I would merely say that in general terms, influences such as those I have mentioned have helped me create a system of exercises which characterise the method.[13]

Strasberg studied with Richard Boleslavsky and Maria Ouspenskaya who in turn had been students of Stanislavski. In 1931, he founded the famous Group Theater with Harold Clurman and Cheryl Crawford, where people from the top grade of North American theatre worked, such as Stella Adhler, Uta Hagen, Hebert Berghoff (who was also an excellent teacher), and others.

All his exercises have a strong content of human development. Among these, the most important are his 'private moment' and his 'overall'. In general, the exercises are structured to lead the performer to a deep revision of his internal and external structures, and to help him take stock of his habits and what chances he has to re-educate himself. Strasberg says,

[W]hen we are afraid of something, that is the clearest symptom or evidence of an area within us which has been hurt. We must revise mainly the conditioning of punishment, the 'I won't do it because I'll be punished', however it is carried out, whether physically, psychically, financially or morally, and develop a reconditioning process so as to overcome these fears which block our movement. This is why there are parts of our body which are asleep, frozen even, due to fears or habits.

---

13   All quotations cited here were recorded verbatim by the author and Helena Guardia in New York in 1978 with the permission of Strasberg.

This is something that a performer cannot allow himself, just as if a violinist were to try and give a concert with a broken violin; we have to recondition our entire body, which is our instrument, and polish it physically and emotionally. Every deep conditioning can only be fought with will and another new conditioning which takes over from it, only that in this re-education, it is the actor who chooses his new conditionings and lives according to a reality which he himself has chosen; he no longer suffers, consciously or unconsciously. This is the best way, because it shows us the relativity of reality, both in and away from theatre.

When Strasberg talks of the relativity of reality, we understand that if we act with safe behaviour patterns, continuous repetition is what will give reality a line of coherence, but this line may be changed, it is not fixed. In fact, it changes on account of the different ideologies which exist as systems, be they political, religious or economic. Reality is always relative, always susceptible to be reprogrammed, or even dramatised, and those of us who work in theatre must be aware of this.

Strasberg's points of view which we will set out below, were taken in New York by Helena Guardia and myself in 1978. Strasberg died in February 1982.

Strasberg's Advice

One of the first steps in the process of the method, I can assure you, is that you will feel confused, so you should not make hasty judgements. The fact that you feel confused is the first healthy step on the road to discovering a wide range of possibilities; it is, so to speak, a way of starting to wonder.

All an actor needs is willpower and control; that is all I would ask you to work on.

All human fabrics and fluids are the actor's instrument; for him to control his instrument, he must develop an exhaustive exercise of understanding and control over it. Sometimes, the actor thinks he is doing the right thing, simply because he thinks so, but often the reality is that his instrument is not responding to him as he thinks it is responding. His muscles and fluids are deceiving him. He must correct this dichotomy, so as to do exactly what he wants to do.

The actor can achieve mental education through concentration. Concentration is the only path open to the actor to turn his evocations into reality. A strong power of concentration always produces an excellent actor.

The function of relaxation is what must come before concentration.

Stanislavski, towards the end of his life, said that we only achieve five per cent of our potential concentration, and that we need to develop the other 95%. I agree wholeheartedly. Relaxation, when it is done properly, accentuates the power of concentration. The actor's concentration must be sufficiently well honed so that it is effective in the shortest time possible. Relaxation shows us how to discover our emotional reserves, so that we can go on to make use of them.

When certain involuntary movements appear during relaxation, it is the symptom of blocked areas which tend to free themselves.

When the actor suffers some sort of interference, instead of putting more energy into the process he must relax; in this way, his relaxation gives him greater powers of concentration and he can then overcome any interference more effectively.

There is a type of relaxation which lies in the habit of relaxation. We must break through this habit, which is false relaxation.

The purpose of re-educating the actor's attention is that he should be able to concentrate, developing various attitudes on the stage and doing so in a natural way, without losing control, as we do in daily life. In life, we drive a car while simultaneously chatting, chewing gum, smoking, listening to music or doing any amount of other things. We do all this without realising it, because we are used to it. That is what we need to do on stage, to use the habits of a character with the same ease with which the latter would do so in real life, without, of course, losing control of the dramatic situation.

Habits create a second nature; the actor must know them well and learn how to handle them.

The main purpose of the method's exercises consists of establishing with the muscles a different type of relationship from the one which they have with the habits, that is to say, we try to break the bonds of our habits, so that sensitivity can flow unimpeded and according to our free will.

Deep-rooted habits form muscular shields which are hard to overcome; to get beyond them, we need the reconditioning of our strength as the principal motor.

The actor needs to develop a series of new habits which will replace many others which he carries through life without even realising it. When the actor has worked on his willpower, concentration, his capacity for delivery, and mastery of his own body and emotions as brand-new habits, he now has the chance to obtain effective and immediate answers to questions on any emotional area.

The actor must fight against the character barrier in his own habits and establish in his theatre the habits of the character he is playing; in other words, the actor must be a human being without habits (Strasberg reminds us here of the influence of Castaneda), with enough ability and will to take on any character script.

With Skinner I discovered, though it may be sad to realise this, that the human being is an animal of conditionings, and that precisely because he is an animal of conditionings, he can recondition himself, that is to say reprogram himself, 're-educate' himself. This is the job of the actor, to restructure his conditionings; moreover, he has to learn a little trick of contemporary psychology, that is, he must know that there are two types of conditioning, the external and the internal. The external one needs to be reinforced continually so as to carry on working; like in advertising, if we stop being bombarded with adverts we forget all about this conditioning. The internal one acts without continual reinforcement, like morality, which comes to form part of ourselves. This is why the development and reformation of conditioning processes are so important to the actor, so that he can achieve maximum control over his instrument.

To change bad habits for good ones, we must first find out which are the bad ones from which we suffer, so as to combat them.

Any habit, however strong, will succumb to the application of willpower; willpower is the only thing which can manipulate habits and change them.

Every deep-rooted habit or conditioning can be combatted only by willpower and a new conditioning to replace it. An interesting scientific fact is that habits form 90 per cent of human behaviour.

The actor discovers himself through certain exercises which must be performed with will and energy.

Pavlov says that there is a basic energy which moves between the mind and the body; the actor's main job is the understanding, formation and application of this energy through willpower.

The process of activating the fluids to achieve different states of mind, must be undertaken by the actor through the discipline of his will and not via external stimuli. Anyone who does so seeking this support, makes the process of emotional evocation softer and ends up losing it, and those who do so through discipline, reinforce their will and the control they have over their instrument, move dynamically on stage, with absolute control; on the stage there is a need for actors who have total control over their actions, because it can be as dangerous as a motorway, onto which nobody should be allowed who is not in control of their vehicle, as they could cause an accident.

Acting is like having a shower: we are free to control the temperature of the water; a good actor never scalds himself - he is in control of the degrees of his reality.

All an actor needs to begin his evolution is willpower. Otherwise, he is like someone stuck outside a door which he wants to open, but makes no move to do so; that way, the door will never be opened we must move along and tackle the problems which emerge with this movement.

It is not the emotions which drive the human being; rather, willpower controls and governs the emotions. In cases in which there is no energetic existence of willpower, the emotions take the instrument prisoner.

When we are faced with a blockage, we reach a point where the individual confronts a duality: whether to give up or to carry on. To give up the work at this point, means having a subjective, not an evolutionary, attitude; we must continue to make use of willpower.

The mind is not the only significant factor in the function of the actor. Nevertheless, he must train his entire body via his mind. The more talent an actor has, the more problems he has in learning.

Looking back over the work of Stanislavski, it can be said that his main concern was that the actor should discover his 'self', 'here and now'.

When somebody says 'I can't feel anything', a huge number of things are happening to him to make him arrive at that decision.

Mental revision of all the parts of the body is the mechanism for achieving complete control over the body.

With his brain and his emotiveness, the actor invents the reality which at the very moment of being performed theatrically, is no longer invented but now becomes authentic.

On the face, just as in all the other parts of the body, we find various areas of expression. We must learn to put our brain into each one of these, so as to achieve automatic control.

It has been discovered that the function of the brain is not affected by the position of the body. Therefore, from any position our body may be in, however uncomfortable, we can make a mental recognition of our entire body and give it orders.

Theatre is the recreation of an experience, not the thought of that experience; it is not something which seems dramatic, it actually is dramatic.

Our muscles and our thought can only do what they are trained to do; in the same way, they may be re-educated.

We must revise our behaviour so as to establish which are the conditions or paths to be followed to reach our aim. Once we have realised what it is we need to do, we must then do it.

The brain is divided into two areas, hence the derivation of no end of behaviour patterns which we need to study.

The mouth is one of the most important parts of the actor's body, as it is where all the ideas registered by the brain are reflected.

When he really gets to hear imaginary bells on stage, and has an honest response to this situation, the actor can then repeat that scene hundreds of times and still be just as fresh and spontaneous.

When the instrument of the actor is blocked and he is working on its rehabilitation, there are generally only two ways for energy to emerge: by laughing or crying.

There are thoughts which get blocked in the muscular fabric. There are exercises, specific movements, which bring about the unblocking and the free flow of energy, and hence the actor, in this flow, can choose the particular character river on which he wishes to sail.

The motivation exerted by an actor on his instrument must be exactly that which is desired; that is to say, in terms of joy, for example: my happiness on Mother's Day is not the same as the joy I experience on the National Holiday of my country, or on New Year's Eve, or when I see a beautiful girl, or a succulent cake. All these experiences may bring about happiness, but they are directed and handled by different centres which we must learn about and gauge.

A blockage is badly-adjusted energy. When we fight against it, we are striving to re-order and understand the natural process of energy.

If, when faced with a blockage, we do not know where it comes from, psychologists tell us that what happens is that we do not want to discover the origins of the blockage, and they are right.

We must fight against tensions for a very simple reason: it is scientifically proven that they are a waste of badly-applied energy. If we relax, we stop wasting it.

In terms of their structure, blockages have a lot to do with the character analysis carried out by Reich. We can learn a lot about this matter from Reich.

At the beginning of *A la Recherche du Temps Perdu*, Proust makes an analysis of affective memory. Tension stops him from remembering; when he relaxes, the whole story begins.

We must revise and be aware that as we try to fight against tension, we should not do so by creating another tension in a different area. In that way, the tension would not be freed, but rather exchanged. Tension is merely a series of forces found in the muscles, and to counteract it, our impulses must be reorganised. As tension creates blockages, it destroys our normal behaviour.

The actor does not develop tensions; he is more qualified to concentrate and hence develop his work better. What is important is not what he says, but rather what he feels. He becomes a virtuoso when, through his performance, he manages to enter reality and, in the conciliation of times, allows living time to flourish through him.

Nobody can know or feel that he has a deep knowledge of the problems of acting, if he has not experienced them.

Acting is all about putting a certain amount of energy in the right place; when we do not achieve what we want, it is simply because the energy is not correctly positioned. Acting, therefore, means placing our energy in the right place.

The actor, like the violinist, must know his instrument and how to tune it. The actor is the violin and the violinist at the same time.

I have discovered that to evoke a character on stage, i.e. to act, a warm-up of no more than five minutes is needed, once the actor has mastered his instrument. We must act not with words, but with emotions.

Any type of action which we carry out, whether consciously or unconsciously, brings about a reaction in our body. When we say 'I can't do it', we are really saying, 'I can't be bothered to make the effort to do it'.

What the actor reveals on stage is a sensation of reality, 'here and now'. The fact that he uses the platform of an imaginary reality is not important; what happens up there 'really happens'.

We do not really know how this sensation of reality happens, but through its exercises, we learn how to understand it, because that is the best domain for it to appear and for us to familiarise ourselves with it; that is, we use the exercises as an investigation into those moments, to develop a greater awareness of the mechanism which makes the sensation of reality appear, and hence we learn how to handle it.

The struggle of the executor with his instrument can be seen in all the arts, always with the aim of achieving the maximum control, that is, virtuosity.

The most typical symptom of lack of consciousness among actors occurs when they see themselves in a film for the first time; they do not recognise themselves, they lose control and find it difficult to adjust to that reality.

To handle his motivation, an actor's needs are strictly individual and selective; for instance, when I need a segment of orange for motivation, this modest segment is better than ten apples; it is not a matter of quantity, but rather of what our emotional triggers specifically need.

On stage, just as in real life, we generally have a domestic action to be getting on with continually, even when the situation takes on a dramatic flavour; when somebody says I am dying, they do not say this and die - they say it and ask for vitamins, or go to the toilet, or blow their nose and so on. In theatre, this type of ordinary attack must always be present so as to give the action more veracity.

One of the first things an actor must ask himself when he is going to play a particular role is: what has the character got which I have also got?; what should I add to it?; or whether I should restructure my entire character-playing, since there is nothing within me which resembles this character.

We must learn to live in danger, because up on the stage anything can happen; it is a highly dangerous area and we must be prepared.

Stanislavski was criticised for being almost exclusively psychological; we do not make that mistake, as we develop physical exercises to complement the development of the actor's psychic structure.

When he is on stage, the actor should ask himself: where am I?; what am I doing?

On stage, the actor should not pretend to do what is done, but actually do it; when he reads, he should really read and not pretend to do so; or when he has to appear drunk, he should really feel intoxicated, and not just try to appear so.

One of the aims of the system is to establish the individual principles of development, to avoid the general rules which curtail the growth of the actor. This is why it is so mobile, a system which is based on principles which bring about individual action, not on rules which produce nothing but obedience, and hence rigidity.

The evolution of the exercises, their continuity and the learning through the system which we use, is infinite, because it is not a finished, I mean regulated, system. When a pianist wants to hear a note, all he has to do is press the key on the piano; the sensitivity with which he does it is another matter, but the fact remains that the note is there when it is played. When an actor needs to produce an emotion, his range should have the same response as the piano - the emotion must appear immediately, regardless of the sensitivity with which the actor wants to handle it.

Acting is like a river: it is necessary to let oneself drift, but even more necessary is the ability to swim to keep afloat and hence be carried by the current.

The character outline of a particular part is to the actor what the score is to the musician: it is the guideline which he must follow in his own individual way, so that it fits in with the general rhythm in a natural way.

Every country has its own character Pathos, as has every individual, every community, ghetto or gang; the actor must study all these codes and understand them to perfection so as to play the characters properly.

Acting has a continuity which must begin before the function and finish moments after the function has ended.

Acting is like crossing a river: we choose the stones we wish to step on, and we look and decide almost instantaneously which will be our next step forward, without stopping. It is possible that if we have crossed that same river several times, we will know the best stepping-stones, but it is also possible that even if this is the case, one fine day the stone we were expecting will not be there; so we have to solve the problem on the spot and carry on, looking for the best way forward.

Here we shall leave Strasberg's comments, but before we move on to another topic, it is important to underline the mechanism which Strasberg developed for relaxation. This is achieved in the following way: we sit down on the edge of a seat and lean against the back, allowing our head to fall backwards, with our arms dangling loosely by our sides; the knees should be apart with the feet away from the chair. The general impression should be that of someone who has fallen asleep in a chair.

We must move our head to the right and the left, loosening all our tensions; our arms and legs should, in principle, move in a wavy fashion, seeking their freedom. Our breathing should be deep, and every time we breathe out, we should loosen all our muscles as far as we are able. This exercise should be done with the eyes closed. Mentally, we revise each part of our body and we order its relaxation; the exercise continues for whatever time is considered necessary to loosen all the tensions.

Strasberg also recommends a type of relaxation which can be used at any time. He says, for instance, that whether we are on stage or anywhere else, we must make ourselves as comfortable as possible and breathe deeply, getting rid of all our tensions; he tells us that we have to develop this type of relaxation sufficiently so as to be able to loosen our tensions when we are standing, sitting down, walking, chatting etc. Once we have understood this mechanism properly, we can easily tell when an actor in a film or a play is using this technique in front of the audience; the best exponent of this is Marlon Brando.

From this, we can detect something of what Strasberg thought as a theatre person. This now remains as advice which could be of use to the performer.

Grotowski

I met Grotowski in New York in 1978, and worked with him on his project called *The Tree of People* in 1979 and the *Theatre of Sources* project in 1980, both of which were in Poland. We worked together in the Mexican mountains, also in 1980, and that was the first time that Grotowski had worked with Mexicans. We also worked together in 1985 at the foot of Iztaccíhuatl. The Mexican projects were essentially subsidised by the National University.

To talk about the work of Grotowski is something which he alone can do. We can merely record our personal reactions and point out that the theatrical renovation which he proposed has been totally misunderstood. A human being's freedom to find another human being has not been accepted. It has been preferable to follow a theatre which celebrates personalities, where the tyranny of an 'innovator' becomes the avant-garde style of the period.

For a theatre with roots, a powerful theatre which is emerging not only in Mexico, but in the whole of Latin America, it is necessary to work with the truth. This theatre cannot ignore what contemporary theatre is working on in terms of rite.

The text which we will now reproduce was written at the end of 1979, after we had worked on *The Tree of People*.

The Sacred Gang

To talk about the new work which Grotowski is doing at the moment in his laboratory in Poland, is to try and draw through language the dizzy atmospheres of an internal movement which has gone beyond the word.

The exercises which he now uses, his ways of approaching his work, his mechanism for keeping space in motion, the premises from which each and every one of the steps which envelop the progress of his work is projected - all this is the result of a quest lasting many years, from when the Laboratory Theatre was built in 1959, to the current day. In such circumstances, numbering the processes would lead us to an analysis of 22 years of continuous changes - something which we feel would be more appropriate to undertake elsewhere; apart from which, as soon as we get around the essence of the quest, the 'being there' appears all the time. From the deepest registers which one can allow oneself, the exercises or techniques are automatically surpassed and we realise that their function is precisely, as Artaud once said, to serve as triggers to find a movement which is irrationally, overflowingly, brilliantly self-contained. We must not, therefore, forget that without these triggers there is no path and that, in this sense, Grotowski is the most diligent researcher there is nowadays, in terms of techniques or processes in the development of the actor - human being - and that it is thanks to his long experience and unquenchable desire for a constant quest, that some form of synthesis has now begun.

But what exactly is Grotowski looking for now? In short, I would dare to say that he is seeking complicity, genuine, deprogrammed, delicate complicity with the other human being. His work has the fullness of one who guarantees that reality materialises in his hands in such a way that it can only be an immense act of magic which he needs to share.

But with whom and how? Participants' internal development mechanisms and external acceptance mechanisms have been rigorously established. Hence, the Laboratory Theatre has, in the last few years, 1979-1982, been through processes of research with a basis in work such as the *Special Project, Mountain of Flame, Beehive, Special Tree, Specialized Programs*, together with various workshops, where work is done with new methods on the discipline of the actor, culminating in the *Theatre of Sources*, a project which finished in about 1984. Some of these projects have been undertaken in forests, in rivers, on mountains, or even in urban areas or in certain spaces at the headquarters of the Laboratory Theatre in Wroclaw, seeking all the possibilities of ritual fact and the validity of those contents in our modern world, coming to discover through investigation the path for the development of what Grotowski calls an active culture. With this, a new route is uncovered and its strange, magical code of communication is gradually established.

In 1970, Grotowski announced that he would not be undertaking any more productions, and that he was leaving the world of theatre. Indeed, *Apocalypsis Cum Figuris* was premiered in 1968 and is, to this day, the only set which the Laboratory Theatre has kept, having suffered a series of internal transformations which make improvement very difficult within conventional theatrical schemes. *Apocalypsis Cum Figuris* has turned into a type of sacrament, a starting point for Grotowski, together with his Laboratory Theatre, to organise the mechanisms of a new language.[14]

Grotowski did not so much abandon as revolutionise theatre. For instance, in the project *The Tree of People*, the performer is involved in a process of intimacy in which fields of reflexion, favourable for internal growth, are gradually established. After a day of preparation, we are slowly and individually taken inside the Laboratory Theatre building. We are given some premises about the use of space in the building, which is totally empty. It is freezing, -35 degrees, and the paltry heating is insufficient. One is committed to staying in there for several days - nobody knows exactly how many. There are no clocks, and all contact with the outside world is interrupted. On the second floor there is a special room, the work room.

All the members of the Laboratory Theatre are involved in the experiment, including Grotowski. The initiatives for the work seem to leap out at us anarchically one by one, suggesting that we take part and accepting our own initiatives; some members of the Theatre suggest guidelines. Grotowski takes part and as the hours and days pass, we develop a form of global complicity. Sometimes, the group turns like a single body and movement transcends us. We sleep on the floor, a few hours or scarcely at all; we work exhaustively, eat once a day and there is also a larder where we can go and take what we want.

Through the work, we lose the coherence of time. There is no reason to digress; movement brings us up to date, and in our minds times are reconciled and we discover the instant in which we are living; we are deeply and powerfully involved. There is neither past nor future, but rather a present which happens spasmodically, amid prolonged silences, noises and climatic outbursts of energy. At the end of the week's work, one is certain of having definitively detected the first signs of an essential language. Grotowski, with

---

14 The final performance of *Apocalypsis cum Figuris* took place in 1979.

his by now classic scruffiness, dressed in a mixture of clothes, sitting in a corner, smiles with the severe completeness of a new-born faun.

In this world which is continually bombarded with manipulation, the performance of an active experiment such as the one we have described becomes rather secretive, subversive. That is why this new code of communication belongs in principle to a type of sacred gang, because Grotowski knows the effort and the fight which are necessary to shake off all the automatisms and reach the necessary levels to establish contact. To begin the flight, we need to surrender ourselves as a sacrifice, where freedom moves itself, where the body becomes an instrument which achieves what is sacred and communicates it.

Grotowski and Brook speak of the monk who burns himself, as an example of this type of rigour. Fabulous. I can also see this in the poet and, of course, in that active member of a gang of desperados who through their play regard themselves as sacred: the actor. Grotowski the actor is alive and well in the real great world theatre, because he has discovered that life is a dream, and that all we have to do is learn to dream.

The following lines were published in the cultural supplement of the newspaper *Unomás Uno*, when Grotowski agreed to come to Mexico in 1980.

What is Grotowski coming to Mexico for?

He is coming to work on a project with the National University.

What type of project?

It is supposed that he had already left the world of theatre and had joined a monastery or something similar, and that his theatre-related activities had led him to an area far from the stage itself. So what really happened?

We must be aware that when Grotowski became internationally famous in 1968, all he needed to do was repeat the formula of his quest ad nauseam, to play himself as much as he wanted, since the market was established; simply being there would have guaranteed him a lucrative lifestyle and the label of being the avant-garde of international theatre, a label which was highly sought-after by those who were interested in avant-garde theatre. So what happened? Instead of sitting down and consolidating his stature as a famous man and seeing his advertising and economic dividends grow, Grotowski decided to throw himself into the honest quest for new propositions or paths towards the better development of the human being, using theatre as a vehicle of ascertainment to evolve our current condition, acknowledging that he was a novice on this new path. We could, therefore, repeat that Grotowski did not leave the theatre, but rather revolutionised it.

He aimed to bring together a group of people who came to his theatre, moved only by their keen, intimate desires for internal development; to be aware that the work of a new form of theatre does not stand up to competition, fraud, imposition, censorship or bad faith, and that from a starting point of the mutual need for development, we try to abandon our castle where we are armoured, and seek to come into contact, in principle, with our own organism. From there, we seek the relationship with the other human being and with the environment so as to try and re-establish the channels affected by fear.

What is Grotowski coming to Mexico for?

To live, to work, to share with a group of people the opening up of new communication possibilities. To fight to rescue - for those people who cannot avoid being caught up in the claws of prudence, competition, progress, war or success - the organic possibility of people facing each other in good faith, fighting against our deformations, becoming gradually more aware of how to find out the unknowable by intuition, so as to flow peacefully.

This type of work is an emergency call to combat reason. Would that these lines could serve to provoke whoever agrees with the aforementioned propositions.

Our offer for Grotowski to come and work in Mexico emerged from the need for communication and the reopening of our theatrical aims.

What exactly do I mean? If certain people who work in theatre know that many of the solutions to our spiritual, social and cultural numbing can be found here, in our country, who would be bothered? If we know that the West is suffering from the fateful agony of a failed culture, and we try, through theatre, to recapture the essences of original rhythm, who would listen to us? If we firmly believe in a theatre of recovery, the recovery of our sources, the recovery of our spirit, the recovery of the original meaning of our lives, so as to find ourselves one day in a theatre of joyous expansion, who would believe us?

When I speak of recovery, what I mean is the awareness which is implied as we realise that whoever is the son of western culture is sick, and that the only way out for him is by 'recovering'. When I talk of the recovery of our sources, I do not mean an archaeological return to our origins, but getting back in touch with our essential vitality. Thus we are able to reinvent the games needed by our spirit, and we can mature our condition as human beings, righting our wrongs and, one day, celebrating the disappearance of our conditioned fear.

When we show the possibilities of a theatre with these characteristics, is when concurrence leads us to share common experiences with Grotowski, not because we want to adopt him as our leader, for on this path the work always makes us look at ourselves as solely responsible for our lives, but because within the aesthetic discipline which chose us to serve it, we feel that his intentions find an echo in our own. We do not want to compete, nor to be afraid of one another, because we want to live and help each other to be happy. If I am wrong, it is not in bad faith, as I genuinely want to be with my brothers there one day. I want to work towards that. That is the path which we recognise and which we are learning.

Conscious of theatre's social obligation to provide nourishment for the spirit, and aware that, in this sense, we are currently starving; and aware too that we must try our utmost to satisfy our needs, the *Taller* which I direct has drawn up a quest for our dramatic contents with a view to strengthening our theatrical possibilities.

It is in this process that we feel, I repeat, the concerns of Grotowski coincide with our own. He is currently looking into the sources of theatre and its ritual phenomenon, among other things. That is why we invited him.

When Grotowski arrived in Mexico in January 1980, bringing his international theatre group, we had already done some previous work with the group which was formed via a meeting called by the University. Grotowski revised the work plan which we had prepared and accepted it.

This work was the first that Grotowski had done with Mexican actors. I shall now set out briefly the way in which the work was done.

In principle, to get through the interviews for the people who had signed up, Grotowski suggested that we should do them away from the city. 'So as to work in the appropriate atmosphere and in freedom', I offered him the only reliable place at my disposal which was near the city. We went to see it, and he told me that we should stay there for at least an hour so as to see if it was a suitable space. We kept quiet while various things were going on, we walked around the hill and its environs, until he eventually stated, 'it is a good place'. We made the necessary arrangements for people to come the next day and then we went back to the city for a dinner hosted by Professor Fernando Benítez.[15] At this meal, we talked about Grotowski's aims on arriving to make contact with the Huicholan mountain range. Benítez explained every single detail he deemed suitable for us to go ahead with the project. They talked of the different ecstasy techniques which they knew and discussed the disciplines which, due to their exacting nature, could be considered as such. We all mentioned the benefits which theatre can extract from research like Grotowski's. We summarised the origins of art as a sacred function and its current confusion, and Grotowski and Benítez agreed on the need to safeguard the almost extinct sacred values which still exist. They concluded unanimously that it is possible, as the poet says, to 'find the threads which unite us with the stars', while Professor Benítez mentioned the efficiency of the experience with the 'Divine Luminous', and Grotowski told us of some opening experiences with entheogens, and emphasised the conviction he has of being able to reach these states of consciousness without having recourse

---

15 Professor Benítez is an anthropologist, journalist, and renowned defender of Indian rights.

to anything other than certain exercises.[16]

The following day, after making a few special arrangements relating to the place, and giving a few work premises, Grotowski interviewed the first half of the group in a field.

One day later certain changes were made, and the second half of the group had their interviews. Many of them did not know, and I am sure they do not to this day, why they were going out into a field; they did not understand the meaning of some of the movements and positions. Grotowski informed me, nevertheless, of the development potential of many of those he had interviewed, and he chose eight people to take part in the experiment in the mountains.

On January 7th, Grotowski gave his first conference at the Central University of Theatre in front of about five or six hundred people. Grotowski set out the basic principles of the *Theatre of Sources*, and explained that,

> The modern-day human being in the big cities is atomised, wrapped up in a film which separates him from organic reality, and he does not have any direct contact with the world or with any other human beings, because he is isolated, atomised. What I am telling you is not fantasy, but scientifically proven reality. Given these circumstances, what the *Theatre of Sources* actually is, is a path towards making a hole in the wall and hence making contact with reality. Only by means of a huge effort and disciplined work will we be able to achieve some results. Learning Zen Buddhism, or even yoga or any other discipline, must be a lifelong task, but what can we do, who are the result of a timeless culture and consigned to live life in a hurry?[17]

He said that he had performed an arduous task in grouping together, in the

---

16 "Divine luminous" is a Huicholan term for peyote. Entheogens is a term used to define mushrooms and peyote as a contact with the divinity; it means God within me.

17 All quotations cited here are reproduced from audio documentation of Grotowski's conferences in Mexico in 1980, recorded with his permission.

Theatre of Sources, all the exercises and techniques to which he has had access.

Now I am beginning to see clearly the path to the east, and I am totally convinced of the chances that city-dwellers have to begin this journey; the only thing that the *Theatre of Sources* can offer is to act as a bridge, a process, a path.

During the conference he stressed his particular interest in not interfering in the Huicholan rites, not going with the idea of eating peyote, and only wishing to work in 'charged' places. After the first hour and a half of the conference, some people began to leave the room, perhaps because what they were listening to was of no use at all to their theatrical interests. The conference went on for seven and a half hours, and I got the feeling that everyone heard what they had to hear.

Some people say that Grotowski's theatre is a type of stale romanticism, plagued with esotericism, which has nothing to offer either to the development of society or to the evolution of the discipline of theatre. From this point of view, not to understand the theatrical use of Grotowski's proposition is to fall into childish radicalism; if the highest postulates (in any discipline) are the integration and the development of the human being, I cannot see the discord in Grotowski's proposition. Is he not looking for the same thing? If the immediate aim is to improve our social condition, is he not looking for a path for us to defend ourselves and cure our deformations caused by the continual bombing we suffer in the big cities. Is this not social work? This sanitation process to make contact with our original state is what Grotowski's proposition offers. Not to understand it as a social commitment is not to want to be aware of our deformations; to say that that is no longer theatre but therapy, or worse still, a pseudoreligion of which Grotowski is the 'guru', is not to understand the effort being made by highly qualified people to help to blend the best fruits of the human being. On the other hand, it is easy to understand this disagreement from another angle. For example, we all know that the majority of theatrical schools and trends which exist in our country serve only to supply the entertainment industry with human material. The trend which Grotowski is developing would hardly qualify people to be saleable within the industry, and perhaps this is one of the motives of the disagreement, since it is public knowledge that the majority of people in our theatre, even those who have been to university, study or invent the best way to sell themselves to the commercial system. In this sense, Grotowski has nothing to offer. In saying this, I do not wish to set out a defence of Grotowski's aims since, luckily, he can defend himself; I merely wish to clarify my own particular point of approach to this type of work, since if for some people his ideas are out of the ordinary, for other people, on the contrary, they represent the strength of a theatrical proposition which has not been properly understood.

While we were getting ready for the trip to the mountains, Grotowski interviewed various groups of people interested in going to work in Poland.

We went as far as Ixtlán in a bus, and from there a plane took us to San Andrés Cohamiatán. As soon as we arrived, and as the group of 16 people was very large, the local authorities wanted to know the reason for our visit. Grotowski asked me to explain that we were an international group on a pilgrimage around different parts of the world, charged with energy, and that all we asked was their consent to get on with our work. 'Yes, but what specifically have you come to do?' asked the Huicholan governor. 'To make contact with the earth, stones and trees', replied Grotowski, and this sparked off a misunderstanding with the authorities who, resentful as they are of the exploitation they suffer, thought that if we were interested in stones and trees, we must be engineers in disguise who wanted to examine the land. Their suspicions got more acute when they realised that we were not carrying any form of permit to enter this area. We explained that it was not our intention to assert ourselves through a permit, as the possibility of doing so existed, but we had rejected it, as if we carried a permit, we would have nothing to ask them. As the owners of the land, it was they who had to decide whether or not to accept us. They refused to believe that we were coming in such good faith, especially as they had suffered attacks to cut down their forests and other things. When they related our pilgrimage to the one that they themselves made to Viricota, they understood the reason for our visit slightly better, and agreed, not without certain suspicion, to give us their permission to carry on. They commissioned two Huicholans to accompany us on our work; Grotowski agreed and invited any villager who wanted to join our group. It should be mentioned that the intervention of the rural experts was extremely important for the Huicholan authorities to understand the reason for our being in the mountains. In the end, they charged us a minimal sum per head, for the benefit of the community, 'since plenty of people come and even do business with photos and the stories which people tell them, without giving us anything in return'. We paid the sum and began our work. We were warned that if we were carrying any cameras or other equipment, we should not use them. We all agreed, as we had maintained from the very start that nobody would take anything of the sort.

We undertook the work in principle on the plateau of San Andrés, in lengthy exercise sessions in the morning and the afternoon, in separate groups and with precise aims, led by Grotowski's monitors and supervised by Grotowski himself; the directions for each exercise were given individually by him. As the work advanced, we began an exchange among the different groups until we had established a circuit. The most important thing in this work was the sediment which formed in each person. The essential content will never, in terms of communication, find the path of explanation or description; we could do a cold dissection of the mechanism, like somebody making an analysis of a bullet and seeing the gunpowder on one side, and on the other side the shell, and the lead, and hence all the different parts of the pistol, an analysis which would not allow us to understand the strength of fire in motion when it is fired at its target. What we can say is that the exercises, perfectly defined, require a complete surrendering of the body, since only by going beyond the limits (as anyone who was there could confirm) can we receive an organic knowledge of which we are unaware in our current state.

Later, the work moved to Las Guayabas in Coamiata and the surrounding area. The Huicholans approached us, particularly in search of medical assistance; we gave them all the help we could, but some other Huicholans nevertheless warned us that it was risky to give them medicine, because many of them do not pay due attention to the required dosages and we could be held responsible for any mishap. We went to speak to the Huicholan governor and he agreed that only stomach illnesses should be treated, as dysentery is a widespread problem, especially among children.

From time to time *mara'akames* [Huicholan Shamans] would appear, seeking contact with the group, and we found out that certain places unmarked by any type of building, but important to them within their religious cycles, had been detected by us as places in which to work. At the end of our stay in the mountains, Grotowski invited a Huicholan who collaborated with us to work on the rest of the project, in Poland. He agreed and, together with four university students chosen from the eight who had worked in the mountains, he was a co-creator on the *Theatre of Sources* project carried out in the forests of Poland.

On our return from the mountains, back in Mexico City, Grotowski again interviewed groups of people interested in working with him, and he gave his second conference on January 27th, also in the Central University of Theatre, in the company of Professors Oscar Zorrilla, Luis de Tavira, María Sten and yours truly.[18]

Grotowski's summing-up of the work done was clear and his general evaluation positive. Professor Sten asked him what possibilities he saw in the people with whom he had worked, and Grotowski replied that he had been pleasantly surprised at the ability of many of them, 'I feel it as yeast growing: the possibilities are enormous'. Professor Zorrilla asked him if he thought Mexican theatre might be able to follow the path which had been so effectively developed by disciplines such as Mexican poetry, painting and literature. Grotowski replied that he had seen that possibility as a latent concern in our midst, and that it was unquestionably a path which offered good possibilities. Somebody else in the audience asked whether, given the

---

18 De Tavira is a Mexican theatre director. Sten is a specialist in Nahuatlan theatre.

illness and defencelessness of the Huicholan people, he did not consider it his duty to do something more than simple theatrical work, to which Grotowski replied, 'my duty is to do everything my hands are capable of doing, and that is what we did. My duty is also to say this in public, as I am doing through this conference, so that you, Sir, as a Mexican, can do something'.

Grotowski talked of the attitude of Professor Tavira, who declared himself to be a person utterly devoted to theatre, with a clearly defined political position, but who, far from adopting a partial attitude, said that he understood and accepted the different options a culture has in order to develop. Grotowski said, 'how good it is that we realise that if the human being has feet, he also has hands, and if he is involved in a social circumstance, stones, trees and stars also exist as organic entities relating to us'. Somebody in the audience again contributed by saying that Herzog, in order to make a film in the Amazon region, had requested military aid to make sure that the natives did not stop him filming; had the same thing happened with the Huicholans? The answer set out clearly each step we had taken, and emphasised that if the Huicholans, without any type of pressure, had not accepted us, we would have moved away immediately. Grotowski ended the conference after replying to the audience's questions.

To understand the mechanism institutionally represented by Grotowski, we must be aware of his quality of exception, which allows him to act with freedom, whilst keeping up a continual fight to assert his right to demonstrate and get sufficient subsidy.

This process of struggling between trends with work objectives and institutions which by their structural formation are committed to research and development of culture, is repeated continually, and it is only by a guarantee of quality, as Grotowski gives, be it in the training of actors or the structuring of performances, that talks with these institutions can be harmonised.

In relation to this, it can be said that here in Mexico, not much preparation is required to make commercial television or theatre, but there are other theatrical possibilities, be they Brechtian, Meyerholdian, Vakhtangovian etc., which need subsidies so that sufficiently qualified groups can be formed to work in these areas. No trend excludes any other; all, within their need for complete training, give each other reinforcement and feedback. Looking at this any other way would be as if music opted to include Beethoven and leave Bach out; it is one discipline with different interpretations.

Visualising the possibilities we have in Mexico to assimilate disciplines like the one proposed by Grotowski for the education of the actor, leads us to the revision of the different options theatre gives us for this delicate task. One path is, as we have already said, to learn the different propositions as well as possible, so as to be able to adapt the best of each system to our own particular idiosyncrasy and give a personal answer. We will achieve this when we are familiar with enough material to allow us to attempt a synthesis. Straight away, we can say that Grotowski's exercises - in direct relation to the training of the performer, in terms of concentration, sensitisation, projection, in the sense in which it was proposed by Stanislavski: 'Imagine that rays emerge from your body and flood the entire theatre', and work done on blockages which obstruct the 'being here, now' - are marvellous and after Stanislavski, nobody has designed such a strict system of preparation. Making use of this, not to imitate it but rather to combine it with other valuable contributions to this area, is our work, which we hope will lead us to demonstrate that we are people wholly involved in Mexican theatre.

A few days after his second conference, Grotowski left for India to continue his search and complete the group which worked on the Polish phase of the Theatre of Sources project. We met up again in the forests of an impatient Poland; what went on there, through the hard months of continuous work, we shall talk about in another section. Nevertheless, for the moment we can mention what, in our opinion, were the objectives of the experiment:

- To accentuate concentration.
- To develop our knowledge of our own body.
- To develop our psychophysical possibilities.
- To educate our willpower.

- To seek contact with the 'internal' accumulator and make use of its energy.
- To complete our entire metabolism at the rhythm of the currents of water, air, fire and earth.
- To make these processes internal and participate.
- To understand the need for 'service' with our energy.
- To achieve harmony with all our companions, whether they be Chinese, Indian, English, South American or African.

These were the basic objectives which were reached with continuous work, through exercises done during the day and at night.

The group made use of country houses built at the edge of vast woods, in which almost all the exercises were done. A description of each of these exercises would, as I have already said, require a separate text, although there is already a text which describes this type of work excellently: *On the Road to Active Culture* (Kolankiewicz, 1979), edited by the Laboratory Theatre itself. We would recommend this text to anybody who is more deeply interested in these exercises.

In 1984, Grotowski left Poland to live in the United States. He is currently directing his Objective Drama project, at certain times of the year, at Irvine University in California. In 1986 he set up the Workcenter of Jerzy Grotowski in Italy, where he has been carrying out his research to the present day.

The research we did in the forests of Poland, promoted by the Laboratory Theatre, has therefore gone down in history and can only be remembered by those who experienced it.

Here we have outlined what we consider to have been the aims of the work we did. We are grateful to Grotowski for his generous teaching, and are aware that this is only a brief sketch, as our need to develop our own mechanisms take up all of our time. Nevertheless, we know that the sediments of this teaching, added to various others, will always have an obvious influence on our work, which proves that true learning is to be found on our own path.

Here we shall leave our discussion of western theatre. We would repeat that this short analysis is based on a personal perspective, and our intention has not been to include all western theatrical trends and characters. We have merely taken the necessary points of contact to explain our work. We have to adopt this perspective in order to understand why, when we are talking about western theatre, we should only consider Stanislavski, Brecht, Strasberg, Grotowski and the Old Vic.

So what about Artaud, Vakhtangov, Jarry, Beckett, Barba and all the others missing from the list? Have they not influenced our work? Of course they have, and there is no excuse for not including all of them, from Aristotle's Poetics to the research of the Squat Theatre in New York. If we have not included them, it is because our research leads us to concentrate on certain areas and pass by many others.

4 ANTHROPOCOSMIC THEATRE

There is a Sufi story which says that we should leave theories to one side and enter the tea-house of experience. We are convinced that experience is the most efficient channel through which to learn anything.

The difference which we make between a system and a guide lies in the fact that we consider the system to be a strictly rigid mechanism, in which experimentation is relegated, if not totally excluded. The guide, on the other hand, proposes feasible options for reconsidering or transcending with the same direct work. We see the system as a closed process and the guide as an open one. We therefore recognise in the open mechanism a suitable atmosphere to ponder our concerns.

For the performer, true learning does not lie in systems. Systems which make schools, or schools which work with systems do not teach us anything; people who rest exclusively on what they have learned from such schools, are limited and consigned to strengthen their foundation with an unproductive orthodoxy. In other words, they must mechanically praise the schools' values, without questioning them, and without having them as a point of contact of a knowledge which transcends them, because they cannot recognise in the systems and the schools their real space - that is, if what we are interested in is true theatre.

How we can become true performers is via the sole, key concept of having to prove and polish ourselves, and using the sole tool of experimentation as a base.

What, for us, is a performer? It is someone who accepts the commitment of learning, in as much depth as possible, about his psychophysical instrument. If he understands it technically and organically, he becomes a doctor; if he learns about it behaviourally and emotionally, he becomes a psychologist; if he investigates it spiritually, he becomes a mystic; if he recognises it in his sensitive possibilities, he becomes a poet, painter, musician or dancer; if he discovers it in its entirety, he becomes a performer, a performer in the world which surrounds him, in which existing is being and being is performing. For this phenomenon to take place, the work must be done in a group; this gives forth the possibility of collective confrontation and contribution to individual development.

Each one of us is committed to searching for and developing our personal performance technique, and we will only find it by working in a group. This apparent contradiction of working in a group to find something individually does not exist; there is no contradiction. That is merely what one understands before becoming involved in this type of work.

Groups working in schools are generally de-activated and numbed by academic orthodoxies. Often, groups which get together because they need to, away from the schools, keep alive their growth process in a much more effective way than those who meet in school because they have to. Rather than respecting schools, we should take them by storm, grab hold of the good aspects and get out. We should remember the difference between information and knowledge; many schools for performers have nothing but information, and they offer nothing documentary, but merely gestural, emotional or behavioural information. The true creative process, as we all know, takes place through knowledge, in other words through direct experience, which cancels out any type of information. It exists in its own right, and cannot be transmitted. Direct experience is a long way from being worked on in an institutionalised way or using a system, and hence it is a long way from being used in schools.

Nevertheless, as we look again at the forms through which we learned about theatre, the following question arises: here in Mexico, we have received our theatrical education via systems structured abroad, and this is one of our most serious conflicts. We sometimes see personal interpretations of these systems made by certain professors, that is an interpretation of a system which then becomes another system; this still happens, even today. Most of these interpretations are unsuccessful because they are feeding commerce, preparing or fabricating people for commercial consumption. However, the good or bad interpretations of our professors are not sufficient; we need a complete process which recognises the performer as a human being in the world.

Few professors look upon the performer as a universal entity; most subordinate him to a series of circumstances which give a particular line to his performance, which generally ends up in commercial theatre. With what line of performance do we, as Mexicans, work? In the area of conventional theatre, people have worked for years in the style or line of the old Spanish school; at another time, with the school of Stanislavski, very much according to the interpretation of the Actor's Studio; there have been other attempts and there will surely be more to come, such as the Brechtian and the Artaudian schools. But we, as present-day Mexican performers, are concerned with investigating and developing our own line of work - it is a commitment common to all of us who work in theatre.

In the area of theatre/festival, the principal orthodoxy adopted has been the catholic one, although there are still some original trends in which rite survives. This means that here in Mexico, within conventional theatre, we are subordinated and manipulated by cultural fashion which imposes a style which generally comes from abroad, and in nonconventional theatre we still have a mechanism which can revitalise us. This is nothing new: Artaud came almost fifty years ago to confirm it, and today we are still tied to the pattern of western culture. Everybody knows that part of the western system is useless, simply because it believes that it is the only one and refuses to recognise nor even to give other types of performance a chance. It is not plural, but closed, childish and dictatorial. It had found it very difficult to open up to the East, and even harder to open up to pre-Hispanic thought.

We, as performers, resent this most directly. The ways of learning theatre here in Mexico generally separate us from our specific reality, bring about a certain type of schizophrenia in us, and divide us, because they oblige us to behave with attitudes, clothes and ways of viewing the world which do not correspond to our reality. We are not European, nor are we fair-haired; we are dark, and we live in Mexico. How can we avoid the harm that these systems can do to us, and yet at the same time take advantage of them? I think this is possible. The harm lies in their way of disorientating us; the benefit in their particular exercises. Let us imagine that these systems are divided into two circles. On the outside is everything that is said about the system: modes of behaviour of people working with it, rumours, clichés or apparent fashions in everything related to the ideology of the system; all this periphery is what could bring on deterioration, and it must be crossed by those who really want to work and benefit from the contact with the inner circle, that is to say, with the exercises themselves. Graphically, it could be represented like this:

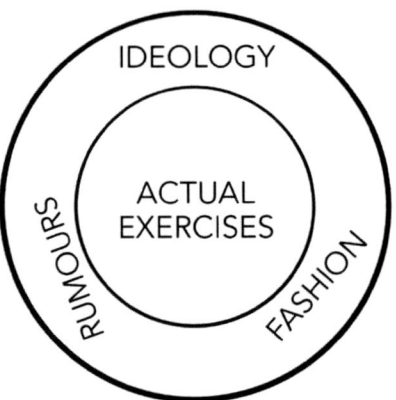

Figure 1

The periphery is localist, classist, semi-stimulating and strictly commercial; the inner circle is universalist, direct and far from the possibility of commercialisation. To benefit, we must dare to get to know these systems and, without paying any attention to the influences of the outer circle, concentrate on the work of the inner one. We must work keeping to that direction and, as time goes by, through experience, allow the development of each of the propositions we find and develop as a personal mechanism there, without falling into the trap of thinking we are inventing a new method, but rather leaving the work process open. In this way we can benefit from these systems. Our suggestion would be to concentrate exclusively on the inner circle.

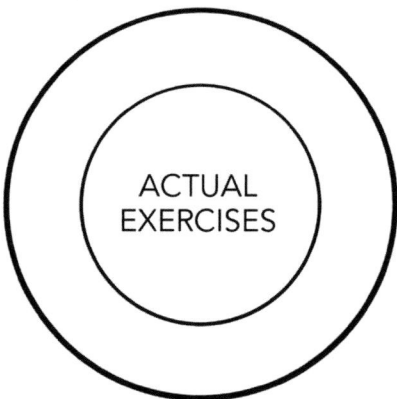

Figure 2

Once we have worked with this circle for long enough, we will surely, without realising hit upon the creation of the second circle, very possibly repeating the aforementioned diversions. The difference is that this time, the atmosphere will correspond directly to us, turning imported affectations into national ones. At this precise moment, we must focus on the struggle we will have on our hands to get rid of these new affectations, although they are ours. Hence, even if the distortions of the outer circle appear, we will have taken a further step towards ourselves, towards recognising our own vices and distortions which, whilst they are still the same as the vices or distortions of any other human being, have their own characteristics, according to our particular geographical, political and historical conditions. It is these conditions which determine our behaviour, which we cannot overlook; this behaviour, be it good or bad, is the one we have, and it is our starting point for genuinely restructuring something. To overlook this behaviour would be to overlook ourselves. Where am I? Who am I? Where am I going? As performers in Mexico we have a desire for global resonance; without nationalism, the performer's country is his own body, and anybody who is not sufficiently aware of himself, has no country. Our primary identity is our body open to its cosmic resonances; this is the performer's true resonance. This is the guide which we are interested in developing.

We start off from the confidence of knowing that all of us who take part in the work are accomplices in the same adventure, that of recognising our workspace, wherever we seek it and for however long, a special place where the competition is excluded, where nobody has a reason to be afraid of anybody else, and where our only commitment is to give ourselves over to the development of our work, be it individually or in a group, in private or in public, aware that there is no censorship and that we can always rely on the help of our accomplices when our process needs it; knowing that we have the respect and understanding of everyone who is involved in the work. Here, there is no room for destructive criticism or mockery, accepting that an attitude worthy of respect is when somebody gives himself over honestly to researching and developing himself, however grotesque or stupid his attitude may seem to us at first sight. This respect is essential to our work and that of other people.

In principle, we use the following premises, taken from Nahuatlan thought:

We have come to get to know our faces.
It is not by chance that we are here today.
To be a perforated mirror.
To read ourselves like a piece of writing.
To converse with our own hearts.
Here and now to look at the stars.
My heart is a flying bird.

Each of these premises acts, for the performer, as a means of isolated reflection, interconnecting, or as a general sensation which he must develop in field experiments, or in other, specifically designed experiments.

ANTHROPOCOSMIC THEATRE

To begin the process of recognising and developing his instrument the performer must work in silence on these premises, accompanying them with physical sensitisation exercises. To make our consideration clearer, let us imagine a performer who is beginning his work with us. Let us suppose that this performer is in the most difficult emotional situation in which we can possibly set a performer capable of working on himself. This performer could be represented like this:

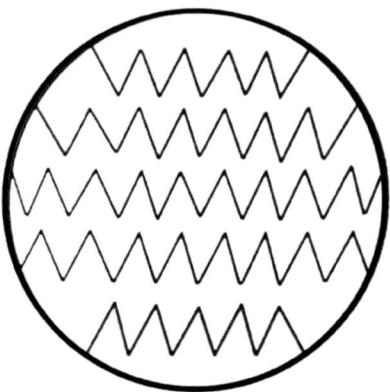

Figure 3

In him, the only movement is of an infinite series of external frequencies which depersonalise him. His self has not evolved, and he is in a *nepantla* state [in the middle; undefined; which is neither on one side nor the other]: he does not know what he is doing, nor why he is doing it, but merely reflects the manipulations exercised upon him from the four cardinal points of his world; he moves, so to speak, without realising. The most suitable process is to formulate our work in such a way that he provokes the coming of his real *self*; when he achieves this, the graphic would change from the first to the second:

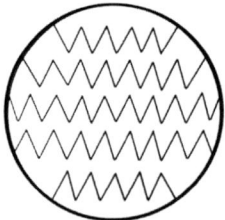 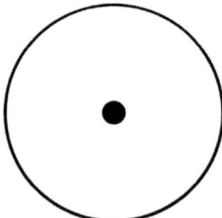

Figure 4

After achieving this starting point (*self*), we find ourselves with work to do so that this *self* can come into contact with the performer's emotions, as it is possible that he may feel isolated from them or not really be aware of them. In other words, he comes into contact with them accidentally, but the representation remains permanently more or less like this:

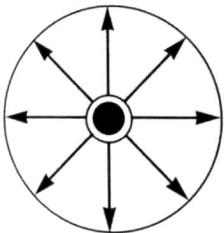

Figure 5

Here we will develop a process of sensitisation which allows the performer to learn to recognise his emotions and structure the path; knowledge which will help him to know what his emotive triggers or blockages are.

Another type of performer is the one who discovers that he has easy access to some emotions and it is harder for him to reach others; we could see him more or less like this:

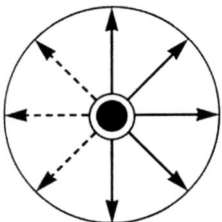

Figure 6

There is also the type of performer who suffers from an emotional structure which is overdeveloped in certain areas - let us remember certain performers' easy access to tears. A graphic representation of this emotional state could be the following:

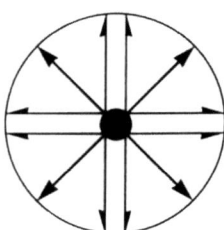

Figure 7

There are other levels of sensitivity to which a performer can have access on positive ground. If we are seeking the complete development of the performer, bearing in mind that any human being can get to be a performer, the ideal state would be when this performer learns to regulate himself. When he achieves this, he will move from his centre towards the whole range of emotions contained in the structure of the human being; graphically, this would be the representation:

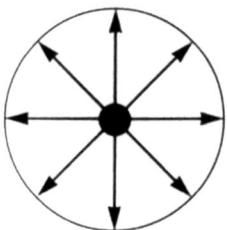

Figure 8

The performer could even come to develop states of energetic eloquence mentioned occasionally by Stanislavski; graphically:

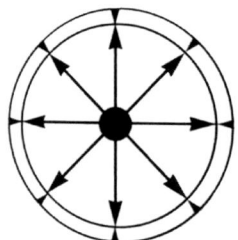

Figure 9

If the limited scheme of these drawings does not help the reader to understand our aim, he will be helped by looking at the windows of certain cathedrals, or studying an oriental tapestry, or any mandala with enough energetic eloquence to transmit the sensation of that flow of energy which, starting from the centre, expands and goes back to the centre, like in the mandalic conception of the Aztec calendar.

The reader will have realised that up to this point, we have only set out the steps which we follow to consider possible states of performers and indicate graphically the evolutive possibilities of their tools. We should make it clear that we know that many internal schemes are not included which could correspond to a multitude of states of the performer; we have merely intended to offer a brief sample of our approach mechanism, so that the performer can understand, draw, recognise or try to visualise his personal situation.

The next step is to know, precisely, what sort of practical work we need to do so that any type of deficiency in our instrument can be corrected, or reinforced, as far as is possible, in its entirety.

In our work, the performer has the chance, if it is his case, to design his re-education process and a method for getting to know himself, in collaboration with people who have experienced the same needs as he has, that is to say that the practical exercises may be proposed by him and supervised or developed in conjunction with more experienced accomplices.

Where am I? Who am I? Where am I going? What we are trying to do in our work is to answer these questions deeply and organically. One of the triggers we use is the text *Psicología de la posible evolución del hombre* (Psychology of Man's Possible Evolution) by Ouspensky (1973). This text, together with our field exercises, where we work at sensitising our visual, olfactory, auditory, tactile, taste and intuitive areas, along with a few essences of Nahuatlan thought, is part of the introduction to our work.

We cannot specify all the exercises we use; nevertheless, we can observe that the exercises with which we work are derived principally from direct work carried out with Grotowski, Schechner and Strasberg, not forgetting other sources such as our contact with theatrical researchers, like Jean Pradier of the University of Paris VII, or the influences of Nahuatlan or Tibetan theatre, as well as texts which show us the possibility of developing concentration mechanisms which are necessary for the performer to structure his process. This, added to the research work of our own group, is what joins together the proposition of our exercises.

I shall mention here, so that the reader has an idea, an experiment which we carried out continually for 24 hours. We call this exercise *Nictémero* [from the Greek term nychthémeron, meaning a period of twenty-four hours].

We met up at the Sculpture Centre of the National University in Mexico City, on the day of a full moon, just a few minutes before the sun rose. At that precise moment, our work began, and it continued until the sun rose the next day. We must bear in mind that this particular place is in the open air and the only thing it contains is volcanic lava. The space is round and its internal diameter is 92.78m. We observed the following work guidelines:

Silence
Read the sun (with movement)
Read the moon (with movement)
Read ourselves (with movement)
Read the space (with movement)
Clean, both inside and outside

We avoided sexual stimuli as well as any type of drug which would distract us from the central aim of our work. The absence of drugs and sex, during our training, works as a basic rule so that we can concentrate more deeply. Some of our members will now comment briefly on their impressions of this nychthémeron, an experiment which some of them were doing for the first time.

I play my snail shell, so do I therefore exist?

It all seems perfectly clear when we realise we are faced with 24 hours of non-stop work. We believe we have enough experience behind us so as not to be afraid of a nychthémeron (as we were later told was the name for this experience of a day followed by its night). We arrived at the place just before daybreak and imagined that what would happen from then on would be the result of a continuous exercise of consciousness (or self-observation and self-memory, to use the Gurdjieffian terms). The sun emerged from behind some volcanoes and strangely-coloured clouds; from the very outset, it was difficult to believe that we were really 'awake'. The *atecocolli* (sea snail shell) was played to wish for a good day for us all. Then we were faced with the first problem: I play my snail shell, so do I therefore exist?; to try to persuade ourselves that we had woken up was to listen to our own air turned into the voice of the snail, a voice which did not sound good, which we had to 'work on' impeccably. We went into the sculpture centre with our minds open to the unknown. That mystery of not knowing how long the willingness to work would last was the second problem, because in a way, when we work in conventional theatre, we go to a rehearsal and know at least that there will be a programme of two or three hours in which the guidance of the director will be a determining factor in whether or not we maintain frank attention. But in this type of work, where there is no schedule and certainly no director, we have to find our own motivations to keep the willingness alive to do something which has no laws other than those of Nature herself. The third problem: how do we recognise said laws, since, as we have discovered, to be in order we must be in agreement with ourselves? This is how the work began inside us. But there was always the companion, the other human being who in a way was an accomplice in the 'sacred gang', as one of our members would say. The subsequent work was therefore directed towards contact with the other person. Finally, within this circuit, there was the group itself, who on principle naturally recognised the first two premises of self-recognition.

What exactly happened? We realised that there really was a lot of soot to clean out of our rational chimney, and our house, which is our own being, was in a state of absolute disorder which did not correspond to the order we were trying to recognise. We began by looking for actions which would cover every minute of a cycle which had already begun and which was beginning to get devilishly boring. We realised that there were no useful experiences behind this. The most difficult action was bringing ourselves up to date with the do-nothing, remembering Don Juan we had once read without realising its organic meaning. We knew that outside the circle of dolmens another reality was going ahead in apparent order, where bricklayers were going about their business simply and plainly. Did they have as many problems as we had? Then we caught a glimpse of cosmic order: the bricklayers were there and they looked at me. I was there and I looked at them. Something was happening between them and us. A mystery. The following day they would have found us right there and been surprised at such a picnic out of time and place. Nobody went against the law. They 'split their sides' as the 'mad-men' played the snail shell and moved about in a strange way. The sun would have continued along its path (as indeed it did), the moon would have followed it (as was also the case), and the rain would have fallen at dusk to accompany the fullness of the moon. We would all have suffered from the heat, or enjoyed it, as well as the rain, the people, the cold and the constant slapping ourselves on the cheeks to remember ourselves. A month after the experience, we would say: that was quite different from anything else. I tried to be at all costs. I wanted to be in a constant here and now. I did not manage it, but at certain moments I think I existed and I was there. Something within me moved and was still. That is the mystery which I love.

Jaime Soriano

At certain times I felt a connection

I had the feeling, as Brook said, of turning the invisible into the visible. I was quite afraid but wanted to face the risk (individually and collectively). There was a series of premises which were, I feel, the vehicle, not the end itself to get to...

I wanted to energise myself (mistake!). I realised that energy was constantly running through me, and that I was part of that energy without having to want to. I looked, perhaps for the first time, at a microcosm (my body) and a macrocosm (which was over me) and at certain times I felt a connection between the two.

My doubts and questions, such as: what am I doing here? what am I? what will I be? and what will I do? were not felt with the accustomed mundaneness; I think they actually went beyond me. These questions had acquired a deeper, far-reaching strength. The answer I found to these questions is partial and personal, and is only valid for me.

At times I felt like a child, and was ashamed of this.

At a given moment, looking at the sky, I unconsciously exclaimed (to myself) how beautiful life is!

The best moments, and those during which I experienced the above, were at night. When the sun came up the next day, I felt tiny, but at the same time I sensed a huge, internal greatness.

These are fragments of what I can put down in words; the rest, I would find difficult to express.

Juan Maya

A 'nychthémeral' experience

My attitude was good. I wanted to distance useless thoughts and the waste of energy. I wanted to 'be'. Perhaps something happened to me (us). But the reality is harsher than what we imagine, and once more I confronted my level; all I have yet to come across, all I have yet to learn. It is a matter of keeping silent, and knowing how to wait. Things happen differently from how we are expecting, and the reality is richer than we can ever think.

Something happened within me which I cannot express in words, and I still do not know what it is. But there I can see the moon and its entourage of stars, lighting up the night, and the deep blue sky, fired by the sun. And there are we, seeking our place in the Universe.

Helena Guardia

A fish in this flow and movement

> *My snail is singing,*
> *I am swimming along in the volcanic sea*
> *heading northwards. My molecules explode*
> *at the epicentre of the sculpture space*
> *and the blood of my grandparents makes me new again.*

*I thrust my obsidian's dagger
into the centre of the sun
and
I am volatile rock
hidden in the cave
of the centre of the earth:
And I saw you
put on your white ankle-socks,
you were the ebb tide of yourself;
then youthful and growing
you showed off your silvery skirt.
Today, my love, you are full,
little moon, little moon
going along with your astral retinue
murdered by the final, well-aimed flint
of your full brother,
naked and crippled
you tumble down the steps of Tenochtitlan.
Whither goes tonight's flame?
Whither creeps the feathered snake?
Whither heads my heart?
To the navel of the world,
to the perfect circle,
the scene of life and death,
my pores and my teeth tremble
this eternal, fleeting day,
a day of sunshine and a full moon
I want to bury myself with my own nails
in Mother Earth,
and recognise my dual father
in the rhythmic blows of the stony rock,*

I am a castaway on this blue sea,
a fish in this flow and movement,
and I want to reach Mictlan
where my spotted dog awaits me.

Xaviér Carlos

The luxury of walking barefoot on the earth

Who in this day and age is prepared to re-encounter that womb-nature, our primary origin? Ancient cultures could accept that there are fluids or cosmic currents which, when our bodies and minds are in that flow, make something happen; now is the re-encounter.

The moon, that celestial body which visits us every night, even when it is hidden in the shadows of the earth's body. Meeting the moon at its fullest and most radiant, and scarcely perceiving it, is only part of the real crimes we have committed against our own being.

It is not a question of going to look for new, extraordinary experiences, but merely of re-establishing contact with the cosmos, without striving for more, and accepting what is destined to happen. For 'subsistence' may no longer be so difficult in this small, civilised world in which we have enclosed ourselves and from which we must escape. It is as easy as living with what we have around us, regardless of whether it is just a case of being allowed the 'luxury' of walking barefoot on the earth; perhaps, therefore, we may be allowed to find its rhythm.

The Sun, as the closest source of energy to us, now stops shocking us and it is the beings whom we underestimate most, children and animals, who will be able to teach us to understand it.

I have tried to 'be' with this world, with this universe, for only 24 hours, and if I had to say anything it would be that I have, in these few hours, attempted to 'live'.

Héctor Soriano

Here for just a while

I throw myself into where the singing is,
I have reached the Earth,
the place of my anguish and my fatigue.
Here for just a while.
In your song is the blue water,
the yellow water at daybreak
sings to you, my love,
food of the world.
Here for just a while!
We have just come here to play on the Earth.
We have just come here to dream that
we are dreaming that we are on the Earth.
Here for just a while!
My snail shell sings,
and in its song lies my joy,
flowers and song.
My sorcerer dances,
the dance of life against death.
Here for just a while!
My heart is a flying bird,
and in its flight
it sees clean hearts
which are still like jades and turquoises.
Here for just a while!
I still do childlike things,
I sing and dance,
I am lying on the grass.
I lose myself in my song,
I play my snail shell,

its song is my spiral towards myself.
Here for just a while!
On the Earth,
I am carried by the wind
I am carried by water
I am carried by fire
I am buried by the earth.
Here for just a while!
My mouth is like Earth
my face like stone.
Your song is carried by the winds.
The night, the sorcerer, the tlatoani.
Here for just a while!
The skies split in two,
the earth opens up;
you hide in a corner in the darkness.
Here for just a while!
Intoxicate yourself, get drunk on your song
and your dance.
The mirror which makes things appear
Is here now.
I know, at least,
that the corncob will feed me;
surely my home is here.
Here for just a while!
The affliction is growing now,
smoke and mist,
fame and glory.
Here for just a while!
Are we really dreamimg?
Are we really here?

*Certainly
the house where we all live
is not on the Earth.
Here for just a while!
My heart is a jewel
of the wind in the form of a spiral.
My snail shell sings,
my body dances;
it is in the Omeyocan
There is eternal abundance to be enjoyed.
Here for just a while!
You are here,
they are here,
we are here.
Here for just a while.*

Juan Allende

That is the end of the accounts written by some of the members of our group about the nychthémeron held in February 1982 in the aforementioned place. This nychthémeron was designed as part of a gelling process for the work we were doing at the time, *Tloque Nahuaque*, [the God of Closeness and Togetherness].

Once we opened it up to the public, they worked in the same space we used for the nychthémeron, from dusk until well into the night. All the work took from one and a quarter to one and a half hours. We used the first part to tell the myth of Quetzalcóatl, without words, establishing the masculine-feminine duality as the generating sources of our world. In the second part we sensitised ourselves with some physical actions which allowed us to develop a process of active culture which we tried to share.

In the following section, we shall include some accounts written by external participants (i.e. members of the public), so that the reader can relate them to the comments made by the internal participants and hence get a more complete picture of our work.

My soul was shaken by the sound of the snail shell

Like a phoenix my decadence touched rock-bottom, at a time when I could go no further. I could no longer tolerate living in the tangle of ideologies and philosophies of the twentieth century urban jungle.

So, just like in a children's story, a group of people invited me to meet up with them so that we could see our faces, feel our hearts like a bird on the wing, and relax in a place where natural and cosmic elements are united.

So I went. When they came out to greet the *pirul* tree, it all began for me; there was complete silence: I looked at them, they looked at me, they touched the branches of the tree and stroked its trunk. Several glances made me follow them into the area of dry lava, testimony, life and protection. At certain moments, both inside and outside, my mind asked, why? why? This disappeared due to the time of day: it was dusk, and I was in a 'dangerous' place, full of rocks which I had to jump over and negotiate carefully. When we got to a flat place, they surrounded me; suddenly, they all shook my soul in unison with the sound of their snail shells. There was nothing more to think of; there I was, drifting with them. They were dancing, shouting and tearing around the place like free, fulfilled animals, but they were men, and I was there.

At the end of the magical, fleeting ceremony of the birth of the free, wise and warlike man achieved by the god Quetzalcóatl, a look beckoned me, and the journey began. I was walking behind this look, without fear, over headlands, brushing against shadows, to the rhythm of a drum which invited me to carry on. With the look I touched the earth, and saw an eagle, a face, an altar; with it I stroked the rocks and crawled through tunnels of time; I burst out laughing, and loosened my body in dance; with the look I drew sounds and music out from stones, while it constantly lulled me with its song and its grief.

Then, a call back. We returned, and were met by a Nahuatlan song, a taste, an aroma, a haven of hearts, and once again the sound of the snail shell; once again we looked up to the sky and let ourselves drift through those moments.

Ana Luisa Solís Gil
(This participant later became a member of the *Taller*).

They are telling an ancient myth

This evening I went to an event at the Sculpture Centre, a moving, impressive place comprising 64 gigantic triangular mounds with slight openings at the four cardinal points: Stonehenge, but at the same time on a human scale. The human order surrounding the flow of nature in frozen lava. Nature uncovered, the double meaning of ritual: having order and having fluid. In this place, a paratheatrical piece where sincere people are working.

What is brought together and shared here are basically good feelings, positive feelings: they are telling an ancient myth, but telling it in an up-to-date way. They are doing this through atmosphere, sound, movement and personal contact. I am therefore very grateful to them, and wish them something more than good luck: I wish them truth in their work.

Richard Schechner

Drawn by the sun or by the moon

Warriors by day or by night,
who seek nothing and at the same time almost everything,
bodies almost float by this space, their space,
our space; they fall slowly on their own hands and on
our very hearts, which after the time has passed
are the same (they are flying birds),
they fly slowly, scarcely moving,
scarcely feeling the strong legs which support all their wisdom. Warriors almost

are they, are we, almost stone ...
Sculptures and shadows search and are confused with the earth,
with the song of the earth which is the same for all.

Drawn by the Sun or by the Moon
or by the Earth
or made by both or all of these things;
green and red warriors
or simply blue like night,
stars. Explainers of life...,
have reached my heart, and reminded me of what a stretch
of my own life I have forgotten,
my eyes have reached me,
they have touched my body,
they have met my face,
I have met the face of each one of them.

And they are still there, as if waiting
for the beautiful new Moon,
to translate it into a soft Nahuatlan song,
to translate it into sighs sent up to the sky.
Warriors who beckon my heart to fly high,
to find what I have really missed since I first thought I was
a man; now I can say that I am beginning to be a man, after
realising that I want to be a warrior like them,
that I want to fight and strive with my arrow and my heart,
to start to know (simply to know), to be
(simply to be)...

I forget my quotations and my dirty words
and my intolerable verses dampened with lies;
now I want to be a warrior.
Farewell and forever yours, space travellers,

the experience is not over yet,
the gaps are open as they never were before,
(and their hearts too)
which our souls could not see before.

And so I have to ask the heart of the sky to let me
thank it, thank it for being or for trying to be.
Farewell and forever yours, warriors of more than
a thousand nights,
the path is made of earth and has a simple aroma,
the mornings are red
as their own hearts are suns,
the nights are blue and black
just as what we do not yet know.
Soon it will be seen at this time, these days, in these hands,
in these hands, in this place: Here and Now.

Emiliano Gutiérrez Sandoval

Through this, we want to introduce the reader to a general aspect of our work; we can say that we work in forests, in deserts, in the mountains, as well as in enclosed spaces.

We are keen to point out the attitude which is necessary for this type of work since, after all, the exercises are not too difficult to find or make up. The real problem, when the performer detects certain exercises, is the inability to keep to them. They generally get forgotten or fade due to laziness or inconsistency; it is not that the performer does not know exercises, but rather that he cannot keep them active inside him due to a lack of discipline. This is the real problem, not having the discipline to keep the simplest exercise alive. Nevertheless, the performer is interested in more sophisticated exercises, perhaps even just to use up his mechanism and then forget the exercises, declaring his inability to function, without daring to recognise that we ourselves personify inefficiency, as we overlap, by force of habit, a ramshackle mental structure which is not trained well enough to make something work.

The performer who comes into contact with our work must requestion the idea he has of theatre and accept the seriousness of daily discipline. The romantic idea, or rather the ill-fated practice of a theatrical performer only practising his instrument when he is actually in work, is outdated and useless. The theatrical performer has the same commitment to his instrument as any other artist, such as the dancer or the musician; if he does not practise daily with discipline, he will always get substandard, unexpected results.

Of course, there are thousands of ways of working, and we all know that every head is a world. Remember when Sartre asked, 'Is the colour I see the colour you see?', and the scientific impossibility of answering this question. If there is no scientific mechanism to make us certain that the colour I can see is exactly the colour you can see, if all we can do to relate to each other is rely on an established code which lets us identify red and what both, or all, of us understand by red, without ever being able to ascertain whether red as I feel and understand it is the same as the red you see, then we can talk of the passion of giving ourselves over to work on the growth of the performer, and everybody will have their own point of view. We can understand how important it is to develop a complete structure which allows the performer harmonious access to all his emotions, however he sees or understands them, and it will only be our own personal interpretation. Despite this relativity, however, we can establish an open work device which unites us as performers with a single objective: to investigate our instrument, polish and develop it in keeping with our particular conditions. That is the red which we all agree on in our work, knowing that it is only a relative point from which to start.

This relativity of colours, or of ways of approaching theatre, brings us close to the thinking of Einstein, who helped us to become the conscience of our universe in a more sober, keenly more scientific and unquestionably magical way. As we touch on this point, we could mention the possibility of the performer-magician, the one who once again takes a path to sacrifice as he acts as a bridge between the sacred and the profane; a performer announced by Einstein, sought by Jung, visualised by Stanislavski, embodied by Artaud, researched by Grotowski and known intuitively by the majority of people who work in theatre. This type of performer is the one that corresponds to our age, the one we must seek in our work. Einstein would surely sympathise with this sort of performer as he was, in my opinion, one of the best performers in recent times, since this type of performer does not necessarily have to live in unbearable circumstances, such as those sustained by Sisyphus. Or if we are consigned to such circumstances, we should not forget the recommendation of Camus - we must try to imagine a happy Sisyphus.

Now, we would like to share with the reader three schemes of participatory theatre.

The first, *Aztlán* (the Lost Paradise), was developed in various parts of the forest of Chapultepec, strictly in the open air. The second, *Tonatiuh* (Sun), was formed exclusively indoors (in a dance studio) at the Casa del Lago, UNAM, in the Chapultepec forest. The third, *Huracán* (Hurricane) we arranged both in the dance studio and in open spaces in the forest. Although we have developed other schemes, in different circumstances, these designs for participatory theatre - open, closed, closed/open - can be representative and illustrate the way in which we do our work. It must be said that when we began our exploration there were no schemes or guidelines to help us work in participatory theatre. In conversations with researchers such as Grotowski, Schechner or Pradier, we could always see the option of participatory theatre as unexplored terrain. In the workshop we took the risk of exploring this terrain. As the years have passed, we have built up, through practice and research, certain models which we have tested in action and which we can now share, in the hope that they can be of some help to anyone who wants to learn about designs for participatory theatre.

Aztlán (the Lost Paradise)

This work was carried out in the Forest of Chapultepec in Mexico City (a sacred forest in pre-Hispanic times).

The participants were called to one of the entrances to the forest (The Roundabout of Flowers) at 5.30 in the morning. They were asked to turn up wearing work clothes (tracksuit) and training shoes.

At exactly 5.30, when it was still dark, the group met up, and the work conditions were briefly explained to them:

1. Anybody who has come in search of a show is in the wrong place and is free to leave.
2. *Aztlán* is a work of participatory theatre. Its structure is designed exclusively for participants, not for observers.
3. We are going to perform in an allegorical way the mythical return journey to Aztlán. During the journey, we should sensitise ourselves and charge ourselves up with energy to offer up when we arrive.

You will realise where *Aztlán* is and where we have to get to.

4. The conditions which, as participants, we must follow are:
   a) From this moment onwards, and until the work is done, keep silent and be attentive here and now.
   b) Be aware that we all form a single body in which, for the duration of the work, social and sexual differences are suspended.
   c) Do exactly what the monitors do and follow their instructions.
   d) Try to keep your look open, that is to say, do not focus on anything.
   e) Let us realise that at this very moment the Earth is spinning at a rare speed in space, generating through its movement a fluid. We must try to get into that fluid through the exercises.

Straight after that, the group was taken into the forest. We made contact with water, we crossed the border between masculine and feminine, and we walked around an ancient tree planted by Quetzalcóatl, according to the legend. We sought permission from the entities of the forest by performing a pre-Hispanic dance, and then the 'contemplative trot' began. When the trot began everything was dark. A female voice accompanied the start of the trot, until the group was lost, trotting round the base of Chapultepec Castle hill. When this exercise was almost over, the light of day was upon us. Then, the participants were shared out among the monitors, who from that moment on directed their own personal action (sensitisation exercises designed and tried out beforehand), each of them heading into the forest in a different direction. We worked for about 40 minutes on this exercise. When the snail shell sounded all the monitors, and the participants in their individual groups, came from wherever they were to a circle drawn on the terrace of the Casa del Lago, UNAM. As the groups arrived, they joined in a communal dance and when we were all together we performed the conchero dance 'of the Sun', which finished just as the latter was rising. At that moment, we allegorically offered our hearts to the Sun, through a fire in the middle of the circle. The work finished with exercises to greet the sun, allowing the participants to reflect in silence, so that each person could reply to himself and decide what point he had reached on the road to Aztlán. On the horizon, the rising sun was growing.

Later on, we specified exercises such as the 'contemplative trot', or some sensitising exercises controlled by our monitors. Hence, with this sketch the reader will get an idea of the work involved in Aztlán, a design for participatory theatre which brings the participants to look over certain luminous areas of themselves and their coordinates with the Sun.

Now, we shall deal with the second scheme:

Tonatiuh (Sun)

Tonatiuh was performed in a closed space, in the dance studio at the Casa del Lago, UNAM, which is in the centre of the forest of Chapultepec, Mexico City.

The participants were called to the entrance to the room at seven in the morning. We had asked them to turn up wearing work clothes (tracksuit), and ready to take part.

At seven on the dot the doors opened. The group formed next to a diagram and the work conditions were explained to them.

1. Anybody who has come with the idea of seeing a theatrical performance, is in the wrong place, and we would ask them to leave, since...

2. *Tonatiuh* is a strictly participatory work, and its design does not allow observation of any type.

3. *Tonatiuh* is an allegorical offering of our hearts to the sun. This allegorical offering which we are interested in recovering, is how the Toltecs did it in ancient times. The specific offering of the heart belongs to another stage of history. Our aim is to try and align our own individual energy with the energy of the sun, and through this allegorical offering, feed ourselves back with its fluid, to make contact with the best of ourselves. The work guidelines are the following:

   a) From this moment, and until the work is finished, we must remain silent and be attentive in the here and now.

   b) We must be aware that during the work we form a single body. We will try to suspend social and sexual differences.

   c) We must fight against physical interferences, in other words our poor attitude or weakness.

   d) To fight against psychic interferences, i.e. lack of attention to keep ourselves in the here and now, if possible, repeating our internal chant. The internal chant is a word or a sentence which we repeat internally, and which helps us to be present in the here and now. If we do not have an internal chant, this is a good opportunity to be alert to what is happening within us, and to start to look for it.

   e) To start the work, we must cross the threshold (a poster at the entrance to the room). If, after reading this text, you agree with what it says, you go into the space, take your shoes off and do whatever the monitors do. If you disagree, you can leave at this point, and nobody will be offended. The text, taken from the poem

Piedra de Sol by Octavio Paz (1957)[19] was the following:

the rotten masks
which separate man from men,
man from himself, fall away
for a huge instant and we glimpse
our lost unity, the helplessness
of being men, the glory of being men
and sharing bread, sun and death,
the forgotten wonder of being alive.

f) Once you are in the space, try to be alert to the rhythm of the group, seek to join in with it, do not impose your personal movement or rhythm. Feel it as a river running round, and fuse in with the fluid generated by the Earth as it spins in space.

g) Just before the end, we need to make a supreme group psychological effort. You will realise when that moment arrives, and then we must offer up our energy and go on to...

h) *Tonatiuh*. If only one of us makes it, the rest of the group will benefit. That is our intention with this participatory theatre: to align our hearts with the heart of the sky, *Tonatiuh*, Sun, to make contact with the best of ourselves. We get to *Tonatiuh* by offering up our hearts.

Once we were in the space, we did a relaxation exercise divided into four parts: lying down, sitting up, standing still and beginning a slow walk. Then we soberly began the contemplative trot, which we did for 30 minutes. We ended the trot with the 'whirling' exercise, beginning to work on the voice in full whirl, going on to work on the voice with the snail shell. After that, we formed two circles, the inner one basically with monitors and the outer one with participants and monitors. Then we made a chain with one single

---

19 This poem, which is quoted frequently by Núñez throughout this book, can be found in an English translation in Paz, 1988.

conchero dance step which gradually gave each circle its own flight. At the critical point of this flight, when the signal was given, we stopped suddenly and worked on the 'cry'. We did an exercise to balance our energy, shared out segments of orange, thanked the participants and ended the work. The whole *Tonatiuh* circuit lasted one and a half hours.

We have set out here the general scheme of *Tonatiuh*, our 'master plan', through which the reader can get an idea, albeit superficial, of what participatory theatre is. For a more complete vision, the reader must get to know and experience some of the tools which we use, like for instance the 'contemplative trot', which is a trot/meditation. The ideal conditions for doing it are the following: we trot floating through the area, relaxing at every step, avoiding the tension in the arms which one gets in a running race, and do not try to advance, since there is nowhere to reach and nobody to beat. We keep our look open, i.e. without focusing, and the same goes for our active internal chant; we must feel that we are hanging by a thread which comes from the crown of our head and is tied to the stars, and flow at our own pace in a constant here and now. The results obtained from this trot, if it is done properly, are tremendous. We know this both from our own personal experience, and from the proof we obtained from our participation in the colloquium 'Theatre and Sciences in Life', held at the University of Paris VII (1984). There we proved that after 20 minutes of this type of locomotion, the organism produces substances called endorphins, which energise the body in a surprising, natural way. That is why the 'contemplative trot' is designed to work with the inner fluids through locomotion and concentration. Even with this explained, the reader is far from understanding something which he can only achieve through action and correction. This is why we deliberately avoid going into our exercises in great detail. We have schematically set out the 'contemplative trot' so as to give merely a sample of the type of tools we use. It took us several years of research to gel a tool like the trot, as was the case for various other exercises, such as the vibration of the snail shell and of the voice; others are still at the development stage, but they are definitely tools to be shared in practice and not to be talked or written about in abundance.

In the next participatory theatre scheme we shared, *Huracán* (Hurricane), we used a laboratory instrument, an *ascid* (inducer for changing states of consciousness). This mechanical instrument is totally harmless and scientifically proven for transpersonal psychology. Its effectiveness helped us, in our scheme, to get deeply into the exercises. It would be too technical to set out how this device works in conjunction with our exercises, as would a description of the field work we undertook in Yucatan and Quintana Roo to give *Huracán* more substance. We would prefer to invite anyone who is interested, to enter into the practice of our work and then describe our design here, schematically, in order to do so with a greater general understanding.

Huracán (*Hurricane - the heart of the sky*)

As part of the training for this work, we toured around Yucatán and Quintana Roo, seeking to make contact through our experiences with the essence of places like Chichén Itzá, Uxmal and Tulum. McLuhan says, 'we are what we behold' ([1964] 2003:21), and this is true. We contemplated these places from different angles, seeking to give ourselves over to our work by contemplating the processes of these sunny groups of people. We allowed ourselves to drift through our research, to try and discover our 'self', as the poet Carlos Pellicer says, 'treasured by a fixed ray which fulfils my being pore by pore' (2018).

Before setting out the *Huracán* participatory scheme, I would like to share the impressions of this preparatory experiment of three of our members:

Luminous Auguries
(Yucatán/Quintana Roo)

We set out on a pilgrimage, searching together for the Heart of the Sky which, like the Blue Bird, is in our own homes, inside our hearts. Nevertheless, we must walk the necessary paths to begin to understand that what we desire has never left us. The paths are like sources of experience which are markers along the road.

Hurricane, Heart of the Sky, immense blue sky. Paradise which expands the look and the soul. Serene centre of balance in contemplation and action. The spirit is near its home.

But for white to exist, black must exist too, just as day and night. So Hurricane, Heart of the Sky, cannot be reached without effort: throughout the journey egos are injured, because they must die. Then comes the challenge to ourselves: do I accept and work on my mistakes, here and now, in the face of such a specific conflict?; am I capable of recognising myself in others and in their growth, as a growth of their own, without suspicion, without envy?; am I really seeking to escape from my own limited person/consciousness so as to expand on the other side?; am I acting without ulterior motives?

To pray, to act as a bridge. To purify the heart, to awaken God in oneself. To grow one's soul and consciousness, to broaden one's horizons and look; to lose one's fear and warm one's heart with love and deep respect. To learn to contain Heaven in our breast. That is the task, step by step, without resting, without forgetting.

Outside - on a path beneath a sun which boils the innards; there are mosquitoes more ferocious than their innocent appearance would suggest; the inevitable personality conflicts emerge. All manner of daily obstacles to work.

Inside - the effort to polarise the attention of the conflict to the overcoming of the conflict = work with oneself and with others.

Outside - luminous auguries, gifts: Sun, sky and deep blue sea, intense white clouds, winds. Glow-worms inundate and light up the path, little stars at arm's reach. A dew out of nowhere presents us with a smile, the rainbow, son of the sun and the rain, burning water. The swallows tell us of flowers in bloom, of the sweet, welcoming fort: Uxmal, source of starry palaces, workplace in the consciousness; Chichén, the geometric, cosmic place, with architecture receptive to the universe; Tulum, its doors open at daybreak - deep, shining night which fuses the stars with the sea, and the waves with feet, body and sands. Dawn of sun and moon, rocked in the ocean of harmony. We have a shape to cultivate shapes and non-shapes. Infinite presence of presences. Spaces/gates to the heavens. Friends.

Inside - communion.

We are not alone. It is a moment of change, of transition to a new stage in human evolution. Let our work be one of the many 'molecules which begin to change rock to glass'.

'With the invisible God who knows the secret of everything in silence, the sincere man's heart takes communion with the earth'.

Helena Guardia, 1984

Changa (To all the gang) (Yucatán/ Quintana Roo)

The glow-worms are stars
just as up is down.
Their light is eternal
on this Mayan track,
how I would like to die this dusk,
just like that,
without images
without fallen fruit
naked to the prickings of insects.
Jungle of the great Ceiba,
wavy root in the taste of the Earth.
- We only came to see the stars -
to follow the glow-worms,
pilgrims on ancient paths,
the Giver of Life of the
four corners, blow this
wind rain,

this father Sun which loses itself,
roar of the earth which envelops me,
which eats upwards
brilliant constellations,
which eats downwards
glow-worms everywhere.

Mayan Area

What are we looking for?
A centre, but what type of centre?
A divine centre, a catalyst of energy, a polarisation
of thought-movement-rest. To be
offerers of our conscious energy, for the
cosmogonical support of the generating
nucleus of our solar system which is the red Tonatiuh.
Comfort is no use in this work, only
friction, movement, the watchful state, getting out
of your state of perpetual sleep, your stereotypes,
your mental weakness, is finding the symbol which operates
inside you. It is not taking anything for granted; it is
finding attention in what is invisible in the cosmic rhythm.

Uxmal

Uxmal, a luminous point
facing the soothsayer,
a symphony of stone
and Mayan silence.

We are clearing our souls
with the blowing of water and wind,
a horizon of birds and trees

name the unnameable, swallows
guests on sacred pyramids.
I sell my eyes
facing the God Chac,
I say my prayer
– I bring you here my snail shell,
my flute, my bird of black mud,
I bring you here my tenochca, my love
I have climbed your steps,
I have crossed tracks
and wide, sunny rivers,
my feet naked of dust
and greedy ants;
my dark skin
imprinted with the Yucatán sun,
my eyes white with looking so much
at the navel of the Meztli Moon;

Here I am with my song,
with the beat of the others;
it is the tinkling river itself
which sings to me.

To this great pyramid,
to your liquid eyes of fire,
stone of Chac and birds which
warble to you this morning,
will my heart break in the Sun?
Only the soothsayer's cave knows.

Xaviér Carlos, 1984

ANTHROPOCOSMIC THEATRE

Sunny Wind
(Yucatán/Quintana Roo)

In the effervescence of the great cosmic soup in which we are all submerged, if one tries to make a pilgrimage with one's eyes open, prepared to recognise the internal fluids in colours, in the quality of internal and external landscapes, it is not a madness which one discovers while swinging on a rainbow brought by the dawn: rain without clouds which feeds our knowledge.

Finding contact again with the textures of such an utterly blue sea, with an exuberance which saw its own thought gelled in monumental structures of solar celebration, imposing pyramids like modest sunflowers. Bridges of contact with stars which do not lose the rhythm, maintaining their faultlessness of always being on time, with every beat of our own heart of the sky.

Hurricane flies to the full, falls in on itself, amid ever-dissolving tracks, devoured by a rhythm of green palpitations, amid constellations of glow-worms/stars, amid the complicity of silences shared at the thrones in the forest, in the invisible threads which wove the night from the arrival at the port of Tulum tossed by the Hurricane. Wind of sun, sand, looks and wills gazing upon the sea, gazing upon our bodies with sunburnt skin, wills which looked in the 'near' and the 'together' of themselves for the chance to share the rhythm spinning in the dizziness of a group dance which, in a moment of absolute contemplation, presented us with the certainty of being and existing, and made us recognise the thresholds we had passed in the baths of the sacred wells, from where crocodiles watched us as we passed by naked.

Recognising in each of the madnesses which were pre-designed by destiny, the 'fields of friction' necessary for the stars inside and outside us to keep their place, is learning to share effort and complicity in growth.

Ali Ehécatl, 1984

Huracán was performed both in an enclosed space (the dance studio of the Casa del Lago/UNAM) and in open spaces in the Forest of Chapultepec in Mexico City.

This is the only open/closed participatory theatre scheme we have performed.

We called the participants to the ground floor room of the Casa del Lago annexe at seven o'clock in the morning. We had asked them to turn up wearing working trousers, sports shoes and a *fichu* (blindfold).

At exactly seven o'clock the doors were closed and three monitors split the participants into three groups of equal numbers. Then we explained the work conditions:

1. If anyone has come to attend a theatrical show, they are in the wrong place and are free to leave now, as *Huracán* is a work of participatory theatre, and its design does not allow for observers of any type.

2. Through *Huracán* we are going to embark, allegorically, on the mythical journey down to darkness so as to come up into the light. All cultures have this myth. In order to go down into the darkness and come up again into the light, we need, in principle, all your trust.

3. Each of the impacts you are going to experience has been professionally checked; you are in no danger whatsoever. On the strength of this certification, we would ask you to put yourselves in our hands with total trust.

4. *Huracán* is basically a device with impacts to allow you to give yourselves over, through this journey, to your own internal spectacle. It will be as spectacular and gratifying as you are capable of experiencing it. Our aim is to unify the energy of the Hurricane Heart of the sky with the Hurricane-Heart of our internal sky. All the monitors are merely a support to enable you to experience the spectacle which is within you.

5. We are going to ask the participants in the centre to follow, at the appropriate time, the monitors with the green wristband; those on the left should follow the monitors with the red wristband, and those on the right should do whatever the monitors with the white one do. It is important for you to know which group you belong to, so that when we do three interconnected actions, you will know which of these actions you should do.

6. From now until the journey is over, we will keep silent and try to be attentive in the here and now, aware that the Earth, at this precise moment, is moving through space at an incredible speed, generating through this a fluid which we should try to enter fully.

7. During the work, we all form one single organism; we will therefore try, for the next two hours, to suspend social and sexual differences. Any type of contact with a person of the opposite sex you should feel and handle in good faith, as part of yourselves.

8. Try, at the appropriate time, to keep your look open, i.e. do not focus.

9. As soon as we begin, we would recommend that you maintain your internal chant. The internal chant is a phrase or word which we repeat internally; if you do not have an internal chant, this is a good opportunity for you to find it. The internal chant should help us to keep our attention focused on the here and now.

10. Lastly, we are going to ask you to keep this a secret. That is to say after you have undergone our impacts you become, in a way, our accomplices and you should not talk outside about anything which happens to you here. This is so as to keep the impacts fresh. If you know of anyone who is interested in coming, do not spoil their surprise, as that is an important element in the correct performance of this allegorical journey which you are about to begin.

We then called them together straight away outside the dance hall and wrapped around them the fichu which we had asked them to bring. We guided them individually into the hall and sat them down somewhere. We burned resin and asked permission to begin the journey - door to the being, open your being. With these words, said by a monitor and followed by the beating of a *huehuetl* (drum), the adventure really began. We then sang a litany in Nahuatlan to accompany the process. Each participant was lifted into the *ascid* (an acronym for an instrument used to achieve an altered state of consciousness), left there for two minutes, and then guided down into a bag made of fabric, where they lay back and relaxed for several minutes. The Nahuatlan litany, at this point, became a murmur, and it was kept going by a single female voice until it was time for silence. The participants began to be revived by a cascade of *ayoyotes* (percussive seed-rattles worn on the ankles), and we lifted them up, got them out of the bag and, still blindfolded, they were put into single file, with their hands on the shoulders of the other participants. They advanced to the rhythm of the *huehuetl*, accompanied by *ayoyotes*, little bells and pre-Hispanic flutes. This human snake danced out of the room and began to wend its way through the forest. The rhythmic ripple carried on until a certain point in the forest, where it curled up into a spiral. There, when the signal was given, the rhythm of the dance ended. We put the participants in a circle, with the monitors inside and the participants facing outwards. We touched various parts of their bodies with the snail shell and, when the signal was given, we took the fichu from their eyes, as up to this moment they had been blindfolded, and each participant had to observe a particular morning angle of the forest. Up to this point, the work had taken a little over an hour. After observing in silence, a monitor said, 'life belongs to nobody, we are all life'. Another signal sounded, and three different physical activities began. Each participant followed his or her monitor: white, red or green. In the centre of the space, a group formed a motionless circle and worked on an energetic Mayan position. From that moment on, it was necessary to keep the look open. Another group formed a circle to move round the first group. This second group faced inwards, and worked on a step from the conchero dance which allowed them to move relatively quickly. The last group circled around the outside, working on the contemplative trot. When the signal was given, we changed activities: the centre group moved to the outside, those from the outside moved to the middle circle, and those from the middle circle moved to form the innermost circle. This change took place several times, until a double signal indicated the beginning of the Dance of the Hurricane. Then we formed a circle of monitors, with another circle outside it comprising participants with a few monitors. We began the Dance of the Hurricane, designed by the *Taller*, using the same body alphabet as the conchero dancers; in other words, this dance in no way alters the conchero dance body code, but its alphabet is adapted in a different way. We use the conchero dance body alphabet, shall we say, without altering it, so as to weave new designs. Our research into these new conchero dance designs is authorised by representatives from indigenous dance. These representatives understand that our research could bring these tools up to date. The dance finished with work on the cry. Then, four monitors positioned themselves a short distance from the group, at the four cardinal points. The participants were spread out in these four directions and there they received, at a tree, their last impact. After they had received this, we thanked them for taking part in the work, and that was the end.

Some people stayed for a little while longer, reflecting in the forest. Others slowly looked for their way home.

One of the most important factors in participatory theatre is that five minutes of instruction for a participant who has never heard of this type of theatre, will suffice for him to play the starring role in a design two hours long. In other words, with only five minutes' instruction, he takes part in a cultural phenomenon which not only integrates him dynamically, but also sustains him so that he can derive his own experience.

Huracán - Heart of the Sky was dedicated to the memory of Juan Allende, an irreplaceable member of our gang, a researcher into and supporter of anthropocosmic theatre, an accomplice among accomplices, a tireless traveller on a never-ending flight, who by harmonising the beats of his heart with the slow beats of the cosmos, positioned himself in the very centre of his being, and surely fled to the Sun.

The Tempest

In the production of Shakespeare's *The Tempest* which we performed at the Sor Juana Inés de la Cruz Theatre in 1987, our aim was to harmonise space on stage and its defined dramatic structure with participatory exploration.

There was one formal, and one participatory, theatrical atmosphere, seeking a way to relate to each other positively, seeking to benefit the observer.

Adaptations and readaptations. Adjustments and dangers. In the end we took on the risk of investigating the make-up of this new dramatic structure, and we discovered that the participatory structure is a dynamic which the public readily accepts, and that the possibilty of developing a selection of participatory models is a risk which promises to pay significant dividends.

The adjustments made for the participation of the public must respond coherently to the dramatic proposition and become a way of 'opening up' the stage so that the participant also becomes an actor without being forced, manipulated or exploited in the service of the show, but in such a way that he finds in the dramatic/participatory structure a model to sustain his action and involve him dynamically in the theatrical phenomenon.

In his plays, Shakespeare skilfully shows us the analysis and exaltation of human passions, for instance love in *Romeo and Juliet*, power in *Richard III*, jealousy in *Othello*, existential anguish in *Hamlet*, greed in *The Merchant of Venice* etc.

In *The Tempest* he shows us the drive which leads us to improve our spirit, to be aware that 'we are such stuff as dreams are made on' and that if the most sumptuous temples and palaces will dissolve leaving 'not a rack behind' (IV.I. 156-157) what is important is to value how precious human life is and train our thought so as to guide our lives without getting trapped in games of power and glory in which we are dazzled by the 'appearance' of reality. To live in reality, not in its appearance. To develop the capacity to master our passions and hence master the forces of nature, to become magicians and have the power to cause tempests. To have enough inner stature to forgive our enemies and not seek revenge even if fate thrusts them into our hands. To invest all our power in the service of the cosmos and hence develop a form of universal responsibility.

For some experts, *The Tempest* is Shakespeare's deepest play and, being the last, a type of testament. This is true; it is not only a gem of dramatic literature but also a real guide to the magical system in which Shakespeare worked on his heart. The golden thread with which all the structure of celebrating the sun is woven can be clearly seen in this play. A quality of light with which the flower and the song of all cultures and all times are woven. At the point of the play at which Shakespeare designed the appearance of the earth's energies, we began our participatory area which, without betraying Shakespeare's intention of fantasy, allowed us to transport our observers blindfolded from the middle of the stage of the Sor Juana Inés de la Cruz Theatre to the middle of the Sculpture Centre. There, around a fire in silence, we looked at the stars and into each other's eyes, and towards the end of the participatory area, amid the vibrations of snail shells, each person captured his image in a solitary mirror. We walked back to the stage in silence along the university paths, and ended up back in the middle of the stage, as if we were returning from the depths of Prospero's magic grotto where we had found our own action, our own reflection, an open sky and, finally, we had captured the richness of ourselves as the most precious treasure.

It was that audience, leaving the production happy, which was able to resist the deficiencies of certain actors stiffened by competence and success who were unable to understand the research in which they were taking part. Nevertheless, we did all the performances to a full house and the general reaction to the experiment of participation in theatre was magnificent.

Italy

We were invited by Il Centro in Rome, Italy, an institution managed by Carolina Salce, to share with the public there some of our sensitisation techniques. Helena Guardia, Virginia Gómez and I went. In May 1988, in the Institute's country house, a mansion on the outskirts of Bracciano, we performed designs such as *Tonatiuh*, *Huracán*, *Citlalmina*, slow walks in the neighbouring woods, research into shamanic tools, together with various other sensitisation exercises. We worked with more than 500 people, morning, afternoon and night.

We ended our month's work with a half nictémero which, given the circumstances of the place, allowed us to light, and keep going all night, two enormous fires and perform various exercises around them. We finished at dawn by receiving the first rays of a sun which had been worked on within us through the arduous exercises of the whole month.

At that moment, the possibility of opening up to establish communication through the sun was obvious, and faced with the symptoms of many of the participants, what we picked out was the certainty of performing participatory dynamics which as well as developing the attention, can also bring us up to date with natural rhythms and allow us to receive the benefit of what this represents.

The good faith, discipline and will of all this group of Italians who work essentially under the loving, effective guidance of Carolina, was all the more surprising as they were not only willing to burn themselves in the fire of internal growth, like modern-day warriors - I remember Adelmo, Romano and Patrizia - but they were also generous enough to offer us a fabulous holiday in Venice. The days we spent there served to consolidate our experience and make us realise that the Nahuatlan attention tools which we are bringing up to date in our *Taller* and which we use to train actors, are not only of use to theatre people, but also have a lot to offer anyone who approaches our work.

Peru - Machu Picchu

In November 1988, nine members of our Workshop set off for Peru: Francisco Lerdo de Tejada, Virginia Gómez, Héctor Soriano, Ana Luisa Solís, Julio Gómez, Xaviér Carlos, Gela Manzano, Cecilia Albarrán and I, plus ten other people who sympathised with our designs and were willing to explore with us our inner space, at various important points of this magical country.

There were, in total, 19 of us seeking tools to tune and increase our perspective of dramatic/ritual technique.

Several members of our group had taken part in our research in indigenous communities such as the Huicholans, the Mazatecans, the Mayans and the Nahuatlans, or with groups of people such as the Tibetans, Poles, Turks, Italians and Indians. Now we were to be enriched by the contributions offered by the Inca world.

We were ready to find themes, rhythm, song, dance, visualisations and invocations which would show us the path to our own vitality, so as not to lose our way to the freshness of the moment. In the design of our participatory theatre tools, contact with groups of people who work on attention exercises has always given us feedback.

So we left for Cuzco, where we were awaited by 84-year-old Don Faustino, an expert in the Apu Inca tradition. This professor, recognised by his own people with tears in their eyes - as we witnessed - as a quite extraordinary person, was energetic enough, despite his age and rank, not only to run through with us the spatial code of places such as Ollantaytambo, Sacsayhuamán and share with us some of his secrets, but also to dance with extraordinary energy to the design of the new sacred dance *Citlalmina*. While we were performing this dance, we were surprised by the presence of something strange in the sky, difficult to define. We all shared, at that moment, the certainty that we are not alone in the universe.

Machu Picchu is 110km from Cuzco. The train takes four and a half hours, and its coaches packed with smells, shoves, women, children, hens etc. make the journey quite extraordinary. When we reached the mythical city we continued to explore our exercises and Don Faustino carried on with his teaching and practical guidance by sharing with us some old Inca chants and ritual convocations and guiding our steps though the folds, caverns and secrets which only a life dedicated to Machu Picchu can reveal.

At dawn and dusk he made us take fantastic thermal baths. Submerged in the steaming spring, surrounded by frightening images, with stars in the sky and monumental mountains all around, it made me question the jump/step/process of a theatre closed in on itself, like in a magic box - which is how most people understand it - to the opening of this box so that it can contain real rivers and mountains, with us included, like at that instant, being immersed in the earth's natural vapours, gazing at the stars. It was like tearing off illusion to discover the magic of reality.

Extraterrestrial intuitions, thermal baths, shamans, mythical magic of Peru, personal reflections. It was clear that we were submerged there to investigate, confront and share the tools and designs of rite; to broaden our vision of the dramatic phenomenon so as to find out in depth what theatre is for.

Don Faustino told us that it has been written since ancient times that whoever comes to Machu Picchu is committed to climbing the sacred mountain of Wayna Pijchu. The ascent must be, at the same time, internal and external. It is an 'analogous mountain' with gorges of more than 500m of sheer drop. One false step can literally wipe us off the map, as the bodies of those who fall are seldom found. If you climb it, it is not in order to conquer the external mountain but rather to master our internal ascent, conquering our fears and deformations. Action, theatre/ritual to be done once in a lifetime. We were lucky. At the summit, a series of group looks as we shared the impulse, turn or flight of our actions which in understandable, up-to-date terms, we call participatory theatre.

A delighted Don Faustino, in reply to our concerns, both theatrical and existential, whispered an old Inca prophecy which defines the meaning and reason of our journey: 'When the eagle from the north flies with the condor from the south, She, the spirit of the earth, will wake up'.

Another moment of open theatre. The magic box now included the Andes, the banks of the Urubamba, Machu Picchu and from the summit of Wayna Pijchu, another instant of startling reality.

All the members of the group vouched for how useful our effort had been. We remained silent. Somebody found in the Inca prophecy the very internal meaning of our university crest.

Citlalmina (the female archer shooting arrows at the stars)

Citlalmina is the name of the Tibetan/Mexican dance which we unified through our research.

At the same time, we performed a participatory theatre production at UNAM's Casa del Lago, in 1989, under the same heading.

We shall now talk in principle about the *Citlalmina* dance. The following is a transcription of the little information leaflet which we used to publicise it.

CITLALMINA
Mexican/Tibetan sacred dance
meditation in motion
Blessed by Tensyn Gyatso,
XIV Dalai Lama of Tibet,
as a tool for mental training.

The sun, the sun,
so deep inside of me I feel it
that my thought acquires a taste of light

Citlalmina is the unification of Mexican sacred dance and Tibetan sacred dance. It is the journey made by a warrior to reach Aztlán/ Shambhala. One of the ways of getting to Aztlán/Shambala is to achieve meditation in motion in *Citlalmina*. For this to happen, we must:

1. Learn the body alphabet of both dances and punctually perform the deprogramming code of its movements.
2. Keep our internal attention alive, tuning it to our breathing, without allowing the mind to wander.
3. Flow with the mandalic design which completes the dance at an organic rhythm which helps us to keep our attention on the here and now.

By basically following these three points, meditation in motion can be achieved.

Citlalmina respects the original structure of both dances which, surprisingly, is very similar. In both Tibet and Mexico, the sacred dance is a battle to conquer a new level of consciousness, and it is therefore a dance performed by warriors. These warriors:

1. Form a circle.

2. Ask permission from the energies to perform the battle.
3. Carry out the dance/battle through a defined body alphabet which deprograms and harmonises the individual.
4. The performer - or warrior - joins his external/internal battle so as to keep himself alert in the instant.

After learning the body alphabet of both dances, the performer learns the visualisation which accompanies them; he mentally evokes the four elements: water, earth, air and fire, and places them inside his body. His dance/battle, therefore, is intended to conquer:

- whatever mineral there is in his body, and eliminate the ego;
- whatever vegetable there is in his body and eliminate the ego;
- whatever animal there is in his body and eliminate the ego;
- whatever human there is in his body and eliminate the ego;
- whatever divine there is in his body and eliminate the ego.

5. At the end of the spiral dance, the warrior offers his conquest to the essences through a cry of rebirth which lines up his organism's vibratory co-ordinates with the rhythms of the cosmos, which will be able to reward him.

The dance is a mandala in motion. As the performer flows with it, he is charged with energy. Certain subtle fluids are activated in our bodies through movement, and these fluids, together with consciously generated endorphine, produce in us a sensation of glowing brightness which purifies and invigorates the organism. These are the benefits of meditation in motion.

Since it has been proved, by people qualified in this particular field, that *Citlalmina* works effectively like a dynamo to raise our energy mentally, physically and spiritually, its teaching, spreading and supervision should be undertaken only by authorised practitioners.

In unifying these dances, both of which are ancestral tools to develop our attention and concentration, we are seeking to collaborate consciously and discreetly with the designs of a new culture.

Origins of *Citlalmina*:

- Mexican dance. Nahuatlan, shell. The four elements, 'Hurricane, Heart of the Sky'. Authorised for this new design by General Teresa. Learned and developed in Mexico City.
- Tibetan dance. 'Black Hat', Lhalhung Pay-dor, belonging to the monastery at Tashi Lhumpo, learned in Dharamsala, India.

These two unified dances form *Citlalmina*, which was blessed as a tool for mental training by Tensyn Gyatso, XIV Dalai Lama of Tibet, on 2nd July 1989, in the Casa Tibet in Mexico. Also formally recognised as an efficient psychophysical technique to develop the attention, by scientists from the Biosphere II project carried out in conjunction with NASA in Tucson, Arizona.

Citlalmina: the female archer shooting arrows at the stars

We dedicated the fruits of *Citlalmina* to all our teachers; particularly to Juan Allende, who taught us how to die with our attention on the sun.

In the participatory theatre production, also called *Citlalmina*, we performed a sensitisation design in which we invited the audience to share an allegorical death and rebirth with us.

We received them in the Rosario Castellanos Theatre in Casa del Lago, UNAM. We asked them to trust our participatory design and brought them up onto the stage. We blindfolded them and took them down through the dressing rooms to the terrace of the Casa del Lago. There we began a sensitisation circuit through the gardens. The participant passed through thresholds of swords in battle, water, fire, questions like who are you?, what is the most important thing for you?

To the rhythm of a drum, they were taken into an open-air stage space and integrated into the stage design of a cosmos from which only heads came out.

We performed a moment of deep vibration with our voices. We then asked them to take off the blindfold, and the dramatic part began when we drank and shared tequila.

We performed critical moments of each of the actors, eager to recognise true reality in a double-sided mirror representing life and death. This mirror, which brought on the visualisation and the performance of the scenes, at the appropriate time, was presented to the audience and at certain times enticed several spectators to share their experiences with us.

When each of the people there, actors and participants, had guessed or confronted his image in the mirror, we did a visual contact exercise in pairs, where a double mirror shot out the sign to learn to see our own face in the other person. Then we went on to perform a circuit of the dance of *Citlalmina*, which ended with a cry of rebirth.

The participation in that production comprised sensitisation throughout the first part; reflective observation of the scenes originating from a mirror in which we all guessed, or contemplated, our own story; and free participation in the dance of *Citlalmina*.

The warmth of the response of the huge number of people who came to all the performances, proved to us once again that participatory theatre is a line of work with a lot to offer contemporary theatre.

Workshop Techniques in a NASA Project

At the beginning of 1990, both the dynamics of sensitisation and the psychophysical dynamics for developing the attention, on which the *Taller* has been working, attracted the attention of scientists involved in the Biosphere II project, taking place in Tucson, Arizona.

The story is simple: in one of our work sessions a scientist turned up, invited by the craziest of our colleagues, and sweated his way through one of our dynamics with the group. He liked both the Tibetan/Mexican synthesis and its body codes, and the results on the body and the mind. He called it an effective process of 'cultural cybernetics'.

I was immediately invited to Tucson, where I worked on a number of our exercises with the members of the project. In these exercises, they found possibilities for their research, and hence our actor training circuit found communication in a scientific context.

Our contact with the project is open and we know that our *Taller* will benefit as we can, in principle, scientifically redefine our training, and approach in a more solid fashion the process of a scientific culture which, as we all know, is the most serious alternative we have at the moment.

The Biosphere II project is considered to be one of the most promising and costly research projects around. In brief, superficial terms, it unites in a space of 14,000 square metres six different atmospheres: a rainforest, a desert, a savannah, an ocean, a salt marsh and a human habitat with intense farming, together with various farm animals and eight human beings; the community is sealed up, and observations can be made on the development of this whole process of encapsulated life so as to determine countless unknown factors related to ecological balance. On the one hand, it is intended to develop a platform for a series of experiments and analyses which will be of use to ecologists from over the world and hence strengthen the new ecological, or ecotechnical, technology, and on the other hand, it will take the first steps towards establishing self-regulated cells, and hence achieve a chain of life to populate the universe in the future, starting with the Moon and Mars.

It sounds mad, but it is really happening and the first step will be taken in March 1991, when four men and four women are shut away in Biosphere II to live together for two years.

The daily life of these researchers seems to be submerged in a science-fiction story, where the highest levels of scientific technology are mixed with the desert, the sun, starry nights which lend themselves to quiet personal reflection high up above the Golden Canyon.

All this allowed me a peep at the sensitivity and humane quality of a group which, using the highest scientific advances, brings into play its guesses regarding the future and reckons on the conscious expansion of life in the universe.

I was shaken by the voice of a member of the gang, nicknamed 'the ray of Apan', who revealed to me the similarity between the impulse of Biosphere II and that of our Nahuatlan forefathers, who sought to give over their hearts to the sun, which is nothing more than - as Nahuatlan philosophy points out - 'collaborating consciously with the development of the cosmos'. This is a meaning of life inherited, alive in the present and projected towards the future, and it is well worth banking on it.

A Guide

The most important factor for the performer is concentration. One way of helping to develop it is to establish the discipline of self-observation. We have found a very simple exercise which can have good results in heightening the concentration; we call it the *Last Judgement* and its structure is the following: the performer is asked to imagine he is being filmed from all angles, twenty-four hours a day, by certain bodies in charge of making the film of his whole life, which will be shown on the day of the Last Judgement. With this idea, the performer can heighten his self-observation. As we are continually aware, as performers in time with our role, doing whatever we have to do in this life, in the 'here and now', our self-observation increases, as does our power of concentration.

The following scheme - called *getting to know oneself* - is the result of several investigations carried out with the intention of helping the performer to get to know or recognise his psychophysical instrument. Once the performer is clear about the difference between acting technique and interpretative reception technique (bearing in mind the above scheme), we can move him on to the next phase. Six steps must necessarily take place consecutively.

1. Will to work

The performer must define his strict attitude and be committed to the work in order to progress to the next phase. Without this definition of will to work being clearly established, it is futile to attempt anything else. He must take on the 'good pain'.[20]

2. Contact with obstacles and distortions
When the performer has to confront certain psychophysical exercises, and we ask him to be constantly aware of his witness to the Last Judgement, he can begin to make contact with some of his obstacles. Here he must begin to develop a form of cartography of his blocks, in other words realise that it is difficult for him to be aware of why the difficulty exists. For instance, when he says 'I am afraid', he must be ready to ascertain why he is afraid.

3. General scheme of our distortions
Once the performer has worked on the majority of his psychophysical areas, his cartography must show him an image of which of his areas have been hurt, sufficiently completely for him largely to contemplate himself. At this point, the performer must do exercises and translate them into his cartography until he can establish the general scheme of his distortions.

4. Greater energy to recognise and overcome our fears and distortions
Once the performer has a general scheme of his distortions, he must begin a restructuring process, aware that in order to change his habits for new ones, he must first have chosen the habit with which he wants to replace the one he wants to remove. To introduce this new habit he must be aware that he must do it at a higher energy level than the previous one; otherwise, no change will occur. In other words, let us imagine that I have a bad habit that I wish to change; it operates in my organism at an energy level of 40. In order to replace it, I must introduce the new one at an energy level of 50. I must do this at the very moment at which the one I want to change appears, and give it a higher energy charge so that the old one is wiped out and the new one imprinted in my consciousness. The time needed to change one habit for another one is relatively short if it is done in the right way and with the correct energy.

---

20 See p. 274 below for Núñez's discussion of the concept of 'good pain'.

5. Removing other people's stares

At this point, the performer must work on his concentration, so as to get rid willingly of outside interferences, like when you go into a place full of people and get the feeling that everyone is looking at you; all the looks which we think we are receiving are working as interference. If we make the effort to look up and confront what we are imagining with reality, we will realise that the latter is different, and that the main interference lies in the deformed ideas which we have of reality; in other words, I think everyone is looking at me, and that is not the case. In any case, learning to remove other people's stares is avoiding being manipulated by external interferences.

6. Stop staring at ourselves

Here the performer has to focus on his process of fighting against his own self-observation and overcome it, that is, to get back to zero, empty, where external interferences have disappeared and even internal dialogue cannot be heard. This is a state of very high energy.

These six points make a column:

1. Will to work
2. Contact with obstacles and distortions
3. General scheme of our distortions
4. Greater energy to recognise and overcome our fears and distortions.
5. Remove other people's stares
6. Stop staring at ourselves

An arrow can add another point to this column, divided into three phases. The first is *Who am I, where am I, what am I doing*. The second is *here and now*. The third phase is blank so that it can always contain the action we are performing at a particular moment. These premises at the tip of the arrow should become a type of organic shock which allows us to develop the consciousness of who am I, where am I and what am I doing, here and now, in an organic, simultaneous way, more as a sensation in the body than an analytical position. The scheme for getting to know oneself would be represented as follows:

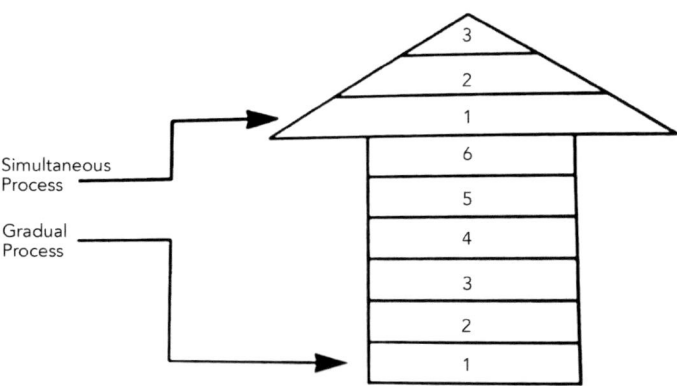

Figure 10

Another clear example of psychophysical work is the lemon exercise, which is divided into two phases:

1. You take one lemon per participant and give it to them in their hands; you emphasise its volume, temperature, weight, colour and smell; a moment later, its taste. The concentration of the exercise aims for the performer to recognise readily the direct effect of a stimulus which he must keep registered in all the fields of his perception. He must memorise these sensations and register all the processes carried out automatically by his instrument, which in this specific case concentrates on the saliva glands.

2. Now, without lemon, we evoke each and every one of the qualities which we registered directly before: volume, temperature, weight, colour, smell, until we reach the moment when we must evoke the lemon's taste; then we will be clearly aware of whether or not our evocation has been correct. As we evoke the taste our glands must respond automatically, secreting saliva as if the lemon really were in our mouth.

With exercises of this type, we can head for a general recognition of our capabilities, working on our five senses, or six for those who have developed a sixth.

Finally, what is the meaning of theatre for those who do it, for those who participate in it and for those who *need* it?

We could say, without fear of being mistaken, that understood as a molecular accelerator,[21] theatre can liberate us from the stasis and the density of our domesticated spirits. I mean that it can help us to live life to the full; without fear, without resentment, without prejudice or judgements, for it helps us to remove the rigidity of protocols and fundamentalisms, and teaches us how to flow with the natural/universal/cosmic rhythms in which we are immersed.

This is, precisely, the intention of Anthropocosmic Theatre - to make us conscious of the fact that *we are the cosmos*. In this awareness, the rigid paradigms of any belief system begin to dissolve, helping us to be present in the here and now, with innocence.

Who am I?

When we try to answer this archetypal question in an ordinary way, the first impulse is to perform a horizontal movement in order to find the answer. In this movement, the 'Who am I?' attracts, in response, name, address, possessions, credit cards, profession, successes and failures, etc., etc., etc. The recognition of who I am is based on externals.

When I ask myself, within the context of the Anthropocosmic Theatre proposition, 'Who am I?', I make, instead, a *vertical* movement; I go inside myself in order to discover our common roots and the strong rhizomatic connection and interdependence I have with reality as a whole, physically, psychically and spiritually. I discover, then, that *I am the universe*. With the strength of this awareness, my quality of being increases and is transformed, revealing new colors in life.

I no longer look for the answer out there, now I can simply be what I am, and what I am arises from within. The poet says: 'I could be bounded in a nutshell, and count myself a king of infinite space' (Shakespeare, *Hamlet*, II.ii. 253-255).

---

21 This term is explained in 'Mandala' in Part Two (p. 293 below).

The authentic meaning of theatre reveals to us its relational aspect: this vertical movement inside myself takes me to the roots that connect me with all, and this, necessarily, has to be carried out in the company of accomplices - whom we call the 'sacred gang'. Then the connection to the 'cosmic' appears, along with the consciousness of *being* the universe. There we find love and kindness, peace, serenity and joy, in the acknowledgement that *I am the universe recognizing itself in your gaze.*

To finish, we could stress the need to work on our body, considering it to be the basic genuine instrument of the performer who wants to get more deeply into an anthropocosmic process.

By recognising our body as a basic instrument, we could end our text with this short poem, in which the speaker recognises themselves as an instrument, in three crystal-clear stages. As an open question, I ask the reader by asking myself, in which stage do we recognise ourselves?

Lord, make me an instrument of your song.
Lord, if I am an instrument of your song,
do not play me too hard, for I fear I will break.
Lord, play me as hard as you like, what does it matter if I break? (Anon)

REFERENCES

Aziz, Barbara N. and M. Kapstein (1986) *Soundings in Tibetan Civilization*. Delhi: Manohar India Pub.

Dalai Lama (1984) *A Human Approach to World Peace*. London: Wisdom Pub.

Eliade, Mircea (1961) *Images and Symbols*. New York: Sheed and Ward.

Hauser, Arnold (1982) *The Sociology of Art*. Trans. Kenneth J. Northcott. London: Routledge & Kegan Paul.

Horcasitas, Fernando ([1974] 2004) *Teatro Náhuatl*. Mexico City: UNAM.

Kolankiewicz, Leszek (1979) *On the Road to Active Culture: Grotowski's*

Theatre Laboratory Institute. Trans. B. Taborski. Wroclaw: Papers from the 1978 Symposium.

McLuhan, Marshall & W.T. Gordon, ([1964] 2003) *Understanding Media: the extensions of man*. Corte Madera, CA: Critical edn, Gingko Press.

Ouspensky, P. D. (1973) *Psychology of Man's Possible Evolution*. New York: Random.

Paz, Octavio (1950) *El Laberinto de la Soledad*. Mexico City: Ediciones Cuadernos americanos.

Paz, Octavio (1961) *The Labyrinth of Solitude: Life and Thought in Mexico*. New York: Grove Press.

Paz, Octavio (1957) *Piedra de Sol*. Mexico City: Tezontle.

Paz, Octavio (1988) *Collected Poems 1957 - 1987*. Trans. Eliot Weinberger. Manchester: Carcanet Press.

Pellicer, Carlos (2018) *Tierra Santa, Invitación al Vuelo* (Ed. Alberto Enríquez Perea). Mexico City: El Equilibrista.

Wasson, R. Gordon. *Maria Sabina and Her Mazatec Mushroom Velada*. New York: Harcourt, 1976.

PART TWO
BEYOND ANTHROPOCOSMIC THEATRE

Edited by Deborah Middleton & Franc Chamberlain

INTRODUCTION TO PART TWO
Deborah Middleton

[T]he theater of the *Taller de Investigación Teatral*, UNAM, founded by Juan Allende, Helena Guardia and Nicolás Núñez in 1975, is like a pyramid buried in the heart of the Mexican metropolis (Fernando de Ita in Núñez, 2007: 45).

For more than forty years, Núñez and the *Taller* have gathered together, three mornings a week, at Casa del Lago, a cultural centre in Chapultepec Park in the centre of Mexico City, to engage in a process of theatrical research and sharing. In the early mornings, participants engage in one or other of the 'dynamics', Núñez's unique psychophysical structures that are offered both as actor-training, and as vehicles for personal, psychophysical development.

In **Part One**, which covers the period 1973 to 1990,[22] Núñez described some of the earliest 'dynamics' (not yet known by that name); *Tonatiuh*, *Huracán*, and *Citlalmina* were described as workshop explorations of participatory devices which were then shared in theatre experiences of the same names. This new section of the book provides an overview of Núñez's work since 1990, during which time the participatory devices developed as free-standing training structures - 'dynamics'.

Part Two opens with Deborah Middleton's 'At Play in the Cosmos', an essay which was originally published in *TDR* in 2001, and which serves as an introduction to Núñez's work as it evolved out of the researches and early explorations detailed in **Part One**. The ritual frameworks within which Núñez operates are explored, and examples are given of two of his actor-training dynamics.

---

22 The time spent at the Old Vic in Bristol predated the establishment of the *Taller* in 1975, and some sections of the chapter on Anthropocosmic Theatre were added to later editions of *Teatro antropocósmico* (originally published in 1987).

Middleton's 2008 article, 'Secular Sacredness', and a new piece of writing, 'Defining the Dynamics', extends her analysis of the dynamics; the former by addressing them in terms of the cultivation of numinous experiences; the latter by giving an account of the genesis of the dynamics and attempting to provide a comprehensive definition.

Throughout the first half of **Part Two**, these chapters are interspersed with short snapshot reflections on the dynamics by a range of participants.

Franc Chamberlain's essay, 'Plotting a Path for Later Steps: Tuning in with Núñez, Rancière, and Sologub' provides a bridge between the chapters focusing on the dynamics and a broader consideration of the work of the *Taller*, including the productions.

In 2007, Mexican author, Antonio Velasco Piña noted that:

> [T]he *Taller de Investigación Teatral* has staged more than thirty plays. Every one of them has been the outcome of an earnest investigation which would need an extensive analysis in order to fairly evaluate it. It is enough to say here that the work of the *Taller*, since its foundation, represents an admirable effort and a great adventure which has propitiated a change in consciousness in numerous people, contributing to the construction of a more balanced reality (in Núñez, 2007: 114).

A decade on, the number of productions by the *Taller* continues to rise, with Núñez producing work on a more or less annual basis. Whilst it is beyond the scope of the present book to provide the extensive analysis of the productions that Velasco Piña suggests is merited, the second half of **Part Two** includes brief case studies of four of the theatrical productions from the period 2000 to 2018, as well as the performance text for *Mandala* (2014). Written by Núñez, and set in a theatre workshop or seminar context, this script also serves as a vehicle for exploring some of Núñez's principal ideas about the role and function of theatre.

This theme is continued with three further chapters of Núñez's writings, not previously available in English. 'High Risk Theatre' was originally published in Spanish in a book of the same name (*Teatro de alto riesgo*) in 2007, but is based on Núñez's unpublished pamphlet prepared for the major theatrical production, *The Flight of Quetzalcoatl*, in 2000. 'Theatre as a Secret Source' was originally presented as a paper at the Symposium of Performance and Mindfulness in Huddersfield in 2016, and accompanied a workshop of the same name. 'Cosmic Manners' was originally presented as a paper in Huddersfield in 2018, and reflects, in part, upon the creative process for the contemplative forest performance, *El Ensueño de los árboles* (2018).

REFERENCES

Núñez, Nicolás (2007) *Teatro de Alto Riesgo*. Mexico City: Consejo Editorial del TIT de la UNAM.

ANTHROPOCOSMIC THEATRE

AT PLAY IN THE COSMOS: THE THEATRE AND RITUAL OF NICOLÁS NÚÑEZ[23]

Deborah Middleton

In 1975, Nicolás Núñez founded the *Taller de Investigación Teatral* - Theatre Research Workshop (TRW) - under the auspices of the National University in Mexico City (UNAM). Throughout its history, the TRW has functioned as a center for research in the fields of both theatre and ritual. Working closely with Helena Guardia, and other members of the group, Núñez has explored the connections between theatre and ritual by researching within a number of traditional and contemporary performance conventions. In particular, the group has worked extensively with indigenous Mexican traditions, but this heritage has been considered through a prism of performance forms from other cultures. For example, in 1986, members of the group traveled to India to study for one year at the Tibetan Institute of Performing Arts to examine the theatre and rites of a culture they considered spiritually close to their own. Their research has also taken them to the heart of Western theatre - drawing from Stanislavski, studying with Strasberg, working for a year with Grotowski as 'co-responsibles' during his Theatre of Sources period. From each of these ventures, Núñez has sought guidance for the creation of a ritual theatre - a theatre that is inspired by sacred practices but transplants those practices into a secular theatrical context. Guided especially by the indigenous performance traditions and philosophies of the Náhuatl Indians of Mexico, Núñez seeks a theatre that may serve as a vehicle through which participants can experience the ancient tradition of offering their hearts to the sun—literally making one's own sun, the heart's sun, rise.

Núñez published *Teatro antropocósmico* in 1987. This record of the TRW's many adventures outlined the theatrical phenomena to which their research

---

23 Originally published in *The Drama Review* 45, 4 (T172), Winter 2001

had brought them: 'anthropocosmic theatre'—a theatre of the human in the cosmos. [...] Núñez's book describes the TRW's work as 'devices of "participatory theatre" which give back to our organism its capacity to be the echo box of the cosmos' (p. 7 above). The centrality of the cosmos within Núñez's theatre is a direct result of the group's research into their pre-Hispanic cultural roots. The heritage they uncovered from the ancient peoples who built pyramids, designed calendars, and studied the universe was a religio-philosophical tradition that aligned the hearts of men and women with the life of the stars. Accordingly, the theatre that Núñez and his group have evolved is designed to put participants in touch with a sense of their cosmological context. This is approached through recourse to ritual practices believed capable of altering consciousness and perception, and through mythological imagery that evokes concepts of nature and the forces of nature. If this seems like an ambitious objective, then it is one that Núñez, seeking a performative tradition for contemporary Mexicans, found irresistible.

Participation is central to the work of the TRW, and is seen as the key to investing theatrical structures with the potentials of ritual. Accordingly, the work consists largely of interactive 'dynamics', structured sequences of psychophysical actions in which participants play an active part and through which they may access altered states of experience. While a particular dynamic may form the basis for a large public event, such as *Citlalmina* (1988), the dynamics are more generally available to participants through the weekly open sessions of the TRW at UNAM's theatre space, Casa del Lago, in Chapultepec, Mexico City, and through pedagogical workshops given at home and abroad. Since 1993, Núñez has carried out seven workshops in Britain;[24] my attendance at these workshops, along with my involvement in Núñez's work in Mexico during three research trips to the country, form the basis of this analysis.

In addition to the workshops and dynamic-based public events, the TRW also produces theatrical performances in which participants may play a more

---

24 At the time of publication, Núñez has delivered 12 workshops and 4 productions in the UK.

or less conventional spectator's role. In these works, the objective is essentially the same as that of the dynamics: in Núñez's words, 'to involve the spectator in the raising and focusing of energy, and in a journey of self-knowledge' (p. 3 above). Productions such as the TRW's *Cura de espantos* (Cure for Fears, 1998) incorporate both aspects of the work within a dramatic structure that effectively combines a traditional actor-spectator relationship with full audience participation. Through careful structuring, spectators are gently guided between two different roles: witnesses to the theatrical presentations, and active participants. Having witnessed and reflected, participants are typically offered the opportunity to engage with a holistic ritual activity within the confines of the theatrical event.

Núñez has forged a theatre that attempts to provide an active arena for those individuals who seek personal individuation, communitas, or the experience of the sacred dimension in their everyday lives. The TRW carves out a sacred space in the context of an urban, cultural institution. To some extent, the work may function as a kind of 'performative religion' (Grimes [1982] 1995: 266). However, Núñez is particularly careful not to invest the actions and experiences of the dynamics with any overt ideology. The TRW professes no particular belief system; the search for 'meaning' and the imposition of defining conceptual frameworks remain the responsibility and personal quest of the individual participant. In place of ideology, the *Taller* offers experiences; ludic, dramatic, psychophysical activities anchor the participant quite firmly in the realm of theatre, but also support the transformative potential of ritual. The TRW specializes in play, but these are 'serious games', and like all games, when played seriously, they may have real consequences (Núñez 1999).

Núñez's theatre consciously seeks to explore and exploit the connections between theatre and ritual in order to emphasize the transformative potential of performative experience - to use theatre as a secular framework for ritual structures. In Victor Turner's definition, ritual is:

> a transformative performance [...] transforming social and personal life- crises [...] into occasions where symbols and values representing

> the unity and continuity of the total group were celebrated and reanimated. [...T]hrough its liminal processes, it holds the generating source of culture and structure (1983: 223).

Núñez's theatre attempts to create transformative rituals that respond to life crises within the individual. Indeed, his pedagogical workshops and performances are frequently introduced with a note to participants that the work is designed for those in personal crisis; like Grotowski's theatre and paratheatre, this work is intended for an elite defined not by social status, but by spiritual or emotional compulsion. The work of the TRW is designed to effect psychological, physiological, and spiritual change through the dissolution of negative psychophysical modes of behavior, and through the embodied experience of life-affirming symbols and processes. It seeks both to enable participants to generate their own personal mythologies, and also to assist in a wider campaign to recover indigenous cultural symbols.

Like many theatremakers who share the impulse toward ritual, Núñez has been influenced by shamanism. Sometimes familiar to those in industrial societies via the popular and academic literature which is available on the subject, shamanism provides an appealing model of the performer as healer, myth-maker, and 'technician of the sacred', a model that many Western practitioners have sought to appropriate by means of literary investigation. In Mexico, however, shamanic and other ritual practices persist as functioning rites or cultural forms in a number of indigenous traditions. For the TRW, the model of the shaman - or the Huichol *mara'akame* - has been both a conceptual ideal and a source of practical research and training: a working model. When the group infuses their theatrical performances with ritual structures, they do so with the full permission of the relevant tradition's authorities, having been first initiated into those practices within their religious contexts. Nevertheless, the significance of the work lies less in its authenticity with regard to traditional practices, and more in its ability to generate new ritual models. The central work of the TRW has been the search for ways to safely and effectively transplant religious rituals into contemporary secular cultural forms, maintaining their psychophysical and numinous potential beyond the matrices of their belief-system of origin.

Núñez's theatre follows the shamanic model particularly in its methods of training participants in techniques of raising energy, accessing and leaving alternate states of consciousness at will; in the imageries of descent and ascent, and of animal guides (*nagual*); and in the use of certain energetic bodily positions and actions. In Núñez's secular and theatrical context, however, there is no attempt to replicate shamanic belief systems, nor is it necessary for participants to believe in a spiritual realm. Núñez deliberately refrains from placing the participant's experiences in explanatory contexts, in order that the work can be as free as possible from an imposed ideology. The participant is free to interpret her own experience in the light of belief in a God, a spirit world, Jungian psychology, or creative visualization. Thus, the work might be seen as an arena in which participants encounter, explore, and generate their own imaginal, and perhaps spiritual, inner worlds within the framework of their personal, and private, belief systems.

The Dynamics

Núñez's research within the field of ritual and psychophysical practices (particularly among the Huichol and Náhuatl peoples of Mexico, and in contemporary bicultural traditions such as *conchero* dancing[25]) have enabled him to develop a series of structures through which personal ritual contact with the self and the cosmos may be possible. He calls these structures 'dynamics' because their primary effect is upon the energies within an individual, a group, and the spatial surroundings.

To date, there are 21 dynamics,[26] each with a different psychophysical emphasis, a different imaginal content, and each utilizing the 'tools' of the

---

25 The *concheros* are dancers who are members of highly organized groups, the aim of which is to preserve the traditional ritual dances of pre-Hispanic Mexico, and to perform at seasonal festivals.

26 Please see pp. 225 - 227 below for a discussion of the number of dynamics at the time of going to press.

TRW in different ways. Each dynamic consists of two scores: an external score of physical actions and an internal score of meditations and focusing images. In practice, these two scores work closely together, each facilitating the other - their interplay being the essential aim. Each dynamic is internally supported by a mythological image from the pre-Hispanic pantheon that acts as a focusing device and provides a conceptual—even philosophical—center. For example, we have Quetzalcóatl, the Feathered Serpent; Tonatiuh, the Sun God; and Citlalmina, the Archeress who shoots arrows at the stars.

Primarily, the dynamics have been developed as devices for actor training. The ritual aspects of the work encourage participants toward a profound self-knowledge through tools that develop mental, physical, and energetic discipline, and through the development of skills for accessing and leaving altered states of consciousness at will.

Through practical research, the members of the TRW have discovered what Núñez considers to be the key features of the dynamic: continuous movement, continuous mental focus on one's experience, changing rhythms, and alternation between tension and relaxation. These are the underlying principles within each dynamic, discovered through practice and through careful attention to the effects of the dynamic as experienced subjectively by group members. Thus, a dynamic consists of a continuous sequence of alternating psychophysical actions throughout which participants remain in continual motion. These actions include slow walking, whirling, 'contemplative running', the corporeal alphabets of certain sacred dances (notably from the Mexican *conchero* and Tibetan monastic traditions), and movements - such as running backwards with eyes closed - which are designed to 'deprogram' daily behavior patterns. These tools are juxtaposed in such a way as to allow their differing rhythms and energetic demands to create dynamic frictions within and between participants. At all times, the participant should work with strong attention, with a constant focus of mind on body, and continually struggling against the dispersal of energies.

These three challenges draw the participant into an experience of intense presence within the moment - what Núñez calls 'the actualized instant'. For Núñez, it is precisely this concept that forges a navigable bridge between the worlds of theatre and ritual (1996b) [see Figure 12 on p. 272 below]. He sees the relationship between the two as centered upon an essential axis, a common dependency on the actualized instant; that is, at the center of each is 'the moment'. Both theatre and ritual are activities which take place in a spatial and temporal terrain and which require the 'enlivening' of time through focus and action, full psychophysical presence in what Stanislavski called 'the here and now'. Núñez has identified Stanislavski's here and now as an 'archaic mechanism of rite'; a 'vehicle to arouse another reality' (p. 54 above). He sees in Stanislavski's work the rediscovery of the essential element that allows theatre to cross from the profane to the sacred sphere. Being fully present in the present moment is both the actor's means of energetic, emotional, imaginative power and the hierophant's means of accessing other levels of consciousness, aided by the faith and imagination of the Stanislavskian 'as if', itself a door into other realms of reality. Making contact with the here and now is, by necessity, making contact with oneself, and with one's experience. I Wayan Lendra reports that Grotowski used to assert that one should 'see that you are seeing and hear that you are hearing' (1991: 126).

Access to enlivened time, to full experience of the moment, is built upon a foundation of training techniques, whether for the actor or the hierophant. In many cultures today, actors use their techniques for commercial and profane reasons; hierophants traditionally use theirs for sacred and cosmic purposes. Yet, as Richard Schechner has shown and discussed, the hierophant's techniques, under particular circumstances, may in fact relate us not to the cosmos but to commerce (1988: 106 - 152). Likewise, as Grotowski's theatre exemplified, the actor may relate us to the sacred dimension - the nonordinary modality of numinous human experience. It is Núñez's intention to find theatrical games that will allow ordinary participants to access the realm of the sacred.

Núñez describes the struggle to remain actively in the present moment as 'epic' - not in a Brechtian sense, but rather to connote an effort of impressive, even 'heroic', proportions (1996b). The epic effort involves a struggle with oneself: overcoming one's limitations and obstacles; becoming, as Núñez terms it, the 'warrior' in one's own personal battle (1993). During the contemplative run, for example, the battle is against the temptation to give in to the physical and mental discomfort that arises, for most people, from running for extreme periods of time. So, too, the ritual dance, *Citlalmina*, is a 'warrior dance':

> You are like a warrior, and you are going to give your battle, you are not going to dance, you are going to fight. And this fight is against the ego. [...Y]ou have to conquer your body, you have to conquer your mind, and then you might try to conquer, maybe to know, your spirit. But if you do not conquer your body and if you do not conquer your mind, you will never find out what to do with your spirit (Núñez 1993).

Unless a participant encounters this opportunity for personal effort within the practice, he will achieve only physical exercise through the dynamics. When the work is performed with an epic psychophysical struggle to inhabit the moment and to overcome weaknesses of will, then energy and strength are invoked in the participant. Further, the experience teaches an important life lesson: through hardship and effort we encounter the best in ourselves; through going down into the darkness, we give ourselves the possibility of emerging into light.

In Turner's model of social drama (1995: 8-10), interpersonal conflicts provide the pivotal points in the life of a community and lead to reflexivity, redressive action, and either reintegration or recognition of the need for change. In the dynamics, the conflicts that arise are within the individual psyche (although they may, at times, be aroused by interpersonal relations through the experience of working intimately with a partner or being part of a group). It is the epic struggle that is instrumental in urging the participant toward self-reflection and a redressive process. Without the latter, a participant would feel only a sense of inadequacy, perhaps despondency or frustration. However, the dynamics and the public performances are designed to carry willing participants into an arena in which they may initiate their own process of transformation. Significantly, in Turner's model the redressive phase of social drama includes ritual, among other processes. The ritual process, according to Van Gennep (1908) and Turner, is comprised of three phases, each of which may well involve performative means to realize its function. These phases are separation, transformation, and reaggregation. The dynamic as a whole may be seen to fit this pattern. Separation from daily life is begun with the formation of a circle, suspension of social roles (silence, alternation of males and females in circle), and frequently the use of a vibratory chant to charge the space and internalize the participants' attention. The closing sequence of each dynamic restores the participant to the circle, to contact with others, and to a sense of the outside world. The energy and focus that has been generated is released, and frequently a yogic 'balancing' position is assumed.

The central actions of the dynamic are liminoid and ludic, and may involve contact with, or enactment of, 'sacred' or unconscious materials. Within this structure, participants may make use of the supporting actions and images of the dynamic, as well as other personal imagery that might arise, in an attempt to overcome personal inner conflicts.

Turner describes liminality as:

> a fructile chaos, a fertile nothingness, a storehouse of possibilities, not by any means a random assemblage but a striving after new forms and structure, a gestation process, a fetation of modes appropriate to and anticipating postliminal existence (1990: 12).

In the dynamics, there is typically a certain 'looseness' of form; participants are not given detailed formal instructions but rather find their own way to perform the actions. That is, they seek out their own means of utilizing both personal imagery and the imagery inherent in the specific dynamic in order to make sense of the experience in their own terms. This openness provides a liminoid context in which new forms, images, identities, and behavioral patterns may be forged. Rather than functioning as a positive induction to new modes of thought or behavior, the dynamic provides experiences through which one might strip away, or learn to refrain from, habitual modes. Thus, while entering alternate modes of consciousness might be an immediate tool within the dynamics (giving access as they do to deeper levels of imaginative and unconscious material), the dynamics might also be seen to initiate alternate modes of being, that is, more permanent behavioral changes.

Turner recognized theatre as an 'inheritor' of ritual, potentially capable of fulfilling some of the latter's reflexive, liminoid, and transformative functions, but requiring, if it is to do so, 'power sources' which are 'often inhibited or at least constrained in the cultural life of society's "indicative mood"' (1990: 12). Núñez's theatre involves a number of the routes to power which Turner identifies: the body—use of energetic positions derived from ritual practices; long-durational actions that raise endorphin levels; meditative techniques; and driving techniques of the kind identified by Eugene d'Aquili and others (d'Aquili et al. 1979), for example, in the use of drumming, vibratory chanting, and rhythmical repetitive actions. Indeed, it could be argued that the main thrust toward 'power' lies in the use of such techniques to bring about a unified presence in the here and now. Meditative techniques in this work are performed within and through physical actions; physical actions are accomplished via meditative focus; driving techniques themselves are identified as a means of harmonizing bodily rhythms. Thus in all cases we might identify these techniques as means by which to bring disparate aspects of the whole being into harmony. This is in itself a central means of tapping into power within the self - accessing energetic and psychological potentials that are normally beyond our immediate grasp. Centrality in the self and in the moment coupled with the motivating, arousing, and reflexive potentials of the epic struggle empower individuals to go beyond their habitual limitations within a context that is at once imaginal and actual. Transformation is, theoretically at least, possible on psychological, emotional, and physiological levels.

Within *Tonatiuh*, *Citlalmina*, and the other dynamics, I believe it is possible to identify a series of practical objectives that effectively act as a kind of ladder - each rung facilitating access to the next. The participant's attainment of each rung is also an important end in itself since it is the attainment of a level of psychophysical development. This structure is reminiscent of the ritual 'ladders' of certain religious practices; for example, the seven chakras of Tantric Kundalini yoga through which the yogi progresses, cultivating at each stage a more developed form of consciousness and psychophysical presence. As with the chakras, each rung in Núñez's dynamics leads to the next, but like the Hasidic ladder to Heaven, one can also reach enlightenment at any stage by a jump in consciousness.

The first rungs of work within the dynamics comprise the epic struggle. Participants are encouraged to: (1) silence the rational mind and banish distracting thoughts—perhaps using a mantra, creative visualization, or rhythm to assist in controlling the mind's tendency to wander; (2) be present in the here and now, avoiding thoughts of past or future, and focus on the somatic sensation of one's bodymind within the particular spatial experience; and (3) focus physical and mental energies, and work with the image of raising and controlling energy through the psychophysical actions. These three challenges go hand in hand, the attainment of one helping the participant to progress with the others. When the intellectual properties of the rational mind, which serve to distance us from reality by 'interpreting' it, are temporarily silenced, a more intuitive and immediate mode of consciousness emerges. In this state we can begin to directly inhabit our own experience, to experience ourselves fully in the here and now. Given that in daily life we are mostly accustomed to mental withdrawal from the present moment (thinking forward or backward in time, but rarely focusing on the present), the attainment of this state, which Núñez calls 'the actualized instant' (1996b) is an empowering and energizing experience in which we feel our mental and physical resources to be fully activated.

Tonatiuh (1984)

Of the 21 dynamics which the TRW currently utilizes, two provide a particularly fruitful source for analysis and discussion. *Tonatiuh* (Tonn-ah-chew; 1984), the oldest of the dynamics, is the simplest to learn and the one in which meditation in motion is most clearly discernible. *Citlalmina* (Seet-lal-meen-ah; 1988) is the most complex of the dynamic structures, and the best example of psychophysical cultivation by means of 'deconditioning'.

Since the action in *Tonatiuh* is broken down into clearly defined sections, each of which comprises a single psychophysical activity, it can quickly be understood by simply following the instructions of the leader. Each activity is accompanied by a simple meditation, which is also easily explained and incorporated. This is of great importance to Núñez since his work is designed for theatrical and workshop situations in which it is desirable to have exercises that participants can experience after a minimal induction. Nevertheless, full embodiment and, particularly, full mental presence are cultivated only through repetition over time.

TONATIUH

External Score	Internal Score
lying on the back	meditate on all that is mineral within you
sitting	meditate on all that is vegetable within you
slow walking	meditate on all that is animal within you
contemplative running	meditate on all that is human within you
whirling	meditate on all that is divine within you
vibration: vocalization and playing of conches; rhythmic group action with drum and rattles; closing circle	focus is now brought to the self as a whole, and to the group as a whole - the sense of communal experience is heightened in these final three sections

In this dynamic, activity is gradually elevated from a supine state to sitting, and then slow walking. In the TRW's version of slow walking, the participant aims to move as slowly and smoothly as possible, taking exaggerated steps so that there is a maximum of activity in the muscles of the supporting leg. The participant's attention is quickly drawn to balance, and to her shifting center of gravity as she moves slowly forward in space. The pace of the walk has a calming effect and breathing is slowed and harmonized accordingly. Throughout the walk, the participant must ensure that her attention is not allowed to wander but instead is fluidly fixed upon the sensation of the body in motion, and upon the imagery that arises from the instruction, 'meditate on all that is animal within you'.

On a given signal, participants gently transform the slow walking into 'contemplative running'. Also referred to as the 'contemplative trot', this run functions as a dominant tool in almost every dynamic (with the notable exception of *Citlalmina*). Núñez developed the contemplative run while working with Grotowski on Theatre of Sources in 1980, as a form of meditation in motion: a means of focusing and quieting the mind, and at the same time centering consciousness on somatic experience. Within the dynamics, the run is also instrumental in forging a sense of group rhythm and communal activity. Núñez describes the tool in *Anthropocosmic Theatre*:

> [W]e trot floating through the area, relaxing at every step, avoiding the tension in the arms which one gets in a running race, and do not try to advance, since there is nowhere to reach and nobody to beat. We keep our look open, i.e., without focusing, and the same goes for our active internal chant; we must feel that we are hanging by a thread which comes from the crown of our head and is tied to the stars, and flow at our own pace in a constant here and now (p. 119 above).

Most significantly, the continual movement of the contemplative run is achieved only through an equally continual effort of the mind. The runner must struggle to achieve 'mental polarization', the focusing of the mind's energies on the run itself. As the participant runs, she encounters, moment by moment, the tendency for the mind to wander, the desire to let the body give in, the craving to be in another place, at another time. Artaud wrote at length about the inability, as he perceived it, to inhabit his own existence, to achieve 'constant concert' (1968: 40); in Núñez's work, participants run into their own lives, run to find themselves. As Ronald Grimes has pointed out in his analysis of Grotowski's Theatre of Sources, statements such as this are often interpreted as pointing toward a narcissistic introversion on the part of the participants. In light of this, Grimes suggests that Grotowski's term 'work on oneself' is better phrased as 'work as oneself' ([1982] 1995: 181). In Núñez's work also, 'finding oneself' is achieved not through self-oriented deliberation, but through heightened awareness of one's own psychophysical presence. Thus, the contemplative run is not contemplative in the sense that one contemplates ideas while running. Rather, it is contemplation in the sense of meditation, a total focus of the mind on the body, on the experience of the run. As Claudio Naranjo has suggested, meditative practices involve the cultivation of a state that is markedly different from 'normal' activity and 'normal' consciousness:

> While in most of one's daily life the mind flits from one subject or thought to another, and the body moves from one posture to another, meditation practices generally involve an effort to stop this merry-go-round of mental or other activity and to set our attention upon a single object, sensation, utterance, issue, mental state, or activity (in Naranjo and Ornstein 1972: 10).

Meditative mental focus requires, and cultivates, what Naranjo calls 'a sustained openness to the present'; one cannot turn away from one's immediate experience, the challenge is simply to face it. In the dynamics, the primary task is to experience the moment fully and directly, without the interference of a distancing rationality. While running, you cannot think of running 'somewhere'; there is no goal to reach. This is one distinction between contemplative running and athletic running, and it is of essential importance. Participants do not think ahead of themselves any more than they think of past events; they focus here and now—not running to, and not running for, just running. In this sense of 'goallessness', it is similar to other meditative practices, such as zazen, or Zen sitting, as analyzed by Grimes: 'Zazen is not a preparation for anything, even enlightenment. There is no difference between practice and goal [...]. One's goal is to sit without goals' ([1982] 1995: 94).

There is no difference between practice and goal; the running is all there is. In my own experience, I found that any thought of an arrival while in the contemplative running brought with it the danger of a complete relapse into habitual modes of being. Only in abandoning the notion of goal, arrival, achievement, or finish line, does one begin to inhabit the experience for itself. As with Grimes's description of zazen, I found the long periods of contemplative running 'excruciatingly painful'; the mind did indeed want 'to fly, or fill up' ([1982] 1995: 94 - 95), to sidestep the problems of 'polarization', staying still with nowhere to go. Eugen Herrigel's description of his Zen apprenticeship in archery includes an account of this difficulty:

> As though sprung from nowhere, moods, feelings, desires, worries and even thoughts incontinently rise up, in a meaningless jumble, and the more far-fetched and preposterous they are, and they less they have to do with that on which one has fixed one's consciousness, the more tenaciously they hang on (1985: 53).

So it is in the contemplative run, and in other tools of the TRW such as slow walking; participants continually encounter their inability to simply be in the present moment. However, persistently making the required psychophysical effort (which, of course, may be a withdrawal from 'effort'), without thought of reward, may indeed bring rewards. Phillip Zarrilli has identified the sense of 'presence' that can be achieved through psychophysical practices whereby the energetic '"blazing flame" of an active, inner, vibratory perceptivity' is apparent to a spectator (1997: 109). The dilation of energetic presence may be accompanied by a dilation of self-awareness; the runner comes to new understandings about the self, about his weaknesses, habitual tendencies, willpower, fears, etc. Energetic flow within the body, and the places where that flow is blocked or misdirected, become apparent to the mindful participant. Further, the experience of focusing the mind, and quieting mental chatter may lead to a state of nondual awareness, and with this, a different form of perceiving and experiencing.

Etzel Cardeña, a psychologist and theatre practitioner who has researched and published widely within the field of altered states of consciousness, has described his experience of nondual consciousness in relation to Núñez's practice:

> Dual consciousness is one in which your consciousness is separate from your body, separate from others, separate from the surrounding environment. While working [with Núñez and similar practitioners] this separate dual consciousness starts breaking down at times. [...A]t one point there will be no observing self that is separate from the action that is occurring. [...I]f there is a movement that has to happen [...,] instead of a thought preceding the action there is a consciousness in action, or an action in consciousness (1998:*np*).

In this state, participants experience both a unified sense of mind and body, and also a sense of the intrinsic unity of self with others, with the world around them, even with the cosmos itself. The run becomes effortless, a sensation of space opens up in the mind, and a feeling of calm, high energy, perhaps ecstasy, pervades.

Tonatiuh is one example of a dynamic that employs a ludic strategy of imaginal association. The imaginal and energetic force of 'as if', which Stanislavski identified at the heart of theatre, is, for Núñez, a key element in moving from the domain of theatre to that of its near relative, ritual. In *Tonatiuh*, by addressing that which is mineral, vegetable, animal, etc., within them, participants make imaginative leaps, approaching the task in the way that is most meaningful for them personally. In other dynamics, participants might similarly evoke imaginal environments, animal guides, or representations of natural forces. And in all of Núñez's work, theatrical games are played as if they were real; as Núñez would say, we play 'with the seriousness of a child' (1999).

Turner has described this 'subjunctive' mood of 'as if', in which both theatre and ritual exist: 'Subjunctivity is possibility. It refers to what may or might be. It is also concerned with supposition, conjecture, and assumption, with the domain of "as-if" rather than "as-is"' (1983: 235).

As a meditative and somatic exploration of images of the self as mineral, plant, animal, and divinity, *Tonatiuh* provides participants with an imaginal experience of oneness with nature and the universe. While the concept that humans are an integral and continuous element within a cosmic whole is derived in Núñez's work from ancient indigenous Indian practices, a similar philosophical position is expressed by Meister Eckhart of the European mystical tradition: 'The soul is all things. She has being with the stones and growing with the trees and feeling with the beasts and understanding with the angels' (in O'Neal 1996:86).

In *Tonatiuh*, participants simultaneously encounter themselves as complexes of physiological and psychological weakness and resource, and as imaginal beings mythologically interconnected to a universe of elements and energies. Eckhart, here, is expressing that *unio mystica* which meditative and mystical practices aspire to, while *Tonatiuh* is an imaginal game, a 'metaphoric identification' (Grimes [1982] 1995: 257) more likely to shed light on the participant's individual psyche than to produce a mystical experience.

Citlalmina (1988)

In contrast to the simple structure of *Tonatiuh*, *Citlalmina* comprises a complex corporeal alphabet; whereas one can be fully engaged with *Tonatiuh* on a first encounter, *Citlalmina* can be learned only through extensive practice. The complexity of the form raises challenges different from those of the simpler dynamics, while the central premises remain the same. *Citlalmina* may be seen as the TRW's warrior rite *par excellence*, as a highly effective transformative ritual, and as a vehicle for developing mental focus and energetic control. This ritual dance was born of the TRW's research in Náhuatl and Tibetan cultures, and is the marriage of a warrior dance from each tradition - a Mexican Náhuatl conchero shell dance (*danza conchera*), and the Tibetan 'Black Hat' dance (*Lha-lhung Pay-dor*). It has been officially recognized and authorized by the religious authorities from each tradition: by General Teresa of the concheros, and by the Dalai Lama who blessed it as a 'tool for mental training' (p. 137 above).[27]

In *Citlalmina*, neither of the source dances is interfered with, nor are they combined, but rather placed next to one another; the upper-body fluidity and lightness of the Tibetan dance in its entirety is nested between cycles of the Mexican dance with its powerful, grounding, step-based actions. Both dances are performed in circles, moving in a clockwise direction. Together, as *Citlalmina*, the sequence takes about one hour to perform.

Núñez tells us that the two sacred dances of which *Citlalmina* is formed are each 'ancestral tools to develop our attention and concentration' (p. 136 above). In performing the corporeal alphabet of *Citlalmina*, participants must adhere to two principal instructions:

> Keep our internal attention alive, tuning it to our breathing, without allowing the mind to wander; Flow with the mandalic design which completes the dance at an organic rhythm, which helps us to keep our attention on the here and now (p. 135 above).

Thus, *Citlalmina* is structured to support the psychophysical demands of meditation in motion through such methods as repetitive aural rhythms, changing physical rhythms, complex actions requiring close attention, and circling and

---

27 For a discussion of *Citlalmina* as a translation from Vajrayana Buddhist practice, see Middleton and Plá (2018) 'Adapting the Dharma: Buddhism and Contemporary Theatre Training,' *Journal of Global Buddhism* Vol. 19 (2018): pp. 113-125.

crossing actions. The body alphabet itself comprises movements that have the effect of 'deprogramming' the bodymind, thereby allowing the harmonizing of mental and physical energies and the dissolution of habitual psychophysical blockages. The deprogramming or deconditioning actions work against daily, habitual physical processes, for example, left- or right-handedness, and forward-motion. Circling, stepping, whirling, and the simple yet confounding combination of directional turn and sided action in, for example, the step called Quetzalcóatl, all have the effect of disrupting physical expectations. Movement becomes less automatic, and physical awareness is resensitized. Nonhabitual actions also have the effect of awakening muscular and emotional responses that may otherwise have lain dormant, thus influencing participants' subjective experiences of their own bodyminds. As with other bodymind practices, participants are enabled to see themselves anew within the frame of the unfamiliar, becoming aware of conditioned, habitual, and detrimental uses of the self. As Naranjo tells us in relation to meditative practice:

> What the meditator realizes in his practice is to a large extent how he is failing to meditate properly, and by becoming aware of his failings he gains understanding and the ability to let go of his wrong way. The right way, the desired attitude, is what remains when we have, so to speak, stepped out of the way (in Naranjo and Ornstein 1972: 9 - 10).

In texts on the Theatre of Sources—a project that Núñez and Guardia were involved with for one year—Grotowski spoke of the suspension of 'daily-life techniques of the body' as a means by which to bring about the 'deconditioning of perception':

> Habitually, an incredible amount of stimuli are flowing into us [...] but we are programmed in such a way that our attention records exclusively those stimuli that are in agreement with our learned image of the world. In other words, all the time we tell ourselves the same story. Therefore, if the techniques of the body, daily, habitual, specific for a precise culture, are suspended, this suspension is by itself a

deconditioning of perception (1997: 257 - 258).

For Grotowski, such a deconditioning—which he refers to elsewhere as an 'untaming' (in Kumiega 1987: 229)—returns us to the state of the 'Beginner' (229), that is, childlike immediacy and vibrancy of experience. Presence in the here and now is heightened, perception sharpened, and consciousness expanded; we escape from the 'prison' of our own 'babbling' (Grotowski 1997: 254), that internal monologue which suspends us between the past and the future, and insulates us from the present moment.

While, over time, repetition of any of the TRW's dynamics provides participants with the opportunity to cultivate their bodyminds in action, the pre- cise external form of *Citlalmina* represents the challenge to conform to technique and to discover one's own inner processes through a set external form. However, while *Citlalmina* consists of a complex corporeal alphabet, it is not taught by Núñez in such a way as to involve strict adherence to specific features such as alignment, center of gravity, etc. Although, clearly, the accomplishment of energetic positions in their finest detail will bring about specific and positive psychophysical states and experiences, here the emphasis is more firmly placed on the overall process, and on attention to one's mental journey through the process.

Grotowski considered that there were two ways in which to approach the state of Beginner: either through training in a technique or through 'untaming', as mentioned above (see Kumiega 1987: 229 - 230). Núñez has largely followed the latter route, stressing individual response and responsibility, and encouraging participants to find their own way of performing set actions, rather than following prescribed routes. The dynamics tend to function more as structures than as set sequences, and it is common to see great variation in the style, energy, and pace of any given action even among the most experienced members of the TRW. *Citlalmina* involves a significantly more detailed and complicated structure, but it is still, importantly, one in which each participant finds her own feet, so to speak. This has several positive effects, among them a sense of liberation and the creation of a nonjudgmental atmosphere for participants, and the displacement of attention from external form to internal discipline. It also means that *Citlalmina* remains an experiential activity and not an aesthetic spectacle. Perhaps it could be said that while training in a specific form one's mental activity is focused through attention to external form, in *Citlalmina* and the other dynamics one's physical activity is accomplished and dilated through attention to internal presence.

Cura de espantos (1998)

Throughout the long history of the TRW, the work of researching and creating actor-training dynamics has been accompanied by the work of creating participatory theatrical productions, exploring and experimenting with the ways in which theatre can be used as a matrix for ritual activity. In 1998, the group produced *Cura de espantos*, which translates, awkwardly, as something like '*Cure for Fears*'. According to the theatre critic and playwright Victor Hugo Rascón Banda, the piece successfully employed theatrical and ludic elements as a springboard from which to move beyond the bounds of representation: 'Theatre is the path taken', he tells us, but 'What at first seems like a game, turns into an impressive, unforgettable experience. [...] Is *Cura de espantos* theatre? It must be. [...] Is it a religious act? It is that, too, due to its deep spirituality' (Rascón Banda 1998: 39).

Cura de espantos is designed for an outdoor, woodland setting—in Mexico City it was performed in the ancient forest of Chapultepec—and comprises a journey to the underworld, inspired equally by Dante and by the myth of Quetzalcóatl. The journey begins with the audience being blindfolded and then led deep into the forest by the TRW's monitors (guides who construct and manage the participants' experience). This induction provides an effective means of crossing a threshold from the real world, to the world of 'as if'. Further, the experience of being led blindfolded encourages an immediate introspection and self-reflection on the part of the individual. Thus, when the blindfolds are removed and the audience members find themselves deep within a fairy-tale forest, there is a clear sense that this will be an experiential form of theatre, with personal implications for its participants. In the forest, the participants encounter four lone figures; each performs a monologue, expressive of archetypal human concerns in answer to the question, 'What is your story?' Drawn mostly from Shakespeare, but also from de Sade, Dante, Calderón, Náhuatl poetry, and other texts, the performances epitomize areas of common existential conflict: self-doubt, anger, jealousy, lust. The four figures wear chains as a reminder of the extent to which our unresolved human passions can imprison us. It is clearly the intention of the TRW that spectators identify with one or more of the figures, and furthermore, that they reflect on the significance of the material in relation to their own lives. In order to facilitate this, the TRW includes an unusual and highly significant space in the performance—a space for self-reflection. For a few minutes, the actors and monitors leave the audience entirely alone in the forest, with the instruction that it is a time for silence and personal contemplation.

It is from this point of recognition and self-reflection that the theatrical event opens up to the participant an opportunity to begin the work of 'working *on* oneself', 'working *as* oneself'. The next stage of the experience is a 'rite' developed from a Náhuatl cleansing ritual in which members of the TRW have been initiated (and which is shared with the permission of the religious authorities). For Rascón Banda, this is 'the most interesting, emotive and disturbing part' of the experience, 'and closest to the postulates of anthropocosmic theatre' (1998: 57). Here, audience members are invited to participate in contemplative running and in a simple, rhythmical dance; to make contact with the earth, and with themselves; and to enact a gesture of forgiveness—first, forgiving another member of the audience for 'whatever they have done', and then forgiving themselves. The assumption is that we free ourselves of unhelpful emotional constructs when we learn to accept ourselves and to forgive ourselves for the events that have damaged and limited us. The ritual actions serve as an opportunity to enter into an imaginative act of self-acceptance and self-liberation. The rite builds upon a foundation of emotional and imaginative readiness that has been created through the earlier parts of the performance. Having been touched, and perhaps troubled, by identification with the performed sections, audiences seem eager to participate in the physical actions of running, etc., and this in turn further involves them in an acceptance of the interior workings of the ritual.

I experienced *Cura de espantos* in Mexico City in May 1998, and afterward wrote this:

> My mind turning alone in the still moment in the forest cannot find a path, but in movement we raise other energies, we run into the here and now. I look into my partner's eyes: the look of I and Thou that Martin Buber wrote of, which transforms the other into a holy being, in which we recognize the humanity, the tenderness, of the other behind their daily garb. I touch my partner's heart and I forgive him for whatever has caused his pain, his fear. It's a simple trick, for having made my best effort to forgive him with all sincerity, I am invited to forgive myself. And if I can forgive him, why not forgive myself? (1998).

If this ritual is effective for its participants, then it is because the theatrical journey has first of all brought us to a point of recognition. We recognize our own need for emotional or spiritual change, and we are offered a ludic means of transformation. Significantly, the rite of transformation is itself both physical and contemplative, both communal and personal, both social and cosmic in its references.

Rituals of transformation, however, are not usually produced in isolation from supporting belief systems, communities, and ongoing ceremonial structures. Is the potential for meaningful personal transformation really within the scope of a theatrical game such as *Cura de espantos*? For Rascón Banda, *Cura de espantos* moves beyond the confines of theatre and achieves the status of ritual:

> [The TRW] achieves a genuine communion between the participants and nature, the earth, their atavistic roots [...]. Spirituality is reached [... and] an encounter takes place with the spirit, meditation in silence and

> the quest for one's roots [...]. In an imposing silence, the participants hug the earth, are purged and discover the light which illuminates the way back to their starting point (1998: 39).

Thus, for Rascón Banda, the experience itself creates a temporary but profound *communitas*, and provides archetypal symbols and enactments that serve to provide us not with doctrine or a specific set of beliefs but rather with a numinous contact with nature, and with the self.

I would suggest that for many contemporary, alienated individuals, uninhibited exploration of the states and actions offered by the TRW is a mode of being that requires cultivation over time. Nevertheless, in my own experience of witnessing several performances of *Cura de espantos*, I was struck by how very frequently participants appeared to let down their defenses, to become more wholehearted and less inhibited during the running and other actions, and to make genuine and compassionate contact with one another in the forgiveness rite. Further, if an individual participant cannot fully engage with the ritual during his first encounter with it, he may, at the very least, have equipped himself with some new ideas and experiences relating to his personal growth. After my first experience of *Cura de espantos*, I came away with a strong sense of having been given the tools with which I might continue my own process of transformation. In my journal, I wrote:

> In the fairy tale, the adventurer is often given magic gifts, and here they are: the 'here and now', given in the running; the 'other', given in the looking; 'Mother Earth', given in the embrace with her; and of course my 'Self', returned to me in the forgiveness (1998).

In *Cura de espantos*, as in Núñez's dynamics, the participant has access to 'technologies', which can be employed beyond the confines of the immediate performance or workshop. These are, specifically, tools that allow us to make active psychophysical contact with mythological symbols as we might encounter them in ancient stories, ritual enactments, the natural environment, or daily experience. And it is precisely through such an opening of consciousness toward mythology that Núñez's work can attempt to function as ritual.

Between Theatre and Ritual

Núñez sees all of the work of the TRW as following a structure of: Theatre → Epic → Myth → Ritual [see Figure 11 on p. 270 below]. We have already discussed the epic proportions of the work, and we might see that it is this struggle, this warrior's battle, perhaps even 'sacrifice' in the Grotowskian sense of revealing oneself through a process of stripping away 'life masks' (1968), that allows the theatre format to support the transformative potentials traditionally associated with ritual. Through struggle, effort, strong energy, and willpower, the individual participant may begin to find that which is beyond the daily experience for most of us. When we go beyond the epic struggle, we come to a level of experience that Núñez describes as 'mythic'. That is, the epic challenges of the work bring us to a state of consciousness in which we can work meaningfully with archetypal, mythological imagery.

Núñez's theatre has been greatly influenced by his readings of Carl Jung, Joseph Campbell, and other mythologists, and it is, in great part, a desire to explore mythology and symbolism that motivates him: '[T]he myths are really a deep, inner, and beautiful fruit for the human soul. So I think that our dynamics can give [participants] the possibility [...] to search for their own roots' (1993). In the dynamics, and in the participatory sections of the theatre productions, Núñez utilizes actions that allow participants to embody images and mandalic designs relating to mythic source-ideas and images. Mythology is actualized through the participants' active psychophysical engagement with images that assist them in the epic struggle required to achieve personal transformation and the experience of nondaily perception and consciousness. For the TRW, working as they are with theatre as the point of departure, presence in the fleeting moment becomes both the means by which participants can holistically engage with the imaginal world of myth, and also the experience to which mythology may bring us. Thus, participants *experience* rather than *think about* the meanings embodied in the myths. Anthropocosmic Theatre, then, might be described as a kind of mythology in action.

Turner paraphrases Lévi-Strauss's identification of myths as encapsulations of the problem of reconciling the dualities with which we live: problems such as 'life and death, good and evil, mutability and an unchangeable 'ground of being,' the one and the many, freedom and necessity' (1983: 231). The multiplicity of meanings inherent within mythological images and story-structures allows us to experience dualities in such a way as to undermine apparent contradictions in the face of meaningfulness on an a-rational level. And rituals provide an opportunity to physically embody the working-through of the mythic image or situation. In the dynamics and theatrical productions of the TRW, contact with the mythological image both empowers participants to make an epic struggle, and also provides access to alternate means and modes of understanding the universe. Through specific actions, and through the psychophysical experience of the mythic imagery and inherent concept of a particular piece of work, participants may begin to move into a different experience of 'understanding'. At this level, they may arrive at knowledge that is beyond the self, may even negate the notion of self. Each turns outward toward the group, the world, the cosmos, so that individual focus moves from introspection to full awareness of others. Only when intention is correct in the ways outlined above does the action become more than action; only then does the dynamic cease to be theatre and truly become rite. Thus, for Núñez, the journey from theatre to ritual is: Theatre → Epic → Myth → Ritual. Through the epic struggle and the mythic image, the dramatic structure of the dynamic becomes a vehicle to transport us into other realms.

For Núñez, theatre has the potential to support ritual processes, structures, and tools with which to interrogate the deep wisdom of the mythologies, and to activate our own latent psychophysical resources. As such, operating out of the base of a secular, cultural activity, Núñez's work moves into fields usually associated with religion: 'You can make a theatre of reflection, political theatre, personal theatre, whatever...but also, the theatre has the possibility to open the gates for you to see your situation in the cosmos' (1993).

Participants begin to 'see their situation in the cosmos' by experiencing themselves in relation to mythological imagery, and to mythological themes embedded in ancient corporeal codes and designs. The heightened sense of presence and the development of nondual consciousness bring with them an experience of our interconnectedness with the energies of the natural world, indeed the Universe.

Importantly, though, this is a spirituality that disregards doctrine. If Núñez's works can be described as rituals, then they are rituals of personal transformation within which each individual makes his or her own private journey. The work is clearly presented as a form of 'secular sacredness', and the practices are firmly rooted in the ludic context of theatrical games, 'serious games' (Núñez 1999).

This is a theatre in which we *imagine* that we are dancing the designs of the Universe, that we are making journeys in inner and outer space, that we are working to conquer those rebel parts of our bodies and minds that we may become whole. We imagine it, and in imagining it, perhaps we make it true. We touch the divine in ourselves and in each other when we run, metaphori- cally throwing off the garments of society, opening our eyes to the look of I-Thou from another, literally arriving at a sense of the self as we begin to understand that there is no arrival, and that we are already here.

REFERENCES

d'Aquili, Eugene, et al. (1979) *The Spectrum of Ritual*. New York: Columbia Press.

Artaud, Antonin ([1956] 1968) *Collected Works. Vol. 1*. Translated by Victor Corti. London: Calder & Boyars Ltd.

Cardeña, Etzel (1998) Interview with author. Huddersfield, England, 13 December.

Grimes, Ronald ([1982] 1995) *Beginnings in Ritual Studies*. Columbia:

University of South Carolina Press.

Grotowski, Jerzy (1968) *Towards a Poor Theatre*. Holstebro: Odin Teatrets Forlag.

Grotowski, Jerzy (1995) 'From Theatre Company to Art as Vehicle' in Richards, Thomas, *At Work with Grotowski on Physical Actions*, London: Routledge, pp.115-35.

Grotowski, Jerzy ([1980] 1997) 'Theatre of Sources'. *The Grotowski Source Book*, edited by Richard Schechner and Lisa Wolford, 250 - 268. London: Routledge.

Herrigel, Eugen ([1953] 1985) *Zen in the Art of Archery*. Translated by R.F.C. Hull. London: Arkana.

Kumiega, Jennifer ([1985] 1987) *The Theatre of Grotowski*. London: Methuen.

Lendra, I Wayan (1991) 'Bali and Grotowski: Some Parallels in the Training Process'. TDR 35, 1 (T129): 113 - 39.

Middleton, Deborah K. (1998) Unpublished manuscript.

Naranjo, Claudio, and Robert E. Ornstein ([1971] 1972) *On the Psychology of Meditation*. London: George Allen & Unwin Ltd.

Núñez, Nicolás (1987) *Teatro Antropocósmico*. Mexico City: Árbol Editorial.

Núñez, Nicolás (1993) Interview with author. Mexico City, 19 November.

Núñez, Nicolás (1996a) *Anthropocosmic Theatre: Rite in the Dynamics of Theatre*. Translated by Ronan J. Fitzsimons. Amsterdam: Harwood Academic Publishers.

Núñez, Nicolás (1996b) 'Theatre As a Personal Rite'. Workshop at the University of Huddersfield, England, 26 - 30 October.

Núñez, Nicolás (1999) 'Theatre and Transformation'. Workshop at the University of Huddersfield, England, 6 - 10 April.

O'Neal, David, ed. (1996) *Meister Eckhart, from Whom God Hid Nothing*. Boston: Shambhala Publications, Inc.

Rascón Banda, Victor Hugo (1998) '*Cura de espantos*'. *Proceso*, 1 February: 57

Schechner, Richard ([1977] 1988) *Performance Theory*. New York: Routledge.

Turner, Victor (1983) 'Body, Brain and Culture'. *Zygon* 18, 3: 221- 245

Turner, Victor (1990) 'Are There Universals of Performance in Myth, Ritual, and Drama?' In *By Means of Performance: Intercultural Studies of Theatre and Ritual*, edited by Richard Schechner and Willa Appel, 8 - 18. Cambridge: Cambridge University Press.

Van Gennep, Arnold ([1908] 1960) *The Rites of Passage*. Chicago, IL: University of Chicago Press.

Zarrilli, Phillip (1997) 'Acting "At the Nerve Ends": Beckett, Blau, and the Necessary'. *Theatre Topics* 7, 2: 103 - 116.

ANTHROPOCOSMIC THEATRE

SNAPSHOT 1: THE COMMUNAL SELF
John Britton

In *Anthropocosmic Theatre* [Part One], Núñez writes of a night-long ritual he attended in the mountains of Mexico:

> The imposing austerity of the mountains, protected by a sky full of stars, and the murmur of human warmth giving itself over to the energies of the light, instilled in us a deep sense of brotherhood….. There we were in small groups, high up in the mountains, gathered in small groups around a fire…. Looking at the spectacle from outside, it seemed like a group which was too exposed, vulnerable, extremely fragile and delicate, and at the same time blessed with unique strength and beauty, like the orchid (p. 49 above).

When first I read this, it thrilled me, made immediate and tangible notions I had first encountered when reading about ritual performance - notions of 'communitas' and 'liminality'. The evocation of humans carving out a shared and structured space within the vastness of the geographical, the galactic and the spiritual, opened doorways of perception for me.

Some years later I attended a training session led by Nicolás. Running, endlessly, in circles, losing and finding myself in the spaces between my heated body and those around me, mediated by the drum. I found my edges by feeling them dissolve against the edges of others. Provoked into engagement with mythologies that, until then, had been entirely 'other' to me, I imagined myself (though it was more than that - it was a deeply lived imagining) simultaneously connected with and distanced from the ancient knowledge and cultures Nicolás brings to the studio. I encountered an imagined community across time with those who can only ever be entirely other to me.

One evening, some time later… I am sitting in a chair in Nicolás' living room. We are drinking tequila. He laughs and tells me that I am sitting in the chair Maestro Grotowski sat in. I realise how strongly he occupies the community of our lineages - in his practice there is an interweaving of strands from Tibet, Europe, India, North American, the Contemporary, the Ancient, the Scientific, the Esoteric.

I once asked Nicolás to give me a definition of one of my own obsessions - ensemble. He said it was, to him, a dinner party that people attended having first removed their social masks. A social gathering that can contain nothing but truth and revelation.

I think of him - three times each week, running early morning training at the *Taller* in Mexico City, providing a place of refuge, meeting and transcendence for all who wish to attend: a practical and conscious construction and maintaining of living community.

In 2008, Nicolás attended a workshop I ran. He was skilled and powerful, as one would expect, but also impish and funny - neither denying the enormity of his energetic and intellectual presence, nor allowing it to separate him from the flow and conections of the room. He carved for himself a unique place in a shared community - of it and not of it, integral and other.

Across so many of my encounters - personal, cultural and intellectual - I find myself considering this notion of community; between peoples, within homogenous and heterogeneous gatherings, across time, across culture, through lineages. I consider the notion of the 'anthropocosmic' - the idea of the human in the centre of the universe. This does not evoke for me a sense of self-importance or of unfettered individualism. The individual here is an individual-within-collective, the communal self. S/he is the centre of an awareness that finds its detail by contact and contrast with the other. S/he is the single star, separated by vast distance from all others, which, in relationship, creates the infinity of the mountain night sky. It is the communal individual who has found her/his place in a biosphere, a galaxy, in the nexus of time and space that is now.

In Núñez, I find expression of a deep truth of performance and of life: that to know oneself - and to embrace the reality that the truth of ones experience is found only through knowing ones experience - requires also a knowing of everything else. I find myself by taking my place in the community of everyone and everything I am not.

The clarity of dawn slowly uncovered the other reality, the everyday one. Shapes regained their volume and colour, and certainty tentatively built its path back to reason, to common sense. Nevertheless, in our stomachs, there was still a feeling that linked us to emptiness (p. 49 above).

ANTHROPOCOSMIC THEATRE

SNAPSHOT 2: SWIMMING IN THE INNER SOURCE: A WORKSHOP WITH NICOLÁS NÚÑEZ

Cassiano Sydow Quilici

In 2016, on the occasion of the 'Performance and Mindfulness: International Symposium' at the University of Huddersfield, I had the opportunity of participating in a workshop led by Nicolás Núñez. Even though the workshop lasted for just a few days, I quickly noted its depth and realized that it was the fruit of many years of research. Throughout the week, I was able to absorb precious procedures and principles, both on a personal level and in such a way that led me to consider new perspectives on my own work. I would like to underline three aspects that were particularly important.

First, there is the contextualization of the exercises within a 'cosmology' that defines different states and ways of being: the quotidian state, the hero state and divine state. The idea is that the training of the actor not only represents a set of strategies for creating a heightened experience of body-mind, but it is also a perspective for understanding the world beyond the everyday. When an exercise is situated within a broader field we are able to understand the horizon of the practice.

Secondly, the specific exercise of 'contemplative running' resulted in an interesting personal experience. Running here is a form of relaxing the body, strongly connected with the group, for a long period of time, in circles, allowing us to experience a change in the quality of energy, expressed in the form of running itself. In the beginning, my impression was that the whole group was galloping, based on an awareness of the contact with the ground and the energy of the earth. As I began using my arms, as if gliding, my energy was renewed and the image that appeared was that of a flock of birds moving through the sky, leading to a transformation of a dense sensation into a more subtle experience. The idea of human body as a complex structure that connects dense and subtle energies can also be found in the practice of *tai chi chuan* and other traditional practices.

Finally, my contact with Núñez and his work brought me greater clarity about the possibilities of dialogues between Eastern contemplative practices and the wealth of pre-Colombian indigenous cultures. He himself emphasized this connection, having worked with traditional forms of Tibetan dance, some aspects of which have been incorporated into his proposals. All of this strengthened in me the desire to develop a new approach to the question of 'mindfulness' that takes into consideration the context of Latin America and its singularities. I am extremely grateful to Nicolás Núñez and the University of Huddersfield for having this opportunity.

'SECULAR SACREDNESS' IN THE RITUAL THEATRE OF NICOLÁS NÚÑEZ[28]

Deborah Middleton

> Núñez has forged a theatre that attempts to provide an active arena for those individuals who seek personal individuation, communitas, or the experience of the sacred dimension in their everyday lives. The TRW carves out a sacred space in the context of an urban cultural institution (p. 155 above; Middleton 2001: 43).

The work of Nicolás Núñez and his collaborators at the *Taller de Investigación Teatral* (Theatre Research Workshop/TRW) in Mexico City offers an activity that responds to both ritual and theatrical imperatives and that integrates religious sources as transferable psychophysical practices. Núñez calls this an 'anthropocosmic theatre', a theatre of 'high risk' for the purposes of personal transformation (See pp. 267 - 287 below; Núñez 2007). He locates the work within a pan-cultural 'secular sacredness', which seeks to reconnect theatre with its archaic ritual sources.

I first began researching Núñez's work in 1993, after encountering his training 'dynamics' at a conference on Performance, Ritual and Shamanism at the Centre for Performance Research in Wales. The article 'At Play in the Cosmos', quoted above, was the result of eight years of engagement in Núñez's work, in residencies that I organized in the UK and during research trips to Mexico. In that period, and since, I have had open access to workshops, daily training, rehearsals, planning meetings and performances. There has been ample opportunity for formal interviews and long informal conversations with Núñez and his collaborators. My role in the work has been that of participant-observer, attempting to maintain that careful line between immersion in experience and the critical distance of the scholarly engagement.

---

28   Originally published in *Performance Research*, 2008, 13:3, pp. 41-54 (https://www.performance-research.org/).

In 'At Play' I was interested in framing Núñez's practice as a ritual activity, elucidated by recourse to ritual structures and concepts and defined by an imperative towards sacrality. In this paper I have explored bases for an understanding of the psychophysical causes and effects of sacred experience within the practice. This paper arises out of my deepened experience; I am now in the second half of my second decade in the work, a chapter characterized by, among other things, periods of immersion in the dynamic *Citlalmina* (since in 2000, Núñez authorized me to practice the form independently). This writing is informed by my phenomenological experience of the work over time, but for reasons of academic distance, I have preferred to draw directly on the experience of other participants as illustration and evidence.

Núñez's project, and indeed my own engagement with it, are essentially intercultural explorations. While I acknowledge the ethical questions surrounding that aspect of the work, the focus in this article will be on the ways in which such a theatre functions as 'a sacred space'. By identifying the culturally syncretic context in which Núñez lives and works, I hope to provide a perspective which both normalizes and legitimizes the intercultural aspects of his project.

Furthermore, I will approach Núñez's religious sources, as he does, as performance practices that embody pre-cultural frameworks that may be uncovered to produce sets of transferable principles and psychophysical technologies.

To this end, I will explore religious experience per se through a consideration of the consciousness-states and structures involved. Through ascertaining the bodily correlates and mental factors that are found to be instrumental in producing religious – or 'altered' – states (and structures) of consciousness, I will propose a model for producing – or increasing access to – culturally 'unformed' psychophysical experience. Against this framework of ideas, I will map the phenomenological experiences of participants in Núñez's practice, asking to what extent they might be termed 'religious' or 'spiritual' experiences and under what special conditions this aspect of the work flourishes.

A Mestizo Theatre

Núñez's project, since founding the TRW under the auspices of the National Autonomous University in Mexico in 1975, has been to create a theatre for contemporary Mexicans – a *mestizo* theatre, which draws on indigenous as well as European cultural heritages and which reflects the ancient anthropocosmic impulses of the Toltec-Mayan people. Indeed, Núñez calls his an 'Anthropocosmic Theatre'. It takes the form of a series of participatory 'dynamics', used independently as a kind of training and embedded in theatrical devices and structures as a ritual theatre.[29]

The legitimate theatre in Mexico has long been dominated by European influences. At the same time, pre-Colombian ritual performances have survived among the many indigenous peoples of Mexico, often doing so through processes of acculturation. The TRW's imperative has been to create a Mexican theatre which reflects the cultural background of the majority of the population (*mestizo*) by combining European and indigenous Mexican cultural forms. To this end Núñez has intensively explored such ritual sources as the Nahuatl conchero dance tradition, Huichol shamanic (*mara'akame*) practices, psychophysical energetic positions derived from phenomenological research into the ancient practices suggested by archaeological artefacts, and imagery derived from the rich pre-Colombian mythologies, notably that of the culture hero, Quetzalcóatl.

This is a complex set of cultural sources; Núñez navigates a terrain characterized by religious and cultural syncretism. Indeed, Timothy Light, a scholar of Comparative Religion, considers that Mexico's national symbol, The Virgin of Guadalupe, is 'as epitomizing an example of syncretism as can be found' (2004: 334). This national symbol, who is both Mary and the Nahuatl fertility goddess or Nature symbol, *Tonantzin*, is appropriate in a

---

29 Here, we will be concerned mainly with the activities that fall within the training sphere of Núñez's work, the 'dynamics', and will not address the further problem of whether individuals encountering the work only through a single experience of a ritual theatre production might also have heightened access to what might be identified as the 'religious' form of an altered state of consciousness.

country where pre-Colombian and colonial religious and cultural forms are intricately interwoven. Widespread cultural syncretism is a lived reality for contemporary Mexicans. The conchero dance tradition, so central to the TRW experience, is, like *Maria-Tonantzin*,[30] a tight knit of pre-Hispanic Nahuatl performance and Spanish Catholicism.

It is beyond the scope of this essay to explore the politics of colonial hegemonies, cultural adaptations and resistances. I would, however, like to identify religious syncretism as a context for the work of the TRW. For, as we shall see, Núñez and his collaborators have embraced that tolerance for synthesis and extended it to religious practices from beyond their own mixed cultural heritage.

The TRW might be described as a kind of theatre/anthropological investigation, in Barba's sense (1991), in which attention is focused on the fundamental performative technologies within the sources, eliminating all contexts but the psychophysical.[31] This essay seeks to understand to what extent religious practices can be stripped down in this way, and represented as theatrical devices which are, nevertheless, designed to cultivate a wholly secular spiritual experience. I have previously claimed that 'Núñez is particularly careful not to invest the actions and experiences of the dynamics with any overt ideology. The TRW professes no particular belief system' (p. 155 above; Middleton 2001: 43). This has been challenged by Antonio Prieto Stambaugh, who responded,

> While *Taller* members indeed avoid imposing a religion or an ideology on participants, there's a particular corpus of beliefs underlying their work. The TRW is intimately associated with a movement of spiritual nationalism known as Nueva Mexicanidad (New Mexicanity), which spans everything from Carlos Castenada to *conchero* dancing... One of the main leaders of this movement is Antonio Velasco Piña, who is cited in the TRW's playbills as a key advisor (2002: 8).

---

30 In 1998, five members of the TRW, working under the direction of long-term member Ana Luisa Solís Gil, created the dynamic 'Tonantzin/ Maria'.

31 For a description of two of Núñez's dynamics in these terms, see pp. 157 - 173 above; Middleton 2001: 46 - 56.

It is true that the TRW engage with both Velasco Piña and the practices mentioned. While I am not aware of Núñez himself having a strong involvement with that movement, some members of Núñez's circle of close collaborators are deeply involved in conchero dancing and other forms associated with the Nuevo Mexicanidad movement. And, as we shall see later, Prieto Stambaugh identifies the work of the TRW as a collective pursuit more than one authored by Núñez himself. Thus he makes a strong connection between the personal orientation of members of the group and the group's practices. In my extensive experience of the TRW's work since 1993, however, I would argue that Núñez's collaborators play a significantly different, though absolutely crucial, role in the development of the dynamics. Núñez, himself, talking about his long-term partner in the work, Helena Guardia, described the relationship thus:

> I direct the *Taller* [Workshop] and its actions. Helena supports and enriches them. I'm responsible for the outside and Helena is a kind of internal catalyser... nothing the *Taller* has arrived at could have been achieved without her (Núñez 1997:*np*).

Similarly, the phenomenological reports of collaborators of being inside the work have fed Núñez's research into the precise psychophysical forms, rhythms and meditations that have the potential to create numinous experiences. We will explore below the exact nature of the relationship between belief systems brought to a practice and the fundamental nature and efficacy of the practice itself; between religious experiences that are 'formed' by culture and those that are pre-cultural and 'unformed'.

Núñez appropriates from religious and spiritual contexts only psychophysical practices and anthropocosmic intentions; in the absence of any further instructions or ideological contexts, he offers these to participants as 'theatrical games that will allow ordinary participants to access the realm of the sacred' (p. 159 above; Middleton 2001: 47). If Núñez's collaborators and participants experience the work through personal cultural constructs and belief systems, it is Núñez's task to identify the core physiological and cognitive processes that will facilitate the core experiential state itself.

In this way, Núñez has explored and integrated ritual and performance sources from beyond Mexico, notably the Tibetan Buddhist monastic 'Black Hat' dance, which forms one half of the dynamic *Citlalmina*, alongside a *Nahuatl* conchero, or shell dance. Núñez uses these sources with the express permission of the Dalai Lama and the leading religious authority from the conchero tradition (pp. 169 - 173 above; Middleton 2001: 54 - 66). In both cases, Núñez learned the forms as they are taught within their respective religious contexts. In creating *Citlalmina* from these sources, he respected the 'body alphabets', structures and rhythms exactly but abandoned costumes and other artefacts where they did not play an essential role in the psychophysical experience of the form. For example, the vibratory qualities of each dance are preserved; the Nahuatl shell, seed anklets (*ayoyotes*) and rattles are used in *Citlalmina*, the bone trumpets of the Black hat dance are replaced by a vibratory vocalization (the sacred syllable *Hu*). *Citlalmina* is a cornerstone of the TRW's practice. Performed weekly throughout the year in Mexico City and open to participants who range from students of acting to ordinary Mexicans wishing to engage with their cultural heritages, it represents a major vehicle for Núñez's participants to engage in a secular pursuit of sacred experience.

Secular Sacredness

Before addressing Núñez's practice in any further detail, then, we need to understand the parameters of the term 'secular sacredness'. What is it, first of all, that we refer to when we say 'the sacred'? While recourse to the presence or power of a God is a usual and convenient shortcut, there is something necessarily circuitous in this, since our experience of that which we call 'God' *is* or is *via* that which we call the sacred. Within the field of Religious Studies, there are a number of definitions of the sacred: that which is 'wholly other' (Durkheim 1995 [1912]); 'absolute' or 'ultimate' or of the highest (transcendent) value (Eliade 1957); that which inspires 'awe', the *mysterium tremendum*, the 'numinous' (Otto 1923 [1917]); that which conveys a profound sense of the connectedness of an ultimate reality, believed to underlie daily reality (Huxley 1944). These are not exclusive categories but rather differences of emphasis and approach.

For Durkheim, Eliade, Otto, Huxley, and for William James (1960 [1902]), the 'sacred' does not, by necessity, imply a deity, nor is it definitively bound up with the domain of religion (which I take, here, to imply both divinity and organized belief system). Let us, then, look more closely at the key characteristics of the sacred, as experienced and articulated across cultures.

The 'sacred' is inferred [either through lived experiences, or by conceptual processes:[32]

by **PHENOMENAL EXPERIENCE** (which suggests conceptualization) →	by **CONCEPTUALIZATION** through contrast with the 'known'
of **awe, the numinous,** *mysterium tremendum* ↓	described as **other, absolute,** **ultimate, highest** ↓
which conveys experience of **profound connectedness** ↓ cognized as →	characterized by - unity of all things
and equates to **'being'** in contact with →	believed to be **underlying reality**

---

32 The table has been slightly amended from the original to improve clarity.

Thus, our sense of the sacred seems to be forged on phenomenal experiences that are of an order 'wholly other' to those of daily – mundane – existence, from which we infer categories relative to that of mundane existence. Those categories are either articulated in qualitative terms, or they imply realities that are, by definition, beyond the range of our conceptual scope. And yet, despite this reaching into a conceptual void, the world's religious, spiritual and transcendentalist literatures represent a surprising coherence. Arthur Deikman, a psychiatrist researching in the field of consciousness and mysticism, states,

> Profound connection is what the word 'spiritual' properly refers to... At its most basic, the spiritual is the experience of the connectedness that underlies reality (2000: 84).

The spiritual quest is one that attempts to draw the subject into relation with a sacred realm, in which we experience a connectedness to an underlying reality that is itself one of profound connectedness between all things.

Thus, the 'sacred' represents for us a ground of being that the world of daily, subjective existence cannot provide. For Eliade,

> [r]eligious man's desire to live *in the sacred* is in fact equivalent to his desire to take up his abode in objective reality, not to let himself be paralyzed by the never-ceasing relativity of purely subjective experiences, to live in a real and effective world, and not in an illusion (1957: 28).

As we shall see later, the sacred as objective reality may be understood as an experience brought about by a perceptual shift from a daily mode to one that is not bound by instrumental object-consciousness. From our isolated subjectivity behind veils of perceptual and conceptual consciousness, we are understood to break through to a reality that our daily modes of being can never reach. In that reality, the mystics tell us, the illusion of separateness is destroyed.

For Eliade, 'the sacred is equivalent to a *power*, and, in the last analysis, to *reality*. The sacred is saturated with *being*... religious man deeply desires to be' (Eliade 1957: 12–13). Thus, contact with the sacred infuses us with an ontological certainty and energy that is not supported in the mundane world. Our phenomenological being-state is intricately connected to our engagement with an objective Universe. Contact with the sacred releases us from the isolation of a world in which we are doomed to perceive only 'fragments of a shattered universe' (24). For Eliade, the experience of the sacred 'founds the world' and thereby creates 'cosmos' (23, 29).

As we know, Núñez identifes his theatre as 'anthropocosmic' – a theatre of the human in the cosmos. Guided by pre-Hispanic mythological sources, Núñez sees a theatre for Mexico as necessarily embracing the ancient practices believed to assist people in 'aligning themselves with the cosmos'. Núñez's professed aspirations are to provide participants with experiences in which they may achieve a sense of connectedness to an underlying reality. Psychophysical experiences, supported by mythological imagery, are designed to act as imaginal 'thresholds' or 'portals' to an experience of reality that will, in Eliade's terms, 'sacralize the cosmos' (Eliade 1957: 17) and increase access to 'being'. For Núñez, the Actor is a sacred animal, alongside the bull, the deer, etc. The sacrality of the Actor resides within the ability to access heightened states of being in which perception alters, such that we feel that we bypass cognitive conceptualizing and directly encounter the cosmos. Núñez tells us,

> we have to make clear that the shaman or the actor is someone who, at will, can go into an altered state of consciousness, go in and out at will… [T]he mind has two main functions; the first one… is to intellectualize or rationalize… the second one is to perceive reality directly with no interference of any kind of thinking, to intuitively catch the reality – not what we think it is – see what it is (1993).

The Actor, then, is seen as a hierophant or shaman with the technologies to make a bridge from the 'shattered universe' into the unified ground of being.

In Núñez's work we find an emphasis on the triad of sacrality, being and cosmos, which our sources have identified as the fundamental religious imperatives. How then should we understand an activity such as that of the

TRW, which divorces anthropocosmic technologies from their religious contexts and espouses a secular sacrality?

In *Das Heilige* ('The Holy' or 'The Sacred') Rudolf Otto introduced the term 'numinous' to describe the experience of the 'sacred'. His *mysterium tremendum* is the experience of awe, of overpowering presence and energy, and of enrapturing fascination in the face of that which is 'other'. For Otto, the experience of the sacred is one to which humans are predisposed. That predisposition can find expression in – or be projected onto – the natural world or an imputed supernatural world. Thus, for Otto, the numinous experience is a natural capacity, prior to and not by necessity associated with religion *per se*. The experience of the sacred – or the impulse to imbue aspects or artefacts of experience with sacred connotations – is not exclusive to the domain of religion (Eliade 1957).

One of the primary functions of religion, however, according to Durkheim, is to create a division between the sacred and the profane. His sense of the sacred is not synonymous with the divine since there are primary forms of worship of the sacred that do not involve divinities, and it was one such (indigenous Australians) on which Durkheim based his explorations. While ultimately Durkheim sees the totem as symbolizing a sacred reality, which is itself a projection of a social reality, it is pertinent to note that the sacred has a fundamentally non-religious connotation for him (1995 [1912, 1915]). William James notes that

> [t]here are systems of thought which the world usually calls religious, and yet which do not positively assume a God... the Buddhistic system is atheistic. Modern transcendental idealism, Emersonianism... Not a diety *in concreto*, not a superhuman person, but the immanent divinity in things, the essentially spiritual structure of the universe, is the object of the transcendentalist cult (1960 [1902]: 50).

'Secular sacredness' might sound, at first hearing, like an oxymoron. Yet the opposite of the sacred is not the secular but the profane. The concept of the sacred forms a polarity with the concept of the profane, each defining and delineating the other. It is worth noting, as Eliade does, that the poles do not equate to a positive and negative; each may contain both – the realm of the sacred consists of evil as much as beneficent powers. The secular pertains to that which is not the religious life or order, thus to permit a secular sacrality, we must only allow that the sacred may be found beyond the bounds of that which we determine to be the domain of religion. As our definitions above suggest, we might well expect to experience the absolute, the wholly other, the interconnected universe without an organizing principle in the form of religious structure or belief.

Before we leave our discussion of the parameters of the 'sacred', it is worth noting that for Durkheim the sacred also referred to a context greater than the individual and the mundane – the collective life of the community (1995 [1912, 1915]). This will be discussed further below, where we shall see the biological benefits accruing to a practice of service to the community, and shall relate this to the group-basis of Núñez's practice and to the development through that of communitas.

Experiences in Consciousness

We have then, a definition of the sacred that allows for secular contexts and emphasizes modes of ontological being, phenomenological states of perceiving and of cognizing the cosmos in which we exist. Experience of the sacred, then, may be seen as an experience in consciousness. Indeed, there is an emergent field of study of precisely this – the consciousness of religious experience – a field that:

1. gives us a framework for analysis (below)

2. establishes the pre-cultural aspects of spiritual practice and experience, which support Núñez's hypothesis

3. provides an insight into the kinds of methodological research that pertain to analysis of religious experience (and, indeed, to the

construction of such experiences, and therefore provides a support for Núñez's methodology).

For Andresen and Forman, editors of 'Cognitive Maps and Spiritual Models' (a themed edition of the *Journal of Consciousness Studies*), religious and spiritual experiences may be seen 'not solely as cultural phenomena but as phenomena that can be related to human physiology, and a kind of pan-human technology of human spiritual development' (2000: 7). Consciousness studies allow for neurological and phenomenological perspectives on the modes of being and states of experience that we associate with the sacred. It is these perspectives that better allow us to understand the complex interplay of culture and biology in the emergence of religious states. '[C]onsciousness' stands as the mediating term between the qualia, or felt experience, of the subjective, and the 'hard' reality we refer to as 'the external world' (8).

Andresen and Forman point out that causal vectors move in both directions between consciousness and culture. Cultural constructs including language influence our ability to have specific experiences, but individual subjective experiences also shape culture: 'Culture and consciousness interact with, and reflectively influence, one another, and so do biology and consciousness' (9). This essay will assume both the viability (indeed necessity) of a methodology that incorporates subjective experience and the primacy of measurable physiological and psychological factors within even the most mystical of religious states.

For Perennial psychologists, mystical experiences of sacred reality across cultures 'share certain common underlying experiential cores'. Andresen and Forman specifically identify those instances as 'non-dualistic', as 'largely, or perhaps even entirely, unconstructed by cultural language and background' and as 'unformed' (8, 12).

The emerging picture of religious experience is of 'a particular kind of consciousness' which possibly 'reflects pan-human correlations at a deeper level than conceptuality – electrical activity in the frontal and temporal lobes of the brain, the stimulation of hormone flows and the ceasing of random thought-generation all may be seen as cross-cultural technologies of spiritual experience' (13). At a physiological level, these are 'unformed' states, but how these states are experienced, conceptualized and articulated will largely be shaped by culture and language.

We might, then, understand mystical and shamanic ritual practices as 'technologies' of mental and energetic means by which to generate 'religious' or cosmological consciousness. These are Eliade's 'technologies of the sacred', which Stanley Krippner identifies as 'a group of techniques by which practitioners deliberately alter or heighten their conscious awareness' (Krippner 2000: 98).

Núñez's cross-cultural researches have explored precisely this terrain, as a result of which the 'tools' of the TRW are a set of psychophysical techniques that can be combined in different ways, and with different mythological imageries, to create the interactive 'dynamics'. The 'tools' include: slow walking, whirling, 'contemplative running', corporeal alphabets and energetic positions. The dynamics are constructed around four fundamental principles, also derived from the research sources: continuous movement; continuous mental focus on one's experience; changing, specific rhythms; alternation between tension and relaxation. The intricate interplay of mental and physical strategies in the dynamics is such that we can describe them as techniques of 'meditation in movement' (pp. 157 - 173 above; Middleton 2001: 46–56).

From the Profane to the Sacred

Arthur Deikman's analysis of mystical technique delineates three useful polarities within which we can locate Núñez's practice:

Instrumental consciousness – Receptive consciousness
Object consciousness – Unboundaried sense of self
Survival self – Spiritual Self

These in turn highlight three important factors for consideration: intention, attention and perceptual deautomatization (2000: 75–99). Deikman tells us that there are different modes of consciousness to serve our basic intentions – they are functional. To act on the world requires a sharp discrimination between self and others and between self and objects... an acute sense of linear time is needed... In contrast, to take in, to receive from the world calls for a different mode of consciousness, one in which boundaries are more diffuse, the Now is dominant, and thought gives way to sensation (79–80).

Deikman points out that normal human cognitive maturation involves the development of capacities for object-recognition, boundary-perception and conceptualization. These capacities and their related skills (with regard to space, time, causality and self) become automatic in normal childhood development. Meditative and mystical practice involves, in Deikman's analysis, a deautomatization:

The meditation activity that my subjects performed was the reverse of the developmental process: the percept... was invested with attention while thought was inhibited. As a consequence, sensuousness, merging of boundaries and sensory modalities became prominent. A *deautomatization* had occurred (77).

Deikman's meditators were intentionally shifting their consciousness from a daily mode, which has evolved for instrumental and survival purposes, to a 'spiritual' mode of receptivity. The mental apparatus of instrumental consciousness itself creates a 'barrier to experiencing the connectedness of reality'. In contrast, a shift to a receptive mode of being enables both perception and experience to shift also. Deikman identifies that this is fundamentally 'a shift in intention away from controlling and acquiring and toward acceptance and observation. The emphasis is on taking in instead of acting upon' (78–80).

The elements identified by Deikman are common to many meditational practices: focused attention upon a percept, the intention to accept and observe [which in turn implies a cessation of ego-activity], the quietening of conceptualization, the dilation of sensory and perceptual activity. In

Núñez's dynamics, attention is focused in the moment-by-moment somatic experience through intentionality, breathing technique or use of mantra. Receptive consciousness is engaged through the necessity to remain within long-durational activities, abandoning end-gaining strategies and time-consciousness. Conceptual activity is subdued, partly through intention, and partly through the psychophysically strenuous tools of running, energetic position etc. Energies are dilated through physiological effects (such as adrenalin and endocrine release), and this in turn intensifies the somatic nature of the experience. Deikman has already identified the perceptual deautomatization involved in the shift from one mode of consciousness to another. In Núñez's dynamics we also find a complementary deprogramming on the physical plane. Many of the dynamics involve physically counter-intuitive actions, such as running backwards with eyes closed, or some of the complex turns in *Citlalmina*. This, too, helps the participant to remain in a state of alertness and presence, vigilant to the necessity to maintain a non-habitual attentional energy.

These, then, are psychophysical structures with the potential to facilitate a meditator's refusal of ordinary consciousness, with its inherent limitations and filtering constructs, in favour of what Deikman calls 'a mode of consciousness responsive to [reality's] connected aspects' (89). Or, rather, a mode of consciousness that does not, by nature of its developmental apparatus, prevent the experience of objectless, unboundaried connection.

It seems, then, that we may access what we are calling 'religious' states of consciousness, in which to experience cosmos, simply by utilising technologies of mind and body. We must be mindful, however, that those states will be experienced and conceptualized in ways that depend upon the cultural and language backgrounds of the subjects. Karoliina Sandström, who has for two years been participating in the experiences of *Citlalmina*, which I run at the University of Huddersfield, writes:

> So for me there exists a quest for 'being' in the universe, which I will approach from a particular individual and societal stance. Even though

each individual's understanding of 'being' differs, the practice of, for example, *Citlalmina*, facilitates a group participation in which there is the possibility of such a quest taking place. And for me this quest for 'being' (or warriorship) can in some degree transcend cultural and societal contexts to allow for possibly very different yet still related spiritual experiences (Middleton 2008).

In 2006, Núñez led a group from the TRW in a 'high-risk theatre' training exercise comprised of ritually walking the *camino*, or pilgrimage, to Santiago de Compostela in Northern Spain.[33] Lee Rickwood, an Australian actor who joined the company for that experience and went on to work with them in the subsequent theatre production, *Cacería de Estrellas* (2007), describes the ways in which the group were facilitated in accessing and understanding the experience as a secular pursuit:

> The approach that Nicolás had devised for the group was held together by the image of Quetzalcoatl, the feathered serpent… The major historical 'story' of the Camino is that it is a Christian pilgrimage… Yet walking in the serpent allowed us to have an experience of the Camino outside this dominant narrative, creating our own, shared, secular sacred experience. We were a group joined not by a religious order or set of beliefs, but by our imaginations… and in walking it becomes a psychophysical sacred experience (Middleton 2008).

In Rickwood's analysis, both personal imaginative response to archetype and the psychophysical effects of ritual walking facilitated a numinous experience, which she defined as entirely secular, divorced from the 'dominant narrative' adhering to it. Eilon Morris, who has experience of the dynamics both with Núñez and in my use of them in England, describes his practical strategy for encountering the forms in a way that acknowledges cultural contexts:

---

33 I joined the TRW halfway through their forty-day pilgrimage to Compostela and, beyond it, to Finisterre on the west coast, a point considered by some to be the end of an ancient pre-Christian pilgrimage into the West.

> My personal experience is that through approaching these forms with humility and respect and an understanding of some of the principles that underlie them, I am able to engage in a personal relationship between myself and the experiences revealed through their practice. This engagement occurs without an in-depth knowledge or personal connection to the cultures that they are drawn from. There is the risk, I am aware, that if the forms are performed purely as physical movements and body positions, they may only function as physical exercise and or dance moves. Therefore I feel there is a need for some form of personal connection and commitment to the work (Middleton 2008).

As with meeting another person, we can have an authentic encounter with a performance form, even across cultural, experiential and linguistic divides, when that encounter is forged in humility, respect and a pre-conceptual level of engagement. Morris's principles, derived from work with Núñez and others and through which he accesses the dynamics, orient him to an approach that reduces the risk of cultural imposition and facilitates receptive consciousness in Deikman's terms. Morris writes:

- a vigilant approach to working with my attention in order to support my intentions in the work
- ongoing search for the living potential within the form
- finding and drawing on a personal inner mantra
- relaxing my vision, allowing it to move freely throughout the work
- listening to the sounds and rhythms of the rattles and the steps and allowing these to work through me, rather than attempting to control them (Middleton 2008).

It is clear that psychophysical forms are constructed not purely from physical actions but from the interplay of those actions with highly specific attitudinal foundations. Núñez's 'meditation in motion' requires the same disciplining of mind as can be found in other forms of sitting or walking meditation. Ultimately, indeed, the interior orientation is the most important element.

As Deikman explains,

> [a] student can meditate for years focused on breathing sensations but if she is inwardly trying to grasp enlightenment, to possess it, that acquisitive aim will lock her into the same form of consciousness with which she had begun. That is why mystics say that 'the secret protects itself'. No cheating is possible because it is the interior orientation that is critical (2000: 78).

One might say, too, that appropriation of sacred forms through acts of cultural piracy or vandalism are also protected against in this way. It is only when engaging with an authentic interior attitude that a person can be said to be actually performing the form and, indeed, benefiting from it. Otherwise, as Morris suggests, it is simply 'physical exercise'.

The meditative, or spiritual, path is itself a vehicle for moving towards the attitudes of inner orientation that are crucial here. Andresen and Forman describe the ways in which such practices centrally consist of an incremental movement away from culturally formed consciousness to the unformed pan-human levels of mind activity mentioned earlier.

> One begins a spiritual practice, of course, utterly enmeshed in the historical world... As meditation slowly moves one away from sensation and thought, the formative role of background and context slowly slip away. One becomes less aware of one's surroundings, thinks with borders that are less and less defined... [I]n some branches of Buddhism and Hinduism, practitioners are believed to have become less and less enmeshed in samsara, the cyclical mundane world (2000: 12).

This, however, brings us to a critical distinction between experiences of altered states of consciousness on the one hand and incremental processes of spiritual development on the other.

States and structures

According to Ken Wilber's extensive survey of religious experience in Eastern and Western psychological systems, 'a person at virtually any stage or level of development can have an altered *state* or peak experience – including a spiritual experience' (Wilber 2000: 149). When these are developed into 'permanent traits' to which the individual has 'more-or-less *continuous* and conscious' access, 'these transitory states are converted into permanent structures of consciousness' (150, 154). Access to altered states of consciousness appears to be an innate capacity, but the related structures of consciousness, which would enable these states to become permanent traits, must be developed through a staged evolution (165, 153). Further, Wilber points out that

> the ways in which these altered states will (and can) be *experienced* depends predominantly on the *structures* (stages) of consciousness that have developed in the individual (154).

While I have proposed that Núñez's practices meet the criteria for creating conditions for the arising of spiritual states of consciousness, we must now ask whether the work also provides for an ongoing developmental process through which those temporary states could influence the individual's ongoing experience. If a practice facilitates the arousal of states but does not provide a developmental process, what are the implications for that practice as a spiritual vehicle? As a means of providing access to 'secular sacredness'?

For Helena Guardia, Núñez's long-term collaborator in the TRW, these are also central questions:

> What's the use of dynamics and practices that take you so energetically to the right side of your brain, that raise your energy so powerfully and make it soar, that open new scopes and give a deeper and more joyful meaning to life, if we do not extend this and produce a real change in our daily affairs. These practices put us in contact with our Being, that place where we can feel that it might be true that we are one with the 'ten thousand things'... If you practice but cannot control your depressive emotions, is it useful? What's the use of ritual if we cannot 'transport' this dimension into our everyday lives, in order to 'transform' them? (Middleton 2008).

In what ways, then, does the work of the TRW encourage not only immersion in transient being states but the development of those states into altered structures of consciousness? Robert Forman explains that

> [the] discriminating feature is a deep shift in epistemological structure: the experienced relationship between the self and one's perceptual objects changes profoundly. In many people this new structure becomes permanent (1998: 186).

Thus, while the wisdom literature of the world records numerous examples of sudden 'Road to Damascus' experiences producing permanent epistemological changes, we might also expect to find long-term repetition of practice, as well as incremental internal processes of engagement. I have previously identified within the TRW's dynamics a series of practical objectives – like a ladder, 'each rung facilitating access to the next. The participant's attainment of each rung is also... the attainment of a level of psychophysical development':

1. silence the rational mind; control the mind's tendency to engage in discursive and instrumental activity
2. be present in the here and now and focus on the somatic sensations of the bodymind
3. focus mental and physical energies and work with raising and controlling energy (p. 163 above; Middleton 2001: 50).

At each of these levels, the participant enters into relationship with aspects of the self (thoughts, feelings, energies), thereby dissolving habitual identification with that aspect and developing the 'observer self' of meditative practice, which enables a profound epistemological shift away from ego-consciousness into the active receptivity that Deikman identified as crucial to the mystical path.

For Núñez, actor training requires an incremental process akin to that of the spiritual path. He writes that

> [t]he training tools of a true actor go hand in hand with the training tools of the spiritual warrior... [T]he actor has to train his mind, his speech and his body through discipline, intent, concentration and

intelligence, exactly as, for example, the Tibetan Shambhala-tradition warrior, or the warrior from the Meso-American Nahuatl tradition... Both are disciplines of spiritual warriors with the same aim of becoming channels for the sacred (Núñez 2000: 21; see also p. 277 below).

Thus it is that the activities of the TRW attract both actors in training and individuals seeking personal and spiritual transformation, both Mexicans making contact with their own cultural heritages and non-Mexicans for whom the work provides structured and accessible experiences at a pre-cultural level.

Theatre is literature and spectacle, play and catharsis, but it is also an initiation ceremony. Núñez and his colleagues have striven to re-introduce the sacred dimension into theatre (Octavio Paz, p. 9 above).

Núñez sees the history of theatre as a development away from ritual efficacy and towards entertainment (See Figure 11 on p. 270; Núñez 2007: 14; see also Schechner 1988: 106–52). He tracks a historical trajectory from early ritual contact with 'pure energy' into the conversion of that energy into deity, and from there into the personified epic culture hero. When the culture hero 'becomes a human being... he performs no more extraordinary feats and now he has emotional conflicts; his rank is theatrical' (Núñez 2000: 11; see also p. 270 below). The history of theatre, for Núñez, is one of descent from the sacred to the profane.

The work of the TRW has been to reinvest contemporary theatre with ritual potentialities and sacred connotations, to move from a foundation in theatrical activity into the realms of the epic and the mythic and from there to the experience of pure energy and cosmos that we associate with archaic rites. In Núñez's analysis, contact with the sacred is the birthright of the theatre, and the actor and hierophant are like twins who share common energetic and imaginal capacities to access other realms of being, other levels of consciousness (2007: 17; see also Figure 12 on p. 272 below). In recent history, Western theatre has aligned itself with commerce and the profane;

only in some isolated examples (notably that of Grotowski, with whom Núñez trained and worked [Núñez 2000: 51–64]) do we find the Actor using their trained potentials to access cosmos.

And yet, there are ways in which the core characteristics of theatre continue to provide a natural environment for a sacred pursuit. Helena Guardia writes,

> It is possible to enter altered states of consciousness through any form of art, all of them take you beyond time and space, as meditation does, but only in theater – as ritual (for it involves participation) – can you share the precise, living instant of soaring, and the mutual commitment deriving from it (Middleton 2008).

As a fundamentally communal art form, theatre provides a space in which one's meditative and energetic training may be supported by a congregation-like body of mutual initiates. This is important in two ways; one, encounter with the 'other' facilitates the pursuit of 'being' mentioned above, and two, the group experience of communitas supports individual effort and equates to what Deikman saw as a biologically adaptive characteristic of spirituality: 'service'.

On the role of the other in ones individual journey, Karoliina Sandström tells us

> [t]here is a strong sense of shared experience, which, for me, not only relates strongly to the possibilities of developing one's engagement in performative work, but also suggests another possibility of engagement in the universe… There are times in the work when I feel that the dynamic and the group are helping me to meet myself and the world… I see a strong link between the work and… meeting [another] person… and being present in ones performative practice (Middleton 2008).

Many of the TRW's dynamics place the individual in profound contact with another. In the midst of techniques that shift our identification away from ego-self, meeting another person can represent a rare opportunity for undefended presence – being – which we see reflected in the partner's eyes (p. 175 above; Middleton 2001: 58). Often, the contact with the other involves facilitating their experience, as many of the dynamics include tools, such as running backwards with eyes closed, that require the presence of a vigilant partner. The TRW's aim may be to provide rituals of personal transformation, yet the work can never be individualistic or self-centred. One operates within the group as within a theatrical ensemble, fitting ones energies and actions to the group needs and relying on that group, in the long-durational actions, for energetic support. This creates a strong sense of communitas, even among large groups of strangers meeting in the work for the first time.

In dynamics such as *Tloque Nahuaque*, participants move in repeating rhythmic patterns of coming together and moving apart, in such a way as ultimately to blur one's sense of boundaries and separateness from the other. Lee Rickwood describes her experience:

> I moved from a sense of separateness to a sense of connectedness to a sense, midway into the dynamic, of an ongoing interconnectedness, whether in the cluster or moving separately. For me, this experiential interconnectedness was an experience of communitas and sacred space ... energizing, expansive and empowering (Middleton 2008).

As Deikman has noted, mystical practices 'help a person "forget the self", to diminish the extent to which survival needs dominate consciousness' (2000: 83). We have already considered the role of meditation in doing this; Deikman also offers an analysis of the practices of 'renunciation and service', each of which dissolves self-centredness and encourages a receptive mode of being and an experience of interconnectedness. The aim of the TRW is to create experiences in which participants can align themselves with the cosmos, and this is achieved through the cultivation of a strong internal discipline, necessary for 'serving the task' (what Deikman calls 'true service' [85]). It is for good reason that Antonio Prieto Stambaugh draws attention to the 'collective nature of much of the [TRW's] activity' (2002: 7).

With his collaborators in the TRW, Núñez has carried out a phenomenological research across cultures in order to establish the parameters and principles of an anthropocosmic theatre. The result is a paradigm forged upon psychophysical practices, which are supported not by religious ideas or doctrines, nor by conceptual ideologies, but rather by technologies of attention and intention, modes of relation to self and other.

REFERENCES

Andresen, Jensine (2000) 'Methodological Pluralism in the Study of Religion', *Journal of Consciousness Studies* 7.11–12: 17–73.

Andresen, Jensine and Forman, Robert (2000) 'Methodological Pluralism in the Study of Religion', *Journal of Consciousness Studies* 7.11–12: 7–14.

Barba, Eugenio (1991) *A Dictionary of Theatre Anthropology: The Secret Art of the Performer*, London: Routledge.

Deikman, Arthur (2000) 'Methodological Pluralism in the Study of Religion', *Journal of Consciousness Studies* 7.11–12: 75–91.

Durkheim, Emile ([1912, 1915] 1995) *The Elementary Forms of Religious Life*, New York and London: Free Press.

Eliade, Mircea (1957) *The Sacred and the Profane*, San Diego, New York and London: Harcourt.

Eliade, Mircea ([1964]1989) *Shamanism: Archaic Techniques of Ecstasy*, London: Arkana.

Forman, Robert (1998) 'What Does Mysticism Have to Teach Us About Consciousness?' *Journal of Consciousness Studies* 5.2: 185–201.

Huxley, Aldous (1944) *The Perennial Philosophy*, New York and London: Harper.

James, William ([1902]1960) *The Varieties of Religious Experience*, London and Glasgow: Fontana.

Krippner, Stanley (2000) 'Methodological Pluralism in the Study of Religion', *Journal of Consciousness Studies* 7.11–12: 93–118.

Light, Timothy (2004) 'Orthosyncretism: An Account of Melding in

Religion' in Anita Maria Leopold and Jeppe Sinding Jensen (eds) *Syncretism in Religion*, London: Equinoz, pp. 325–47.

Middleton, Deborah (2001) 'At Play in the Cosmos: The Theatre and Ritual of Nicolás Núñez', *TDR* 45.4: 42–63.

Middleton, Deborah (2008) Unpublished interviews and personal correspondence.

Núñez, Nicolás (1993) Conference address at 'Performance, Ritual and Shamanism', Centre for Performance Research, Cardiff, Wales.

Núñez, Nicolás (1996) *Anthropocosmic Theatre: Rite in the Dynamics of Theatre*, Amsterdam: Harwood.

Núñez, Nicolás (1997) Personal correspondence with the author.

Núñez, Nicolás (2000) *The Flight of Quetzalcoatl*, Unpublished pamphlet.

Núñez, Nicolás (2007) *Teatro de Alto Riesgo*. Mexico City: Consejo Editorial del TIT de la UNAM. Translated by Helena Guardia.

Otto, Rudolf ([1917]1923) *The Idea of the Holy*, trans. John W. Harvey, London: Oxford University Press.

Prieto Stambaugh, Antonio (2002) 'To the Editor', *TDR* 46.3: 7–8.

Schechner, Richard (1988) *Performance Theory*, New York: Routledge.

Stewart, Charles and Shaw, Rosalind (1994) *Syncretism/Anti-Syncretism*, Oxon: Routledge.

Wilber, Ken (2000) 'Methodological Pluralism in the Study of Religion', *Journal of Consciousness Studies* 7.11–12: 145–76.

ANTHROPOCOSMIC THEATRE

SNAPSHOT 3: WHAT THE *TALLER DE INVESTIGACIÓN TEATRAL* REVEALED TO ME

Etzel Cardeña

Deborah Middleton's loving invitation to contribute to the new edition of *Anthropocosmic Theatre* could not have come at a better time: I was in the midst of writing an academic paper on altered consciousness and enhanced psychophysiological functions and had considered including my personal experiences. I decided against it because I wanted the reader to focus on the research evidence. Yet, in various interviews throughout the years I have stated that my interest in the psychology of alterations of consciousness sprang from my experiences doing experimental theatre during my 20s, initially in UNAM's *Taller de Investigació*n Teatral, led in the late 1980s by Nicolás Núñez and Helena Guardia (my theatre activities as director and actor have naturally also been also informed by this work). Here are two examples that stand out:

One late afternoon, the *Taller* members (besides the leaders it included Marcela Camacho, Alejandro (Bracho) Rojas, Jaime Soriano, and a few others) went to a nearly 4,000-meter high dome volcano to the south of Mexico City, El Ajusco. It was a fairly cold afternoon even at the bottom of the volcano and our goal was to walk up the volcano silently and mindfully. As I started my ascent, I experienced that my body was effortlessly moving as a harmonious and agile unit, as if my legs knew exactly how to climb this new terrain, without any need to think about what I was doing or even look at the ground in front of me. Contrary to my typical physical caution and awkwardness, I was climbing with an assurance and speed I had not experienced before, and the cold did not bother me. This body know-how felt so natural and in tune with the surroundings that I decided on the spot to feel less encumbered and take off my clothes, shoes, and socks to continue the ascent. Some members of the *Taller* told me then that I would get injured and/or sick given the considerable cold and stones and other obstacles on the way. I responded that as long as I remained in the state I was in everything would go well (as, in fact, it did). This was years before I had even heard of the concept of *flow* (a state of full immersion, effectiveness, and enjoyment in an activity) or meditative techniques such as G Tum-mo that allow Tibetan monks to dry clothes dipped in freezing water on their backs after generating bodily heat, but some part of me was already aware of this (see Cardeña, in press, for a review of research on the topic).

The other event was even more striking to me and I proudly bear a scar to prove it. Two other members of the *Taller* and I prepared a scene using a text by Samuel Beckett. The scene we performed at one of the theatres of México's National University was an invocation of the devil (I apologize retrospectively for completely mangling the text by Beckett, which had nothing to do with our performance). The reinterpretation was that I, as magician, would draw a magical circle and summon the devil, whom I would only observe through a mirror because it would be very dangerous to see it directly. In the background, a *Taller* member was playing a drum and my friend Alejandro started coming down from the back of the audience space onto the stage impersonating the devil. I was intensely absorbed in the scene and suddenly, for no reason I can think of, the framed mirror I was holding shattered. One large shard pierced my hand, which started to bleed profusely, but I felt no pain whatsoever. In the midst of that droning darkness, relieved only by lit black candles, we finished the scene, after I had just enough energy to blow out the candles. It has been my most intense performance experience, and it would be some years before I read that intense focus on hypnosis, meditation, and similar contexts can dampen or even eliminate pain and affect bleeding, and that there is scientific evidence that mental intentions may affect matter directly (Cardeña, 2018, in press).

These two experiences occurred within a larger personal transformation that owed much to the work in the *Taller*. I had been a precocious child and teen, but my development as a person had been very slanted towards intellectual endeavors. My body felt somewhat alien despite my being a good table tennis and tennis player, because in sports I only 'employed' my body instrumentally to carry out specialized movements to obtain some goals (e.g., win the point).

I did not experience my body as the centre of my sensual and living universe, and felt almost always a split between my intentions and their bodily enactments. Even before becoming a member of the *Taller*, I had discovered what I later called the *truthful trickery* of acting, how the Stanislavskian 'as-if' (or in the same construct in hypnosis, a 'believed-in-imaging') can turn an initial falsehood into an experiential and physiological reality (Cardeña & Beard, 1996). Yet it was still a very long way for me to become aware of the gift I had and to trust and enjoy my vibrant body/mind, undivided in itself and in its encounter with others. The challenges of the *Taller* (and later in training with Stephen Rumbelow and others), like mindfully running or doing other activities well beyond exhaustion, silenced my inner monologue and tapped a state of greater endurance and awareness. Engaging in risky actions that demanded full attention and commitment short-circuited my (ir)rational meandering and physical hesitations, allowing for the emergence of potentials far surpassing my conscious self. My body was no longer a vehicle to 'use', but a source of astounding revelations and sensibility, preciously unique but also part of a much larger process 'within' and 'without'. Gradually, and at times punctuated by fulgurating experiences like those described earlier, I became a far more integrated human being, and for that I will always be grateful to the *Taller*.

REFERENCES

Cardeña, Etzel (in press). 'Derangement of the senses or alternate epistemological pathways? Altered consciousness and enhanced functioning'. *Psychology of Consciousness: Theory, Research, and Practice.*

Cardeña, E. (2018). 'The experimental evidence for parapsychological phenomena: A review'. *American Psychologist, 73*, 663-677.

Cardeña, Etzel, & Beard, J. (1996). 'Truthful trickery: Shamanism, acting and reality'. *Performance Research, 1,* 31-39.

SNAPSHOT 4: AND I SANG
Edward McGurn

I first met the work of Nicolás Núñez at a workshop in Glasgow, that I attended on a whim. I knew instantly that I had begun the process of experiencing the 'seat of my soul'. Soon afterwards, before I knew it, and without any rational thinking, I was travelling over 5,000 miles to Mexico to participate further in work that I was not sure that I understood in any way. In the workshop in Glasgow, I was a mess; I was terrified to close my eyes, I sent my partners crashing into others, I was stuck, and out of flow... in hindsight, I was depressed.

In Apan, Núñez's workshop space in rural Mexico, I learnt of the root of my depression. In one session, a participant asked how she could engage in the work whilst suffering from an injury, and Nicolás responded by referencing the words of a poem: a human must be *a tree that dances*.[34] Unconventional as this advice appeared to be, the image clearly made perfect, and personal, sense to the person asking the question. In that moment, I also understood the root of my depression, of which I had not been conscious until this point.

Gabrielle Roth once said,

> In many shamanic societies, if you came to a medicine person complaining of being disheartened, dispirited, or depressed, they would ask one of four questions: When did you stop dancing? When did you stop singing? When did you stop being enchanted by stories? When did you stop being comforted by the sweet territory of silence? (Roth & Loudon, 1989: xv)

This statement encapsulates the depressed state I found myself in at the first workshop; I had stopped being enchanted by stories! I had turned my back on the acting profession, due to the profane nature that the art form

---
34 A reference to *Piedra de Sol*, Octavio Paz (1957).

seemed, to me, to have adopted. Theatre no longer seemed to be posing the question, 'What does it mean to be a human being?' Staged work no longer appeared to give us the opportunity to deeply communicate with others, or to be ambassadors for any meaningful message in relation to questions such as, 'How must we act as human beings?' and 'What must I do as a human being who is alive here and now?'.

Prior to arriving in Apan, I was stuck, numb, operating on automatic; I was a high-functioning depressed person - I did only the activities that were necessary to keep my life operating and no more. A few days into the workshop, I could feel something begin to shift. Nicolás talks of us being like a closed box that needs to begin to allow energy to pass through, so that we can be in the optimal state of 'flow'. Whether this process began to happen for me, or whether it was through the work and the contemplative practices allowing me to feel more grounded in the earth, my levels of inspiration began to return. One day, whilst standing on top of a hill with the group, in silence, after completing one of the dynamics, I looked over and saw a cactus that had clearly, at some point, caught fire from the blazing sun. The mantra, 'Just because I've been weak doesn't mean I can't be strong', entered my mind, inspired by the evident areas of regrowth that surrounded the heavily burnt areas of the cactus. Its suffering and rebirth became, in that moment, synonymous with my own. I was beginning to yield to the life-breath that was ever present around me and the mantra, discovered that day, still lives with me and has seen me through further challenging times.

On one of my last evenings in Apan, when I felt most settled in myself, whilst sitting around a burning log fire, one of the other participants spontaneously and with no prompting asked me to sing. Until that point, I had danced gleefully, been enchanted by stories and been comforted by the sweet territory of silence; however, I was yet to sing.

I learnt in Apan that to 'love' - both self and others - is our authentic mission in life. With this, I also inadvertently found the answer to those questions that I had been struggling for years to answer through my art form;

'What does it mean to be a human being?', 'How must we act as human beings?', and 'What must I do as a human being who is alive here and now?' And I sang.

REFERENCES

Paz, Octavio (1957) *Piedra de Sol*. Mexico City: Tezontle.

Roth, Gabrielle & Loudon, John (1989) *Maps to Ecstasy: Teachings of an Urban Shaman*. Mill Valley, California: Nataraj Publishing.

DEFINING THE DYNAMICS
Deborah Middleton

This chapter further expands upon the analysis of the dynamics contained in 'At Play in the Cosmos' (2001) and 'Secular Sacredness' (2008), drawing on my further practical experiences, conversations, and interviews with Núñez and Guardia over the last decade. I attempt here to bridge the gap between Part One and 'At Play in the Cosmos', by offering some further insight into the genesis of the dynamics; I also publish here, for the first time, a full list of the dynamics, and both summarise and extend what has gone before in terms of delineating their defining features.

Although the term 'dynamic' barely appears in Part One of this book, in the chapter on Anthropocosmic Theatre, Núñez introduced some of the principles underlying the dynamics - the anthropocosmic frame, the notion of sensitisation exercises, and key tools of the *Taller* such as vibration and contemplative running (or 'trotting'). Part One also includes accounts of theatrical events which carry names later used to designate specific dynamics; for example, *Tonatiuh* and *Huracán* are described as 'schemes of participatory theatre' (p. 114 above), *Tloque Nahuaque* is mentioned in passing as a 'work' (p. 108 above), and *Citlalmina* is described as a 'tool for (mental) training', and as the basis for a participatory theatre production in 1989 (p. 137 above). Within the descriptions of *Tonatiuh*, *Huracán* and *Citlalmina* as participatory productions, it is possible to discern the core structures that represent the dynamics of those names: *Tonatiuh* (pp. 116 - 120 above) seems to have consisted largely of the series of actions which I described in 'At Play in the Cosmos' (pp. 164 - 169 above); *Huracán* is described as involving a number of devices and experiences which were unique to the theatre event, but the core *Huracán* dynamic - which consists of a sequence of alternating cycles of contemplative running and the construction of a complex rhythmic pattern of three moving, concentric circles - is described as forming one part of the experience (pp. 126 - 129 above).

Similarly, the theatrical event, *Citlalmina*, included 'a circuit' of the dynamic of that name within a broader aesthetic experience (p. 138 above).

From the earliest explorations, Núñez and his collaborators were, in fact, developing sequences of psychophysical actions which could be embedded within participatory theatre events, or shared in workshop settings (indeed, prior to the adoption of the word 'dynamic', the practices were simply referred to as workshop sessions (Middleton, 2018, *np*).

According to Núñez, 'Every dynamic was born from the contact with a sacred tradition; [from the] techniques of ecstasy that Eliade talks about' (Middleton, 2018, *np*). The earliest researches within performative spiritual traditions to have influenced the dynamics include Núñez's exploration of Gurdjieff's work, and Guardia's practice within the Sufi tradition, as well as their collective exploration of conchero (shell) dancing. Guardia told me, 'The dynamics began to appear through contact with the concheros, whirling dervishes, howling dervishes...' (Middleton, 2018, *np*). From these initial sources, they derived 'breathing exercises, singing, praying, whirling exercises' (Guardia in Middleton, 2018, *np*).

Between 1978 and 1981, both Núñez and Guardia worked with Grotowski[35] on experiences which would richly feed and support the development of the dynamics. In Theatre of Sources, Núñez developed the contemplative run, which would become a dominant technique in the *Taller*'s toolbox. Guardia worked on 'The Movements'[36] - 'a flowing sequence of yoga asanas, performed slowly, with open visual awareness in a multi-directional pattern' (Middleton & Núñez, 2018: 226). This sequence provided the *Taller* with 'a kind of anthology of asana-like postures, or psychophysical "gestures"' (Middleton & Núñez 2018: 229) for further exploration, and with a model for a form of meditation-in-movement through energetic positions that

---

35 In 1978, on Tree of People in Poland; in 1979, in the Mexican sierra; in 1980 - 1981, on Theatre of Sources in Poland; in 1985, at Iztaccíhuatl, Mexico. (See pp. 72 - 87 above)

36 The relationship between 'The Movements' and its later development as 'The Motions' in described in Middleton and Núñez, 2018.

could act as a kind of 'key' to deeper dimensions of experience (Middleton & Núñez 2018: 228).

In 1984, the first dynamic - *Tonatiuh* - was created. Described above (pp. 164 - 169), *Tonatiuh* synthesised these various early influences in a sequential meditation-in-movement form that included contemplative running from the phase with Grotowski, whirling derived from the Sufi training, and a closing sequence from the conchero tradition. As I explored in 'Secular Sacredness' (and as was Grotowski's model in Theatre of Sources), the practices that were derived from spiritual traditions were approached as pan-cultural, psychophysical techniques. The essence of the action was rigorously maintained, and practices were brought alongside each other (never mixed) in a containing structure.

The term 'dynamic' was introduced in the late 1990s to distinguish between a participatory sequence designed for a specific purpose within the aesthetics of a production, and such a sequence refined, set, and repeatable as a free-standing structure. Just as the key tools of the *Taller* - contemplative running, slow walking, (and various directional and other versions of these two), the use of closed eyes, conchero rhythmic stepping patterns, the Sufi whirling, vocal vibration - are the building blocks for dynamics, so too the dynamics themselves can be combined with other devices and performance materials to provide the participatory heart of the productions.

By 1997, Núñez had developed eighteen distinct dynamics (personal correspondence dated October 1997), each of which created a different energetic experience and embodied meditation for its participants. By 2001, when 'At Play in the Cosmos' was first published, twenty-one dynamics (p. 157 above) were being practised in the thrice-weekly morning sessions, and also shared by Núñez in his workshops in Europe, Mexico, and Central and South America. Impressive as that total might be, it does not tell the whole story.

In 2016, speaking in Huddersfield, Núñez gave the total number of dynamics as 24 (p. 311 below) and in March 2018, I noticed that his working notebook contained a list of 28. When asked, however, he continues to specify that there are 21 dynamics! In fact, the corpus of dynamics is in a continual process of refinement. Whilst *Citlalmina*, arguably the cornerstone of the *Taller*, is practised every Wednesday morning without fail, on the other mornings, Núñez cycles through the various dynamics; working with different emphases in different periods, exploring and refining existing sequences, and sometimes building new ones. He describes this as a 'chaotic', rather than a systematic process (Middleton, 2018, *n.p.*), and no doubt it is guided to some degree by the demands of the productions he is working on at any given time, by the sources he is currently studying, or by the needs of the particular individuals attending the *Taller* sessions at a given moment.

To be included in the official list, a dynamic must satisfy certain conditions: it will have been fully developed and refined, will have been given a specific name, and will be active in the *Taller's* current repertoire. For various reasons, a dynamic which might once have served an important function in the evolution of Núñez's practice may be set aside for a time. One example of this is the dynamic, *Tensegrity,* which was personally transmitted to Núñez and a small group of other Mexicans[37] by its originator, Carlos Castaneda, in Mexico City in 1986. When Núñez presented workshops at the Centre for Performance Research symposium, 'Performance, Ritual and Shamanism' in Cardiff in 1993, *Tensegrity* was included, but by 1997, preferring to distance himself from commercial developments by Castaneda and his followers, *Tensegrity* had been withdrawn.[38] In the past few years, however, Núñez has re-explored what he sees as the core of the exercise, sequencing it with the *Taller*'s sensitization tools, and creating a new version of the dynamic, now called *Nahui Ollin* (*Nahui* - Four, *Ollin* - Movement in Nahuatl).

---

37 The group included Ana Luisa Solís and Helena Guardia, Núñez's long-term collaborators; Marco Antonio Karam, founder and director of Casa Tíbet in Mexico City, and Jacobo Grinberg, a Mexican scientist and writer whose disappearance in 1994 is the subject of ungoing speculation.

38 Personal correspondence from Núñez to Middleton, dated October 1997, lists 18 dynamics, with *Tensegrity* crossed out.

At the time of going to press, there are 22 dynamics on Núñez's official list. Since he expresses a preference for the 'auspiciousness' of the number 21 (Middleton, 2018, *n.d.*), the following, currently definitive list of the dynamics follows the example of the Tarot Major Arcana with numbering beginning at '0'.

The Dynamics

0. **Citlalmina**	11. **Huracán**
1. **Tonatiuh**	12. **Kikiriki**
2. **Queztalcoatl**	13. **Moyocoyatzin 1**
3. **Cadoceo**	14. **Moyocoyatzin 2**
4. **Nahual**	15. **Mictlantecutli**
5. **Nanahuatzin**	16. **In Ixtli In Yolot**
6. **Olmeca I**	17. **Tezcatl**
7. **Tezcatlipoca**	18. **Monotza**
8. **Ixpapalotl**	19. **Tloque Nahuaque**
9 **Teozintle**	20. **Xochipilli**
10. **In Teotl**	21. **Nahui Ollin**

Defining the Dynamics

In 'At Play in the Cosmos,' the dynamics are described as: 'structured sequences of psychophysical actions' (p. 184); with an inner and outer score (p. 189); involving a pre-Hispanic mythological image; and combining the tools of the *Taller* in various ways (p. 189). The key features are identified as 'continuous movement, continuous mental focus…, changing rhythms, and alternation between tension and relaxation' (p. 193).

In this short section, I would like to go further in exploring the defining features of the dynamics, by discussing three aspects which Núñez identified as crucial in an interview in 2018. These are: the inner score of foundational attitudes and inquiries; the pre-Hispanic names/images; and what Núñez describes as 'the raising and focusing of physical and mental energies' (Middleton, 2018, *n.d.*). References to all three of these aspects can be found throughout this book; my intention here is to bring together some focused discussion with brief descriptions of some of the dynamics, by way of illustration.

Inner Foundations

The particular steps, sequences, repetitions and rhythms of a given dynamic emerge through assiduous practical research and are carefully refined; nevertheless, as psychophysical technologies their efficacy cannot be reduced to physical protocols. The inner score is essential to the dynamic. *How* a dynamic is carried out is, for Núñez, more important than its physical dimensions. In guiding a practice, Núñez rarely gives detailed instruction on the physical actions, but continually coaches the participant with regard to the sustained mental and attitudinal activity that constitutes their inner work. Typically, there are repeated prompts regarding, for example, 'mindfulness', the raising of energy, and the sustaining of the 'will to work': *Pay attention! Don't automaticise your work! Here and Now! This is Working Time! Free [mental] association is not allowed!* This constitutes a continual call to mindfulness, the practice of which has formed a key part of Núñez's work from the earliest beginnings.

Each of the dynamics contains a core of personal challenge structured around three incremental stages of inner inquiry, (some dynamics emphasise one stage over the others in their overall function). These are:

- Know Yourself
- Control Yourself
- Project Yourself - 'I can because I think I can'.

In 'Mandala', Núñez attributes these directives to the three-part structure of both the Eleusinian rites and the ancient Mexican rites of the cult of Tlaloc (p. 298 below). They form the basis for an inner score - a contemplative inquiry which is carried in the embodied actions of the dynamic, and which asks the actor to make an honest encounter with herself. The fundamental task of the actor in training begins, for Núñez, by looking within.

Know Yourself

'Know Yourself' is the first - the foundational - directive for the participant, but it could also be seen to be the over-riding inquiry to which the dynamics cycle back time and again. At the most basic level, the participant is asked to bring their attention to bear on their present moment experience, and to discover what they can of their own tendencies and distractions - what Núñez often calls 'distorted perceptions' and 'ego games'. This is not to suggest a process of self-analysis, but rather a close observation of oneself in action. In this way, the inner structure of the dynamics functions as a form of meditation.[39]

In his book, *Rhythm in Acting and Performance*, Eilon Morris describes his first encounter with the dynamics in 2004, and the way in which they acted upon his self-knowledge.

> The work confronted many of my understandings of performance and acting, as well as the philosophical and spiritual ideas I had regarding how I related to the world and to myself within it. We were repeatedly asked to let go of preconceptions and expectations, to break out of our automatic patterns of behaviour and to surrender control while also attempting to master our physical and mental behaviours. While, at the time, I struggled to grasp many of these propositions intellectually, my practical encounters – the ways in which I was directed to perceive and engage with myself and my environment – had a profound impact on my embodied understanding of myself as a performer and a person (Morris, 2017: pp. 167-168).

The *embodied* nature of the self-encounter offered by the dynamics is crucial to an understanding of how they function; the self-knowledge that can be arrived at is an embodied knowledge, and thus represents a transformation

---

[39] For an analysis of Núñez's practice in relation to Vajrayana Buddhist practice, see Middleton, D. & Plá, D. (2018) 'Adapting the Dharma: Buddhism and Contemporary Theatre Training', *Journal of Global Buddhism* Vol. 19, 2018, pp. 113 - 125.

of the individual's experiential bodymind. This sense that the dynamics represent an arena for personal transformation was reflected in the title of a workshop Núñez taught in Huddersfield in 1996 - *'Theatre as a Personal Rite'*; the concept is discussed in 'High Risk Theatre' below (pp. 267 - 287). It is also evident in some of the snapshot accounts included here, such as acting teacher Edward McGurn's description of finding a source of personal healing in a residential workshop with Núñez in 2015.

Control Yourself

'Control Yourself' points to the challenge to sustain self-discipline and will-power. The dynamics, which each last approximately one hour, are often physically strenuous and require continual mental focus. The effort to avoid distractions and tiredness, and to go beyond one's first threshold of perceived limitations is implied in 'Control Yourself'.

The dynamic *Moyocoyatzin 1: The One Who Constructs Himself* gives a very clear example of the challenge to control oneself. The central action of the dynamic revolves around holding ones arms in the air for a long time. For most people (especially those carrying a lot of shoulder tension), the muscles quickly tire and begin to ache. This is, however, an example of what Núñez calls 'good pain' - not a sign that one is injuring oneself, but, rather, an intense somatic sensation which offers the invitation to engage ones determination and the power of mental focus (See pp. 274 - 276 for Núñez's discussion of good pain). In many of the dynamics, we come face to face with our own strength - or weakness - in relation to determination and self-control.

Control, though, should not be misunderstood as 'controlling'; indeed, Morris above refers to 'surrendering control'. It is not by egoic force, but rather by an internal process of renegotiating one's usual behavioural patterns, that the dynamics offer up their effects on the bodymind.

Through mindful observation of the self in action in the dynamics, the participant encounters the possibility that they might 'control' - that is, resist and even dismantle - those habitual impulses and self-limiting beliefs that do not serve them. What those impulses and beliefs are becomes abundantly clear through the immediate feedback provided by one's own mind and body on a moment-by-moment basis in the crucible-like container of the dynamic.

Project Yourself or I Can, Because I Believe I Can

Thirdly, and having taken these steps, the actor can present herself, and can project her presence and her energy in relationship with others, including an audience, and in performative ways. 'Project Yourself' includes the idea of creating so strong a mental intention that others (audiences, for example) can be moved by it. This is embodied in the dynamic, *Tezcatlipoca*.

Tezcatlipoca - the Smoking Mirror - (evoking an image of the shadow side), takes the form of a small, personal ritual of forgiveness (a version of the central mechanism of this dynamic was used in *Cura de espantos* - see pp. 173 - 177. Participants are given the task of forgiving each other through a symbolic action of removing sorrow and regret from their partner's heart, and metaphorically burning it. Núñez urges the participant to believe in the symbolic fiction; if we believe it, he tells us, then the ritual is effective - *I can, because I think I can*. This is the sense in which the actor 'projects' herself - entering so fully into the 'as if' of her creative illusions that she makes them believable, and makes their effects tangible for herself and for others.

In fact, for Núñez, the notion of *I can because I think I can* is, at one and the same time, the Stanislavskian 'as if' and the technique 'used in rituals as vehicles to arouse another reality' (p. 54 above). Aligning Stanislavski with ritual devices, and understanding the power of meditative focus, Núñez takes very seriously the transformative potentials of the actor's art. To achieve this level of focused attention and inner commitment, however, it is necessary for the actor first to have worked through the levels of Know Yourself and Control Yourself.

The process of inwardly crossing the three thresholds of Know Yourself, Control Yourself, and Project Yourself constitutes the inner score of the dynamic, and is supported by cultivation of the foundational attitudes of mindfulness and focused intention. These foundations are themselves supported through an additional layer of imaginative engagement - typically in an image derived from pre-Hispanic mythology.

Pre-Hispanic Names

Almost all of the dynamics have a name drawn from pre-Hispanic mythology,[40] in which is embedded a particular story or principle. Locating the work in pre-Hispanic Mexican culture is central to Núñez's project; from the very beginning, his research sought to redress the imbalance of the European influence on theatre in contemporary Mexico. Beyond this, the pre-Hispanic names key into the poetic and mythic philosophy and cosmology that provide the foundation from which the practices arise. This creates, for participants, a very particular kind of container for the psychophysical experiences that the work offers; whilst usually only lightly, and often playfully, evoked, the mythic figures and symbols create an invitation to participants to shift into an extra-daily engagement. In keeping with the language of the secular spiritual warrior which he also employs (pp. 277 - 278 below), the mythological dimension provides a strong impetus to, and support for, the will-power and serious play required to meet the challenge of the dynamics.

In his workshops and training residencies, Núñez generally introduces the dynamics without lengthy discussion or instruction. Sometimes the name alone is evocative: *Ixpapalotl* is the Solar Butterfly, and thus the 'flying' action that each participant is facilitated to explore in the course of the dynamic is imbued with the qualities of the lightness of a butterfly in sunshine.

Sometimes the dynamic has a particular story attached to it, and in sharing the story informally before the dynamic begins, Núñez also gently prompts the participant's imagination, and sets the metaphysical dimension for the experience. *Kikiriki*, for example, which is named after the Mexican onomatopoeic word for the cry of the rooster, is prefaced by a story about a conversation with a shaman in the Sierra: 'What is this life all about?' Nicolás

---

40 The current exceptions are 'Kikiriki', which is an onamatopoeic word used in Spanish, and 'Cadoceo' (caduceus), for which Núñez expects a pre-Hispanic name to emerge in the future.

asked the shaman, 'What is the meaning?' In that moment, a rooster crowed, as if in response. 'That', said the shaman, 'is the meaning'.

'The rooster knows what his role is', Nicolás tells us. 'He does his job and helps the flow of the Universe. We no longer know what our own Kikiriki is; we have to find it' (Middleton, 2016). The subtitle of *Kikiriki* is 'Find Your Life's Action'.

When Núñez tells this story in workshops, it is intended to cue participants to understand that the form of the dynamic is there to give them an opportunity to better know themselves through the revealing experience of working alone, in the context of others. The central action of the dynamic consists of moving, with eyes closed, in close proximity to the other workshop participants. Each person must find their own form of movement whilst having to negotiate around the other moving bodies nearby. The presence of others in this dynamic might be experienced as a hindrance, or as a helpful catalyst, or even as a support. (The interpersonal dimension is particularly heightened in *Kikiriki*, but the group is an important context throughout all of the dynamics).

The dynamic embodies, in a simple task, the necessity to find and sustain one's own authentic impulse whilst also adapting to an inter-personal context. Prefaced by the story, participants are unlikely to treat the dynamic merely as an improvisational exercise; the story seeds the invitation to reflect on one's experience allegorically; to treat the dynamic as a form of contemplation in movement.

Another example of a dynamic that is enhanced by its association with a story is *Nanahuatzin*, named after a character from Aztec mythology who volunteers to be the one to 'jump into the fire' and become the sun. When stronger, younger, seemingly more heroic warriors refuse the challenge, it is Nanahuatzin, a weak, old man, who reveals the inner strength and courage needed to make the sacrifice that will ensure the rising of the new sun (Nanahuatzin becomes the sun for our current epoch). Such stories provide an inner support to the participant in the challenge to 'make one's fight', as

Núñez repeatedly describes the inner work. (In the snapshots that follow, Tray Wilson and Karoliina Sandström both reflect vividly upon their experiences of engaging in *Nanahuatzin*).

The mythic imagery embodied in a given dynamic is also a prompt to the imagination; and in some dynamics, the imagination plays a central role. In *Nahual*, for example, the participant makes a long, disorientating imaginary journey, with eyes closed, until the appearance - in imagination - of an animal guide. In *Tonatiuh* (described on pp. 164 - 169 above), the participant imaginatively identifies with various elemental aspects of their being. It is also not uncommon for participants to describe the appearance of spontaneous images as they are working, and this perhaps explains the poetic nature of so many of the responses and snapshots contained in this book.

Energy

Structurally, the dynamics present in microcosm an invitation to participate in the *Taller*'s overarching trajectory, as described by Eilon Morris,

> Within these processes the performer/participant often seeks to raise their energy from that of everyday 'life' to a 'heroic' or 'epic' level of being. Núñez located these qualities along a vertical spectrum, the pinnacle of which is 'pure undifferentiated energy' (Morris, 2017: 173).[41]

If this schema, and the notion of verticality, suggests a linear direction, in fact the movement of energy within the dynamics is much more organic. Each dynamic is structured in such a way as to create an overall arc of energetic engagement through waves of alternating pace, intensity, expansion and contraction.

Brazilian scholar, Cassiano Sydow Quilici, noted, in his snapshot above, the experience of moving from a 'dense sensation' to a 'more subtle experience' during a workshop with Núñez in 2016. Similarly, Morris notes that the 'transformation of energy can be understood as a qualitative transformation,

---

41 For the schema to which Morris refers see Figure 11 on p.318.

in the sense of moving from "coarse to subtle"', and identifies that it is this qualitative transformation that is described through the notion of 'verticality' (Morris, 2017: 173). As Quilici pointed out, there are traditional practices which operate within the concept of the 'human body as a complex structure that connects dense and subtle energies' (pp. 187 - 188 above). One such tradition is Vajrayana Buddhism, from which Núñez derived the Black Hat Dance which forms one half of *Citlalmina*. He tells us that,

> As the performer flows with [the dance], he is charged with energy. Certain subtle fluids are activated in our bodies through movement, and these fluids, together with consciously generated endorphine, produce in us a sensation of glowing brightness which purifies and invigorates the organism. These are the benefits of meditation in motion (p. 136 above).

Arguably, the other dynamics also function as meditation-in-movement forms with the capacity to activate effects on the level of the subtle or energy body which is seen to underlie the gross physical body.[42] Thus, the 'raising of energy' does not refer merely to a process of becoming more physically energized, but rather to the refinement and cultivation of the subtle dimensions of the bodymind.

The dynamic *Olmeca 1* embodies an image of raising the quality of energy - from a dense, earth-bound, horizontal plane to an uplifted, vertical 'flight'. The dynamic begins with participants in a supine, resting position, then moves to an exploration of the spine against the floor. From here, the central section of *Olmeca 1* consists of a series of asana-like positions, all of which have been derived from pre-Hispanic statuary, and through which the participant moves incrementally from being horizontal on the ground to the final Eagle position, in which is the spine is fully vertical.

---

42 For a discussion of Citlalmina as an adaptation from Vajrayana Buddhism, see Middleton, D. and Plá, D. (2018) 'Adapting the Dharma: Buddhism and Contemporary Theatre Training' in *Journal of Global Buddhism* Vol. 19 (2018): 113-125

Olmeca 1

Supine, resting position. Arms by the sides, palms down. Raising arms and legs, the spine is snaked and rubbed against the floor.

Chac Mool - reclining on the forearms, with feet on the floor and knees raised, head turned to the left. The body creates a 'u' shape.

Xochi Pilli - Sitting with legs crossed and feet raised off the floor, balancing on the sitting bones. The arms are held in front with the hands in a position that suggests the holding of invisible sticks or poles. The chin is lifted and the head dropped slightly back.

Squatting - with feet flat on the floor, elbows are against the inside of the knees with hands in prayer position, spine elongated.

El Acechador [the hunter/stalker] - Standing, angled forward from the hips, knees slightly bent. The arms reach slightly back, palms facing backwards. The chin is slightly tucked but the gaze is lifted.

La Águila [the Eagle] - Standing on tip toes, knees bent, arms raised overhead.

Contemplative Running.

In this way, the dynamic is designed to allow the participant to explore the evolution from a horizontal orientation to the ground to a vertical orientation. This is an embodiment of the mythic image of Quetzalcoatl - the feathered serpent - an image which encapsulates the notion of the transformation of earth-bound, dense energy into the subtle dimensions of spiritual flight. The 'flight' that is embodied in the raised wing position of the Eagle is released into full expression in a closing cycle of contemplative running.

Each of the positions in *Olmeca 1* is challenging to sustain, but, mindfully inhabited, they also hold the potential to act as psychophysical catalysts, releasing areas of tension and blockage and intensifying the participant's energetic presence. The 'asanas' do not follow immediately one upon the next, but are alternated with short periods of relaxation and release (and repeated in cycles of three). This alternation of contraction and release, intensification and relaxation, is a key principle of the dynamics (p. 158 above), and contributes to their energy-generating effect.

Rhythm plays an important role in conducting the energetic flow of the dynamics. Often, the rhythmic temperature is established and modulated through drumming, with Núñez - or, on occasion, an assistant - using a hand-held frame drum. At other times, the rhythm is created by the sound of the group's running or dancing feet.

In his discussion of two of the *Taller's* key tools, slow walking and contemplative running, Eilon Morris writes,

> rhythm can be seen as both emerging from and acting upon the performer and the group. As they move through the space (sometimes slowly, sometimes fast) each participant generates their own rhythms and begins to tune into the rhythms of the others. This attunement (an entrainment of sorts) is one of the tools by which the performers become 'present', existing in the flow of the moment – what Núñez refers to as the 'actualized instant' (Morris, 2017: p.168).

The interplay of intra- and inter-personal rhythms that Morris describes is indeed both a focus for attention and a support to the stabilising and intensifying of that intention. The group's rhythmic attunement is, however, not solely the result of the group's interaction. Guiding the dynamics from within, Núñez drives the rhythm of the group, side-coaches to encourage continuous focus, and models, through his own participation, the process of raising, sustaining and modulating energetic output. Each individual, and the group as a whole, should be carried through waves of increasing and decreasing intensity and repeated cycles of action, until the dynamic culminates in a final release of energy. This involves a skillful conducting of the process by Núñez, and a conscious balancing of surrender and persistence by each participant; to lose control in the sense of giving way to a mindless and exhausting frenzy of movement or 'trancing out' is not desirable. Rather, heightened awareness is to be continually maintained: 'You have to watch your mind, it's like a meditation in movement, you have to be alert' (Núñez in Middleton & Núñez, 2018: 223).

All of the dynamics end with the same closing process: from a final phase of contemplative running (in an anti-clockwise direction), and without stopping, the group come together, stepping clockwise, in a close circle. The step is derived from the Mexican conchero tradition and involves alternately crossing the right foot in front of, and then behind the left. This creates a centripetal-centrifugal pulse, at the same time as the rotation of the circle. With arms crossed in front of their moving bodies, the participants link hands and the circle turns with increasing speed until a final cry of *Awa!* (*Now!*) halts the movement, and the raised energy is released in a loud cry.

Defining the Dynamics

In closing, I would like to try to draw together these comments with the analytical summary of the dynamics with which I began, and to offer a definition of the dynamics that contains all of the characteristics that have been variously described as essential:

> *A dynamic is a meditation-in-movement form comprised of energetic, attitudinal and imaginative gestures performed through a structured sequence of psychophysical actions. The sequencing entails continuous movement, changing rhythms, and alternation between processes of tension and relaxation, or contraction and expansion. The essential attitudinal foundation is one of continuous mindful focus upon the cultivation of inner qualities, as experienced through the lens of an embodied mythological image.*

The dynamics represent more than forty years of assiduous practical research at the intersection between theatre, ritual, and meditational traditions. As such, they function equally as devices for actor-training and as devices for personal development. In Part One, Núñez wrote that with his understanding of 'here and now' and 'as if,' Stanislavski had 'left implanted in contemporary theatre a path which will lead us to the heart of the human being' (p. 54 above). The work of the *Taller* has also been to rigorously and tirelessly explore the creation of a path for the actor which leads to the heart - to the inner dimensions of our being. The dynamics are the central devices on that path, opening into the depths of experience and insight more usually associated with the world's meditational and ritual traditions.

REFERENCES

Middleton, Deborah (2016) Personal Notes from *Swimming in the Inner Source: A workshop with Nicolás Núñez*. University of Huddersfield, England, 31 May - 1 June 2016.

Middleton, Deborah (2018) Unpublished interview with Nicolás Núñez and Helena Guardia. Mexico City, 10/04/2018.

Middleton, Deborah & Núñez, N. (2018) 'Immersive Awareness' in *Theatre, Dance and Performance Training*, 9:2, 217-233.

Morris, Eilon (2017) *Rhythm in Acting and Performance*. London: Bloomsbury Methuen.

ANTHROPOCOSMIC THEATRE

SNAPSHOT 5: CONTEMPLATIVE RUNNING
Daniel Plá

The first time I heard of Nicolás Núñez was during a meeting with scholars and artists at the University of Huddersfield in 2014. I was introduced to the practice of *Citlalmina* by Karoliina Sandström. It was a hard challenge to go through all the cycles as it is a very energetic form. So, in the summer of 2016, when finally I met Nicolás, I found myself a bit concerned about the training and about how an overweight man in his 40's like me would be able to engage in such intense activity. That was my spirit when I walked into the studio to start the workshop.

After the usual introductions, we started with running meditation. I started slowly, just a bit faster than walking. Travelling anti-clockwise, I drew my senses inward, feeling the pulsation coming from my movement, speeding up as the energy rose. In front of a me, a partner ran. The walls passed by me from time to time while I kept the rhythm, attending to my breathing and the sensations coming from the body. The first signs of tiredness started to arise, and I decided to keep running. My breathing began to get faster and shorter.

Looking to the group running with me, I started to see us as warriors, each running their own path, and I was magnetized by my partner. It was as if I was not me but the shadow of that person. After a while, my breath started to become heavy; I am not sure how long we had been running by that time. Fear started to arise, but I decided not to stop. Feeling the pulsation of my body, I noticed a place in myself where I could find rest in the middle of storm. Running became my meditation object, a source of a great variety of sensations, emotions, formations. Running was a support for my consciousness which started to become sharper. Thoughts, feelings, emotions passed in front of me, reflected on the running mirror. The more I ran, the more deeply I travelled inside myself, and the more my impulses gained space and time in the room.

Meditative running.

Back home in Brazil, I introduced my students to this process. Running together, we discovered a way to enliven the body. Through relaxation in response to the intensity that running promotes, we found an effective tool for looking inside and for freeing impulses from the body into actions - a way to put the internal world out, into time and space.

SNAPSHOT 6: CITLALMINA AND NANAHUATZIN
MEXICO (2010 - 2016)
Karoliina Sandström

The following texts were written in response to the actor training dynamics, *Citlalmina* and *Nanahuatzin*, and reflect two features of the work which I have come to consider tremendous wells of understanding and learning with regard to the process of being an actor. One of these is the manner in which, through the dynamics, one can learn to become more attentive to the observer self, and the internal mechanisms of the construction of a habitual self. The other is the sheer power this work can have for an individual, in enabling them to transgress their personal, habitual, physiological, psychological and energetic limits.

There are few teachers of acting who embody over 40 years of experience of generating, expanding and directing energy, as can be said of Nicolás Núñez and Helena Guardia. And here much could be observed regarding the recent investigations which show that the teacher's embodiment of psychophysical practices such as mindfulness, sitting meditation or meditation-in-movement transmits a knowledge of embodiment and being to the student, even when meditation is not being taught. In my experience of this training numerous doors opened, and others closed. I am forever grateful to my teachers who showed the way of transformation.

Citlalmina

To be present in every step, present but without grasping. To be here yet to know here is nowhere and everywhere.

Sweat, sweat and confusion, a battle against thought. A battle against thought manifested in form, in the limits of form. A constant noticing. I think I am here Now, but know Now is already a concept. It is already one step removed. I find myself full of mind. Attempting my best to be the space in which experience happens. There is confusion; What is life? What am I? What can I hang onto if I have no time to construct the usual, the known, the controlled?

There is a sense that at this speed, the natural ways of distraction, habits of mind, come forth like a speeding train with all kinds of crazy folk on board - apparitions of self hanging out of the window, shouting out their shopping list of complaints to an innocent bystander! There is no escape from being able to see the mechanisms at work in being me.

...

The dancing goes on forever, because forever is eternal. The universe flashing by in all its glory, constellations, stars, planets and black holes, and my brain with more nerve connections than there are stars in the sky. When I think I cannot go on, I remember I already have. There is always another wall to break through, another feather to watch floating in the air. There is always more depth, more width, more closeness and more space.

...

Dancing is home; it has become home, and it has shown me I am always home. I am home. There is no outside and no inside, yet the dance of the earth joins with the dance of my bones; the flight of the stars is knitted together into the light of the dancer. Dancing is home and home is now - this I learnt in Citlalmina. *Citlalmina, bow bent towards a shooting star, intention bent on burning the tales of mind, so well practiced.*

Nanahuatzin

I saw various suns pass before me; I saw them close their eyes, turn their soul to its next trial. The flow of life emanating from their twirling force as they turned into the next sun. The next light to guide the way of man. Women gifted their life energy like Nanahuatzin, to illuminate the lives of others.

We ran, and ran, in the river trail of sunlight, spiralling through the space.

She came to me – my mother, my grandmother, my bloodline of life force, the lineage of light I had been born from.

My number was up.

I was calmed, hands reaching out for me, to hold me as I fell, as my self fell away from me into the ground. Into the dark soil of my childhood. Chunks of me fell away, to mould into compost. I let myself go and was lifted into the air, empty. Unleashed into a million hands, into a multiplicity of directions unknown, to be buried. Turned upside down, inside out, so another one could stand. Could find her way, in the path of those before her. Women, finding their light, their radiant flight.

And then I flew beyond myself, beyond the molecular walls of my cells. I traversed every body, and pillar, every wall and wood; twirling without centre, a body in the sky. Sound escaped, and all levels of being were shone by this new light.

Direction was taken, held between these two pairs of arms. You ran – I was not there. I had been undone. Life had taken my place. Force, power and love had taken my place.

after

I kept breathing and breathing. Like breath had opened a door into a savannah and there was no end to the inhalation. I had been restored, rebuilt, re-cognized and recognized, for the first time. Woman. Sun. Unlimited, running. Running without legs, taking her first flight.

After still

Gratitude is boundless. The reinvention of the *conquistador* – the conqueror of oneself. One turns into a warrior in the hands of the greatest teachers.

ANTHROPOCOSMIC THEATRE

SNAPSHOT 7: BEING THE SUN - NANAHUATZIN
Tray Wilson

We run as a group, finding the group rhythm, helping one another with our collective energy. We fight the good fight to stay present in our bodies as we run, charging the space with our will to work. There is a collective responsibility to engage in this serious play 'as if' it is essential. I watch as the first woman is placed in the centre, she is guided by Nicolás as she roots her feet, then falls into waiting hands which allow her to 'burn off her outer shell' as she is passed forwards and backwards within a circle before her feet are lifted off the ground and she is flown upside down through space until she is placed again on her feet. In this transformation, she has become the sun and she is encouraged to spin and whirl and to gather up the energy of the sun. In her fast whirling she cries out - an ecstatic cry of something releasing or awakening in her. Her spinning reaches a climax and she is helped by watchful hands to run again, as before, but to share all that she has received as the sun; running with renewed vigour and energy through the space.

On the next cycle, the sun will be me. I feel the anticipation and responsibility rising in my body as I prepare for the role. I want to do my best for the others, to let myself be the sun without fear or self-consciousness which might draw me away from the experience. I am placed in the centre of the waiting carers who stand with arms outstretched to catch me as I allow my body to fall from this rooted position. As I am caught and moved through the space, I hear Nicolás guiding me to allow the outer layers of my humanity to burn away. I feel as though all that I use to define who I am - my age, my gender, my experiences and beliefs - burn away; layers of skin or armour peeled off to reveal essence, spirit, light. It is not difficult to let them go; they fall freely and quickly and I am still present.

As I am lifted and turned through space, I am light and essence. I am transformed from known places to a new dimension. I start to spin as if it is my compulsion, my specific task. The spinning seems to have a life of its own; I do not spin but rather align myself to the spinning around me. As I spin, I find moments when I connect with a line of energy, a vector stemming vertically through the space, connecting me to the source. When I meet with it I am charged with energy and I cannot move from that place. I am connected through the centre of my body to an axis which extends through and beyond me. I vocalise a sound which tries to emulate the experience of this connection, a sound wave reaching out. A complete release and freedom of body, mind and spirit.

At some point, I let go of my physical awareness in the space and there is a moment of flight, of nothingness, of silence… but then I hit the ground with my body! The impact awakens my physical senses to the studio, the others… they help me to find my feet on the floor. I am physically supported as I find my footing, and I start to run. The running at first feels too slow and cumbersome for the energy that I still feel rising in my body. I feel myself break free from my helpers and I run with the energy as it wants to soar, projecting me through the space. My body is open and alive and full of energy; I am flying around the space, not as a bird but as a ball of energy or fire, expanding into the space, creating a vortex for others to flow in and feel.

I use my arms, wide open in the space, to allow this energy to flow out of me into others and the space around. I am giving it all away; there is nothing held back. I run like this for a while, feeling the charging of the space. Slowly I start to become aware of the breath in my chest and the pounding of my heart, my feet running furiously along the ground as if they can barely keep up with the speed at which I am travelling. A thought enters my mind: that I could collapse or die if I continue - I will not be able physically to sustain this level of intensity forever. I make a decision to slow my body down and to allow the energy to dissipate to a more manageable level so that I might sustain the running and not die in that moment. There is no real fear in this dying or burning up, but it is a choice that I consciously make, to be able to continue. I feel myself lowering back to the ground. I make a conscious effort to feel my feet and to run as a horse, with the awareness of the ground beneath me tying me back into this world. I re-join the group. I run with them again, but with the knowledge of having soared. I have made a huge jump into unknown territory and now that I have been there, I will know how to return.

ANTHROPOCOSMIC THEATRE

PLOTTING A PATH FOR LATER STEPS: TUNING IN WITH NÚÑEZ, RANCIÈRE, AND SOLOGUB

Franc Chamberlain

ONE

Nicolás Núñez and the *Taller de Investigación Teatral* have developed a series of immersive or participatory structures and scores to transport participants into an imaginal realm where they have the possibility to slough off their everyday selves and safely enter altered, ecstatic, states of awareness. As the main body of *Anthropocosmic Theatre* articulates, these practices were developed through a range of encounters with different lineages including Tibetan Buddhism, Stanislavskian actor-training, Grotowski's post-theatrical actions, and an embodied reconnection with a pre-Hispanic, Nahuatlan, current.

Does this mean that participants in the performances and trainings of the *Taller* lose touch with their embodied reality? Not at all: the practices are designed to assist participants to transform their relationship to reality through progression along a vertical axis from everyday life up through epic/mythic, theistic, and ritualistic levels with the aim of reaching the level of 'pure undifferentiated energy' (Morris, 2017: 173). Without a grounding in the actual practices involved, this can easily sound like a process of spiritual ascent and disembodiment; absconding from material reality into a realm of dreams and fictions and progressively losing touch with our body. The *Taller's* work, however, aims at synchronising body and mind with the intention of enabling individuals to 'have the energy and the courage to maintain [themselves] in the living instant' (Núñez, p.277 below). The journey is an embodied one which requires an intense psychophysical commitment from the participant, a willingness to generate the energy to attempt a leap to the next level. Each leap, if successful, offers another perspective on our lives, our relationships and the world but, I would suggest, that this perspective isn't one of 'looking down' on our previous view but of 'opening out' to a wider experiencing of self, other and environment (or cosmos).

Ultimately, 'pure undifferentiated energy', the term used by Morris, stands in for a core element of *Nahua* metaphysics, that of *teotl* a process of perpetual generation and regeneration which we might also consider an ongoing creative and autopoetic process of becoming (Maffie, *IEP* n.d,). *Teotl* manifests in complementary polarities and is in that way superficially similar to the Chinese idea of the ten thousand things being generated by the complementary opposites of yin and yang emerging from the *dao*. Everything is, in some way, *teotl*, including people, and the direction of development in the *Taller*'s processes would be for the participants to become more fully themselves *and* more in tune with others *and* the cosmos. It would seem that becoming attuned to pure undifferentiated energy does not involve the loss of differentiation but is an awareness of the vital energy that is present in all processes of becoming.

That one becomes 'more fully oneself' and more 'in tune with the cosmos' seems a rather big claim to make, particularly if we imagine that participants in one of the *Taller*'s performances might only be with the group for a couple of hours at most. Indeed, Núñez doesn't make the claim that these changes *will* happen. In his introduction to the performance of *Cura de espantos* in Huddersfield in 1999, for example, he explicitly stated that 'some of us may get something…some of us not' (Chamberlain in Yarrow *et al* 2007: 178). Without adequate context this could be read in a judgmental way implying that only the 'worthy' will 'get something' and those who don't 'get' anything, who don't feel themselves to be more 'fully themselves' or 'more in tune with the cosmos', have somehow failed. But this would be the logic of a cult not of a Theatre Research Studio, and Núñez and his 'gang' are explorers, inviting participants to carry out their own research to see what happens. Maybe we get something today, maybe not. It's possible that we might become aware of how distant we are from ourselves and others or how disconnected from the environment we feel. Paradoxically, perhaps, that would a good outcome as we would have become more aware of our situation; a discovery that is potentially disturbing but which still offers the opportunity for creative development.

The *Taller*'s work has strong affinities with Grotowski's Art as Vehicle or Ritual Arts, an 'attempt to create a performative structure that functions as a tool for work on oneself' (Slowiak and Cuesta, 2018: 53). Such a structure (or score) would enable 'energy transformation' from coarse to subtle by working on the body, heart and head of the participant (Slowiak and Cuesta, 2018: 53; Grotowski, 1995: 122).[43]

TWO

Núñez and the *Taller de Investigación Teatral* are firmly situated within the tradition of theatre laboratories that began in 1905 in Russia with Stanislavski's first experiment in setting up a theatre laboratory. This laboratory (or studio), led by Meyerhold, focused on problems in staging symbolist dramas such as Maeterlinck's *The Death of Tintagiles*. For a variety of reasons, including the artistic differences and the impact of the 1905 Revolution, this first experimental studio was short-lived but, in 1912, Stanislavski set up the First Studio which became established as a key component of the Moscow Art Theatre and stimulated the creation of theatre laboratories throughout the world.

As Schino points out, however, theatre laboratories are 'not a genre or a uniform category' (2009: 7) and terms such as theatre laboratory, studio, workshop, *atelier*, or *taller* are neither fully interchangeable nor precise translations of each other. Whilst this is important to bear in mind, there are also similarities that can be identified and Chemi refers to a 'laboratory turn' in the theatre, asserts that the First Studio of the Moscow Art Theatre can, indeed, be defined as a theatre laboratory, and articulates the key characteristics of such laboratories as a 'sustained, free and explorative mindset with the awareness of and commitment to a research programme' (Chemi, 2018: 5).

---

43 The notion of transformation of energy from coarse to subtle is also mentioned by Cassiano Sydow Quillici (pp. 187 - 188) and Middleton (pp. 234 - 235).

A laboratory's research may create public performances but the work is not driven by a production schedule. As Stanislavski noted:

> Laboratory work cannot be done in the theatre itself, with its daily performances, its concerns over the budget and the box office, its heavy artistic commitments and the practical difficulties of a large enterprise (Chemi, 2018: 5; Schino, 2009: 101; Stanislavski, 2008: 301).

Theatre laboratories, as Stanislavski suggests, need to be free from the demands of both the market and the public. This requires access to either private or public funding and a building where artistic research can be carried out with few strings attached. It would be expected that the some of the work would be shared and that the experimentation would further our understanding of the theatre. Grotowski's Theatre Laboratory was funded by the communist regime in Poland, for example, and the government in the Soviet Union had earlier funded a number of studios after the 1917 Revolution. Universities were also places where a theatre laboratory might be established and allowed to conduct research free from the demands of the market and Núñez and the *Taller* were able to secure a base at UNAM in Mexico City in 1975 and have remained there ever since.

One aspect of the theatre laboratories, including those of Stanislavski, Grotowski, and Núñez that is perhaps less often noted than it could be is that they aim to create sacred spaces with an atmosphere which would demand a different level of attention from participants and engender a quality of experience which was markedly different from their daily lives. Stanislavski and Sulerzhitsky imagined developing a 'spiritual order of actors' (1980: 537) and the Theatre Studio was their laboratory in which these experiments could be carried out.

Stanislavski had set up the Studio partly because he had struggled to find a way to stage the plays of Maeterlinck - a problem he shared with others in Europe at the time. August Strindberg, for example, had struggled with the plays of Maeterlinck and debated whether or not to include them in the programme of his Intimate Theatre in 1908 before deciding that it was best to avoid them. A key problem, for Strindberg, was the absence of actors who had the ability to 'gain entrance into this poet's marvellous world' (1967: 301). This ability, according to Strindberg, could only be acquired by passing through what he called the Inferno, a disturbing, but ultimately transformational process, that he'd experienced in his own life prior to writing his most innovative works such as *To Damascus*, *A Dream Play* and *The Ghost Sonata*. Strindberg, however, lacked any training programme that would enable the development of the kind of actor he felt was necessary in order to stage Maeterlinck.

The idea of an actor being transformed through an inferno experience is implicit in Artaud's image of actors as being 'like victims burnt at the stake, signalling through the flames' (Artaud, 1958: 13) and Grotowski believed that this image contains the 'whole problem of spontaneity and discipline' in the theatre (2002: 125). The high intensity of energy contained in the image of the actor burning is matched by the discipline and precision needed to shape the signals effectively and these aspects of high intensity and precision are also present in the work of the *Taller de Investigación Teatral*.

The initial focus of Stanislavski, Strindberg and Artaud was on the training of the actor to stage plays and the audience would still be separate from the doers. Artaud imagined different configurations of the theatre space to adjust the relationship between actors and spectators but the two roles were left untouched: actors were doers and spectators watched what was done (even if the aim was to cross that boundary with an affective athleticism which infected the audience). In Grotowski's work on productions prior to the mid-1970s there was also an attempt to use an altered spatial relationship to effect a change in the spectators themselves. In his *paratheatrical* experiments (1973-1978) Grotowski sought to abolish the distance between actor and spectator in order to open up a space of collective creativity where participants were able to drop their habitual behaviours and discover new ways of relating to themselves and each other. Ultimately he was unconvinced of the viability of this approach and moved on to explore techniques from a range of cultures that were designed to have precise effects on participants and had a long history of doing so. This period of exploration was known as the Theatre of Sources and it is during this period that Núñez and his colleagues collaborated with Grotowski (see Middleton and Núñez, 2018).

THREE

The possibility of turning spectators into active participants was not something unique to Grotowski or Núñez, of course, and Rancière sees the aim to transform the spectator from 'passive voyeur' to 'active participant' (2011: 4) as a defining aspect of theatrical reform since the early part of the twentieth century. This process of transformation has two different goals which are sometimes complementary and sometimes in conflict. One aim is to transform the spectator into a 'scientific investigator or experimenter' (Rancière, 2011: 4) whilst the other is to transform her into a participant who is 'in possession of all her vital energies' (Rancière, 2011: 4). These two tendencies are represented by Brecht and Artaud respectively and it's possible to insert Grotowksi into this second lineage and, at least by association, Núñez and the *Taller*. What both approaches have in common, beyond the aim of transforming the spectator from a so-called passive into a so-called active position, is that they accept the idea that theatre is, in some sense, false – whether inherently or contingently. Spectators are captured by the illusions of theatre which render them passive; they are stupefied. If theatre is intrinsically false and disempowering then it would be necessary to move beyond theatre to effect a transformation, but if it is only contingently false then it is possible to use theatre as a way of questioning or analysing itself. In both lineages there is also a belief that theatre was once more than it is and can be so again. All of this is based on the commonly held notion that the spectator is passive and needs to be reconstructed by the performance and Rancière rightfully calls this notion into question.

Acknowledging that the reformers often return to the roots of the theatre in Ancient Athens, Rancière points to their desire to return to the theatre as the 'active body of a community enacting its living principle' (2011: 5). A century earlier the Cambridge anthropologist Jane Ellen Harrison wrote in her *Ancient Art and Ritual* that:

> There is no division at first between actors and spectators; all are actors, all are doing the thing done, dancing the dance danced... No one at this stage thinks of building a *theatre*, a spectator place. It is in the common act, the common or collective emotion, that ritual starts. This must never be forgotten (Harrison, 1913: 126).

This return to ritual, or at least a reference to the theatre's ritual roots, runs throughout the past one hundred and fifty years. Five years before Harrison's book, in 1908, the same year as Strindberg decided that Maeterlinck's plays were 'unstageable', Fyodor Sologub, seeking to restore the ritual dimension to the theatre, wrote:

> the rhythm of liberation is the rhythm of the dance [...] the dancing spectator both male and female will come to the theatre and at the threshold they will leave behind their crude petty bourgeois clothes, and race along in the light dance... So the crowd, which has come to look on, will be transformed in the round dance [...] (Sologub 1977: 99).

In Sologub's vision the spectators would no longer be separated from the action, passively watching, but involved in a round dance returning to the origins of the theatre in a resurrected mystical community. Sologub believed that we had lost the playful creativity that we had as children and, asking what we wanted from the theatre answered that it was the same thing that we wanted for our play when we were children: 'fiery ecstasy, ravishing the soul from the tight fetters of our boring and barren life' (1977: 88).

Sologub's vision wasn't actualised, and nor was the *Mysterium* of his younger, and even more visionary contemporary, Alexander Scriabin. The *Mysterium* would also have transformed spectators into participants who, at the end of a seven-day ritual in the Himalayas, would 'achieve spiritual unity with the divine cosmos' (Gawboy, 2015).

Accessing the 'pure undifferentiated energy' that Morris and Núñez refer to sounds, at least superficially, akin to Scriabin's aim and the links between Sologub's vision and Harrison's archaeological assertion are evident. Influencing the thinking of both practitioners and theorist there is the current flowing from Nietzsche whose work had such a profound influence on the theatrical innovators of the twentieth century with his conceptualisation the twin forces of Apollo and Dionysos in *The Birth of Tragedy* (1872). These complementary opposites suggest the *daoist* pairings of yin and yang and the dynamic oppositions of *teotl* but Nietzsche's thought owes more to Schopenhauer's concept of the Will which is the force that propels all human activity and which he was later to reconceptualise as the Will to Power (Smith in Nietzsche, 2000: xxx). There can be a temptation to simply assume that the primordial source of these varied polarities is the same, that the names are simply nothing more than labels placed on identical phenomena. There is also the risk of assuming that the experiences of the individuals involved in these processes of transformation will be identical.

FOUR

Sologub wanted to break down the barriers between performer and spectator and restore a sense of community. Rancière claims that there is a 'presupposition that theatre is in and of itself communitarian' (2011: 16). But if this were the case then why would the reformers feel any need to transform the relationship between spectator and performer? Surely the visions of Sologub and Scriabin, or the practices of Grotowski and Núñez make the assumption that this communitarian aspect is either buried and needs to be uncovered, or needs to be created and the role between spectators and performers transformed. The theatre is a machine for making and transforming communities, but the transformations that it effects need not be identical in each circumstance. Nor is theatre only a machine for making and re-making communities.

Rancière's concern is that by focusing on the communitarian dimension of the theatre those who wish to turn spectators into active participants not only undermine the importance of spectatorship for the theatre, but also forget that 'there are only ever individuals plotting their own paths in the forest of things, acts and signs that confront or surround them' (2011: 16). Yet Rancière assumes that in any process of turning the spectator into a participant or of generating a temporary community, the aim is to erase the experience of the individual rather than to place the individual within a new set of circumstances or, at least, a set of circumstances that are different for those in which they live their everyday lives. Perhaps the individual's experience within these events will lead to changes in her everyday life, perhaps not.

Being part of a community or an ensemble doesn't mean giving up one's ability to plot one's own path or construct one's own narrative within a set of given circumstances, whether those circumstances require us to remain seated in our red chairs or to walk through a wood in which various characters appear to articulate their suffering or to join in the round dance.

FIVE

It is the 'blurring of the boundary between those who act and those who look' that is the meaning of emancipation, according to Rancière (2011: 19). It could be argued that this is exactly what theatre has been experimenting with for the past century. Different ensembles and practitioners have experimented with different kinds of participation and made different demands on the spectator/participant, whether they are invited to join in a dance with Núñez and the *Taller* or to enact a potential solution to a social problem in the work of Augusto Boal.

Grotowski (1995) distinguished between Art as Presentation and Art as Vehicle. The former is the way in which we normally think of art – as something that takes shape in the perception of the spectator – whereas the latter emphasizes the experience of the 'doer' (1995: 120). Grotowski's emphasis from the mid-1970s onwards was on the doers, whether there were external witnesses to the action or not. This emphasis on doers runs throughout the archipelago of studios and workshops, *tallers* and laboratories that are dotted around the globe.

At least some of the *Taller de Investigación Teatral*'s performance events can be seen as a hybrid of the Theatre of Presentation and the Theatre as Vehicle. For example, in *Cura de espantos*, the audience begin as participants but there is a sense in which they are not agents. Middleton mentions the 'monitors' whose task it is to 'construct and manage the participants' experience' (p. 173 above).

The participants are invited to step into the skeleton boat, place a tube of tissue over their heads so that they are effectively blindfolded and move with the boat into the wood where the tissue tube is removed, and then they are guided around the woods to witness four solo performances by figures who tell their stories of suffering. Up to this point the participants have made a decision to join in but their choices from that point are quite limited in terms of action. There is a clear set of actions that they are invited to carry out. Even the moment where the participants are given time for silent contemplation, after the encounter with the four figures, could be seen as directed action rather than self-initiated action. But they aren't compelled to stand in silent contemplation, it is an invitation rather than an instruction, and they have the possibility of doing something else. This moment of contemplation opens up a new possibility between the idea of the active and passive spectator and points towards a contemplative theatre.

REFERENCES

Artaud, Antonin (1958) *The Theater and its Double* (Trans. Mary Caroline Richards), New York: Grove Press.

Chemi, Tatiana (2018) *A Theatre Laboratory Approach to Pedagogy and Creativity*, Basingstoke: Palgrave Macmillan.

Gawboy, Anna (2015) '*The Mysterium*' programme note for *Scriabin in the Himalayas*, Ladakh. http://www.scriabininthehimalayas.com/about accessed 11th October 2018

Gerould, Daniel (1977) 'Sologub and the Theatre' in *The Drama Review* 21 (4) pp.79--84

Grotowski, Jerzy (2002) *Towards A Poor Theatre*, London: Methuen.

Grotowski, Jerzy (1995) 'From Theatre Company to Art as Vehicle' in Richards, Thomas, *At Work with Grotowski on Physical Actions*, London: Routledge, pp.115-35.

Machon, Josephine (2013) *Immersive Theatres: Intimacy and Immediacy in Contemporary Performance*, Basingstoke: Palgrave Macmillan.

Maffie, James (n.d) 'Aztec Philosophy', *The Internet Encyclopedia of Philosophy*, ISSN 2161-0002, http://www.iep.utm.edu/, 11th June 2018.

Middleton, Deborah & Núñez, Nicolás (2018) 'Immersive Awareness' in *Theatre, Dance and Performance Training*, 9:2, 217 - 233.

Morris, Eilon (2017) *Rhythm in Acting and Performance: Embodied Approaches and Understandings*, London: Bloomsbury Methuen.

Needleman, Jacob and Baker, George (eds.) (1998) *Gurdjieff: Essays and Reflections on the Man and his Teaching*, New York NY: Continuum.

Needleman, Jacob (1998) 'Gurdjieff in the Modern World', in Needleman and Baker (eds.) (1998) pp. 70—85.

Nietzsche, Friedrich (2000) *The Birth of Tragedy* (translated with an introduction by Douglas Smith), Oxford: OUP.

Rancière, Jacques (2011) *The Emancipated Spectator*, London: Verso Books.

Richards, Thomas (1995) *At Work with Grotowski on Physical Actions*, London: Routledge.

Schino, Mirella (2009) *Alchemists of the Stage: Theatre Laboratories in Europe*, Holstebrö: Icarus Publishing.

Slowiak, James and Cuesta, Jairo (2018) *Jerzy Grotowski* (reissue), London: Routledge.

Sologub, Fyodor (1977) 'The Theatre of One Will', (trans. Daniel Gerould) *The Drama Review* 21(4) pp. 85—99.

Stanislavski, Konstantin (2008) *My Life in Art,* London: Routledge.

Strindberg, August (1979) I*nferno and From an Occult Diary* (trans. Mary Sandbach), Harmondsworth: Penguin)

Yarrow, Ralph et al. (2007) *Sacred Theatre*, Bristol: Intellect Books.

CASE STUDY: THE FLIGHT OF QUETZALCOATL – TEOTIHUACAN, MEXICO (2000)

Deborah Middleton

In 2000, the *Taller* performed a major work at Teotihuacan, the pyramid site near Mexico City. *The Flight of Quetzalcoatl* was a durational work in two senses: it crossed the night, beginning at dusk and ending at dawn the next morning, and it was performed on every full moon for the entire year.

The production focused on the archetype of the sun, as symbolised in the Pyramid of the Sun, and articulated in the myths of Quetzalcóatl, a solar deity, and in the story of Nanahuatzin (see p. 233 above), two figures closely associated with Teotihuacan. The mythic trope of going into, and through, darkness in order to come into light underpinned the whole project and informed the ritual structure of the audience experience. In September 2000, I was part of a group who undertook a two-week workshop residency with Núñez and his then assistant, Nad'xeli Forcada, at the *Taller's* base just outside the Teotihuacan archaeological zone. The residency culminated in our participation in *The Flight of Quetzalcoatl* along with other audience members who had travelled out from Mexico City. The following account draws on a description of the experience that was published in *Total Theatre* in 2001 (Middleton: 2000/2001).

The Flight of Quetzalcoatl was structured into three sections, divided by two breaks in which refreshments were available at the *Taller's* base - a rustic building close to the periphery of the pyramid site. Outside the building there was a painted *tonalamatl* platform - a circular stage on which the Nahuatl calendar had been painted. It was on this platform that the performance began and ended.

Our first action is the choosing of a small card which, when turned over, reveals one of the Nahuatl zodiac signs, and determines where we will each stand when we climb onto the painted platform. There is a frisson of excitement, a little nervousness as spectators who have arrived together are separated. I watch my friends smile as they turn their cards over, and discover which symbol they have unwittingly chosen. I receive Ehecatl – the Wind.

> On the *tonalamatl* platform we stand on a symbolic Universe, part of a cosmic order, not the social order. The *tonalamatl* symbol is also the first and most personal piece of information we receive. Each participant can make a personal reflection on the performance from the starting point of their *tonalamatl* sign (Middleton, 2000/01: 21).

From this opening, we are taken, single-file and in silence, on an eight-mile walk around the periphery of the pyramid site. We go clockwise, with the pyramids on our right, huge against the night sky. The monitors wear *ayoyotes* so that their walking creates a rhythm to which our own rhythm can entrain. 'It is a kind of walking meditation, in which the vision of the pyramids flows beside us and through us' (Middleton, 2000/01: 21). When the silent circumambulation is complete, we walk out into the scrubby landscape, and find there a campfire, tended by a solitary actor. We sit with him and he tells the story of Nanahuatzin. The audience listens – quiet and reflective after the meditative effects of the walking.

The second section of the event 'comprises the transformative crux of the work' (Middleton, 2000/01: 21). After a short break, back at base camp, we are blindfolded and led away from the base in a disorientating process which confounds any sense of direction or location. The landscape around Teotihuacan is fairly flat - a large plateau ringed by mountains - so it is with great surprise that I sense a change in the quality of the air and the ambient sounds and realize that we are being led, one by one, into caves. When the whole audience has been seated on the rough ground of the cave, the second performed sequence begins; the story of Quetzalcóatl, the feathered serpent, is told chorally, delivered in darkness against the cave's strange acoustics. It is a story forged on the mythic template of the descent into darkness and the ascent, phoenix-like, into light. We are invited to contemplate the archetype of the feathered serpent, which, as Núñez wrote in the production dossier, 'all of us carry within ourselves' (Núñez, 2000a, *n.p.*).

> When at last we are invited to remove our blindfolds, we find ourselves in a deep, total blackness. For a time we undergo the sensory deprivation of silence and sightlessness... Finally, candles are lit and we find ourselves in a large cavern seated around a huge display of flowers, blooming weirdly there at the dark centre of the earth (Middleton, 2000/01: 21).

We are blindfolded again for the return to the surface, where we are each laid gently on the open ground. At a signal, we open our eyes to the night sky filled with stars. The entrance to the caves is nowhere in sight; the mystery remains.

The final section of *The Flight of Quetzalcoatl* is, ritually, the phase of reincorporation. Here we are invited to consolidate and manifest what the experiences of the night have offered: like Nanahuatzin, we are given the opportunity to 'jump into the fire'; like Queztalcóatl, we are invited to 'be the heroes of our own adventure. With a small effort, we can really make our heart fly' (Núñez, 2000b).

The jump - the flight - is, of course, symbolic, but it is also embodied; to return to the *tonalamatl* platform from which the performance began, we must each jump through a hoop of flaming candles.

> As we prepare to 'jump' we look through the flaming circle and see the sun beginning to rise behind the pyramid of the sun. On the platform, one by one, we join the traditional pre-Hispanic Dance of Quetzalcoatl. Following the dance steps, feeling the rhythms, moving cyclically together we bring the night to an end. The sun comes up. The darkness has passed (Middleton, 2000/01: 21).

Although *The Flight of Quetzalcoatl* is unusual in the *Taller*'s history in terms of its durational aspects, it is exemplary in terms of its use of participatory devices and structures, and in its challenge to audiences. In *The Flight*, Núñez had full scope to develop and express his notion of a 'high-risk theatre'. In fact, the chapter of that name below (first published in a book of the same name in 2007), was partially developed from essays Núñez wrote for the production dossier for *The Flight of Quetzalcoatl*.

The theatre critic Fernando de Ita has suggested that Núñez's audience is 'a group of individuals who do not want to go to the theater, but to live an extraordinary experience' (Núñez, 2007: 46). In fact, what the *Taller's* participatory productions offer is theatre *as* extraordinary experience; and there is, perhaps, no better example of this than *The Flight of Quetzalcoatl*.

REFERENCES

Middleton, Deborah (2000/2001) 'Flight of the Heart' in *Total Theatre*, Vol. 12. 4, Winter 200/2001, pp. 19 - 21.

Núñez, Nicolás (2000a) *The Flight of Quetzalcoatl*. Production Dossier. Unpublished.

Núñez, Nicolás (2000b) *The Flight of Quetzalcoatl*. Script. Unpublished.

Núñez, Nicolás (2007) *Teatro de Alto Riesgo*. Mexico City: Consejo Editorial del TIT de la UNAM. Translated by Helena Guardia.

HIGH RISK THEATRE[44]
Nicolás Núñez

What is the purpose of theatre?

It can entertain, divert, make us dream, create illusions, and help us to forget ourselves. It can also inquire, question, reflect, and discover, or create an expansive reality.

The dramatic structure is so powerful and generous that it can serve both purposes. Through it, we can escape reality or penetrate it, and even if it causes us certain suffering, it can help us to discover the true nature of things.

Theatre has no dogmas. Nevertheless, there are some orthodoxies which validate only certain kinds of established theatre. Some stand for a social theatre, others for a psychological or religious theatre, and still others, for one strictly for amusement.

After more than thirty years of dramatic investigation in our *Taller*, we are now convinced that every theatrical genre has meaning, that each one of them serves its purpose within society.

These words are not intended to bring out any particular structure, but to share with you what might become, in the future, a serious research possibility. We refer to what we have defined as High Risk Theatre.

Why High Risk Theatre?

Because its participatory designs have certain psychophysical requirements which not everybody is willing, or able, to fulfil. In order to go through the different stages of our participatory theatre designs, a certain kind of physical, mental and emotional effort is needed. Certainly, the High Risk dramatic structure demands quite a lot from the participant but, for that very reason, it returns benefits.

---

44 Originally published in Núñez, N. (2007) *Teatro de Alto Riesgo*. Consejo Editorial del TIT de la UNAM. Translated by Helena Guardia.

The main differences between conventional theatre and High Risk Theatre can be seen in these four points:

CONVENTIONAL THEATRE	HIGH RISK THEATRE
1) The audience are observers; they sit in a specific place and watch from there.	The audience are transformed into participants. They sit, stand or walk, becoming an integral part of the dramatic action. Space is multiple.
2) The performance takes place on the stage, and the audience, from their seats, identify with the characters.	The participants take part in the performance which, mainly, takes place in their inner world. Inner landscapes interact with external ones.
3) The spectator draws her/his conclusion and reaffirms, or corrects, behaviours.	The participant has been transported and transformed. She/he began in one place and ended in another. She/he began with one inner status and ended with another.
4) The performance ends after two for hours. The spectator leaves the building and perhaps goes to some restaurant to digest the theatrical experience.	High Risk Theatre can last several hours of continuous involvement. By the end of the performance, a sense of travelor journeying is felt by the spectator, which compels her/him to look for a peaceful place in which to let the experience settle.

Participation in theatre is neither an innovation, nor a novelty. It goes as far back as its origins when, more than two thousand years ago, during the Eleusinian rites, participants were guided through different initiations. We have discovered in our High Risk Theatre designs, such as *The Flight of Quetzalcoatl* - which began at sunset and ended at sunrise, and was performed at the full moon throughout the year 2000, in Teotihuacan - that when the sacred experience is re-positioned within a contemporary dramatic structure – of risk - it regains its capacity to nourish our deepest fibres; that is to say, it actualizes our relation to the cosmos.

The benefits of High Risk Theatre have to do with our necessity 'to know ourselves', 'to control ourselves', and to believe 'I can because I think I can'. Acting based on these three steps ignites passion, and passion has its risks, but it also gives meaning to life. If we take the risk to discover and live our passion, routine will not knock down the scaffold of our existence, colours will not lose their brightness, and forms, tastes and smells will enhance their freshness. The worst pandemonium of the new millenium is not cancer or AIDS, but the death in life. Anyone who lives their quotidian life without a good dose of passion, is condemned to this kind of death. When passion does not assist us, colours lose their intensity and humour dies: the possibility of risk or adventure paralyses us, and the joy of being alive becomes a kind of 'abstract shit', as Octavio Paz says [in *Piedra de Sol* (Paz, 1957/1988)].

With *The Flight of Quetzalcoatl*, we advanced another step in our search for a dramatic structure which, under the name of High Risk Theatre, allowed us to live our passion to such an extent that we launched ourselves in a flight, with the certainty that we would never touch down on the ground again; like a labyrinthine impulse with no return. This experience allows us to share with you the assurance that, at least in the bones of those magnificent seven who gave their battle in order to keep this project alive, one of the most exciting archetypes of humankind, Quetzalcóatl (silently, overcoming many obstacles, with a great many sacrifices, with nobody noticing and nobody caring), channeled the spirit to speak for our race.

Those of us who participated in this experience share the same feeling; a kind of perfumed sensation that rises like a spring from somewhere in the back of the neck - the satisfaction of having the millenary Feathered Serpent, summoned by our High Risk Theatre platform, reassume its flight, in Teotihuacán.

In order to understand our proposal, it is necessary to be familiarized with the aim of our research. One way to do it is through the following scheme:

HISTORY OF THE THEATRE	⇩ RITE ⇧
	⇩ MYTH ⇧
	⇩ EPIC ⇧
	⇩ THEATRE ⇧
	DIRECTION OF OUR RESEARCH

Figure 11

Rite is absolute energy; we cannot understand it because it is beyond our comprehension. In order to approach this idea, human beings converted it into myths. In this form, energy is no longer unnamable, it has now a divine countenance, it has been transformed into a deity, acting within a myth. Descending further, this divine energy leaves behind deity and becomes a hero. The hero is a super human, he performs great feats, but he is not a god. Descending still another level, the hero becomes a human being, he no longer fulfils extraordinary feats, but has emotional conflicts; his rank is theatrical. Humans are the actors of the great theatre of the world. Thus, the specialists tell us, runs the history of theatre.

Our research goes the other way. We begin in the theatre, closely examining our human structure, its delicate and complex emotional circuits, in order to have a clue as to what kind of animal we are. At this point, by way of the good pain - we shall later detail what we mean by good pain - we ask from ourselves an epic attitude, understanding that the hero is someone who acts for the benefit of themselves and of the community. Through this attitude, we ascend to the epic level and become the heroes of our personal story. We will now attempt to perform actions that will draw us near to our inner divinity, accessing, thus, the mythical level. When we become conscious of our own inner deity, we can contact absolute energy. This is rite. When this happens in a strictictly personal way, with no intermediaries or orthodoxes, we call it a personal rite.

We think the future of human sacredness tends in this direction. People are in need of devices to help them contact sacredness in a personal way. They do not want any more mediators, but structures that will facilitate for them the time and the space necessary for this parenthesis in which they can have their own dialogue with the unutterable.

This parenthesis for reflection is what we offer to those who come to our work: we invite them to explore their own potential through, for example, the archetypal myth of Quetzalcóatl, from his human condition to his mythical being.

First, we have to touch our human conditon, attempting to discover who we are. We can then make the effort - good pain - to reach our epic condition and, through this effort, we get closer to what we want to be: the heroes of our own adventure. This effort gives us the strength to reach our mythical, or archetypal, condition by shifting us to the possibility of finding our personal psychophysical sign which, also as a personal rite, will re-link us with absoute energy.

On this basis, the High Risk Theatre actor/participant has to be someone very special who is willing to reflect on himself or herself. They will also manifest their effort creatively, in an aesthetic idea around the process of the serpent which transforms itself into an eagle.

The aim of such a game is to reconnect us, through a cultural, non-religious structure, to the natural rhythms of the cosmos. This is the reason why actors/participants, sensitive to this kind of experience, who conceptually, emotionally and passionately understand the ludicrous meaning of our work, are needed.

We call, then, all those who feel in their blood the desire to be part of this risk, to approach our work.

In order to realize the function High Risk Theatre performs for society, we have to know the difference between theatre and rite. The following scheme will help us to see the correspondences and the differences between them:

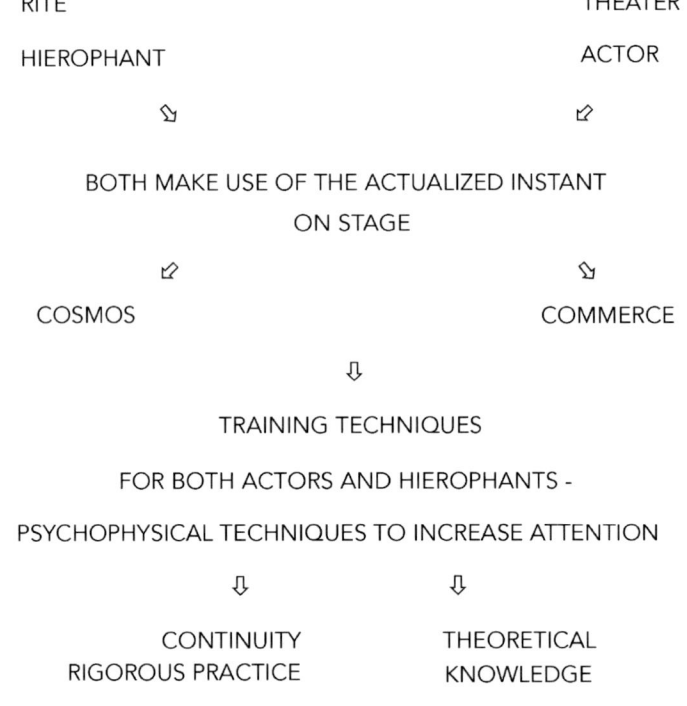

Figure 12

Both hierophants and actors make use of the actualized moment, for which purpose they have a similar training. Through this living instant, the actor relates us to commerce. Hierophants connect us to the cosmos; therefore, their work is sacred. There are, however, also actors who relate us to the sacred, and some hierophants who relate us to commerce.

It has not been easy to put into practice our High Risk Theatre devices. The example, again, is *The Flight of Quetzalcoatl*.

How was *The Flight of Quetzalcoatl* conceived?

It all began almost thirty years ago. As theatre people, we were not satisfied with the conventional dramatic structure which, at that time, did not offer many possibilities, paralyzed, as it was, in a very formal structure. Consequently, we were not in accordance with its results.

Mesoamerican theatre and culture, and the indigenous wisdom, extended our boundaries and opened up for us alternative spaces. Grotowski inspired us with his depth and meaning, reconnecting us to tradition. Artaud gave us the conviction that only through passion can we conquer our madness. Schechner and Turner taught us excellent lessons through their academic rigour and sharpness in their analysis of rite and theatre.

Our urgencies met those of other desperate ones and, together, we intertwined the plot of our participatory actions which, slowly through the years, became our training dynamics. The madness of the gang found shelter under transpersonal psychology, under quantum theory and shamanism; under the startling ceremonies we experienced in the Mexican mountains and forests, as well as the Himalayan mountains, and running after Pachamama on the slopes of Machu Picchu; soaring at Konya and landing our tired bodies on Kashmir to commune with the bones of Christ. All these led us to Quetzalcóatl, in Teotihuacán.

We do not know how we came to risk ourselves with this puzzle, nor from where we got the freedom to quarter - deconstruct - the dramatic structure.

It is only because God is very great, and much is our necessity, that we found these participatory platforms which helped us to define our intent, as well as to gather the sweat of a shared desperation which, slowly, has become our alibi in front of the world, as an alternative answer to the meaning of life.

We are sure that the warmth of the unified movement of our minds and bodies has sometimes allowed our consciousness to burst with the certainty that, though nobody notices and nobody cares, we are working, in a direct and contemporary way, with *la flor y el canto* of our theatre [the flower and the song - a Prehispanic metaphor employed in philosophy and poetry to refer to the essence of art].

Good Pain

Now we would like to talk about good pain. When we seriously observe ourselves, we discover that the mind is a wild, sacred animal, incommensurable, and interconnected with the universe. The great investigators of the mental processes have always taught us how to know, control and direct our mental fluid; for its ferocity can lead us to ecstasy and help us to remain firmly in the light, as well as consign us to the lowest and most destructive hell.

To educate this runaway animal which is our mind, we need discipline, continuity of effort and rigour. We have to be aware that a certain amount of effort, or pain, is necessary to grow healthy. This, which is so evidently understood, is not so easy to practice, maybe because it goes against the core of the belief system under which we were educated. Within this system of beliefs, everything seems to be structured to avoid pain. The triumph of comfort is proclaimed all over the Western world. Let's do the least effort! Rationally, there is no justification for giving any place to effort or pain within our happiness. Therefore, why would it be necessary to make any kind of effort or feel any pain?

Psychology has been characterized by its analysis and healing techniques for multiple illnesses afflicting us, but it has paid little attention to techniques which could help us to sustain the fullness of life. That is to say, a psychology of health, as transpersonal psychology might be. Jung, one of the most outstanding pioneers on this perspective, says:

> Life demands for its completion and fulfilment a balance between joy and sorrow. But because suffering is positively disagreeable, people

> naturally prefer not to ponder how much fear and sorrow fall to the lot of man. So they speak soothingly about progress and the greatest possible happiness, forgetting that happiness itself is poisoned if the measure of suffering has not been fulfilled. Behind a neurosis there is so often concealed all the natural and necessary suffering the patient has been unwilling to bear. We can see this most clearly from hysterical pains, which are relieved in the course of treatment by the corresponding psychic suffering which the patient sought to avoid (Jung, 1966: 81).

How to pay our share of natural pain that will keep us healthy? How not to exceed ourselves, and thus feel unnecessary and useless suffering? Or how not to lie to ourselves, just to avoid good pain? Sometimes it is very hard, because we do not know that conscious suffering is good for us. Could a cultural structure assist us in this process?

Good pain is the mental and physical effort that we know we have to make but, generally, do not make. It is an effort that implies a certain amount of suffering which is not harmful for the mind, nor for the body, but, by demanding from us the necessary rigour to do what we know we have to do, becomes a suffering which makes us grow. As the Nahuatl philosophy says it, 'becoming the sun on the earth'. This painful effort, paradoxically, helps us to be healthy and balanced.

But to make an effort beyond what is necessary is as destructive as not making any at all. What we need is the correct measure. We can feel it when we pay attention to our organism. If we listen carefully to it, we will always know which kind of effort will benefit us. This effort is good pain.

Which is the harmful pain? That which breaks, hurts, deteriorates, mutilates or pollutes our mind and body. This kind of harmful pain, or wrong effort, generally appears for two reasons: the first is due to an excess of rigour, which is the consequence of not understanding the extent to which we should push ourselves (voracity); the second is related to lack of action, which allows the retrogressive energy to drag us down into states of mental and physical dirt. In conclusion, either we go too far, or we do not make any effort at all, sinking in the depression of involuntary movement. We might not like it, but that is how it is.

What does all this have to do with the Theatre of High Risk?

Good pain is related to High Risk Theatre through the effort principle. High Risk Theatre entails a considerable effort. Let us see how, using as our model, once more, *The Flight of Quetzalcoatl*.

In Mexico, Quetzalcóatl is one of our main archetypal images, and contains a complete and rigorous code of inner education. Vigil is, in every tradition, one of the most difficult and most effective exercises for training the mind. To be awake and vigilant all night long is a frightening effort. To perform it through a cultural device is a wonderful warming up - or over-effort - which, on the one hand, helped us to consolidate a reality: the archetypal image of Quetzalcóatl coming alive in the third millenium; and, on the other, it gave us the assurrance that it is possible, if we are awake, to harmonize ourselves in such a way that we can acknowledge our co-responsibility with the rhythms of the universe - cosmic ecology - with all its social and political implications. This might save us from losing more time, since 'we are here just for a while' (Nezahualcoyotl[45]). Because if we do not engage in the passion that sustains the universal dance, in which we are all involved, life loses its meaning and becomes ill.

To carry out this effort through a cultural device, such as High Risk Theatre, is, from our point of view, a way to keep the soundness of our social body as well as to nourish our spirit. Furthermore, it also creates projections of inner growth and plenitude. High Risk Theatre seems to be a logical and natural way to do it, with all its mythical and ritual connotations.

If we re-examine with care the texts of such ethnologists and historians as Mircea Eliade, Joseph Campbell, James Frazer or Arnold Toynbee, amongst

---

45 Fifteenth-century ruler and poet-philosopher from Central Mexico.

others, we realize that the ritual phenomenon has been part of theatre since its origins, almost in the beginning of time. The excellent anthropologist, Victor Turner, is of the same opinion. Therefore, theatre is, in itself, an essential device, co-creator of all religious's festivities. According to their analysis, theatre could be defined as one the oldest sacred devices of humanity.

This theatrical tradition projects itself even into the future. Communication investigators such as Marshall McLuhan and Alvin Toffler acknowledge the rite/theatre dynamic as a very effective possibility to satisfy, in the future, one of the vital needs of contemporary man: the need for action.

High Risk Theatre is action. What is interesting in this kind of action is that it is a secular device of inner expansion. This is what we have referred to as personal rite, with no mediators or orthodoxies, as perhaps corresponds to the culture of this new millenium.

This rite/theatre filiation, which goes as far back as the origins of humanity, and dynamically projects into a promising future is, I think, the living tradition of Theatre.

Actor Warrior

As a member of this theatre tradition, I would like to share with you the idea that the training tools of a true actor go hand by hand with those of the spiritual warrior. The actor has to train his mind, body and speech through discipline, concentration and intelligence, just as the spiritual warrior from, for instance, the Tibetan Shambhala tradition, or that of the Mesoamerican Nahual. Both disciplines belong to the tradition of the spiritual warrior. Their aim is to transform one into an instrument, or channel, of the sacred.

The High Risk Theatre actor is an actor/warrior. They must develop their energy in order to reach the state where being a warrior means to be genuine, and to be a genuine warrior means to be an Actor, with a capital letter. It means to have the energy and the courage to maintain ourselves in the living instant, in syncronicity of mind and body. It is to have the power to remain in authentic reality. To run away from the present, to live as if death did not exist, is cowardness. In the actor/warrior path, it is fundamental to live in the present, with open eyes. It is to celebrate the moment in which the natural hierarchies blossom, and this, too, is part of their training. The actor/warrior feels the authentic melancholy of the artist facing the world. Melancholy arising from contact with the void, which makes the poet say:

> The cloud-capp'd towers, the gorgeous palaces,
> The solemn temples, the great globe itself,
> Yea, all which it inherit, shall dissolve,
> And, like this insubstantial pageant faded,
> Leave not a track behind. We are such stuff
> As dreams are made on; and our little life
> Is rounded with a sleep. (*The Tempest*, IV, i, 152-158)

Now it is, now it is not… This is the melancholy of the true actor/warrior: consciousness of the void. Being, in Nahuatl philosophy, is like a hollow mirror.

The actor/warrior achieves, through their disciplined training, an epic level, moving triumphantly on the stage, celebrating the path. Their battle entails no victory or defeat, just action.

These devices, Eastern, Western or Mesoamerican, designed to enliven the moment, employed at their best, have much to offer to the new synthesis of consciousness.

Western culture considers the East the cradle of wisdom and knowledge. If we go to the east of the East, we find Mexico, and it, too, has a secret to convey to humanity. We are not aware of the fact that humanity forms a living organism which is in perpetual movement. It is never static. And as it has produced great civilizations, so it contains the seed of future, new and unpredictable cultures that might already be pulsating amongst us.

Can we discover - intuit - their pattern through theatre? How can we give an answer to our restlessness and inner needs? How can we actualize ourselves, without demolishing the established traditions, and not making a superficial and useless soup from all of them? How to create the new -

nourished by the old - so effectively that it can induce a real change in us? This is not an easy path.

The answer would be by walking. The map is not the territory; the map has never been the territory.

Some of us know, well or deficiently, the maps of the evolution of consciousness. Almost all of us are semi-experts in the multiplicity of religious or theatrical maps, but we are, mainly, desk experts. We spend time discussing the maps, but almost never travel through them. A characteristic stroke of this actualization is action. Inner action - rectified, controlled, oriented - but action. The ritual/theatrical map in which we are interested entails more doing and less talking or writing about doing. What our present condition is asking from us is to become the actors of our own lives. To live it, not to chat about living it. To better it, not to talk about bettering it. To refine, not to speak about refining.

Maps do not hinder us; they are, indeed, important. They can help us to find our way. But to go to a map is an impulse which carries the danger - and this has to be emphasized - of withholding us from action and keeping us discussing the journey. Information with no action has no effect. Baudrillard tells us that 'instead of transforming the mass into energy, information produces even more mass' (1983: 25). We have to conceive actions that set us in motion, and then re-examine the map. We need to shatter the spiritual numbness into which the dictatorship of our intellect has put us. Ask yourself how much you know about the map, and how much you have walked the path. I am sure that if we practiced one tenth of the knowledge and information we have, we would be an enlightened society. This means we need to become stronger through action. High Risk Theatre is, fundamentally, based on action. And we assume the risk it implies.

In this sense, the theatre we are interested in is one dealing with a set of actions which move us to reflection and change. To achieve this, the recovery of the original and mythical Eleusinian, Orphean or Quetzalcóatlian structure is of great help; the ritual/theatical circumstances of the initiation rites giving us, as our only clue, the task to know and refine ourselves.

In our search for a new theatre, we will harvest the fruit of direct experience only if we use experimentation as our groundwork. Direct experience transforms information; *it is* in itself. It is not theatrical, nor ritual. It blossoms, and its fruit is, for those who taste it, untransmittable. For this reason, direct experience cannot be possessed in an institutionalized or systematized way. It cannot be the property of any cultural or religious group. It is far from orthodoxies and close to poetry.

High Risk Theatre is not orthodox; it is a poetic battle field. In it, you will not find followers but accomplices, equally commited to take, by assault, the luminosity of the instant. It is neither a group, nor a sect, maybe not even a 'gang'. Its code is not written, but it earnestly comes to life with each step on the stage.

I am talking about taking risks in the theatre as a means to acknowledge our inner and outer territory; to realize that the land of the seeker is their own body, mind and spirit, and those who do not take the risk to take root in themselves have no land.

Our first identity, the passport to our deep consciousness, is our empowered mind and body, receptive to their cosmic resonances. This is the true identity of the actor/warrior.

Our departure point in the work of the *Taller* is the complicity we have with our companions in the adventure: the adventure to recognize, in our working space, wherever we convoke it, and for the necessary time, a special place where competition is discarded; where no one has to fear anyone; where the only commitment is to devote ourselves to the expansion of our work, whether individual or collective, with closed doors or open to the public, conscious that there is no judgement, that we can rely on the help from our companions, and knowing that we have the respect and understanding of all those involved in the action. There is no place here for destructive criticism or mockery. We accept the fact that, whenever someone abandons themselves to an honest search, any attitude, as grotesque or stupid as it might seem to us at first sight, is worthy of respect. Respect is essential for the progress of our work.

We use theatre to contact our inner realities. It is only one way to do it. We have searched through theatre, basically, for a path to ourselves. This has produced encounters, caused afflictions, set-backs and criticism, but we know it is worthwhile to go on. So, through these lines, we wish to offer our complicity to any future participants.

We all have urgencies, and the commitment of true theatre is to assist us so we can acknowledge them. For instance, you who read these lines, what is your interest in theatre? What is your urgency in life? Do you know a theatre - or any cultural device - which can help you to recognize it, to inquire into it, and to satisfy it?

A kind of theatre, or cultural device, that teaches us how to take care of our mental fluid, how to observe it and, if possible - through its dynamics - how to control it, is an approach to a culture that could function as a personal rite. This is High Risk Theatre.

The theatre tradition does not fit in the definition of group, church or sect. It is a meeting of accomplices; a 'gang' of the living instant. And who defines it so? The stage itself accepts some people, and not others. Full, genuine action, without dogmas or second intentions, is what counts. The ability to fuction in action.

With its power of convocation, the stage is what reunites and defines us. The work causes an energy leap which alters perception. You walk on the edge, courageously riding the windhorse, keeping up the invigorating moment, joyfully alive. Those who achieve it recognize themselves as members of an unselfish gang, to whom the stage conveys its secret: everything is, everything happens in the here and now.

This kind of theatre is not for everybody. Affinity of needs is what brings us together, or not.

In action, we have certified the effectiveness of our theatrical dynamics in unifying mind and body and increasing, gradually, our capacity to exert ourselves, our resistance, and our attention thresholds.

When we share our restlessness, we want to send a signal to those who feel empathy with our search. We invite them to see if it is a real alternative to the madhouse. Our dynamics, executed within the High Risk frame, can serve to sustain a kind of regulated alteration, a controlled explosion, of channeled anguish and certainty in the emergency. That is to say, can serve to keep away the vigorous and vigilant men in white.

We must make clear that our proposal to search, through theatre, for our personal rite is not psychodrama, but a dramatic game with simple and plain rules. The fundamental structure of rite - death and rebirth - is always present in the actions of this game-theatre-dynamic.

Threshold-journey-transformation-completion-exit. Our game always travels, in a secular way, through the classical, archetypal descent into the darkness and ascension to the light. By secular we mean free of dogmas.

Likewise, we want to clarify what kind of sacredness our work touches. This sacredness has no religious tendency. However, it does have the certainty of an underlying, basic, sacredness. Each one appeals to their own very intimate idea of the sacred. It is from this respectful attitude that people, in good faith, participate in the actions, establishing, among all, a serious game of open, secular, universal sacredness. The stage, shared by all of us, transforms into a poetic battle-field, and we become the actors/warriors of our own struggle. The dynamics are a guide to sustain us with their rhythm, and to signal our way. The degree of our commitment to keeping our mind and body awake and alert is strictly personal. We can fool ourselves, but we can also make our best and most sincere effort -

- To conquer physical territory: our own body.
- To conquer mental territory: our own mind.
- To conquer spiritual territory: our own faith.

Manipulating another's spiritual, mental or physical territory is a crime which has to be assumed by whoever commits it.

Our intention is to play, in good faith; to conquer that which, in our opinion, is the only thing that it is worthwhile to conquer: our being.

This is, in synthesis, the philosophy of the gang.

And who is the gang?

Whoever understands the kind of theatre in which we are interested and joins us. The inner nucleus of the TRW is formed by members who, through the years, have become the monitors in our actions. Most of them began by attending our sessions, coming back again and again, until, almost without noticing, they turned our actions into an authentic, personal training field.

We know High Risk Theatre is not for everybody, but likewise, we are convinced that our search has resonance in some consciousnesses that we want to contact. We do not want to teach everybody to howl, but we wish to tell those who are about to burst that there exists a theatrical alternative in which their howling is welcome and can be refined, celebrated, and become part of a collective flight.

In order to create an adequate working atmosphere, we ask our participants to make the effort, during the dynamic-event-performance, to suspend the following differences:

SOCIAL – Ethnic discrimination is not permitted.

SEXUAL – It is not valid to divert energy from the work to put attention on the legs of our companions.

ECONOMIC – Nobody is to impose themselves through their economic condition.

RELIGIOUS – Respect for the right everyone has to light a candle to the saint of their devotion.

IDEOLOGICAL – To have kindness, patience and respect for the other, though we might be sure, deep inside ourselves, that his wrong point of view is what impedes him from seeing correctly; that is, from seeing the way I do.

The basic rules for participating in our theatre games are plain and simple:

1. To trust and act in good faith. To play each dynamic in depth, making our best effort, as real conquerors of our mind, body and, as much as possible, our spirit.
2. Neither to judge nor to compete with anybody.
3. To permanently observe our mental fluid.
4. To accept that theatre can also be a device to cultivate our heart and our face.

This scenic game that we have called High Risk Theatre, participatory theatre, or theatre as a personal rite, is the result of the effort and dedication of the members of the TRW, whose support has been indispensable for its existence.

Some of you might be surprised to discover theatre as a sacred instrument because, nowadays, it does not peform this function anymore, it no longer convenes the divine, nor does it convert a profane space into a sacred space.

Nevertheless, theatre, even in its most superficial aspect, still holds the virtuous capacity to transform an ordinary space into an extraordinary one. By summoning us at a precise time and place, it heightens our attention. It enspirits the space and, with it, our capacity to be in the moment. It is, still, a dynamo of effective energy, inheritance of its ancient origin.

What does the theatre tradition have to offer to the awakening of consciousness?

I am convinced that, fully employed, theatre devices have much to offer to this end. But how? As we see it now, it would seem impossible.

With theatre, something similar to what happened to the Tarot occurred. It is said that the Tarot contains very deep knowledge. In order for it to survive through the different civilizations, it was handed over to the masses under the disguise of a divinatory game. Only men and women of knowledge knew how to read it correctly, as a key to contact superior energies. Likewise, theatre is used today mainly for amusement, after which we can go someplace to have dinner. But those who know teach us that it, too, has the possibility to link us with a deeper quality of being, reaching the status of a sacred instrument.

This does not mean that we do not care for, or do not have answers for, other problems afflicting contemporary theatre. For example - why would young people make theatre? It is said theatre has no audience anymore - why? One possible answer is that you can find in movies and television mainly the same product, at a lower cost. With rare exceptions, melodramas, sexual and emotional games and suspense form the dramatic content of commercial theatre, movies and television. Their product is almost the same, but television and movies exceed theatre as far as production, recreation of intimate spaces, landscapes, violence and changes of time and space are concerned. In them, the audience watches, close up, a richer variety of costumes and scenography, and such vertiginous impacts that they make them feel as if they were on a toboggan, their stomach twisted with pleasure. Without exposing them, and without moving them from their armoured seats, risking nothing, movie and television offer them many more visual and auditory impacts than theatre.

But theatre, with the living presence of people, can affect them through other areas, or even directly through group actions which awaken them energetically to be in the here and now. Conventional theatre is unconscious of the huge potential underlying the living moment. Theatre is limiting itself when it competes against movie and television and employs their same communication means. Instead, theatre has the opportunity to recover its origins, to return to being a theatre that is communal, tribal, sacred, archetypal.

Alternative theatre has something to offer which cannot be found in movie or television, nor in the commercial theatre. One of the first things is participation; getting involved in a living event happening here and now, exactly in the time and place it is convoked. Something happening only once, that considers the audience not only as spectators, but as members of an action evolving through a dramatic dynamic, untransferable and unique, that gives them the possibility to vivify and integrate mind and body, not limited only to sight and hearing. Something that happens not just *for* them, but *with* them. An active dynamic which is not trivial and superficial, as most pseudo-participatory structures generally are - tricky and cheatingly manipulative.

Commercial theatre, movie and televison, until now, have offered the audience the same role: that of the observer. Here is where theatre loses the game, because people prefer to see more and pay less. In such conditions, movies are full and theatres empty. Millionaire movie and theatre productions have intricate ways to recover their investments, which makes them excellent businesses. But regular theatre has only a small audience to bear the payroll burden. As I said, a theatre performance is unique because it really happens in the same space the audience is sharing with the actors. You cannot programme it in a thousand theatres simultaneously. The economic disadvange is enormous, except for the commercial theatre's toys, which are also very profitable.

We do not have to be experts in Umberto Eco's writings to draw conclusions. Movie and television are two dimensional, limited vehicles of communication. If, in addition to this, you have a content which deteriorates the perceptual structure of the observer and deforms reality, the undermining of consciousness is automatic. In some cases, it even causes loss of perspective and is psychologically disorientating. Television's hypnotic factor is an important element because it captivates the attention, and nothing happens, annulling the possibility of any activity. It does not happen the same way with other two dimensional devices such as books, which do not have the hypnotic factor, and the contents of which, generally, take you to other dimensions. Nor is the movie hypnotic. For this reason, books and good films are considered high culture, with the exception of those which are strictly commercial. Unfortunately, television is, as Habermas says, culturally regressive ([1968] 1984). It has the demon of the hypnotic factor which, in some way, impedes the inner and personal soaring which all high culture offers.

We ask ourselves, do we have the possibility to invent, hallucinate, investigate without manipulating, some other forms of theatre? Yes. How? Finding the paths that give an answer to the authentic inner urges of people.

High Risk Theatre is, for us, an answer, an alternative to be investigated.

REFERENCES

Baudrillard, Jean (1983) *In the Shadow of the Silent Majorities*. New York: Semiotext(E).

Habermas, Jürgen ([1968] 1984) *Ciencia y técnica como ideología*. Madrid: Tecnos.

Habermas, Jürgen (1970) 'Technology and Science as "Ideology"', in *Toward a Rational Society* (Trans. J. Shapiro). Boston: Beacon Press.

Jung, C. G. & Read, Herbert (1966) *The Collected Works of C.G. Jung: Vol.16, The practice of psychotherapy : essays on the psychology of the transference and other subjects*. (Trans. R.F.C. Hull). 2nd ed. London: Routledge & Kegan Paul.

Paz, Octavio (1957) *Piedra de Sol*. Mexico City: Tezontle.

Paz, Octavio (1988) *The Collected Poems*. (Ed, Trans. Eliot Weinberger). Manchester: Carcanet.

ANTHROPOCOSMIC THEATRE

CASE STUDY: CONSPIRACIÓN HAMLET - CASA DEL LAGO, CHAPULTEPEC, MEXICO CITY (2012)

Karoliina Sandström

The 2012 *Taller* production, *Conspiración Hamlet*, was an adaptation of Shakespeare's classic into a participatory experience.[46] The production employed many of the principal soliloquies of *Hamlet*, seeking to work with the themes of doubt, self doubt and lack of action. The production sought to consider these both in the context of the original play and in relation to our own lives. Both in the rehearsal process and in the piece itself, the mirror as object and metaphor was used to evoke various perspectives of an assumed ´self and other´ for reflection. During rehearsals the actors were invited to consider how the struggles and ruminations of Hamlet could serve as a mirror image of themselves. The purpose of this reflection, besides being the groundwork for the creation of the performance score, was to make explicit the intention of exploring through the final production the notion of being true to who we are. *Conspiración Hamlet* asked participants and actors to contemplate what it would mean to be true to our destiny, which in Hamlet´s case is a tragic one, and which, in our own lives, can often be sidestepped in favour of ´musts´ and ´shoulds´. As with so many *Taller* productions, the intention here was to try to awaken, to choose 'to be,' rather than ´not to be´.

The play began in the woods of Casa del Lago, in Chapultepec. The audience were asked to join a circle. The rules of the game were explained: please trust us, please do as we ask, please play honestly, intently, and truly. Only this way may you find something of importance, only this way may you have a genuine experience.

The audience is gathered into a circle whilst the rules of the game are explained and a moment is taken to begin the play. They walk through the

---

46 This is not a strict description of the play's events, but rather a reflection of the shape of the play. As such I attempt to echo its nature as an experience.

woods behind a guide, the one who will take them through to the end. They walk making the serpent, becoming once more part of a whole body, reminding them in movement of their belonging, of their interconnectedness to everything else. They are lead into the woods and through the golden gate - the gate of consciousness and awakening. Then, they are gathered around the great palm tree.

Here is Hamlet, for the first time, holding the frame of a handheld mirror with no glass in it. Hamlet speaks to himself, to himself in the audience through the glassless mirror in his first monologue. There are three Hamlets on stage, and in his/her mirror there are as many Hamlets as there are audience members.

'[…] But break, my heart, for I must hold my tongue' (*Hamlet*, I, ii, 158)

The serpent line gathers again, we walk deeper into the woods to find a path, to come to a castle. To find Hamlet on the brink of the balcony, having seen the ghost.

'[…] Remember Thee'[47]

We follow the guide around the castle and encounter the players. The 'appearance' of life in all its banality, in all its melodrama and superficiality. But when shall we catch ourselves - we who are not even half as alive as these pretenders? When shall we find the courage of acting out our true needs?

[…] But I am pigeon-livered and lack gall

To make oppression bitter, or, ere this

I should have fatted all the region kites

With this slave's offal. Bloody, bawdy villain! (*Hamlet*, III, ii, 572- 575)

The guide moves forward, gives each actor their own sin to bear; the theme of life which does not let them fly free - which binds them by fear to repeating the same patterns of life, over and over. Hamlet speaks again:

[…] But that the dread of something after death -

The undiscovered country, from whose bourn

---

47   A play on the line, 'Remember me' (*Hamlet*, I, v, 91).

> No traveler returns - puzzles the will,
> And makes us rather bear those ills we have
> Than fly to others that we know not of? (*Hamlet*, III.i. 78 - 82)

The guide beckons the audience to follow him. They enter the woods again where they are placed standing in a circle of which Ophelia is in the middle. She cleanses the audience members, one by one purifying them with smoke from herbs and sacred plants. Preparing them to trust the following journey walking blindfolded, to bring their outer attention inside. The blindfolded audience makes a serpent, and walks through the woods, onto a path, accompanied by song, up and up, and into the castle. Now everyone is invited to take part in action, in finding their own freedom to be. They are asked to walk in the space, alone, not next to whom they came to the play with. They are asked to find a place to stand to find their roots, to sense the movement of the planet in the cosmos. A drum is played, the audience is encouraged to find their dance, to liberate their bodies from resistance, to be free in movement. The music intensifies in waves, and the audience find their way back to being. The game is serious, one´s life is at stake. What would you choose? To be or not to be? Each audience member is placed in a pair, facing each other, with their eyes closed still. They are asked to recognise the essence of the other, without judgement, through gentle touching of the other. Eyes slowly open, to see the other, to be with the other, to recognise their true being.

The pirates invade the space; we are not in the castle, we are in the ship that saved our lives! And the actors walk through the audience with the empty handheld mirror, whilst the question is asked, Who are you truly? Who do you see on the other side - is it other, or is it you, as much as you are him or her?

The mirror theme which appeared in the production, both in physical and metaphorical forms, spoke to the account of Tezcatlipoca - the 'smoked mirror' of Mexican indigenous mythology. It spoke of the necessity to work on our clear vision; to see further and deeper than our undisciplined minds, our cravings and grasping. To see our true self, and in that seeing to see ourselves in the other. *In Lak'ech Hala Ken:* I am you, You are me.[48]

---

48 This expression is a Mayan greeting which seeks to express the unity of all beings and energies in the universe. *In Lak'ech*, signifying: I am another you, and *Hala Ken*: You are another me.

MANDALA: THE SACRED ART OF ACTING - A PLAY IN ONE ACT[49]

Nicolás Núñez

CHARACTERS:

MAESTRO   A distinguished theatre teacher, middle-aged
RESEARCHER   A doctoral student, engaged in theatre research, younger than the Maestro

The play begins with an introduction in the theatre lobby, where the spectators are asked to sign a letter of agreement in which they accept the possibility that they might be transformed through the theatre they are about to experience. Those who agree, sign, take off their shoes, and enter the theatre.

*The **RESEARCHER** is onstage. The **MAESTRO** is late and enters the stage in a hurry.*

MAESTRO: (*greeting the **RESEARCHER***) Hi, how are you? Did you have trouble getting here?

RESEARCHER: No, not at all.

MAESTRO: I've just come all the way from Teotihuacan. I was running late, and there was terrible traffic, but I am here now...

*(The **MAESTRO** receives the letter signed by the public).*

MAESTRO: Thank you. I can see that you all entered this space out of your own free will, and I can see that many of you travelled from very far to be here with us, in Tenochtitlan, tonight. Welcome. Splendid! Can we now, please, lock the door?

---

49 This version of the production, adapted for two players, was presented in English in Huddersfield in 2015. Translated by Karoliina Sandström and Helena Guardia.

(On the stage there is a rectangular table with books, notes, a candle, matches, a glass and a bottle of tequila. Next to it, there is an umbrella stand with some rolls of paper in it. Behind the table is a large, old-fashioned rectangular blackboard. To the right of the stage, there is a clothes hanger).

MAESTRO: Thank you. Now, let's finish arriving. What do I mean by this - to finish arriving? Sometimes, I find, the body may be physically in a place, but the mind is somewhere very different, so to finish arriving is to bring all aspects of yourself here - mind and body. Good. So, I assume everyone present is interested in acting, at least for the duration of this session.

In real life, which is the greatest theatre in the world, we are all actors; some of us are good, some of us not so good, and some are ok; but what is sure is that we all have our specific role to play. Some people call this destiny.

Mystics and scientist tell us that there are no accidents, so it is not an accident that we are all here today. For better or worse, in this very instant our destinies come together. Let's begin.

*(The **MAESTRO** draws two big, over-lapping circles on the blackboard. Inside the upper circle, he writes 'Mandala', in the lower one he writes 'Acting'; at the intersection, he writes 'Sacred'. The **MAESTRO** and the **RESEARCHER** ceremoniously light the candle).*

MAESTRO: Why is acting a sacred art? We would like to begin by sharing with you what is for us a sacred art. One of the best examples of a sacred art is the art of making a Tibetan mandala. But what is the Tibetan mandala?

*(The **MAESTRO** uncovers the Mandala hanging at the center of the stage).*

MAESTRO: This is an image of a Tibetan mandala. The Sanskrit word 'mandala' means a sacred cosmogram. You will find that most cultures in the world use some kind of cosmogram.

The origins of the Tibetan mandala, in particular, go back to Tantric Buddhism in India - a tradition that is more than 2500 years old.

Mandalas are tools for the re-consecration of the energies of the world, and for healing its inhabitants. The iconography is based in sacred geometry and ancestral symbols. Mandalas have an external, internal and a secret level of meaning.

The external level presents the divine form of mother earth. The internal level is a map that traces the journey of how the ordinary human mind can be transformed into an enlightened mind. Through the secret level we discover the perfect balance that exists between the most subtle energies of the body and the enlightened dimension of the mind.

This design teaches us how the circulation of the purifying energies in the universe is transmitted. It contains the four directions - represented by the four gateways which lead toward the centre point - each one represented by a specific colour, depending on the mandala in question, because there are an infinite number of mandalas. It could almost be said that each human being is a living mandala, with some aspects in common but each one completely different to the others.

A mandala can be of a regular size or it can be very large. The circles, lines and particular details of the design are created with strict precision. The colours which are used are directly connected with the subtlest energies of the spirit.

Mandalas are created laboriously and with great patience. Sometimes, fine coloured sand is used; sometimes powders made out of flower petals, herbs and corn. Sometimes they are made out of fine painted stones and sometimes even of gemstones. The time that it takes for making a mandala varies between five to seven days, or even weeks, depending on the size.

To create the mandala, little by little, delicate silver funnels are used. It is almost as if, grain by grain, a miracle is being realised. One false movement and the whole process has to be stared all over again.

The monks always begin the construction of the mandala from the centre outwards. During the process, their breathing and their minds are connected to mantras. Mantras are words or phrases with neuronal resonance connected to the Source, the original primal vibration. These mantras help with maintaining, in the here and now, the presence of unconditional love toward all sentient beings.

As the mandala is finally finished, it is a radiant work of art, so charged and beautiful that it enraptures the eyes and soul of anyone who sees it.

The completion of the mandala is celebrated by offering its beauty and its power to the forces of nature. This moment is a turning point. Immediately afterwards, a farewell ceremony is carried out, and in four large spiralling sweeps, the mandala is destroyed. All the sand is collected into one pile and it is placed into the closest source of water; it may be a river, a stream, a lake, or the sea. It is placed there so that its purifying energies may move through the world healing all its inhabitants.

This sacred design teaches us detachment, impermanence, learning to let go. The monks don't construct the mandalas to last forever, because they know nothing is eternal.

Being able to make a thing of great value and beauty, a work of art, and still to have the capacity to let it go is an astonishing achievement. We learn that this letting go keeps us in the sanity of a cosmos which dances with an unexplainable serenity and joy - an infinite cosmic dance, unable to contain or to define itself. When you see the finished mandala, the first reaction is to say: 'it should stay perfectly as it is, no one should touch it, it should be contained like this forever', but you cannot contain reality. Reality is a living act, in constant motion, like the water in a stream, and this is why the mandala is a sacred art. So, we invite you to drink to that.

*(The **MAESTRO** offers tequila to the audience and, having taken their glasses, they all drink).*

Why is acting a sacred art? What is acting

*(The **MAESTRO** picks out one of the rolls of paper in the umbrella stand and opens it).*

This actor is called Johnny Depp.

*(It is the image of Antonin Artaud. The **RESEARCHER** laughs).*

No, this is not Johnny Depp.

*(The **MAESTRO** hangs Artaud's image from the hanger, and takes out another roll. He shows it).*

This is Johnny Depp.

*(The **MAESTRO** hangs Johnny Depp's image from the hanger).*

He *(indicating Johnny Depp)* declared that for constructing a character for theatre you need great discipline, patience, studies, and a vast psychophysical training - the result of which is acting with a very high artistic value, which can be appreciated for the fascination it has over the audience.

When it is done well, acting becomes an art that expands consciousness and brings joy to those who see it. All the effort and perseverance that it took to build this character exist only in the moment when the actor is on stage. When the performance is over ... the character disappears, ceases to exist. And at the end of the last performance, that character which was so painstakingly built – by revealing the true colours of the deepest human emotions – must be released by the actor. In order to stay sane, the actor must let go of the character, so it may return to the emptiness out of which it emerged.

Johnny Depp says the actor has to have the capacity for a very rigorous creative process, and the ability for a deep detachment. The art of acting is to create, nourish, offer and vanish; it does not seek eternity - what is sought is the celebration of the present moment.

Harsh work to construct something that nourishes society, hard work to let it go. This is why acting is a sacred art, just as the art of making a mandala.

And it is in that line that, as a Mexican actor, I would like to share with you a couple of syncronicities, which I feel will be interesting for you to know. You see, we have to know as much as we can in our intention to make acting a flourishing mandala.

You might remember that in Ancient Greece, through a very particular ceremony, and by using divine substances - in this case, ambrosia - the actors came into direct contact with the sacred; right? Well, in Tenochtitlan, also through a particular ceremony, and using the 'enlightened divine' (peyote), and the 'sanctified children' (sacred mushrooms), one would come into direct contact with the sacred. This is the first parallel, or syncronicity: Dionysus in Greece, Xochipilli in Tenochtitlan - big chiefs!

The second parallel - (remember, coincidence doesn't exist!): Those who were chosen to be initiated in the rites of the Eleusis, or in the Tlalocan rites, had to cross the famous three gateways. In Greece, the first one was…

RESEARCHER: 'Know yourself'.

MAESTRO: Exactly. And so, I ask myself - what would be the equivalent in Tenochtitlan? In the Nahuatl wisdom, we find…

RESEARCHER: 'Labra tu cara, trabaja tus facciones, ten un rostro para mirar mi rostro y que te mire, para mirar la vida hasta la muerte' [Work on your face, work on your features, have a face to look at my face and to look at yourself, to look at life until death].

MAESTRO: Very good. The second one in Greece…

RESEARCHER: 'Control yourself'.

MAESTRO: Which in Mexico is…

RESEARCHER: 'Be like a torch which does not leave smoke'.

MAESTRO: That's it. And the third one in Greece is… 'You can do it because you believe you can'.

RESEARCHER: 'My heart is a bird with wings'.

MAESTRO: These are two syncronicities which may be found between two apparently different traditions, both with a strong connection with theatre. So, I ask myself, today, here and now, not only in Greece or in Tenochtitlan but, rather, in any part of the world, what possibility do we have as actors to gain knowledge and understanding, in a deep manner, of our human condition and, at the same time, to touch the sacred? How could we do that?

What could we do, what could we eat or… whatever - in order to cross that threshold?

I have something here… *(The **MAESTRO** looks for something inside his briefcase, which is on top of the table).*

Please, fear me not!

By my judgement - and this is a very personal point of view, nowadays, I think - one of the best, healthiest options is to… work with Shakespeare. Shakespeare - big chief! He always makes us touch deep into our human condition. Please, be attentive of how it touches you *(indicating the **RESEARCHER**).*

RESEARCHER: *(playing a scene from* Hamlet*).*

Now I am alone.

O, what a rogue and peasant slave am I!

Is it not monstrous that this player here,

[…] Could force his soul so […]

That from her working all his visage

wann'd;

Tears in his eyes, distraction in's aspect,

A broken voice […]

[…] And all for

nothing!

For Hecuba!

What's Hecuba to him or he to Hecuba,

That he should weep for her? What would

he do,

Had he the motive and the cue for passion

That I have? He would drown the stage

with tears, […]

Make mad the guilty, and appal the free […]

Yet I, […]

> [...] the son of a dear father murder'd,
> Prompted to my revenge by heaven and hell,
> Must, like a whore, unpack my heart with words, [...]
> [...] Fie upon't! foh!
> About, my brains. Hum – [...]
> [...] I'll have these players
> Play something like the murder of my father
> Before mine uncle. I'll observe his looks;
> I'll tent him to the quick. If 'a do blench,
> I know my course [...]
> [...] The play's the thing
> Wherein I'll catch the conscience of the King. (*Hamlet*, II.ii, 542 - 601)

MAESTRO: 'Wherein I'll catch the conscience of the King'… where I will catch my own conscience… Working with Shakespeare, we will never stop learning about ourselves. So, what do you say if we share now with these actors the scene where Hamlet gives instructions to the gang of actors? But now, for fun… in Spanish.

RESEARCHER: In Spanish?

MAESTRO: Harsh, isn't it? But… you can because you believe you can.

RESEARCHER: Ok, 'my heart is a bird that flies'.

(*The **RESEARCHER** plays the scene among the audience*).

> Te ruego que recites el pasaje
> tal y como lo he declamado yo, con

soltura y naturalidad, pues si lo haces
a voz en grito, como acostumbran muchos
de vuestros actores, valdría más
que diera mis versos a que los voceara
el pregonero. Guárdate también de aserrar demasiado el aire, así, con la mano. Moderación en todo, pues hasta en
medio del mismo torrente, tempestad y
aún podría decir torbellino de tu pasión,
debes tener y mostrar aquella templanza que hace suave y elegante la expresión. No seas tampoco demasiado tímido;
en esto tu propia discreción debe guiarte.
Que la acción responda a la palabra
Y la palabra a la acción, poniendo un especial
cuidado en no traspasar los límite de la sencillez de la naturaleza, porque todo lo que a
ella se opone se aparta igualmente del
propio fin del arte dramático,
cuyo objeto, ha sido y es
presentar un espejo a la humanidad;
mostrar a la virtud sus propios rasgos,
al vicio su verdadera imagen y a cada
edad y generación su fisonomía y sello
característico. Y no permitáis que los que
hacen de graciosos ejecuten más de lo
que se les esté indicado, porque algunos
de ellos empiezan a dar risotadas para
hacer reir a unos cuantos espectadores
imbéciles, aún cuando en aquel preciso
momento algún punto esencial de la pieza

reclame la atención. Esto es indigno, y
revela en los insensatos que lo practican
la más estúpida pretensión.
Id a preparaos[50].

MAESTRO: Thank you, dear; that was very good. (*To the audience*) Sorry, you don't speak very good Spanish? Don't worry, I don't speak very good English, either.

I think that now it might be a very good time to tell our friends what it is exactly that you are investigating here in Mexico.

RESEARCHER: Well, I am currently investigating methods used in Tenochtitlan for the transformation of the actor.

MAESTRO: As you might know, she *[indicating the **RESEARCHER**]* is doing a trandisciplinary investigation, looking for the internal and external connections between different practices which suggest that everything in the universe is interconnected and, also, in a state of constant transformation.

Transdisciplinarity is a part of quantum theory, and it is through this interconnectedness that we can begin to recognise our own lineage as actors, which is based in a profound connection with the forces of nature; that is to say, we belong to the lineage of the God Pan who, incidentally, suffered in the flesh, through the offices of the Holy Mother Catholic Church, so that his image was transformed into a symbol of the infernal beast, the devil himself, *el diablo*, his religion forbidden and persecuted and his heirs, the actors, that gang of whores and bastards, demonized by excommunion, a label which still today hangs over our head. But anyway, that's another story. We, the actors, are still standing, and continue doing our job of communication, because, essentially, the actor is a communicator. Of course, there are different types of communicators, sacred and...

---

50 An archaic expression in Spanish, meaning 'Go to prepare yourself'.

*(To the **RESEARCHER**)* Would you please help me? Could you respond, through movement, to what I'm saying?

*(The **RESEARCHER** nods, stands up and takes off her shoes. She follows the **MAESTRO'S** speech with bodily expression. The **MAESTRO** writes on the blackboard: 'GOLD' - 'LEAD').*

MAESTRO: When you give a lead actor 100%, he only transmits 30%, and he swallows 70%; he is a lousy conductor! On the other hand, you have the golden actor, he is given 100% and he delivers 100%; he is an excellent transmitter. Are they different? Of course, one transmits 30 out of 100 and the other 100 out of a 100. Nevertheless, scientists tell us that the material composition of lead and gold is the same, the only difference that exists - and this is an important point for us - is molecular speed; lead has a low molecular speed and gold has a very high one. Hence, we define our techniques for actor training as 'molecular accelerators'. When people realize that our theatre pedagogy is based on molecular acceleration, usually there is a lack of understanding and resistance to this view; the transmutation of lead into gold is perceived as impossible. However, this process of transformation is an ongoing battle in the training of the actor and nobody notices that this is the very same transformation which is sought for in Nahuatl and Buddhist wisdom.

That is to say, what is sought for is the transformation of an ordinary human mind into an awakened mind: that is the work of the actor! This is the correct attitude! This transformation is a powerful work and we inherited this lineage from those who served, with passion, the tradition of theatre.

And there's more for us - reading carefully, we can learn from people like Mircea Eliade, Joseph Campbell, James Frazer, Victor Turner, Arnold Toynbee, among others, that the theatre is the oldest religion of humanity.

To understand this well we will share with you a map which we have followed and worked on for years. Could you please continue helping me, but, please, now let your hair down... flow...

*(The **MAESTRO** erases the writing on the blackboard and writes: 'ENERGY').*

MAESTRO: In the beginning, say 'those who know', the universe was an ocean of undifferentiated energy, which manifested itself as a runaway river, on whose banks the human being was born and performed acts of gratitude and appreciation. These acts of gratitude and appreciation prefigure, and end up initiating, the appearance of the rite.

*(The **MAESTRO** draws, below the word 'ENERGY', an undulating wave, below which, he writes 'Rite').*

Rite/river - the first religion of humanity, which manifested in a seriously theatrical form, served as a structure to celebrate the flow of the Universe. At this stage, the stories of our origins begin to appear: the Bible, the Popol Vuh, the Kalevala and many others.

This rite or rites - because they appear all over the planet, slowly and gently, in very different ways, depending on time and space - bring forth the myth.

Now it is no longer just a celebration and recognition of pure energy; it becomes a celebration of energy manifested as deities, with specific characteristics defined by the group who perceives and constructs them. To some it would be Zeus, to others Wotan, and others still, Quetzalcoatl. In Tenochtitlan, you might know, we are in the domain of the left-handed Hummingbird.

*(The **MAESTRO** writes below 'Rite', the word 'Myth').*

And so, here, the stories and adventures of the gods begin to appear, and ritual and myth intertwine, making a maze like a network of divine relationships that no one really understands ...

And to make these energies, in our reality, more comprehensible to us, we create the epic stage.

*(The **MAESTRO** writes below 'Myth', the word 'Epic').*

At this point, the sagas, the epic adventures and stories of heroes appear; their battles, their victories and decadence ...

And, finally, theatre appears.

*(The **MAESTRO** writes the word 'Theatre' below ENERGY - Rite - Myth - Epic).*

Here, the passions and desires of ordinary women and men are presented and considered: the wonderful array of lights and shadows of our human condition; our fears, anxieties, pains and jealousy.

All the emotional upheaval that characterizes us is portrayed here, and we are not conscious that this is the lowest level of the original energy. And here we all are, and anyone who says he's not, is lying. And because we are so confused, we are always asking Who am I?, What is this all about? What is important in life? We make a labyrinth of psychological, ideological, political, farcical, tragic, comical, intellectual and pornographic theatre.

RESEARCHER: But also sacred theatre - holy theatre.

MAESTRO: Yes, also sacred actions through theatre. This (*pointing to the diagram on the blackboard*) is the historiographical journey of the oldest religion of humanity and also - at this point - the most prostituted: theatre.

However, it is important to remember that there exists a theatrical lineage which remains connected to the Source. It has survived, and appears, from time to time, in different places - usually in small, isolated and ignored groups, without almost anyone noticing. They move like a sacred gang, and I wonder, what could the purpose of this gang be?

RESEARCHER: To overcome the inertia and restore to the human being, through theatre, her original function.

MAESTRO: Which is?

RESEARCHER: To align us with the Universe.

MAESTRO: But how?

RESEARCHER: From any doorway which theatre might offer to open, in this very moment, I think it is possible to return to our origins. Like they say in Tenochtitlan - Turn our gaze to the sun.

MAESTRO: Turn our gaze to the sun… Saying that, you shine beautifully.

RESEARCHER: But do not stare at me, lest you fall into the abyss I have become!

MAESTRO: Fall into the abyss which you've become ... falling into the abyss which I myself have become... into the abyss which each of us have become.

And there we are, wallowing in the filthy sewer in which our distorted perceptions move...[51]

However, there is still hope. Theatre, in its immense generosity, gives us all a gateway through which to become conscious of our own abyss; to ferociously recognize it and move beyond it. Theatre gives us the chance to reclaim ourselves and, if we achieve the energy level required, we may raise our status from humans to the epic level, and become heroes of our own adventure.

And if we want to move forward still more, we raise our energy once again to reach the mythical level and we become our own gods, and if there is some energy still, we can leap, like solar salmons, to reach the point where we are able to make our own personal rite. Can we do this?

RESEARCHER: 'I can do it, because I believe I can do it'.

MAESTRO: To do this, through theatre, is to make your heart fly, and that is a sacred art. And the way society is today, this art is not at all profitable.

RESEARCHER: But Maestro, theatre, as a cultural product, has to be profitable and make money, because if it doesn't, you can't live off it.

MAESTRO: Really, you think that?

RESEARCHER: You can't live off the cosmic banana!

MAESTRO: My Dear, that hurts… So, if it is not profitable it has no right to exist.

RESEARCHER: I think it would be very very difficult for it to survive.

MAESTRO: What are you looking for, Dear, Hollywood?

RESEARCHER: Why not?

MAESTRO: Is there something there for people like us?

---

51   A reference to Pierre Klossowski's *Roberte ce soir* (1953).

RESEARCHER: Sometimes.

MAESTRO: You are right - sometimes…

RESEARCHER: … would you allow me…

MAESTRO: Please do.

RESEARCHER: I find it is very easy to forget about proper self-defence. And I'm not talking about martial arts or anything like that; I'm talking about the artist's self-defence against certain politicians, economists, governors and businessmen who use terms such as budgets, overall cost, sales and profit margins, as if that was the purpose of theatre. As we all know, when there are funding cuts, the first thing that is left out is culture. The idea that a nice pair of shoes is better than a good book is outrageous. And so, I ask you, when did you last read Aristotle's *Poetics*? You have read it, right? If one really wants to do theatre, we have to read the *Poetics* of ancient Greece, the *Toltecáyotl* of the Nahuas, because these texts define and justify artistic activity as part of our basic nourishment necessary for our healthy development. Obviously there exist artistic activities that may not be profitable but are essential tools for us to become mature human beings. Why? Because theatre, and art, almost always predicts, senses, sometimes defines very accurately, the most subtle social and spiritual changes taking place. In theatre's interiors our future belief system is prepared and this is invaluable, priceless, it cannot be measured in money or gold. This is why it is necessary to learn proper self-defence… May I?

MAESTRO: Of course…

*(The **RESEARCHER** hangs a sign from the blackboard, which says: 'We will be called enemies of morality, but we will only be inventors of our selves' Nietzsche).*

MAESTRO: The thing is - (although it might be out of our reach, I think it is good to mention it) - here, we are talking about the actor and acting with a capital A. The actor sought after by Artaud, Grotowski, Brecht, and, in Mexico, several great masters such as Mendoza, Azar, Gurrola, Valencia,

Darien ... And right here, in this space, now, it is possible that there are among us some who have the necessity and the need to re-invent themselves, to reach the point where 'nothing which is human is alien to us'.

RESEARCHER: If we understand and apply what the Maestro is telling us, we will be using theatre as a vehicle to reconcile our differences - a vehicle of transportation and transformation which allows for the appearance of a cosmic consciousness. (*To the **MAESTRO***) And it is a practical way, right? It is a question of doing....

MAESTRO: Yes, and rather than trying to explain this, if you agree, we will try, practically, to touch this register.

(*To the audience*) We are going to do an exercise of sensitization, including physical contact with our partners, and non-rational communication, ok? Please, let us self-observe, and note which is the nucleus of energy with which we came here today. You may be here with your partner, a friend, an acquaintance, or maybe you came here alone. These relationships interweave as a nucleus - a core of energy. Now, please, consciously, move away and detach from this core. Consciously separate yourself, and look for a place in the space where you are by yourself.

I ask you to play fairly - really do the exercise. We need to open up, be really willing to live this process.

So, I move to an area where I am by myself. (*The audience stand up and spread out in the space*).

There, I look at my hands - the palms of my hands. These are mine. And slowly I raise them to my face, closing my eyes, and touch my face, I observe myself, I touch my head, I touch my chest, my belly, my back, my arms, my legs, my knees, my feet, and I become aware of the fact that I am physically here and now.

I am attentive to my interior. All stimuli I receive from outside awakens personal processes. If someone touches my hand, it is not important to find out to whom that particular hand belongs; it is more important to observe the image, emotions or feelings that that touch awakens within me.

We will cross a space and time, encountering some of the worlds which are within us.

I'm in a group, and I'm safe behind closed doors. I feel the group, but I am aware of myself. I don't make any judgement about the people by my side. I do not know them. I have no idea who they are. I just know that, right now, they are other human beings committed to doing an exercise so as to look inside themselves, and being here together we may help each other to look inside ourselves and so, they are accomplices with good faith.

Please do not open your eyes until I ask you to. Have no temptation to look outwards. Focus on looking inward.

Touching the entire body until we reach the feet and when there, feel how, out of your feet, you grow roots into the ground.

With good faith, kindly start moving in different directions; waving your body like seaweed.

(Silence)

> But love, [is] first learned in a lady's eyes [...]
> They sparkle still the right Promethean fire;
> They are the books, the arts, the academes,
> That show, contain and nourish all the world,
> Else none at all in ought proves excellent. (*Love's Labour Lost*, IV, iii, 323-350)

(Silence)

Let's make a circle.

(The audience sits, forming a circle. The paper with the signature of the spectators and the candle are in the centre).

We are converted into that which we contemplate.

(Silence).

RESEARCHER:

> …and it is not known, if before or after his death,
> He looked into a mirror facing god,
> And god told him,
> 'never stop being an actor,
> Because just as me, you are everything and nothing.
> And through your dreams Shakespeare exists.
> And so do I.[52]

*(The **RESEARCHER** picks up the lit candle and the page of signatures from the centre of the circle. She gives them to the **MAESTRO**. The **MAESTRO** stands up and together they go towards the blackboard which has transformed into a mirror. They look at each other; both touch the mirror. Darkness. In the darkness, we listen to the sound of the mirror shattering. Immediately afterwards, the lights come up to reveal that the mirror has disappeared and the **MAESTRO** and the **RESEARCHER** are on the other side of the threshold).*

MAESTRO: *(To the **RESEARCHER**)* 'I have crossed oceans of time to find you…'[53]

RESEARCHER: *(Looking at the audience)* We have crossed oceans of time to find you…

They walk to the back of the stage. With the candle, the RESEARCHER sets fire to the paper with the audience's signatures, and puts it inside a bowl until it is consumed. Music. The **MAESTRO** and the **RESEARCHER** dance for some seconds. Darkness.

END

---

52 From the poem 'The Actor' by Jorge Luis Borges, in *Poesía completa* (2009).

53 A reference to Bram Stoker's *Dracula*.

THEATRE AS A SECRET SOURCE[54]
Nicolás Núñez

'True culture makes life bloom'
(Antonin Artaud, 1976: 32)

What I am about to tell you is very personal. It is the reflection of a spirit in a state of emergency who grabbed onto theatre in order not to tumble into the depths of desperation to which the distorted values of this modern society have driven us.

The truth is that all of us on this planet, today, are consigned to survive in the time of the assassins.

My name is Nicolás Núñez, and for more than fifty years, I've been working in theatre research in my country - the land of the sun, tequila and mariachi. As Mexicans we are aware that our bandit lineage is what defines us to the world. Some of us burgle gold, others steal hearts, and some others, through art, attempt to take light by assault.

The context of my work is the relationship between ancient traditions and the sacred origins of theatre. Throughout the years, we have designed tools to raise our energy and cultivate attention in order to look towards the Sun; like *Citlalmina*, for example - a sacred Mexican-Tibetan dance for training actors, authorized by His Holiness the Dalai Lama and the General Teresa from the Mexican conchero tradition, or *Slow Walking* and *Contemplative Running* which were developed in the Polish woods, guided by the hand of Maestro Grotowski. These tools, together with our twenty-four psychophysical dynamics[55] – all of them meditation-in-movement techniques – form the training method of the *Taller de Investigación Teatral*.

---

54 A key-note address given at the International Symposium of Performance and Mindfulness at the University of Huddersfield, June 2016. Translated by Helena Guardia.

55 See discussion of the number of dynamics on pp. 225 - 227.

Our teachers have been Shakespeare, Krishnamurti, Gurdjieff, Grotowski, Artaud; also the Náhuatl, the Buddhist, Contemplative and Sufi traditions, as well as the teachings from Quetzalcóatl, and whatever we can understand from Einstein's intuitions. In Van Gogh's paintings we have felt the rhythm of the universe, and we have tried to be moved by this rhythm.

For us it has been of vital importance to be passionately faithful to our research; as Joseph Campbell said, to 'follow our bliss' (remember?); and to realize, thanks to Mircea Eliade, that theatre is the most ancient religion of humanity.

Anthropocosmic theatre, which started in 1975, comes face to face in this Symposium, with the search for 'mindfulness' in the West; a search which, for us, has been informed by people like Jon Kabat-Zinn, in the field of health; by Lee Worley, Meredith Monk, and Marina Abramovic, among many others, in the field of performance; and also by scientists such as Basarab Nicolescu, and his proposition of 'transdisciplinary cosmic verticality'. All of them have enriched our experience and work.

We are very grateful for this opportunity to share with you our reflections:

What is the real meaning of culture, of public health? What is the purpose of theatre?

But do not take too seriously what I'm going to say. Remember, I'm just a Mexican bandito!

From my very personal point of view, the ideas of culture, health, justice, equity, social and political organization have been, in this global society, completely misunderstood and - I think intentionally and wickedly - twisted.

It is clear to us, for example, that commercial medical care and cultural structures dance, amidst grimaces of mutual satisfaction, to the rhythm of the clinking coins. They happily sell their consciousness to the highest bidder, and everything, as the poet says, in exchange for a few 'copper coins and abstract shit' (Octavio Paz, 1957/1988). There are no more ethics; only convenience.

Imagine - the system tells us that to be healthy means, essentially, to be able to 'work' for the system's benefit. Of course! Astonishing! What a terrible thing to say! Breton's howling was not enough. His shout, through Nadja's voice, warning us that we will never find the real meaning of life through conventional 'work', has not yet been heard. If we have to accept it as a burden - so be it. But to glorify it and pretend that this is the way life is? In the words of Octavio Paz - 'Better to be stoned... than to circle the grinding wheel that squeezes the substance of life, turns eternity into empty hours, minutes into prisons, and time into copper coins and abstract shit' (1957/1988).

Should we be healthy and fit merely in order to work like this? For God's sake! We shall be healthy and fit when we assert our right to do our *good* work, the work that celebrates life and makes us upright human beings!

Who or what has misled us?

Some clinical doctors and scientists, nowadays, pretend to play the role of religious leaders, enthroning themselves as the new prophets of the system, when it is clear that their real purpose is to serve only as mere adjusters of the public health, fine-tuning the big machine.

We ask ourselves: what is happiness in an enslaved society? To cherish the chains and bars of our captivity? To cheerfully lick our handcuffs?

We have novel and playful technology, disguised as evolution that makes our work easier, that gives access to information and communication, and besides all that, is fun! True, it works well, very well! But it also distracts us and makes us lethargic. We have become fans of this highly addictive media drug, which truly weakens us by increasing our frailty as we face the greedy beast inside ourselves, whose sole aspiration in life is to 'become someone' in this nonsensical society. Pure ego!

The serpent fooled us again and, once more, we did bite the forbidden fruit – take notice of the logo: we have gladly bitten the apple, and its electronic poison already flows in our blood.

We suspect that most of our cultural, political and medical systems play, wickedly and arrogantly, their role of watchdogs and nannies of this society, *intentionally* keeping us fearful, superficial and handicapped.

Mario Vargas Llosa, in his book *Notes on the Death of Culture* (2015), makes clear the difference between the consumerist culture, the snob culture, and the high culture. High culture helps us to grow, to mature and to free our mind. Is this system collaborating with it? Or quite the contrary? The system is promoting a pseudo-culture which cloys and distracts us from the real meaning of life, selling us the idea that true happiness means only to be a winner, secure and comfortable - making us drowsy and violent.

And if you have some secret needs of any kind, the system advises: you better satisfy them under cover, for your scandal might awake our happy slaves.

To behave hypocritically, and to master a double moral is, they teach us, to know how to do things well. And that is the cheating ethic of our time, to trick the truth; the way, according to them, to happiness and success. We are facing the victory of the elegant crooks.

But let's clear things up a little bit: the real purpose of high culture is to be a tool for conscious evolution.

In this sense, which is our role as theatre workers? What kind of fuel do we offer society? Do we give them sweets - pure entertainment and show? Or do we nourish them - offering a space and a time, auspicious for going within to question and reflect upon themselves, upon life?

As you might know, a human being can live without food, but with water, for about forty days. Without water, we cannot resist more than two or three days. Without air we cannot live for more than four or five minutes. But, without mental impressions, human beings cannot be alive for more than four seconds.

We could say, then, that the subtlest nourishment for a person is mental impressions. We are receiving them all the time.

And theatre, as you know, is a source of impressions, an essential fuel for our health which should be considered, together with all the fine arts, as part of the basic food basket.

But let's be careful in the creation of impressions, for we must distinguish between fission impressions - impressions that break apart - and fusion impressions - impressions that create unity.

Both of them generate energy, but in a totally different way: fission breaks, fusion connects. Fission produces a feeling of isolation and, therefore, fear. Fusion, instead, brings about a feeling of unity. Fission is cold, frigid; fusion is warm and cosy.

In any human activity, by breaking and isolating, fission stimulates selfishness and fosters negative emotions. It hurts, causing suffering and resentment. It tears apart our social fabric, dividing us, making us the prey of hate, victims of a nihilistic and fearful wandering inside a labyrinth leading nowhere. Fission drowns us in non-edifying actions that stimulate a hyper-consumerism in order to mitigate the anguish of being alive, but which never really satisfy us.

A series of fission impressions, metaphysically speaking, turn us into zombies, who behave only 'by the book', blindly following rules and regulations which nullify human criteria, and create many other distortions: irrational violence, nihilism.

Instead of that, we are interested in a culture of fusion - in a theatre that re-connects and opens the way back to our true entanglement: an anthropocosmic, 'transdisciplinary', 'mindful' theatre.

The 'transdisciplinarity' proposed by the quantum scientist, Basarab Nicolescu (2002), is a contemporary scientific model that, in its research, takes into consideration the deep meaning of the flow of life, which is nothing more and nothing less than the consciousness of the transience of life, of the fact that we are here… just for a while, as the Nahuatl poem reminds us: '*sólo un rato aquí*' ['only here for a while'].

Free transit in our thought, speech and action, with no fear, with no other commitment than to honour the authentic hierarchy that rules the universe: that is 'cosmic verticality'.

'Cosmic verticality' is the awareness of a higher consciousness: it is the ladder that 'transports and transforms' you, the dawn of mystery. In it, the natural hierarchies flow freely in a very fortunate way, through the ritual structure which, as Richard Schechner said, 'transports and transforms' (1985: p.3 - 33).

Our theatre research adopts Schechner's premise of transporting the spectator through different external and internal scenarios, knowing that the impressions they might receive during this physical transportation will, hopefully, trigger in them an inner transformation, provided they live the process with 'mindfulness'.

'Mindfulness', this millenarian technique, now naked of all its cultural attachments, alive only in its virtuous innocence is a mental tool to raise the attention. It leads to a secular sacredness that today allows us to change our perception, to be aware of the speed and beat of this universal loving and gentle dance. Because this [indicating the Earth] is moving. The existence of the gravitational waves, as predicted by Einstein a hundred years ago, has just been certified.

Do you know at how many kilometers per second we are spiralling, in a vortex motion, around the sun, at this very moment? At 30 kilometres per second. In addition to that, the sun is spiralling around the galaxy's centre at 200 kilometres per second, and, on top of that, this galaxy is moving throughout the universe at 600 kilometres per second.

This means that we began this lecture thousands of kilometres ago and, in spite of that, the perception of many might be that nothing has happened here. However, without doing anything (pause), we are moving (pause), and fast!

Perception defines reality and builds our belief system. Once triggered, this system of beliefs is crystallised in a 'specific perspective of reality'. Right now, humanity is changing its paradigm, and we are about to understand reality more clearly. As Gorostiza, the Mexican poet says, life 'is a runaway dream looking at itself at full speed.'[56]

And to become conscious of this runaway dream means the acceptance of a constant transformation. But do we know how far this transformation can take us? Maybe to the point of listening to the angels' call, to the mermaids' song, or to the music of the spheres, the gravitational waves?

---

56 From the poem, *'Muerte sin fin'* [Death without end] by José Gorostiza (Gorostiza, 2002).

'The rest is silence' (*Hamlet*, 5.2. 350).

It is known that sound travels at 343 metres per second.

If I tell you, Wake up! and you are more than 343 metres away, my voice will reach you one second later.

Awake! Even if my cry were loud enough to be heard at one thousand metres away, my voice would be heard 3 seconds later.

Now, if I told you, Awake! at the speed of light, which travels three hundred thousand kilometres per second, and if you were one million kilometres away, you would receive my signal three seconds later, because the speed of light loses one second every three hundred thousand kilometres.

But - surprise! The mental synapses make an instantaneous connection through the whole universe. Thought is the fastest and most powerful form of communication.

For this reason, and since the actor is a communicator, he or she has to know how to control the mind, because acting, at its bottom line, is learning to ride the wild horse of our mental wind.

McLuhan says that 'we are what we behold' ([1964] 2003:21). To mentally contemplate something, to sense it, either through an image, a sound, a feeling or a smell, mindfully, is to create it, and that goes hand in hand with Stanislavki's 'as if'.

Have I ever thought or felt myself to be the universe?

As actors, we need to educate and refine our mind with such precision that our thoughts become capable of transforming theatre, by *mimesis*, into a source of cosmic resonances.

I ask myself if it is possible for an actor on the stage, who thinks and feels themselves to be the universe, to expand consciousness to such an extent that we can perceive this universe through her or him. What do you think? Do you think it is possible? The truth is: yes.

In fact, we *are* universe. What prevents us from living this truth is only our rational, emotional trash - pure egocentricity and useless garbage. That's why when I see an actor on the stage, taking his place in the universe, when I see him present in the living moment, I am able to perceive that fullness, the vortex of reality shining. Yes, there is no doubt, when an actor touches this level, by mimesis, he or she reveals to me the cosmos that I am.

In which school are actors and, ultimately, human beings, educated to remember that 'we are universe'?

There is no more Eleusis; no more enrooted theatre; each time it is more difficult, in any artistic manifestation, to find our way back to the Source.

In the field of the performative arts, we have to insist on this because this is our way to health, to joy, to dancing the dance that dances and sings through us.

If we lose the beat of the universal rhythm, we bump and fall, disoriented and feeble. But if we go with its rhythm, its exhilarating enthusiasm intoxicates and enchants us. In that intense joy resides true health. So we can say that the poetic invitation to a cosmic stage is as important as penicilin.

Those who know say that through art you can recognize the authentic health of a nation. The roots of art in ancient México were engaged with cosmic principles - Tezcatlipoca's mirror, for instance; the mirror of consciousness and inner growth.

This mirror allows us to intertwine our actions with the fibres of the universe, and the cosmic lattice is reflected in our eyes.

Can we look into each other's eyes, please? [The audience look into each other's eyes during what follows].

In order to reach our best level, first we need to acknowledge what is wrong in us. We need to realize, for example, that we are domesticated by the fear of being ill, of having no money, no certainty or solidarity; we fear that we will not be recognized, and we feel insecure, rejected. The lack of sense in life attacks us; we become violent and nihilism might appear.

During his last days, Octavio Paz said, 'from Babylon to this day, there is no sense, there is only the search for sense' (Domínguez Michael, 2014: 564).

Today we need to help each other in this search for sense, to recover our full and total action, with all its meaning, its basic goodness, strength and color. We must get back our power to live and die flying in the feast of life.

Close your eyes, please. Get comfortable in your seat.

Inhale, exhale.

And ask yourselves:

Who am I? Truly, who am I? [Pause for reflection]

There is, indeed, a theatre that is a secret source. A transformative theatre based on 'cosmic verticality', whose axis lies on its universal ethics. A theatre that creates events as emergency spaces in which to breath, counteracting the suffocation wickedly produced all around us. Events as platforms to refine ourselves, to transcend our anger, our fear, our frustration and resentment; that bring us closer to our true self, to our sanity, to our innocence and contentment, in order to share with others 'the forgotten wonder of being alive' (Paz, 1957/1988).

Inhale, exhale.

Slowly, please, open your eyes.

I want to thank each and everyone of you for being here, at this very moment.

REFERENCES

Artaud, Artaud ([1971] 1976) *Mensajes revolucionarios*. Editorial Fundamentos.

Domínguez Michael, Christopher (2014) *Octavio Paz en su siglo*. Mexico City: Santillana Ediciones Generales.

Gorostiza, José (2002) *Death without End*. Random House Mondadori, Barcelona.

McLuhan, Marshall & Gordon, W.T. ([1964] 2003) *Understanding Media: the extensions of man*. Corte Madera, CA: Critical edn, Gingko Press.

Nicolescu, Basarab (2002) *Manifesto of Transdisciplinarity*. (Trans. Karen-Claire Voss). Buffalo, New York: SUNY Press

Paz, Octavio (1957) *Piedra de Sol*. Mexico City: Texontle.

Paz, Octavio (1988) *The Collected Poems*. (Ed, Trans. Eliot Weinberger). Manchester: Carcanet.

Schechner, Richard (1985) *Between Theater and Anthropology*. Philadelphia: University of Pennsylvania Press.

Vargas Llosa, Mario (2015) *Notes on the Death of Culture*. London: Faber & Faber.

CASE STUDY: PUENTES INVISIBLES – CHAPULTEPEC FOREST, MEXICO (2016)
Cash Clay

Puentes Invisibles was a contemplative, participatory performance, with text by Deborah Templeton, which took place in Chapultepec forest in Mexico City during November of 2016. Templeton had been commissioned by Núñez to write the story of the creation of the dynamic, *Citlalmina*, as it is described in Part One of this book.

The performance text depicts a fictional seeker - an old man who wandered the world and has a story to tell,

> I have wandered the four corners and the seven seas and seen the 10,000 things on a thousand shores. I have gone deep into the dark interiors of distant lands and climbed, with my breath thin, to the high peaks of the world's holy places. And I have a story for you; a story of bridges and dances and things sought and things found (Templeton, 2016).

In the performance, members of the audience are guided on a contemplative journey of their own, led by the old man, his 'vagabond gang' and the storyteller. The following account is based on my participation in *Puentes Invisibles* as a performer, and includes short personal reflections based on my rehearsal notes.

> *This is a personal journey and Nicolás is my guide. In my role as a performer in* Puentes Invisibles, *I know that I will have to share this journey with strangers at the end of the training and rehearsal process. I am always aware, during this process that I will act as a guide for travellers I don't yet know. We will create and cross bridges and meet one another with all our guards dropped.*

After gathering in a circle on the edge of Chapultepec Forest, the audience are given instructions for the performance and we (audience and performers) form a serpent and begin walking backwards, slowly, towards the centre of the forest. Helena Guardia leads us as we embark on our journey.

The first stage of this journey takes us across a stall-lined pedestrian street that cuts through the park. Next we cross a bridge where we pause and contemplate. The bridge marks the threshold, the spot where park becomes forest – a shift from the everyday world into the world of the performance. The world of the unknown.

> *It seems that each day, as Helena leads us into the sacred forest of Chapultepec, I cross invisible bridges. I am making a many-layered journey from the brash, neon boulevard of materialism on the edge of the forest into the natural world where I share my roots with trees and land and human beings. The bridges appear at moments when I am disarmed - in those split seconds when I abandon myself to the forest.*

We continue to travel, facing forwards now, as a serpent – moving into the deeper forest. We stop at a few contemplative sites and Helena snakes us through the trees. The serpent twists and doubles back on itself so that the audience encounter each other, connecting with humans as well as with trees and earth and sky.

> *As we are led into cool roots and canopies, I am jolted out of everyday sensations. I am forced to open all my senses. When I walk backwards, I stop relying on my sight and feel my way through the soles of my feet on the earth and the tips of my fingers in the air and I forget myself. Bridges appear and I can cross them to enter woodlands of my past and others' pasts.*

As we enter the space in the forest where the old man's story will be told, we gather the audience around a tree whose roots protrude from the earth. I have been chosen to model for the audience a way to make contact with the tree. I physically contact the tree`s roots and trunk and speak about my personal connection. The audience are then invited to find their own tree nearby and make their own physical and personal connection with that tree.

After some time, a bell rings and the audience and performers form a circle in a forest clearing. It is here that we begin to tell the story of the old man and his wanderings, a story of connections between Mexico and Tibet and a story of human connection. We take the audience through actions, contemplations and dances as the story unfolds. In one moment, another performer and I create the image of lovers who meet on a bridge at night.

> *My bare feet, in the cool forest dirt, begin to form a bridge. I cross it and journey into roots and rock of ancestors and beginnings. Looking up into early morning sunlight, another bridge appears and I am connected to the planetary world above. Staring into the eyes of my imagined lover, I cross imagined bridges for all the world's lovers.*
>
> *Vibrations of voice, hompak and bone trumpet[57] wake me up and my cells dance inside me and vibrate with the forest floor and the trunks of trees.*

We instruct the audience to close their eyes and we place our hands lightly on their chests whispering a few lines of text to them individually. Then there is stillness before a trumpet begins to play and performers and audience begin a whirling dance. Finally we all come back together in a circle, as we began our journey, and stand connected for a few moments. The journey is over and we return from the fictional world of the old man, back to the forest clearing.

> *In moments of stillness, I feel the movement of the earth respond to me. In moments of movement, I feel the stillness of my core respond to the earth. Movement and stillness bridge the gap that has formed, over many years, between us.*

---

57 The hompak is a Mayan wind instrument, similar to a didgeridoo, made from the agave plant; the bone trumpet is a Tibetan wind instrument, made from a human femur, used in Tibetan Buddhist rituals.

ANTHROPOCOSMIC THEATRE

SNAPSHOT: EL ENSUEÑO DE LOS ÁRBOLES - A REFLECTION
Ana Luisa Solís

[*El Ensueño de los árboles* was created in an intensive artistic residency in the remote Panamanian jungle village of Armila in the indigenous *comarca* of Guna Yala in June 2017, and premiered in Chapultepec, Mexico City in July 2017. The production took the form of a guided contemplative forest experience, incorporating key sensitization tools of the *Taller*, a central ritual action and poetic text. DM]

Daybreak - it is 7 in the morning and in the humidity and mud left by the night rain, the light is coming, and *El Ensueño de los árboles* (*The Dreaming of Trees*) begins in the sacred forest of Chapultepec.

We are kindly and delicately summoned by a group of actors to a theatrical, ecological tour through the forest.

With the instruction to keep silent and to open our eyes to the green space, we begin to walk paths among roots and trees... silence in the heart and an extended gaze to the whole landscape... attentive, attentive, attentive...

Deeply breathing the green freshness of the early morning, my wild look goes from top to bottom... A wet silence is fertilized by our Intent, inviting us to walk through the soft mud, contacting the shape and the magical, misty atmosphere of the trunks, branches and leaves pierced by thresholds of light. Breathing becomes such that it allows us to be suspended... A cool drop of fresh dew falls on my eye; 'Wake up', it says. But I do not want to wake up; it's a little cold and the path invites me to keep floating in a slow walk.

Once a teacher from India named Babaji said 'We are beings of the Forest'. I remember this and, through that memory, I enter into the experience.

The forest sings and the trees look at us with eyes of water, of hearts, of snakes - with arms extended towards the Earth and Heaven - deep eyes through which I let myself go towards I know not where... Tree eyes... I sigh.

I am attentive to the fresh moment that renews the gaze and the breath. That moment contains everything and there is no word or thought that collapses it.

The body and mind become a delicate antenna that connects the sky with the roots in the Land of Trees. The hands simulate branches and extensions of the landscape, dancing in gratitude.

Everything fits together as we look at the timeless forest; its green jade injecting and healing me - reminding me that we are One in stillness, in calm, freeing ourselves and integrated with everyone.

Embracing the tree, I listen to the shaman's song and the tree sings and sings my heart and we all sing... a litany of wholeness and forgiveness is sent to heaven... *'Find the face you had before the world was made'*[58]. Looking inside, eyes closed, I enter the joyful universe of geometry, colors, light and movement. Joy, pure joy, that is my face before I was born.

I listen to myself telling me 'there are more senses in your body and mind than you imagine'... I discover new senses.

I hover and become space, light, geometry, tree! In this dream we become a tribe, rediscovering the origin of something that perhaps is called Love.

I want to cry with the trees; a weeping offering or a song of forgiveness that helps them to endure and to continue sheltering us... A song cried with joy.

Our breath of grateful audience communing with them.

Someone brought *baraca* [blessing] from the Guna community; yes, they managed to receive and bring back that offering through this dream. They wove themselves in the loom of the same Intent, in the loom of the shaman's song, with the jungle and the forest who are always our brethren.

I celebrate the shared adventure and I thank this tribe of dreamers; thank you for opening your hearts to this dreamlike, ecological, sacred theatre and for sharing it from your own dream...

---

58 This line, quoted from the performance, is a reference to the W.B. Yeats poem, 'Before the World was Made' (in W.B. Yeats (1929) *The Winding Stair*. New York: Fountain Press).

COSMIC MANNERS[59]
Nicolás Núñez

I am going to describe the current state of affairs as I see it, and then offer an alternative perspective, or approach, that arises out of my work in theatre pedagogy, and that offers a model, vision or ideal for actors. I will share it with you. Thank for your patience and attention. You know… I am only a Mexican bandito.

Western civilization is a civilization of spoiled brats. The petulant and arrogant rationalist stance has ended up driving us away from the truth. And now, we are suffocating.

To seek truth exclusively with the eyes of reason is to sink more and more into the meaninglessness of life. For life cannot be 'explained' only rationally. Any attempt in this sense is doomed to failure or madness.

All the mess that we suffer economically, politically, culturally and morally is the result of bad behavior: we were poorly educated. They have been educating us for ages and, to this day, they continue to educate us poorly.

Let it be said that I say this from an English university forum that, accepting a thesis like this, is willing to make the effort to understand what good education really means.

We have been told lies and, out of ignorance, driven away from the true rhythm of the universe. They make us believe that we are separated, isolated, out of reality. Frightening!

I breathe, and through breathing I know that I am here, present, that the consciousness of my presence connects me with my spirit and my spirit does not rationalize… it vibrates. It is here, radiant. And that vibrant spirit actualizes all my human capacity and leads me to be in the present without dispersion, with the mind attentive.

---

59 Paper given at the University of Huddersfield, UK on the 5th of October, 2017. Translated by Helena Guardia.

A few seconds in that silence open certain thresholds of perception that lead me to deeper layers of my being, where I realize that I am not alone; that myself is not only me but that I am all. And there, in that place where we are all together, we are able to remember, as the poet Octavio Paz says, 'to recover our lost unity... the forgotten wonder of being alive' (1957/1988). In that state of consciousness we touch the Source - the Source of Being.

Our tragedy is that this essential being is not connected with our social being. The essence asks us to behave in a certain way, to commit ourselves to the respect for ourselves and for all the energy of the universe; it demands that we behave with dignity and cosmic consciousness, that we should acquire the good manners to know how to behave, not only in society - in the stereotyped red carpet or in the pathetic and sinister meetings of the elite - but in the authentic human society.

Let us recapitulate then:

To breathe with attention is to connect, through the breath, with the spirit; to enter into its vibrational quality means to behave accordingly: to embody, with kindness, a vibration that fuses realities, connecting in all directions, harmonizing people, actions, environments, towns and cities, countries and milky ways, merging. Fusion, not fission.

Good cosmic education, without a temper tantrum. For example, a well-educated scientism knows in depth the protocol of nature and, without disrespecting it, courts it to give us its secrets, without violating it. Science that courts finds and develops the magic of connections. The science that forces and attacks only discovers the mirror of its own limitations; the isolation, the coldness and the solitude of the reason that builds monsters.

In order to survive, we ask for a good education that will make us flourish as an enlightened humanity. Most universities are dedicated to adjusting consciousnesses to fit into the dislocated structure of the status quo. We do not need that education. We need an education that liberates consciences, that allows what is fermented in our interior to flourish: our rooster's song, our spinning of the sun, our inner horse running wild, our solar howl.

If you ask young people today, in any part of the world, what do you study for? She/he answers: to achieve a bachelor's degree, a master's degree, a doctorate, in order to live better.

Doing what?

In a world where almost any profession that is chosen is locked into the chain of production of goods and services, of cost/benefit in the world economic development, this means that the central aim for studying is to make money. I educate myself to learn how to make money. And what does it mean to know how to make money in this world, as it is, in this effervescent 2017?

In short, making money is learning to lower costs and increase profits. How? Well, there is an infinite range of possibilities, depending on the field in which one moves. As a trader, I can slyly increase some air bubbles in certain products, to make it look like you have more than you actually have. Does it sound familiar? Or introduce an obsolesence chip so that after certain hours of service, the apparatus I produce dies - dies an announced death… What could we call that technique? Industrial euthanasia? Or present the products so inflated with cardboard, plastic and useless packaging - which also pollute - for the sole reason of increasing their price. Or I can lower ingredients. Or invent pseudo-scientific lies to put 'healing' or 'revitalizing' products on the market. Or, as laboratories do, invent illnesses and epidemics to profit from public health.

Or invent and celebrate success in life, with the possession of a car… or two… or ten… or a house… or three… Or a trip… or two… or a thousand! Or a plane!

Or signature clothing… Or author's cuisine… Or culture as a fashion show!

And Falstaff? To the desserts!

Or… accounts, many secret accounts in banks abroad, or cash, under the mattress…

In order to enter the 'real' world, looking for success, white, black, brown, red or yellow have to be smart elegant cheats. They believe that they trick each other for their personal financial gain, not realizing that they are cheating themselves.

By achieving a quality of life as superficial and dislocated as their own belief system, they do not realize that their bad education hybridizes life, dislocating and confusing us, causing anxiety and anguish - for it does not give serenity or real satisfaction. It puts us in an excitement of an inappropriate 'happiness', full of an insatiable voracity, which ends up breaking us; it is a lifestyle that generates energy and money by destroying, tricking and fission-ing.

Good education teaches us, in principle, to recognize our own nature: Who am I? What is my physical, psychic, spiritual gift? And, when we have recognized it, to seek its place in the concert of human activities.

But we do not have time or space to do this search; we have to eat, to dress, to sleep - always running after the carrot. They have us all running around, anguished, exhausted. There is no time for anything other than working; that is, licking the iron of the mule's yoke.

Bad education: I only look at my own satisfaction, thus provoking pain.

Good education: I look at my own blessings.

Learning to be: human being

With myself,

With the others,

With the cosmos.

With authenticity, without dislocating anything, without altering, inflating or deflating anything - not egos, not anything. Seeking only to transform ourselves internally and, with that intention, to design, culturally, platforms that allow us to walk that way.

Like the room in Tarkovsky's *Stalker*, where the manifestation of our deepest reality is summoned and flourishes. Or our deepest reality reflected in the geometric designs of the Guna community in Panama.

Here I would like to share with you the research that we carried out last July in the Guna community, in the *comarca* of Armila, Guna Yala, in Panama. This community of Guna Indians is settled in a Panamanian territorial strip that overlooks the Caribbean Sea and is bordered by Colombia. The Guna maintain their territory and their ancestral beliefs with strength and integrity. Their way of relating to the environment makes them one of the most educated human groups on the planet; a true example of cosmic education. They know the language of trees, plants, animals and waters. They live with the consciousness of being with the universe, they know they are the universe and, through their ceremonies, they touch the Source. From the contact with these levels of consciousness emerges their conception of the world: *Purpakana*, the ultimate reality, the place where the basic design of everything that exists is born. The Kunas learn and share a cosmic education that is reflected in their social structure and in their attire. They grow up with an education that keeps them with their spine erect, dignified; they are aware that their work in this life is to help the flight of Mother Earth. From this comes a social ethic that transforms into a communal aesthetic evidently connected to the root and which has much to teach us. From them we learned to connect with Purpakana. We shared this teaching in an immersive theatre piece that we performed in the Kuna community and in the Bosque de Chapultepec in Mexico City. The performance is called *El Ensueño de los árboles*. Through the project we collected the perfume of a tropical jungle, and encountered the conception of a reality in harmony with the good manners of the universe. We discovered that there is the possibility of a temperate and happy life within the paradise which is this planet, which our Western civilization - with its continual bad education - strives to make look like hell.

This paradise can also be found in the designs of the Huichols, in Mexico.

Or in the symbols that adorn the cultures in Babylon, Greece, Rome, Tenochtitlan, Tibet, China, Machu Picchu and many other places in the world, which are the testimony and reminder of the authentic contact that man has with the deepest layers of a universal consciousness. The same Source of circulating energy, in an infinite game of fractal geometry.

Languages may be different one from another, almost incomprehensible to each other. However, the contact with a deep graphic signal uncovers the archetypes that sustain all cultures and unifies our perception of life, revealing our surprising brotherhood.

We are like drops of water from the same spring. I believe that this is the grammar of a universal language, the code to which we all belong. Wasson analyzes it very well in his writings on rituals and experiences of altered states of consciousness. Remember that it was he who made María Sabina, the Mexican shaman, well known all over the world (Wasson, 1976).

So how about a kind of theatre that focuses on taking steps in that direction? Even without the mescaline of Timothy Leary or the *honguitos* of the shaman Maria Sabina; not even with the ancient Greek ambrosia but, anchored to an advanced scientism, a theatre that creates theatrical designs as honest vehicles of transformation of consciousness.

As if we were filthy and smelly, with the urgency to cleanse ourselves by blows of breath and attention. To be self-educated so that, in our friction with the contemporary world, we get as little dirty as possible. Less greed, vanity and lying, less arrogance, personal importance and power. To create a melting atmosphere that slowly boils, bubble after bubble, until the persistence of the fire compels the critical mass necessary to bring us to the transformative boil which we need. No one knows what path it can take, but we do know that its first boilings always manifest through the stage - the stage that is built not with marble and iron, but with the most ancient and solid material it has - the convocation: 'now it is' (silence), 'now it is not'.

These types of platforms are definitely exclusively for spirits in a state of emergency. It is a call to establish a culture of dignified behavior with ourselves, with the other, with the cosmos.

Metaphor is the only boat which can navigate these waters. That is, if we accept that these waters emanate from a spring of endless energy, without beginning or end.

We have to realize that we are simply animals that are nourished by, and live in, an incomprehensible cosmos; and that all of that huge cosmos interacts; that we are all cosmos; that in thought, in blood, in society, on the planet and in the universe, there are streams of energy that circulate constantly, obeying a design that surpasses our human understanding.

Science has shown us that, out of 100% of the reality we perceive, only 30% can enter into a rationally repeatable, predictable, measurable process, and that 70% of it is outside our rational parameters, remaining in the realm of mystery - unpredictable, unattainable.

Do we want to live in an isolated reality of only 30%? Or do we seek to open thresholds? We have to risk entering the current of maturation of who we are, even though we do not know very well what it is that we are.

We fail to understand that the true contemplation of our being emanates from unfathomable strata that surpasses reason. It is not with arguments, but only through true silence that we open doors.

What theatrical current goes in this direction? The one that summons us, in principle, to be together.

Ok, here and now, we're together. With my rational mind I begin to realize that each of us is breathing.

We pay attention -

I'm here, just breathing.

This action engages my intuitive mind, the one that knows more about me than I, the one that perceives the energy of the group. And these two aligned minds, energetically, enhance my perception of the living instant. I open myself to the ability to cross the threshold into deeper states of consciousness and try to connect with the Source, the eternal spring, the fractal geometry - movements, shapes, colors, flowing images - without asking where they come from or where they are going.

We simply observe, without judgment. We close our eyes [*inviting the audience to close their eyes*]. I do not resist. I learn to let myself go in that spring. I gently play in order to learn to swim in that spring.

I interact with these waters, I flow with them.

I get wet in their color and shape.

Who am I ?

Universal energy looking at itself in full run.

What is my job on this planet?

The one that the energy has designed for me.

How will I recognize it?

In deep silence, with true innocence, I fall into myself and surrender to my own being (silence).

How do I know I genuinely touched the Source?

Very simple - I become aware of how I'm feeling. If I feel uncomfortable, angry, tired, speculating, it means I did not touch the Source. How do I feel? Happy, so happy, that if I would have a tail I would be wagging it!

It seems to me that wagging the tail of happiness is a symptom of good health and good cosmic education. That is what universities have forgotten to teach us, to wag the tail. Thank you.

REFERENCES

Paz, Octavio (1957) *Piedra de Sol.* Mexico City: Tezontle.

Paz, Octavio (1988) *Collected Poems 1957 - 1987*. Trans. Eliot Weinberger. Manchester: Carcanet Press.

Wasson, R. Gordon. *Maria Sabina and Her Mazatec Mushroom Velada*. New York: Harcourt, 1976.

APPENDIX I

A SUMMARY OF MY LEARNING
Alí Ehécatl

[This account, ostensibly written by a young performer, describes a process of development through working with the principles of anthropocosmic theatre. It was originally included at the end of the closing chapter of what is now Part One. In fact, in the style of Stanislavski, Alí Ehécatl is a fictional character, allowing Núñez to include something of his own youthful experience. DM]

When I decided to study theatre, my whole family hit the roof. I was eighteen and had barely finished my secondary education. They thought that acting was not a very lucrative profession, in other words actors got to earn nothing or hardly anything, unless they got to be famous, and they thought that there was no chance of that for me. Besides, it was an atmosphere full of homosexuals and prostitutes, where addiction to drugs was widespread. So they tried everything to dissuade me from choosing theatre as a profession.

I was lucky and managed to get some money together. I convinced them of how sophisticated it sounded to study theatre abroad, and as true middle-class people, they understood the cultural prestige that that represented and gave my plans their blessing. I left for London in 1973 and spent a year searching furiously for success, in whichever way. I didn't find it.

The material I studied made me reflect more about the function of Mexican theatre in relation to contemporary world theatre.

When I went back to Mexico, a couple of years passed by amid whispers and echoes of my disappointment abroad, and without my finding an opening to work for a Mexican theatre. Sceptical, and having lost my way completely, and not knowing where to begin to build a truly Central American, and at the same time universal, theatre, I came across the forest of Chapultepec one day in May 1976. In the Casa del Lago I saw that a workshop was about to begin which looked as if it could be novel; it was directed by one Nicolás

Núñez, whom I had not met. Just for the sake of it, I signed up. That was the first contact I had with the proposition of an anthropocosmic theatre.

In the first work session, Nicolás explained to us the general scheme of his proposition; I thought it was pretentious, but I nevertheless let time go by. Anyway, there were two or three women in the group who were attractive enough to encourage me to keep going to the sessions.

'You aren't paying attention', Nicolas said to me during a breathing exercise. I was actually occupied with my mental jokes. 'You haven't understood any of what we're trying to do'. I was irritated by his arrogant, aggressive way of picking on me.

'So what exactly are we trying to do?' I asked sarcastically, trying to deflate his pretentious attitude of attempting to do something important. At that time, the most important things for me were my female companions' bodies, which lit up in the reddish nightfall at the end of July, in a bucolic Chapultepec. Nicolás kept quiet.

In the next work session Nicolás took me to one side. 'You aren't even fulfilling the first premise of our scheme'. I told him he was wrong, and that of course I was fulfilling it; I insisted, stating that my attitude was committed. He looked at me without believing a word, but simply shook his head from side to side and walked away saying to me, 'I hope you realise'. I took exception to his picking on me like that, as after all the only thing I was interested in was meeting up with the group and enjoying the presence of the two girls I liked. Besides, I was totally sceptical in the sense that anything really important could be generated in the workshop.

At the next class, I took along a text which I had written and recited in London. I took it for Nicolás so that he would realise that he could not put the pressure on me so easily. I wanted him to be aware that I had a personal history behind me, and anyway, the text provided a good way of impressing the girls in the group a bit more.

There were fourteen of us in the group, five women and nine men. Of the five, only Esperanza and Fe were attractive to me; the other three were mere teenagers, so I didn't pay them much attention. All of the men, Nicolás apart, were aged between 18 and 23; Jaime was the most spirited in the exercises, followed in terms of work by Alfredo, who was known as 'Chac', and Félix who was Brazilian. The rest of us were Mexican. The text I took for them was the following:

Critical staging disguised as a street demonstration, recited at Speakers' Corner in Hyde Park, in London, on 24th March 1974

Here I am.

London in Spring.

My energy wasted away by the eternal cold.

Extension of paving-stones.

My esteemed and serene body, emancipated, volatile, set in your ways, vice-ridden coagulant friend: I'm telling you this because I cannot hammer a theatre out of your guts, because here, you do it energetically, with chic, and I hate you for doing theatre like that.

Because you pick up emotional charity with exaggerated virtuosity, because you deceive me, deceiving yourself, because you've forgotten to laugh. I hate you for that, too.

Let me also tell you that I have witnessed your infinite range of cheek which never gets revitalised, faces you pull in which your blood's taste of life does not flow. I'm fed up of looking into your eyes, looking to find that my-your (our) spiritual co-ordinate, and all I have found is gags, and any amount of useless projects of modern, industrial manufacture. You really made me sick.

That's how I came to the happy conclusion that your theatre, my dear novel friend, no longer contains that touchstone which talks directly to my guts. For this reason, rather than any other, I really hate you.

I came here from so far away, because I needed to see you close up, get to know you, find out what was the true colour of your emotions. And now that I am here, all I can think of to say to you is that you need to go there, to the valleys of the sun, to the place where looks and tastes of earth still don't freeze: I mean, to Mexico.

I have scoured the sources of Elizabethan theatre, those of the *commedia dell' arte*, of the theatre of the absurd, war theatre, poor theatre, the grotesque, puppet theatre, live theatre, total theatre, political, mystical, of all their origins and their possible evolutions in our age, and until today, in this city, nowhere have I felt the communication of theatre as a manifestation of joy of life; only in some passage or other, for two or three people, have I discovered a fine ray of tortured brightness which connects me to the final guffaw of my personal representation of being human in this world, via and through the instrument of theatre.

By this I do not mean that everything in my travels has been, or still is, in ruins around me; quite the contrary.

Shakespeare is more alive than ever, as are Ibsen and many others. It's just that in every production you do of their plays, in almost the majority I could say (with the odd exception) both to Shakespeare and to any other maker of theatre, your stages full of modern technology are killing them. And I see how you rip their guts and their sex out and leave them in rags, where the colouring and the swelling of emotion are not ruled by bloody blows but by the weakened rouge of make-up.

I do not believe in this type of theatre and I do not accept that type of falsified Shakespeare.

Because Shakespeare, just like anybody else, is not for me a style or a fashion; he is not even a socio-political circumstance at a given moment, but an emotional vibration which swallows the make-up with any other speculation and leaves us naked, clear, illuminated in joy or tragedy, with the only shade of reality which allows genuine communication.

So I believe in a theatre of light, in a theatre of genuine dramatic joy, in which the phallus is not disguised or deformed, and life vibrates serenely and terrifyingly, connecting us with the real co-ordinates of a world cast before our eyes in worrying cycles of joyous vitality, and is eternally transformed, at every step falling, just as at this very moment, living.

One of the most distressing dramas in this atmosphere which surrounds us, my dear friend, happens when we discover, accidentally or by surprise, that our feet are in a world which belongs to us, our veins are full of acts about to be performed, and as we realise this, we cannot find enough courage to experience these acts; we choke to death on gushes of life which we could not get out into the open. This, my dear friend, is our day-to-day drama, both in the theatre and in the big cities.

So where can we find the pleasure and joy of natural hierarchies? How can we re-establish the original rhythm which will give us back our healthy appetite for life and sex.

At this time, when our spiritual concerns find no satisfaction in established rites, when our internal sympathies debate amid the jingling of Krishna, in the streets of New York, or Zen Buddhism exercises in London's West End, or even in the masquerades of those who appear to be illuminated and come to collect our tithes as a weekly jape wherever we may be in the world. At a moment when we know we are alone, when as an individual need we have the quest for a new touchstone which will link us to something magical, at a moment like this - again, we must reinvent theatre, as a frighteningly divine game which is rebuilt from any point, without conditions, without tithes, in a free, natural way.

If I am talking to you like this, my dear friend, it is because I feel that the impulse of vigorous theatre is convulsing in my insides, where I can feel the tuggings of urges caught up in the infinite acquisition of my worlds gladdened to the very limit, till they reach the edge of the silent, changeless universe of death.

That is why I came here. To shout out to you what I feel.

I feel the sun and its energy. I believe in a theatre of the sun. I believe in the light which creeps through the fabrics of our human labyrinth, to make us jump into action and hence be connected to totalising vitality.

I look down on any production which externalises, or which is formed in institutions, just as I look down upon the stupidest theatrical production I have been unlucky enough to suffer: religious and political orthodoxies, as well as theatrical ones.

I am absolutely convinced that internal convulsions and changes which sensitive individuals undergo, when they are the result of honestly and deeply emotional manifestations, consequently form and change culture.

I believe in this type of culture, performed by strokes of stomach and light. I believe in this type of theatre.

I do not believe in the pedantry of bourgeois humour which fabricates with its industry apparent cultural changes in any artistic manifestation, merely producing disorientation and a cloudy ideological colonialism without any consistency; your waste culture, dark, shady, sterile, you know it well, my dear friend; that is your arguable magazine information.

And so we come to realise that what separates some of us from others in this medium is not necessarily a question of talent, but of the budget of having enough time free to reinvent culture step by step. Original sin is the idiotic distribution of our paid time, yours, mine, everybody's. In this manipulation of our simple permanence is the essence of that pigheaded habit of sticking instants in headings, and dusks in photographs, to freeze our soul and turn us into objects, supposed makers of art, where the laid-back cheek of the average man contemplates the vigorous image of the artist's cheek in motion. I do not believe in this exchange of petrified cheeks. I do not believe in this type of theatre.

Moreover, you are committing the sin of obscurantism when you censure and hinder capable people, because at this advanced stage of media evolution, the vitality and internal spell of any artistic manifestation is no longer the patrimony of any group, clan or social nucleus, because if we can no longer ignore the fact that the emotional co-ordinates produced by art are resting under the skin of any human being, it is clear that our responsibility as individual artists is totally committed with the performance of this or that group, other people, everybody. And you are unwilling to realise this.

So I shall now end my journey through your sterile scenarios, full of tricks disguised as magical technology, which never convinces me fully; full of possibilities, worlds which freeze at the moment when they were about to lose control, Saxon precipices and cliffs where you, perhaps due to the climate, become the executioner of your own vitality, as you rediscover your stubborn habit of killing reality through reasoning.

I come from a place where reality has a hot waist, I come from the valleys where Prince Quetzalcóatl began his flight to the sun.

Just as if here, somehow, the words of Gauguin were fitting when he said: *If our life is ill, our art must also be ill, and we can only give it back its health by starting again, like children or savages.* And in such a scandalous situation as this, my dear friend, one of the quickest and healthiest paths would be to gather together your copious and overstructured encyclopaedia and ... burn it.

Nevertheless, you are not solely responsible for this huge fraud which envelops your glamour, my broken-down friend: I also have part of my cheek and my emotions deformed by compulsion. That is the self which at this moment I am snatching from your clutching arms so as to try and rehabilitate it and give it back to life. That is the cheek which discovers itself with these words, independent; acting before you, breathing, with its look and body open, proving that reality is achieved and lost at every moment, that life reveals itself by fusing with the breath of whoever is breathing us, in this way, before you, at this moment.

Two classes later, when Nicolás gave me back my text, he asked me to read it out to the group, and this seemed like a good idea. I began to read it and as I got into it, I understood that I had generated this text in an organic, personal way; when I tried to exhibit it and use it to impress the group, it turned against me. In a certain way I had been totally honest as I wrote it and recited it in England, but now that I was reading it to a group of Mexicans of my own age in Mexico, I was overwhelmed by the commitment of what I was discovering in my own lines. How could it possibly have moved me so far away from myself? For a moment it seemed like a text written by a complete stranger. I stopped a couple of times and Nicolás insisted that I should continue. I finished completely confused, as if I were returning from a long journey.

'Did you really shout that text out in England?' asked somebody, and I answered in an absent kind of way, without daring to look at anybody.

'How is it possible', Nicolás began to say, 'for somebody to have written something like this and yet not have the will to work, merely coming to the workshop to pass the time of day?'

Helena added to this:

'Do you think we don't meet here to try and develop a process appropriate to us as Mexicans, just as you want?'

I did not know what to say. The class ended.

When I got home, I looked for the exercise book in which I had jotted down the work scheme of the workshop, and read: Point number one - will to work. I realised that I had confused my willingness to go to the workshop; I thought it was enough simply to be there, that making the effort to reach the woods of Chapultepec, in the middle of a congested city, more or less on time, was a merit which more than fulfilled my will to work. But that was not the case. The will to work was something else. It was being awake and committed to the exercises, it was not being distracted by other activities such as chatting each other up or thrusting our insidious egos on the others; it was, above all, being attentive and ready to make the best possible use of our work time.

I arrived at the next class a bit earlier than usual and began to play with the people who were there, asking them about the second point of our scheme, i.e. their deformations [distortions]. Chac looked at me inquisitively and I began to walk in a deformed way, as if I were a hunchback. He began to imitate me and we ended up adopting the most extravagent positions and faces one could imagine. By then, the whole group had arrived and were watching us in silence. We ended by slumping to the ground; I felt as if I had passed through ancient places and atmospheres; I had quite a penetrating taste in my mouth, as if my body had generated special fluids. Helena congratulated us on what she called good work. We began the class and I asked myself inside, what were my deformations and how could I detect them. We did the usual warm-up exercises: we stood on our heads, first against the wall and then, for those who had mastered the process, with no more support than the arms; then we warmed up our legs, together with rhythmic breathing. This warm-up is based on Tai-Chi, which originated in China, although some people say that its origins are Mayan. The basic position is bending the legs a little, as if one were sitting on an imaginary bench, with the spine straight; then one breathes deeply, moving very slowly through a form of quite complicated choreography, where the synchronisation of the breathing, the rhythm of the movement and the concentration in the lower abdomen should be a harmonious, fluent whole. Learning Tai-Chi takes many years, but the simple introductory exercises were led by Helena, who knows the 108 positions of Tai-Chi. We continued with some exercises led and developed by Nicolás. Here the contact, recognition and practice of each part of our body were carried out, and it was continually insisted that we paid attention to the source of energy of the human machine, i.e. in the lower abdomen.

For me, this was now a revelation. These were exercises I had been doing mechanically; my attention was on Fe and Esperanza, never on my own muscles and even less on my centre of energy.

I now realised how different it was to do an exercise with the attention alive, and obviously I reaped the benefits. The indifference and inertia disappeared from my soul; I began to sweat in a different way, with the awareness that now I really was working on my instrument.

The warm-up finished and we worked on the voice, i.e. all our body's resonators. Here we used a position similar to the basic one used for Tai-Chi, but with the hands in front, making a circle as if we were hugging a tree. This is the position of Chi-Kun. In this position, we breathed and opened our mouths as wide as possible, trying to let the sound vibrate out of our entire body. We shouted as loudly as we could, without focussing our attention on the vocal chords, but rather on the lower abdomen.

When we finished this class, I really understood that at that moment I had come into contact with the first step of the workshop's work scheme: the will to work. At that moment I began to worry about the second step, which is the contact with obstacles and deformations.

Until this moment the idea that I could have obstacles or deformations had never occurred to me. As far as I knew, I had always been a normal person. However...

Contact with Obstacles and Deformations

Once I had begun to take the scheme seriously, things started to change by themselves. As I looked for my deformations and obstacles through the workshop sensitisation exercises, I understood the enormous number of obstacles I had inside me, and determined a few 'habits' which I thought were part of my nature but were not; they were, in fact, deformations.

I understood the need to re-educate myself, I mean I now understood it organically, not only intellectually. I remember the first exercise of this type, that is to say the first exercises I did seriously. Once we had done all our warm-up exercises, we relaxed and prepared our spirits for the sensitisation exercise. We were lying down on the ground, with our eyes closed; Nicolás asked for our trust so that we could do the exercise. He told us that we were in a safe place where our exact commitment was to work on ourselves as well and honestly as we could. He asked us to stand up with our eyes closed and begin to walk around the place, attentive to the reactions of our organism, focussing our attention on what was happening to us, rather than what was happening outside: if we were pushed or handled, it was more important to detect what that push referred me to, than to try and find out who had pushed me. We all knew that we were working in good faith and that if each person was sufficiently into the exercise, they were not looking to bother or impose themselves on the others. I recall that when I stood up, trying to keep my attention on my own organism, I noticed that I insisted on seeing myself through the eyes of the others; this was now a bit ridiculous for me, as I found myself walking in a way in which my attention was focused on the others. When I made the effort to walk with my attention on myself, I noticed that I began to walk in a different way from normal. I carried on making this effort, and felt liberated. For the first time, I felt free from the pressure of the others; I relaxed; I told myself that however ridiculously I walked, nobody could see me and therefore all I had to do was walk as my body wanted me to walk; I walked numerous times like this round the work space; at each step I felt freer and happier with my own walk. I knew at once that the way of walking which had characterised me up till that point had a tremendous affectation, a type of block which stopped me from allowing my human animal to walk, merely walk, without any more pretence.

I admitted to myself that I had discovered this blockage and promised myself that I would work on it. I had thought I had no blockages of any type, and look how I now realised I could scarcely walk normally without any problems.

Like this exercise to recognize ourselves in our walk, we did others in the areas of smell, taste, touch, sight and hearing, without ignoring the most representative emotional areas of our instrument, such as love, hatred, tenderness or passion.

All this, of course, via a work process sustained in the workshop, i.e. several days of uninterrupted work, so as to get a fuller idea of this type of internal 'cartography'.

Nicolás asked us to jot down in a notebook, in different sections, the problems, blockages or tensions which we discovered, for instance in the head, arms, legs, hips, and then separate further each of these areas: in the head, the eyes, the nose, the mouth, the eyebrows, the teeth, the chin, etc., until we had done a complete check on this area. Of course this took me a long time and I think it is a task which never finishes, since as soon as I think I have got a more or less definite scheme for a certain area, things immediately happen to change it; it is important for us to realise that nothing is ever at rest. Our deformations get worse or weaken, but never remain at the same level of affectation, so it is necessary to establish a continuous revision device, for life. In this sense, I agree totally with Nicolás when he has mentioned that picking up this internal 'cartography' and keeping it up to date is a lifelong project.

Among the habits I discovered which were imposed on me by my environment, was that of drinking during meetings, for instance. I realised that I drank as a challenge, to fit in, so as not to be left behind, to show everybody else that I was very macho, etc. As I gradually discovered the true causes of some of my acts, I abandoned certain attitudes or deformations which, far from being organic, were social impositions which I was unable to put my finger on. That was what so many exercises in the workshop achieved for me, allowing me to get a little closer to my real needs and learn, through my re-education, to get rid of my artificial habits or behaviours.

I learned to reflect organically, to give myself time, or rather to give my body time and let its wisdom guide my actions. I would not claim that I have achieved this totally, or anything close, but for me the important thing is that I realised that it is along these lines that I should be working, both to learn to be better in the world, and to be able to propose 'something', theatrically speaking.

General Scheme of our Deformations

With the time and discipline to carry around in a notebook the notes corresponding to my feelings and blockages, I had my internal 'cartography' in a reasonable time. It had a lot of variations, and was changeable, but despite that I could see certain recurring feelings, some thoughts, always faithful to certain stimuli. In other words, I could basically determine the type of human animal I was dealing with.

Nicolás asked us to do absolutely nothing to change our habits, but merely to recognise them, however horrible they appeared to us, and register them (hence the notebook), using as a help the idea of filming ourselves for the *Last Judgement*. Let us say that it was only a process of self-observation. Of course the better we did it, the better we could pick up the scheme for ourselves (until that time without judgements of any type, simply observing ourselves as continually as we could).

When we finished this stage of the work, some of us had a more precise idea of our uneasinesses, automatisms and feelings in general. For instance, I discovered that I smoked excessively, and the more I observed myself, the more I realised that I did it due to nervousness, as a social process, as a support for when I was with other people, as a substitute for food, etc. I had the impulse to get rid of this habit, but Nicolás asked me to wait a while longer. So it was very revealing to observe the impulses which led me to smoke and become aware of their devices. I carried on smoking, but now I was certain of why I did it. At least I was no longer under the illusion of believing that I did it because I liked it. The cigarette is only one of the many points of observation, through which I began to discover myself. I think that the same thing happened to most of the members of the group.

Greater energy to recognise and overcome our fears and deformations

Once we had picked up our scheme with discipline, after a reasonable amount of time, we were ready for the fourth step: greater energy to recognise and overcome our fears and deformations.

The important thing at this stage was to have a perfect understanding of the mechanism of our habits and realise that, for instance, the habit of smoking came into my body via x need (in fact the cause is unimportant; what matters is the intensity with which it entered the body). Let us imagine that it entered due to anxiety at an energy level of 40. If I want to change this habit, I must 'consciously' choose another habit to replace the previous one. I must get it into my organism at the precise moment at which I feel the need for my former vice. Let us say I feel the need to smoke, and at that moment I bring the new habit into my body, but making an effort of will to begin it, at an energy level of over 40. I decided to stop smoking, and in its place I decided that every time I fancied a cigarette I would breathe deeply at least five times. The day I began the change, I felt the need to smoke and made the effort to raise my energy level, then gave my body the order to register the change. I had set my smoking habit at 40, so I tried to make the level of will about 50 or 60. The first few times were the most complicated; by the fifth or sixth day, I discovered a type of crisis whereby the desire to smoke rose to about 60 or 70, as if the habit were making a special effort to keep going. So I too made a special effort and set my breathing at 80 or 90. Once I had passed through this crisis, I no longer suffered this impulse to smoke, and a certain type of breathing pattern was established in my body which I have upheld to this day.

Aside from this, there were certain fears in my system which, being resigned to them, I had merely recognised, but they were still active in my organism, like for instance the fear I experienced in the countryside at night. Being alone at night in the middle of the countryside was something which terrified me. My decision to overcome this fear led me to promote the design of a special exercise to work on it. Nicolás and I designed it, and we were also helped by Helena and Jaime to complete it.

One Friday evening, the four of us went to a place near the town of Apan. There, in silence, we went out into the dusk and walked onto a huge hill. We walked for about an hour and a half; I had no idea where I was. Night had fallen completely and it was almost totally dark, such that we could scarcely see our hands. At that moment, as we had arranged, the group split up, leaving me on my own in the middle of the hill. All I had to do was resist the impacts of the night and the different entities of the countryside. If I found that I was in difficulties, we had agreed on a signal to call the other three, which I could only use if it were genuinely necessary. The agreement was that I was not allowed to stray far from the place where we split up. In complete silence, I had to be attentive to everything that was happening within and around me. The vast range of small and major fears which appeared almost drove me mad; several times I was within a whisker of making the emergency call, but I was kept going by the need to battle effectively against the fears. I had to make a supreme effort to continue my life with as few fears and as little manipulation as possible.

At dawn I felt a feeling of joy which exploded when the sun came out. I was dancing frantically, with my eyes full of tears and a sensation of fullness which I had never felt before. I had got through the night, I had got through my night and crossed through my fear, and the certainty that my organism, somewhere deep inside, had learned this, made me radiate an immense serenity.

As the sun came out, my guardians appeared, my friends and my protectors, with whose help I was able to come through the darkness. The three of them danced and did exercises to celebrate the sun; they had been sustaining me internally so that I could give myself over wholly to myself. Now we were together again. I felt the great experience which they feel in this type of exercise; they know the why and the wherefore of this type of bridge to lead us to the sun. Throughout this exercise my will was at its limit; so that I could pull through and see out the night I had to use all my external and internal resources, and I know that only with specialised assistance was it possible to do this. We have talked about the risk involved if somebody without this type of training dared to try this exercise, and Nicolás has recommended that under no circumstances should anyone unqualified be encouraged to try it. The design to work on our fears is quite selective, since there is a particular exercise for each fear.

This fourth point of the scheme carries on to be a continuous work tool, together with the other points. That is to say, we must always be attentive so as to be aware of the obstacles and deformations generated in our organism, almost by the mere fact that we are alive. We always need to be working to overcome them; the work is never done.

Removing other people's stares

The important thing here for me was becoming very clearly aware of how many 'interferences' from other people I had on top of me. Did I do what I did because I wanted to, or because other people wanted me to do it? Removing other people's stares from me meant, for me, focusing my attention on the 'I Am' and liberating myself of the physical, animist and emotional stares of other people. I realised that what others expected from me was not what I expected of myself. To stop doing what others expected me to do was part of my work, until the point at which people left me free from their stares. I noticed the incredible sequence of small manipulations, looks, tones and pure thoughts which we give off continuously to make another person do what we want. To stop doing this to others and avoid their doing it to me was part of my task. I ended up with the type of automatic replies to which I was so marvellously conditioned; some people, those who were best able to judge me, were the first to be surprised and say to me, 'you're not the same as you were before', 'what's happening to you?' and so on, simply because I was consciously working to break their little ways of manipulating me. I stopped paying attention to other people's stares and focused, to reiterate, on the 'I am'. This was the best thing, and it helped me most.

After a considerable period of time, I settled down into myself and felt the organic security of the 'I am' in a neat, coherent way, aware that my being did not spell aggression to anyone or anything, that I now had not even the slightest trace of arrogance, that I was simply discovering myself, before my very being, in all my shape and weight as a human animal tangled up in the infinite structures of cosmic animals of which I am also a part.

The exercise I did on the hill was quite helpful in my understanding of a lot of things about my own organism; it helped me, above all, to remove other people's stares. That space, at that moment, was absolutely mine; nobody, other than my three companions, could track my thoughts down in such a place, and they, as I well knew, were busy among themselves, leaving me alone in absolute freedom. For anyone else it would have been less than impossible to get into that type of experience. So, I got through the test, the prison which other people's thoughts imposed on me, and finally managed to get rid of other people's stares.

Stop looking at ourselves

If removing other people's stares is difficult, stopping looking at ourselves needs a super-human effort which can only be achieved by serious discipline. I cannot really say much about this, but what I do know is that the way is open to whoever wants to follow it, whoever feels the need to stop looking at themselves.

What I experienced through a series of exercises and work after observing something about this mechanism, was the explosive expansion of every atom in my body which instantaneously noticed the correspondence with the thread which linked them with the stars. I guessed at the incredible range of suns accumulated in infinity, of which my little body, at that moment, was a tiny, modest echo-box. I can say no more. That is the end of my summary.

Alí Ehécatl

ANTHROPOCOSMIC THEATRE

APPENDIX II
SPEECHES

A speech delivered by Antonio Velasco Piña[60] on the night of 10th September 1984 at the Colegio de México, on the subject of Anthropocosmic Theatre

Ladies and Gentlemen,

What is anthropocosmic theatre? What characteristics distinguish it from other types of theatre? When and where did this attempt at differentiation from on-stage activity begin?

This talk will attempt to answer these questions, and I think the best way to begin would be with a basic mention of the fundamental inheritances which develop in the west what we commonly call 'theatre'.

Classical Greek theatre is, as we all know, the form of theatre which gives us the fundamental bases for the development of this art within western culture. Through the centuries, and particularly since the Renaissance, European theatre has been enriched with valuable contributions coming mainly from Italy, England and Spain.

So, since the beginning of this century, numerous thinkers had started to notice that in the same way as everything to do with the culture of which it was part, western theatre was sinking into a deep crisis.

Among the great figures who throughout this century have questioned theatrical orthodoxy, the most notable have been Stanislavski, Vakhtangov, Brecht and Grotowski, whose powerful criticisms allowed us, principally, to acquire a clear understanding of the degree of decadence to which this artistic activity had stooped, and secondly to begin the search for a new path, whose direction would lead the theatre to regain its essential content.

---

60 Antonio Velasco Piña: Mexican novelist and promoter of Mexican cultural consciousness.

Anthropocosmic theatre fits specifically into these efforts which tend to achieve genuine recognition in theatrical material. The year 1975, UNAM's Theatre Research Workshop and the name of its director, Nicolás Núñez, are the three essential pieces of data which reply to the questions when, where and by whom, referring to the emergence of this new theatrical trend.

To establish the influences which gave rise to the birth of anthropocosmic theatre is a more difficult task, but I would nevertheless dare to state that the main one comes from the determinant influence exercised by the study of Nahuatlan philosophy carried out by the initiators of this theatrical movement.

In a similar way to the conceptions of other grand civilisations of former times, those developed by the pre-Hispanic cultures considered that between man and the cosmos there is a narrow interdependence, such that each is affected reciprocally by the other's actions. That is, in accordance with said conceptions, not only do the heavenly bodies exercise a powerful ascendancy in human beings, but to the same extent, what they do produces repercussions with important consequences in cosmic happenings. That is why the lives of the ancient Mexicans were orientated, as the foremost objective of their existence, towards the formation of a personality capable of harmonising with the universe and collaborating consciously in its growth.

This ancient ideal of trying to develop a personality so complete that it can even feel the bonds which link it to the energies which shape and support the entire universe, constitutes in essence the basic objective of anthropocosmic theatre, which can be said to be deeply traditional and at the same time radically revolutionary. It is traditional because it addresses once more the possibility of creating a time and a space different from the normal ones, a possibility which, as Mircea Eliade has so correctly pointed out, constituted the supreme purpose of all ancient cultures. It is revolutionary because in current circumstances an objective of this nature constitutes something completely novel, which requires whoever practises it to undergo a radical transformation of consciousness.

APPENDIX II: SPEECHES

In the first edition of Nicolás Núñez's book *Teatro antropocósmico*, in the section entitled 'A Guide', various members of UNAM's Theatre Research Workshop relate some of the experiences they have had in the course of their work. I will mention a few sentences picked out from these narrations, as I feel that this material will be particularly revealing in showing us what people feel as they carry out this type of work:

Something happened within me which I cannot express in words, and I still do not know what it is. But there I can see the moon and its entourage of stars, lighting up the night, and the deep blue sky, fired by the sun. And there are we, seeking our place in the Universe.

Helena Guardia

They shook my soul with the sound of their snail shells. There was nothing more to think of; there I was, drifting with them.

Ana Luisa Solís Gil

Here for just a while!
My heart is a jewel
of the wind in the form of a spiral,
my snail shell sings,
my body dances;
it is in the Omeyocan.
There is external abundance to be enjoyed.
Here for just a while!
You are here,
they are here,
we are here.
Here for just a while!

Juan Allende

355

I tried to be at all costs. I wanted to be in a constant here and now. I did not manage it, but at certain moments I think I existed and I was there. Something within me moved and was still. That is the mystery which I love.

Jaime Soriano

I think the deep emotion contained in these sentences clearly reflects the nature and aims of anthropocosmic theatre, which obviously exceeds the purely aesthetic objectives, to try to achieve through action on the stage objectives of a psychological nature, such as confronting the subject with his internal 'I', so as then to make him feel the bonding which links him to everything that exists.

The means which are used to achieve the aforementioned objectives are the same ones which have always been used for this purpose. Music and dance, song and the acting out of ancient myths, the focusing of the attention on the 'here and now'. In short, it is another case of the yearning of the human spirit to go beyond itself and set up a conscious communication with whatever is around it.

Finally, I would just like to mention that in no way are we intending to create a new theatrical orthodoxy under the name of anthropocosmic theatre. Rather, this type of theatre consists basically of a process of research, an attempt to open up powerful trends which, coming from the distant past, can become the renewing strength which begins in our era a real theatrical renaissance. I hope this lofty aim can be achieved. Thank you for your kind attention.

A speech delivered by Femando de Ita[61] on the night of 10th September 1984 at the Colegio de México on the subject of Anthropocosmic Theatre

To answer the question which has given rise to this speech, what is anthropocosmic theatre?, I feel the need to reply first to another question:

---

61 Fernando de Ita: Mexican theatre journalist and critic.

what is theatre in Mexico? The quick answer: it is nothing. I mean, nothing of any real interest to society as a whole; not even to that part of the social conglomerate which, as a professional obligation, should give it some thought.

A while ago, Professor Hector Azar was telling me about the startling contempt magazines and cultural supplements have for work in drama, at a time when the rest of the media confuse it with burlesque shows and spectacles. Theatre is that, of course, but it is, above all, something else. It is, or it ought to be, a place in which the artist's imagination takes shape in order to relate to the imagination of the next man.

Jean Duvignaud has said that theatre is the last sacred place available to twentieth-century man, because although people recently involved in theatre have striven in very different ways to remove the sacred nature from theatre, this act is nevertheless still a rite carried out in a particular place, at an exact time, under previously determined conditions.

This ceremony has varied a great deal in twentieth century western theatre, to the extent that straight after seeking in a thousand different ways to break with its ceremonial meaning, contemporary theatre has returned to the original convocation of ritual theatre, anthropocosmic theatre. In this circular action, it can be seen that the thousand masks worn by the theatre of our times aim merely to bring about the participation of the audience in the game of true-or-false which is theatre. For better or for worse, in the last thirty years western progressive, research and laboratory theatre has established the stage as the true body of dramatic action. In this quest, the job of author first became the job of director, and then a task of collective creation.

We are not here to discuss the advantages and disadvantages of each option, but to indicate that creative theatre in the western world took on new characteristics of space and time, or rather, another dramatic dimension. The vehicle of ideas and emotions of *zom teatrikon*, the theatrical animal, is no longer the voice, the gestures and the rhetoric of the actor: now it is the whole organicism of his body which expresses the crux of the dramatic conflict. We are talking about the sixties and the stage revolution brought about by a Polish director called Jerzy Grotowski, with the idea of a theatre poor in material resources and rich in human tensions which would express, through the activation of all the actor's psychophysical apparatus, the tribulations of the human being.

When the discipline of Laboratory Theatre began to be regarded as the bible of a new theatrical church throughout the world, Jerzy Grotowski announced that as of 1970 he would do no more conventional theatre, so as to devote himself to researching the mechanisms of what he himself later termed Active Culture. From my point of view, the new relationship which the Grotowskian actor had with the theatre, had brought on the need for a new relationship between the actor and the audience. It was simply a case of doing away with the condition that the spectator was someone who merely watched the performers in action. He had to be made to perform, even if in order to achieve this no more theatre was performed. As far as I know, Grotowski discovered that theatre is an arena in which one can only work with actors, while the world is wider than that, and any of its creatures is an actor in his own life.

During their travels, Nicolás Núñez, Helena Guardia and other members of the *Taller de Investigación Teatral* at UNAM, had direct contact with the Laboratory Theatre and worked with Grotowski on various international projects. Previously, these theatre workers had decided to take Mexican identity as a starting point for their first performances. So it was that with the outstanding participation of Juan Allende in this searching process, the workshop staged Octavio Paz's *El Laberinto de la Soledad* (*The Labyrinth of Solitude*), and *Zapata*, a show which we will now call Grotowskian, in which the workshop dipped into the indigenous roots of the Caudillo del Sur.

With the Polish experience already in his rucksack, the *Taller* director arrived in Mexico to study in depth the philosophy of the ancient Mexicans, and found in this the anthropocosmic conception which gave both name and foundation to his subsequent research. The people working in the university workshop found in the Polish forests the psychophysical mechanisms which allow the person who is exercising them to find a better harmony with the environment, with himself and, finally, with the Universe. If we say it like that, it could give the impression that we are commenting on a new *Hare Krishna*, or another form of cultural escapism. On the contrary, the anthropocosmic meaning of the TRW's work is based, as Nicolás will explain in a few moments, on the one hand on the vision of the world as seen in Nahuatlan philosophy, and on the other hand, on the latest scientific discoveries in this field.

The idea is that if, through controlled super-effort, we activate some of the untouched areas of our organism, we can achieve in time a new state of consciousness in which it is easier to reach the psychophysical balance which we often seek in the doctor's surgery or on the psychiatrist's couch. This is the form of the work; its content is described in the eagerness of the first settlers on this earth to have their own image, a whole heart. Nahuatlan philosophy allows us, in an allegorical way, to offer our hearts to the Sun, so that through our symbolic sacrifice the order of the Universe is not yet broken.

You may ask what this type of mental craftsmanship has to do with daily life. Well, the *Taller*'s intention is to offer the public in general a space for participatory work, in which we are all actors in our own action, without the need to follow instructions, to accept dogmas, or have an experience which has been imposed. All this is possible because the field of work is the human body, and the body does not lie. Either it really flies over the work place, or it crashes and falls to the floor. Finding a place in which one simply flies is not bad going in this world of crashes, first of all because the workshop has outlived mistrust in its midst and a lack of understanding at institutional level. As is customary with us, this is work which has been called to question without being known and understood. I would even add that the reason was precisely because the work's meaning, intention and aims were not known. Nobody there wants to be an apostle of a new stage religion. The group's only aspiration is to offer actors in particular, and the general public, a method of participatory theatre which has demonstrated in a practical way its helpfulness, after more than five years of continuous research and training.

For me, finally, anthropocosmic theatre is a work space in which for a few moments we come to be aware that man really is part of the universe.

A speech given by Nicolás Núñez on the night of 10th September 1984 at the Colegio de México, on the theme of Anthropocosmic Theatre

What is anthropocosmic theatre?
Where does it come from?
Where is it going?

We could reply that it is born in response to an urgency.

What urgency?

The urgency to be in the here and now in the fullest possible way.

If to get man onto the moon we need a great deal of knowledge and resources, to get our consciousness up to date in the here and now, no less is needed.

The system of work in our workshop is to investigate possibilities and mechanisms which will help us with this updating.

Rite is the oldest device used by humanity as a vehicle to achieve this updating. Throughout history, a whole range of possibilities and variants have stemmed from rite. Theatre is one of the direct heirs of the convocation of the here and now, only in general terms it has become a type of depository in disguise. What do I mean by a depository in disguise?

We are told that a very old form of knowledge was deposited in Tarot cards so that it could circulate through time without any danger, since in this way it could be passed on from generation to generation, from civilisation to civilisation, disguised as a game of chance. Hence theatre, as we know it, has served as a disguise for the ancestral convocation of the here and now. To remove theatre's disguise and recover its original strength is, for us, to investigate, design, poke tirelessly with tools of breathing, movement, participation and vibration which will allow us literally to set the place alight, so as to have our look and body open to the next man, where the deep breathing of my individual self is united with the consciousness of my collective self, without fear, with the certainty that I only have to be and exist in the world, working, here and now, in good faith.

We believe that this attitude to start off with would be enough to help reorganise the chaos. That is why we think that the workshop's work can help rebuild our trust in our possibilities, that is, those of everybody; our possibilities to work on an image or a heart; our potential to realise, for example, that it is not by chance that we are here today.

Needless to say we went, as you may have realised, for the precepts of Nahuatlan philosophy, precepts which give our workshop its ethical base.

Our projects *Zapata, Aztlán* and *Tonatiuh* are designs for participatory theatre which have been generated over several years of research in various areas. These works are now beginning to find their path in the field of the teaching of theatre.

We could, therefore, affirm that anthropocosmic theatre generates designs for participatory theatre with the meaning of sharing an experience, and that this cultural alternative is currently proving its efficiency, not only in Mexico, but in various parts of the world. Hence space is won for the phenomenon of transculture, i.e. culture in transit, in motion, active, participatory.

Participatory theatre has earned its legitimacy very slowly within the field of theatre. At this moment it is beginning to be looked upon as something more than pure madness. This may be due on the one hand to the fact that scientists have started to look upon us favourably, and on the other to the fact that we have approached our work in a more scientific way.

Now, rather than drawing out a list of the influences and contributions which our work has received, we would like to take this opportunity to thank all the people and institutions who, having come into contact with the group's work, have supported and enriched it; in the same way, we would like to thank all of you here today for making the effort to come and be with us. I am sure that some of you have come out of curiosity, others in solidarity, others still due to your involvement. Whatever the case, I think that the fact that we have gathered together to talk about anthropocosmic theatre can help people to understand that our work is to develop modest designs which drive us to recall natural rhythms; we could, for instance, be reminded that we have a full Moon at the moment. Thank you.

A speech made by Ethel Krauze[62] on the night of 15th December 1987 at the Casa del Libro Universitario, to mark the first edition of *Teatro Antropocosmico*

Good evening. Perhaps I am the least suitable person to begin this launch of a book about theatre, since I have a lot more to do with work on writing than work on the stage. However, I am, perhaps, the most suitable to introduce this theatrical experience from the non-theatrical side of it, that is the part which deals with a normal, run-of-the-mill audience, a spectator, and then those who really understand this field should take over from me.

Nicolás Núñez invited me to present his book, (and I am deeply grateful to him for this), due, I think, to an article I wrote a short time ago in *Excelsior*, where I told of my experience watching one of his most recent performances, Shakespeare's *The Tempest*, performed as participatory theatre. I went to watch and in this article I related what had happened to me. I did not know Nicolás Núñez; I was faintly aware of what he was doing, and my visit to see *The Tempest* was the first time I had been close to his work. There I went through what for me was a very new experience. From the second act I had to get up from my seat, from which I was watching the performance very comfortably; I had to be blindfolded; I had blindly to put my hands on the shoulders of the person opposite me - without knowing who this was - and I had to do what I was told. I had to go out suddenly into the cold night, out of the stage area, with no idea of where I was going. I felt I was going to fall on the stone steps, in the mud, in the bushes; I heard strange sounds, of drums, snail shells, birds and human voices, and had to enter into this experience. So I related this. I

---

62 Ethel Krauze: Cultural journalist for *Excelsior*.

said that it was an experience well worth going through. Nicolás Núñez told me something later which pleased me a great deal, that I had understood what this participatory theatre business meant, because I had had no previous, shall we say, theoretical experience of it. I had experienced it as a spectator and I had understood it. Hence this invitation to launch his book.

I said at the beginning that I had a lot more to do with writing than with the stage. I have, however, obliquely experienced something of the stage. I was once the co-author of a collective theatrical show. I have also been on stage, and have done various things in theatre, although my writing deals basically with other genres. In this first experience of mine in a collective show, which was called *De Mugir a Mujer* (*From Mooing to Being a Woman*), I had the chance to meet one of Nicolás Núñez's disciples, Jaime Soriano, who prepared the group of women with whom we performed this production in 1983, when we were at the Casa del Lago for a time. He gave us workshops on bodily expression and from then on, also for the first time in my life, I understood that we have a body as well as a head and that if we do not get it going, our head will be of very little use. There I learned to allow myself to drift through my senses, to dare to close my eyes, to understand that the strength of the senses is not in our sight, as the major mover of human communication, as has been claimed, but in other things: in our senses of smell and especially touch, and it is in our hearing and in the possibilities of the voice itself. This could appear to sound rather elementary or commonplace: 'Close your eyes and see what you feel'. Nevertheless, whoever has experienced it knows that it is a unique experience. So I had something of a memory of that experience in the bodily expression workshop with Jaime Soriano and, driven on by the need to get into these different orbits from the ones we are used to, I approached the phenomenon of participatory theatre, wrote about it and finally got hold of a text, a document in which all the bases are set out. This is the book which we are presenting today, *Teatro antropocósmico*.

There I discovered where it comes from, why, what it is looking for, in what way it is based on the most ancient traditions and, at the same time, in what way it is renewing the concept of theatre; in what way it is very old as well as being extremely up to date, and how it can involve us all, because I think that is one of the great meanings of this theatre on which Nicolás Núñez and his group are working: the fact that everybody can be involved. It is not only for theatrical people, it is for everybody. If we really open theatre up and put it in a house, in the street, wherever there is a human being, that is where we can have theatre. That is what we discovered with the book which we are presenting today, so I preferred to write a short text which I would like to read out and share with you. So as not to go off at a tangent or go on too long, I noted down a few points which this book suggested to me and which I consider to be fundamental or essential and very synthetic:

Teatro antropocósmico is the result of more than ten years of experience in the *Taller de Investigació*n Teatral at UNAM, founded by Nicolás Núñez in 1975. It is an original, Mexican, extremely up to date proposal, which seeks to renew the concept of theatre and which, at the same time, starts off from the most ancient traditions of three continents. This ability to unite traditional with modern, national with universal, artistic with social, is perhaps one of the most beneficial characteristics of the proposal, which does not come to a close but rather serves as a springboard for new explorations. In this sense, the *Taller*'s *Teatro antropocósmico* proposal is not a particular school or trend whose aim amounts to no more than the field itself, nor is it a specific area of knowledge about the theatrical world; it is, above all, an attitude in which we find its zeal for renewal and its importance. I say attitude because *Teatro antropocósmico* wants to turn theatre into a vehicle of self knowledge, of both the body and the mind, 'so as to give back to the organism its ability to be the echo box of the cosmos', as is said in the text. That is to say, it is not the usual stage where action is performed and fiction is pretended before a number of spectators, but rather in a space where we are going to discover, with all our senses open, what we are and what we have around us. It is, therefore, participatory, and not merely informative or entertaining theatre.

How. Where this attitude springs from. What results have been achieved. How it is done in practice. These are the answers which the book offers us. We learn that the process has been long, winding and meticulous and that its sources are so varied that they range from the ancient East to the modern West via the pre-Hispanic world. The Workshop members recount their experiences in India, where they studied Tibetan theatre, and their discovery of dance and the voice as key elements of rite. They also describe their work in different parts of the Mexican Republic researching Nahuatlan theatre so as to understand our roots in ceremonies, dances, and the use of all the voice's vibrations as a means of purification.

Then comes the western section: Stanislavski's here and now, Brechtian techniques, and the Workshop's experiences at the Old Vic theatre in England, at the Strasberg Institute in New York, with Grotowski in Mexico and Poland.

From each of these sources the *Taller*, or the gang, as Nicolás Núñez calls it, has taken theoretical coincidences and practical tools which form the infrastructure of the book *Teatro Antropocósmico*.

The author says:

> The ways of learning theatre here in Mexico generally separate us from our specific reality, bring about a certain type of schizophrenia in us and divide us, because they oblige us to behave with attitudes, clothes and ways of viewing the world which do not correspond to our reality. We are not European, nor are we fair-haired. We are dark and we live in Mexico. How can we avoid the harm that these systems can do to us, and yet at the same time take advantage of them? I think this is possible. The harm lies in their way of disorienting us; the benefit is in their particular exercises.

These sentences offer a perfect definition of the attitude of assimilation and renewal which the Theatre Research Workshop keeps alive.

All of the members, as Mexican performers - that is how they refer to themselves, and deliberately not as actors - take on the commitment to develop a particular line of work which they define as the possibility of the performer-magician, somebody who takes a sacrificial path serving as a bridge between the sacred and the profane; a performer announced by Einstein, sought by Jung, visualised by Stanislavski, incarnated by Artaud, researched by Grotowski and known intuitively by the majority of people dedicated to theatre.

It is this type of performer who corresponds to our times and whom we should seek in our work.

To exemplify these quests, three schemes for participatory theatre which have been developed over the last few years are explained in the book: *Aztlán*, *Tonatiuh* and *Huracán* were performed in different parts of Chapultepec Forest. There are also accounts written by the participants themselves, in the form of poems, letters, and words which have been said on different occasions about these productions. In other words, it is a very vivid set of accounts, very much flesh and blood, as indeed are all those who belong to this group.

I will only add that *Teatro antropocósmico* is an adventure well worth facing up to against the paralysis of one's body, mind, will, sensitivity and imagination - a paralysis which is imposed on us by today's ways of life. Thank you very much.

A speech made by Fernando de Ita on the night of 15th December 1987 at the Casa del Libro Universitario, to mark the first edition of *Teatro antropocósmico*

I understand that theatre is fundamentally about one man meeting another. I think that in the work of almost fifteen years undertaken by the Theatre Research Workshop at UNAM founded by Nicolás Núñez, what is worthy of particular emphasis is their quest and their way of conducting this meeting. We now know that in all cultures, dramatic performance is born from propitiatory rite in which the community finds itself among the forces of nature, with the invisible forces which have dominated this rite from the very beginning. Theatre is born from rite and then it flees from it as one would flee from a plague.

One of the problems faced by this type of research at the beginning of the seventies, was somehow linked to the horror felt by left-wing thought with regard to any type of artistic expression involving religion.

Midway through this century, the proletarian parties (following, I really feel, the Marxist exegesis that religion is the opium of nations), denied without any previous research any connection between art, myth, rite and religion. Curiously, only recently Heberto Castillo, the presidential candidate for the Mexican Socialist Party, swore that he would defend the right to religion and what is sacred to a people whose very culture depends on this sense of the religious and the sacred.

I turn to the launch of the book in this way because when we first began, a few years ago, to present the work of Nicolás and the *Taller*, certain critic colleagues who wear blinkers when they judge things accused us of being reactionaries for supporting a project which attempts to eliminate the petit bourgeois idea of 19th Century theatre, theatre whose only use is to entertain, on a particular stage. Since the beginning of this research which has followed its winding course - as Ethel correctly said - the idea was how I should meet the next man; how I should establish this relationship in a myth, in contemporary rite.

My role in the *Taller* has been somehow to represent the sceptical, earthly side of things - if I may use the expression - in the sense of linking this quest to the reality of our country and our times.

The *Taller*, as is also stated in the book, and the very research into the concept of anthropocosmic theatre, which could suddenly sound like a puff of opium or a mirage of the mind, actually stems from two very important, extremely verifiable pieces of wisdom. One of them is the use of philosophy, cosmogony, the conception of Central American peoples, of the first settlers on this earth, and the other is the contemporary sense of dramatic action and scientific research. As Ethel also pointed out, these two sources with one foot in the past and the other in the future suddenly produce something which cannot yet be seen and above all cannot yet be understood.

I would like to mention particularly the *Taller*'s underground, obscure, vilified work in terms of the extent to which researchers, critics and theatre people have more or less set about condemning something which they do not know and understand, instead of criticising something with which they do not agree. This is important because it is a beautiful thing to see a group of people who have given their all with passion, delirium and madness, to a project which receives no subsidy - because the fact that the group is involved with the University does not mean that it is subsidised. On the contrary, one of the certainties of this love of one's work is given to us by the fact that the majority of people who work here do so because they are happy to be involved in research, not to receive an emolument for their work. The media, I repeat, have omitted to talk about a *Taller* which for more than a decade has been researching into what could be the rite of our times.

I think that after a very materialistic moment in our society, many groups from many parts of the world, with many different attitudes, are suddenly going to finish the millennium seeking to recapture the original sources of thought and action. Beyond any millennialism there may be in this, what Nicolás and the *Taller*'s work brings to the fore is this need - to use Nicolás's own words - to look into each other's eyes and find in the other person what we have lost, which is from the deep identity of the human being to the, also deep, meaning of life.

I believe that what the work aims to do in its essence is to rediscover the will to be on earth, here and now, and it is a task which we should embrace with pleasure, because it is based on the premises of the pre-Hispanic world, which valued life on learning that its destiny was mortal. In a world of death I really think it is worthwhile believing in a rediscovery of the essences of what we are, what we were and what we will be.

The *Taller*, as is also stated in the book and as Ethel has mentioned too, has a whole range of influences. One of the first reasons for criticism has been the thinking that as it is close to ritual and striving for sacred meaning in life, it is therefore something esoteric, something anthropocosmic and out of place, and no effort has been given to indepth research into what this anthropocosmic proposal is. Why is man, with his body, the echo box of the universe? This sentence, which appears futuristic or hollow, suddenly takes on a deep meaning when we attend the *Taller*'s projects. It must be made clear that this is work which for many years has been devoted to a daily, constant praxis. It is not merely a theory worked on in a void but, basically, work carried out in reality. I think it is here that the critics with no deep knowledge of the work have lost the very meaning of the research.

As they criticise the work because of the sources which the members of the *Taller* pursue, due to their closeness to Grotowski, their ritual meaning - this I would stress - and their refusal to approach daily work, work which people do every day in an extremely disciplined way, they have lost sight of the fact that a research proposal is not only being carried out in theory, in a void, but above all in practice; people are seeking to find through daily practice this proposition that the actor's, or man's, body is seriously an echo box in which a great deal of things explode, from the past to the present and future of man.

I would very much like to invite you to read this book because I believe it summarises a type of research which it is worthwhile to follow in Mexico, a type of theatre which, moreover, does not deny other theatrical trends.

In his presentation of the book, Nicolás says that there are as many theatres as there are performers in the world, and accepts a plurality which he himself has been denied since the time when his research - and I repeat, this is what I would like to emphasise - was dodged, criticised and not properly understood. This is what often happens to us here in this beautiful country of cannibals in which we eat the next person without really knowing who they are, why they exist and what they want. What the *Taller* aims to do - with certain deficiencies, with certain u-turns on the road, with a few revisions which must always happen in this type of research - is simply to find this fundament which man, primitive man, once had, of what was the reason for this rite, this reverence for nature, for rhythmic meanings in life, for natural meanings. Now that we have lost it in a dramatic way, as moreover we really cannot make any more jokes about birds dying in the air, now that the authorities are finally seeing that our world is changing in a dramatic way, that the men and women of this country really are in serious danger of losing their lives, simply due to the atmosphere which we breathe in this city, for example, I sincerely think it worthwhile to read a book which leads us to rediscover fundamental essences of what man is, without aspiring to deal with redemption or religion - in the sense of propaganda - but simply as an act of life which analyses itself so as to propose an action which can really be for the good of the person who does it and the one who sees it.

Finally, I would just like to note that if theatre has always been participatory, if it was born from a communal participation and is performed in this way - although it may have lost this at certain points in history - the interesting thing here is how this contemporary rite is being proposed, how it is proposing to us this breathing of one person with the next, and how research into theatre is being done in reality. There you will see, without much propaganda, that the *Taller* has done a lot of work over a long period of time and I would recommend that you go along, because this research is palpable and can be felt with practice. It is very difficult to talk about this research in merely theoretical terms because the important thing, the secret factor, always happens within the individual and is not transferrable. The best way to read *Teatro antropocósmico* is to experience the *Taller*'s work, as they are open to the public at certain times, and this is when something can happen such as what happened to Ethel, who suddenly found a different way of being at the theatre, a way of being there and participating not only as a mere spectator in her seat but as an actor in a theatrical happening which gives each individual their own experience.

This invitation implies, therefore, that after reading the book you should spread the idea that it is worth following a participatory theatre in Mexico, because I would repeat that precisely because it is Nicolás, and because he has done it in Mexico, this seems to take the shine off the matter. When other propositions suddenly arrive from Denmark, Poland etc, where they are doing the same thing and, in some cases, not with such a good intention nor with such good results, then we really are surprised and we ignore what we are doing here.

I think that people here, certainly in some way, are close to the *Taller* and believe in their work. But the invitation, I repeat, is for you to help this type of artistic manifestation to have a wider meaning, a more concrete diffusion and, above all, a more precise understanding, because we are talking about fifteen years of research and it still feels as if we were in the catacombs. Each of the *Taller*'s projects still requires almost heroic acts to go ahead. From here, I would like to acknowledge the people who have worked for so many years for love of this sense of participation. From here, I offer my acknowledgement to the perseverance of the whole gang with whom I have had some good arguments, with whom I will continue to fight so that this proposition of meeting the next person and looking into each other's eyes may be truer by the day. Many thanks.

A speech made by Héctor Azar[63] on the night of 15th December 1987 at the Casa del Libro Universitario, to mark the first edition of *Teatro antropocósmico*

Nor do I consider myself the most authorised, the most suitable person to talk about this experience, but I do feel I am the most obliged, as a basic commitment to Nicolás.

This obligation has arisen since I bumped into him - for that is the best expression - at a particular moment twenty-five years ago when we did not meet, but rather bumped into each other, quite literally.

We were to see each other again two years later. We were to meet on the stage of the Foro Isabelino - may it rest in peace - through a basic play, because

---

63 Héctor Azar: Professor of Mexican theatre.

it was a play about breaking up, or break-ups, in the plural: Ionesco's *Jeux de Massacre* [*The Killing Game*], in which he was playing various roles together with our dear, unforgettable Espacio 15 Theatre Group, from UNAM. That is where I really saw and verified, or proved to be true, a series of things which I knew by intuition about Nicolás and which suggested to me that any type of relationship, any type of quest undertaken by Nicolás was, in a certain way, tinged with blood-red plasma, that Londonesque, Draculean type which he tried to propose in his first - not very successful, incidentally - book of short stories: that all his quests were going to poke into the most visceral side of the human being.

I am not surprised by the name of his proposition. He wanted, and still wants, to understand, to stretch out his hand and reach the depths of the essential from his skin inwards and the farthest planet from his skin outwards.

My relationship with him has always had this shade of viscerality. I am not therefore surprised that when he began his specifically theatrical quest, when he decided to take on the quality of a theatre animal, he should have gone specifically to the sources, to where theatre is a human experience, to what Ethel and Femando have referred to as meeting and rediscovering. Meeting and rediscovering whom? Other people. Professor Paz has said that all of us are these other people - what theatre has as an essential element. I am not therefore surprised that Nicolás should go to the sources and hit upon the fact that religion and theatre rock in the same cradle in all civilisations. For it is precisely in theatre where the human being has his only chance to re-bind his interests, be they existential, metaphysical, biological, sentimental or sexual. The only chance the human has, the human being of spectacle, is to provoke images which re-bind men in their interests of these types.

Nicolás's quest from his skin inwards is the quest for many images which had brought on the anguish which belonged only to him and which he was trying eagerly to find outside him. That is why at a particular time he goes to situations, places and times so remote as for example Tibet, where he will have had his problems. Coming from an upper-middle-class family, hidden away in mysticisms of the fifth to the tenth order, as we Mexicans would describe it, he goes to the source to drink from the mysticism of the first order. I am not sure if this mysticism can be drunk on a level higher than that of Octavio Paz.

The problems which Núñez surely had when he hit upon all this Tlaxcaltec baggage, all this Chimalpan baggage - and here we pay homage to Tlaxcala and Chimalpa, aside from the fact that it is an unsurpassable painting by José María Velasco - the problems he had, with all his baggage, to get to a source of mysticism, the rising of a troubled sky, re-binding, primary, like Hinduism or Buddhism. Living through these experiences to the full, as he himself indicated at the very beginning, that is how they should be experienced. The scarcely modulated frequency of his vibrations obliges him to get into some really frantic situations in this quest.

After that I have no option other than to go to the spring which nourishes his national condition.

The dialectical process, so to speak, of thesis and antithesis - for that is what they could be: the pre-Hispanic source as a thesis inherent to his national condition, the orientalist antithesis as a presence of the universal - had to take him to convulsions which mean a particular commitment.

I do not know up to what point - Fernando said that it is full of influences and how good that is - but once somebody said to somebody else who was starting to write: that reminds me a lot of García Lorca. The latter somebody replied: of how many people does García Lorca remind us? When you read you should not try to decide what the influence is, but at a particular moment, to what point, in an eclectic, wise manner you can collect the influxes and dodge the rest either elegantly or inelegantly. I do not know the extent of the influences, particularly Artaudian as taught by Grotowski, and to what extent Nicolás affirms the closeness of Artaud himself and his theatre of cruelty with the human sacrifices of the pre-Hispanic world. Artaud was undoubtedly looking from the window of his madness and the pre-Hispanic world functioned from the re-binding need of better emotions and better gratifications to the end.

I find this book fulfilling because it talks a lot about things which Nicolás finds fascinating, because it speaks a great deal about things and to people whom Nicolás and I find fascinating, like Oscar Zorrilla, for instance, our beloved friend who is not absent because we think of him often.

The projects which Nicolás undertook with Oscar ought to be more abundant. That is the real position, as pointed out by those who spoke before me, about having one foot in Mexico and the other in the world. Not only Mexico in the twentieth century, how sad that would be. The foot in Mexico covers 500 years where, through theatre, Europe came to instil into the inhabitants of these regions a way of being and existing which was based on miracle. It was that medieval theatre which was really brought by the conquest, the true conquest of Mexico because it was the conquest of the spirit. It was not the violence of the conquest of Cortés and his captain, which was the same from the bars of Puerto de Palos to the bars of Caádiz, that operated in the conquest of Mexico. It was religious, medieval theatre, through instituted miracles which substituted the religion of the defeated, which means that these people live by a miracle, this theatre of miracles, and live every day through such a miracle. For me, one logical consequence of this proposition of Nicolás's, his gang, his colleagues, is finding the real link between the aspirations of those pre-Hispanic theatrical schemes tinged, transformed, suppressed, conformed by medieval theatre, and coming to deal with findings which, on the one hand, of course, bring up the thing which so worries the current-day Mexican state, national identity, but above all, they bring up conclusions which, derived from the Theatre of Sources, come to speak to us in a clearer way. Theatrically, this is a way of existing and being which characterises our Mexican of today.

The book *Teatro antropocósmico* is a proposition - as I understand it - and a commitment. The way of sealing it is to say this is the sociological, anthropological consequence which can help us to understand this miraculous way of living supported only by miracle, the miracle of life, the miracle of death which characterises our national condition not only from the borders inwards but also in terms of our borders with the rest of the world.

Mexico is a magical country, as is said continually, but I am sure that people say this because the magic cannot be explained and because there are a lot of things which are not explained to us by those who govern us, nor by those who drive us, nor indeed can artists explain them. Magic cannot be based on that.

I feel that Nicolás' proposition is important for that reason, because it relates for us situations from the past which go beyond the estimations of the venerable Father Garibay and the no less venerable Miguel León Portilla, Horcasitas, and so many people who have told us a thousand times that the pre-Hispanic theatre schemes cannot be analysed according to European criticism, and we should delve into the sources. If we go to the sources of other countries, of other, more closed mysticisms - excuse the pleonasm - of other, more impenetrable mysticisms which are of use to us, it is to try and help others in this encounter about which we are all talking. We talk about this because the book beats with this between the lines, in the lines themselves, continually. It is the desire of the author to meet us specifically through something which means theatre, which, due to its audiovisual condition, knows perfectly well that something can be understood more and better if it is both seen and heard than if it is just either seen or heard.

I offer my warmest regards to Nicolás, as I always have done, and wish him every success for his book.

ANTHROPOCOSMIC THEATRE

CONTRIBUTORS

Nicolás Núnez has been director of the *Taller de Investigación Teatral*, based at UNAM, Mexico, for more than forty years. He has created numerous psychophysical performance training dynamics and participatory theatre productions. He is the author of *Anthropocosmic Theatre*, amongst other titles. Nicolás is a Visiting Professor in the Centre for Psychophysical Performance Research at the University of Huddersfield.

John Britton is a theatre director and trainer of performers. He is Artistic Director of DUENDE and of The DUENDE School of Ensemble Physical Theatre, and author of *Encountering Ensemble* and *Climbing the Mountain: The Performer's Journey into Presence*.

Etzel Cardeña holds the endowed Thorsen Chair in the Department of Psychology at the University of Lund. He has more than 300 scientific publications in areas dealing with consciousness, and has delivered international keynote speeches in psychology and performance. He has also worked professionally as theatre director, actor, and playwright in Mexico, the United States, and Sweden. While in Mexico he was a member of the *Taller* and has maintained contact with Nicolás and Helena since then.

Franc Chamberlain is Professor of Drama, Theatre, and Performance at the University of Huddersfield.

Cash Clay lives and works in a meditation center in France. She has worked with Nicolàs Nùñez a number of times since 1995 and collaborated with him as a performer in 2016, 2017 and in 2018. She recently completed an MA (Research) in Drama, Dance and Performance at the University of Huddersfield which focused on aspects of her work with Nùñez.

Edward McGurn is a Drama Lecturer, working throughout the United Kingdom. He has participated in the work of Nicolás Nùñez, both in the UK and in Mexico. He has a strong commitment to the psychophysical training of actors, and has published work on the subject of embodiment.

Deborah Middleton is a writer, and a Senior Lecturer in Drama, Theatre and Performance at the University of Huddersfield. Since 1993, she has published a number of journal articles about aspects of Nicolás Nùñez's work, which she is also authorized to teach. Since 2017, she has written three performance texts in creative collaborations with Núñez in Panama, Mexico, and the UK.

Daniel Reis Plá is a Lecturer in Drama, Theatre and Performance at the Universidade Federal de Santa Maria, Brazil. He has published a number of journal articles on meditation and contemplative practices applied to actor training, and is coordinating the project 'Contemplative practices and meditation in higher education: perspectives for creation and learning in the performing arts'.

Cassiano Sydow Quilici is a Professor of Contemporary Theatre and Performing Arts at the State University of Campinas (UNICAMP), and has published several articles and books related to intercultural studies and performance, particularly about Eastern traditions and Latin American cultures.

Karoliina Sandström is an actor, director and the coordinator of the BA in Theatre at Universidad de las Americas Puebla, Mexico. Since 2006 she has trained in the *Taller* actor training dynamics, first under the guidance of Deborah Middleton and later as a *Taller* member. In 2014 she acquired the authorization to practice the work from Nicolás Nùñez. She has participated in various *Taller* productions, and has functioned as the organizer and assistant teacher for international *Taller* workshops.

Ana Luisa Solis Gil has been a member of the *Taller* since 1980. She is a teacher of the art and history of the ancient cultures of Mexico, and founded the *Escuela de Flor y Canto* in which she shares and facilitates Maya Toltec teaching techniques. In this school a path with heart is travelled for those who seek to achieve a firm face and a wise heart. She has published a book as well as pre-Hispanic music.

Tray Wilson is a performer, and Course Leader in Performance at University Campus Oldham, UK. She has trained with Nicolás Nùñez on numerous occasions since 1993 as part of his visits to the University of Huddersfield. In 2018 she worked with Nicolás Nùñez, Deborah Middleton and Cash Clay on the performance project, *Clouds in the Cotton Weave*.

ANTHROPOCOSMIC THEATRE

INDEX

Abramovic, Marina 312.
Actor (capital A) 58; 197; 210;
    Actor Warrior 277-8; 280; 282;
Actor's Studio, The see Strasberg, Lee
Allende, Juan 44; 108; 129; 137; 149; 355; 358.
Anthropocosmic Theatre 3-5; 7; 8; 55; 56; 58; 59; 89-145; 149n; 154; 174; 177-8; 189; 191; 197; 211; 223; 312; 315; 335; 336; 353-362; 367.
Artaud, Antonin 33n; 53; 74; 88; 91; 114; 166; 266; 256; 273; 296; 297; 307; 311; 312; 366; 373.
Ascid 120; 127.
Aztlan 114; 115; 116; 371; 376.

Baudrillard, Jean 279.
Biosphere Project, The 137; 138-140.
Black Hat Dance see Dance
Brecht, Bertolt 8; 53; 56-8; 85; 88; 91.
Britton, John 183-5.
Brook, Peter 53; 76; 102.
Buddha 11; 14.
Buddhism 11; 12; 22; 23; 30; 80; 170n; 194; 198; 206; 229n; 235; 251; 294; 303; 312; 323n; 339; 373.

Campbell, Joseph 177; 276; 303; 312.
Capra, Fritjof 7.
Cardeña, Etzel 168; 215-8.
Castaneda, Carlos 65; 226.
    Tensegrity 226.
Celebration 11; 15; 19; 20; 22; 30; 35; 40n; 42; 43; 47; 48; 59; 125; 297; 304.
Centre for Performance Research 3.
Chamberlain, Franc 150; 251-261.
Chant 16; 39; 48; 49; 117; 119; 127; 133; 161; 162; 165.
Citlalmina 3; 4; 131; 133; 134-138; 149; 154; 160; 163; 164; 165; 169 - 173; 190; 194; 203; 204; 223; 224; 226; 227; 235; 241; 243-244; 311; 321.
Clay, Cash 321-3.
Communitas 155; 176; 183; 189; 199; 210; 211.
Concentration 7; 15; 22; 25; 64; 65; 86; 99; 119; 136; 140; 142; 143; 170; 208; 277; 343.

Consciousness 23; 27; 42; 46; 48; 54; 55; 56; 57; 70; 79; 100; 120; 121; 127; 135; 141; 142; 145; 150; 154; 157; 158; 159; 162; 163; 165; 166; 167; 168; 172; 176; 177; 179; 190; 191f; 196; 197; 199-203; 205-211; 215; 241; 274; 278; 279; 280; 283; 284-286; 290; 297; 308; 312; 315; 317; 318; 327; 328; 331; 332; 333; 353n; 354; 359; 360; 361.

Conspiración Hamlet 289-292.

Contemplative 151; 175; 188; 220; 228; 260; 312; 321; 322; 325.
Trot/Run 115; 116; 118; 119; 128; 158; 160; 164; 165; 166; 167; 174; 187; 201; 223; 224; 225; 236; 237; 238; 241-242; 311.

Cosmology 4; 24; 187; 232.

Cura de espantos 155; 173-177; 231; 252; 260.

Dalai Lama, The 11; 12; 15; 20; 23; 26 - 31; 135; 137; 170; 194; 311.

Dance 3; 4; 11; 12; 13; 14; 15; 16; 18; 19; 20; 21; 22; 23; 24; 25; 26; 29; 33; 35; 41; 42; 43; 45; 46; 47; 109; 116; 125; 128; 129; 133; 134; 135; 136; 137; 138; 158; 160; 170; 174; 188; 194; 205; 244; 257; 259; 265; 276; 291; 296; 310; 311; 312; 316; 318; 321; 323; 356; 365.

Black Hat 11; 22; 23; 25; 170; 194; 205.

Conchero/Shell (*danza conchera*) 24; 33; 36; 44-5; 46-7; 116;119; 128-9; 157; 158;170; 191; 192; 193; 194; 202; 224-5; 238; 311.

Deikman, Arthur 196; 201; 202; 203; 205; 206; 208; 210; 211.

de Ita, Fernando 149; 266; 356n; 366.

Don Faustino 133; 134.

Dorzong Rimpoche 22.

Durkheim, Emile 194; 195; 198; 199.

Dynamics 4; 132; 138; 149; 150; 154; 155; 157n; 157-173; 176; 177; 178; 189; 191n; 191; 192n; 192; 193; 201; 203; 204; 205; 207; 208; 210; 211; 220; 223-239; 243; 273; 281; 282; 311n; 311;

Einstein, Albert 113; 114; 312; 316; 366.

Eliade, Mircea 56; 59; 195; 196; 197; 199; 201;

INDEX

Emotion 3; 15; 17; 43; 56; 59; 63; 64; 65; 66; 69; 70; 71; 89; 90; 95; 96; 97; 113; 156; 159; 163; 171; 174; 175; 207; 209; 241; 257; 267; 270; 272; 275; 297; 305; 309; 315; 317; 337; 338; 340; 341; 345; 350; 356; 357; 373.

Energy 3; 4; 7; 15; 17; 19; 23; 24; 29; 42; 43; 46; 47; 50; 61; 64; 66; 68; 69; 75; 82; 87; 98; 102; 103; 105; 115; 117; 118; 119; 123; 126; 133; 136; 141; 142; 155; 157; 160; 161; 163; 168; 172; 177; 187; 197; 198; 203; 207; 208; 209; 216; 220; 228; 231; 232; 234; 235; 236; 237; 238; 241; 243; 244; 247; 251; 248; 251; 252; 253; 255; 258; 260; 261; 275; 277; 279; 281; 283; 284; 303; 304; 305; 306; 308; 311; 315; 328; 330; 331; 332; 333; 334; 337; 340; 343; 344; 347; 348.

Ensueño de los árboles, El 151; 325-6; 331.

Festival 13; 14; 43; 91; 157n.

Flight of Quetzalcoatl, The 151; 263-6; 269; 273; 276.

Good pain 141; 141n; 230; 271; 274-6

Grimes, Ronald 155; 166; 167; 169.

Grotowski, Jerzy 8; 53; 72-87; 88; 99; 114; 153; 156; 159; 165; 166; 171-2; 177; 184; 210; 224; 225; 251; 253; 254; 255; 256; 258; 259; 273; 307; 311; 312; 353; 358; 365; 366; 369; 373.

Theatre of Sources 72; 74; 80; 81; 84; 86; 153; 165; 166; 171; 224; 225; 256; 374.

Guardia, Helena 6; 26; 44; 62n; 63; 103; 122; 131; 149; 153; 171; 193; 207; 210; 215; 223; 224; 226n; 243; 322; 355; 358.

Guna/Guna Yala, Panama 325; 326; 330.

Gurdjieff, G.I. 100.

Happening 55.

Hauser, Arnold 54.

High Risk Theatre 150; 189; 204; 230; 266; 267-287.

Hocasitas, Fernando 33-41; 45; 46; 375.

Huichol/an 48; 49; 79; 80n; 81; 82; 83; 84; 85; 132; 156; 157; 191; 331.

Huracán 114; 120-9; 131; 149; 223; 227; 366.

James, William 195; 198.

Jung, C.G. 24; 62; 114; 157; 177; 274; 275; 366.
Kabat-Zinn, Jon 312.
Khamtul Yeshe Dorje Rimpoche 22.
Kikiriki 227; 232-3; 232n.

León Portilla, Miguel 33; 33n; 34; 35; 41; 44; 375.
López Austin, Alfredo 33; 33n; 35.
Los Cenci 3.

Mandala 4; 23; 46; 98; 136; 294-6; 297.
Mandala: The Sacred Art of Acting 6; 150; 228; 293-310.
Mara'akame 48; 84; 156; 191.
Maria Sabina 50; 50n; 332.
McGurn, Edward 219; 230.
McLuhan, Marshall 120; 277; 317.
Meditation 4; 22; 23; 24; 25; 46; 119; 135; 136; 158; 164; 166; 170; 175; 193; 201; 202; 205; 206; 210; 211; 216; 224; 225; 229; 235; 238; 239; 241; 243; 264; 311.
Middleton, Deborah 5; 6; 149; 150; 153; 170n; 189; 192; 192n; 193;194; 201; 204; 205; 207; 208; 210; 211; 215; 233; 224; 224n; 225; 226; 226n; 227; 229n; 233; 235n; 238; 253n; 256; 260; 263; 264; 265.

Mindfulness 61; 151; 187; 188; 228; 231; 243; 311; 312; 316.
Monk, Meredith 312.
Morris, Eilon 204; 205; 206; 229; 230; 234; 234n; 235; 237; 251; 252; 258.
Moyocoyatzin 1 227; 230.
Myth 4; 12; 34; 43; 108; 110; 126; 156; 173; 177; 178; 263; 270; 271; 304; 356; 367.
Music 16; 20.

Nahuatlan: Philosophy 5; 46; 51; 94; 99; 137; 140; 251; 354; 359; 361; 365.
  Song 34; 43; 110; 111; 127.
  Theatre 4; 7; 8; 24; 33-52; 84n; 99; 132.
Nanahuatzin 227; 233-4; 244-5; 247-9; 263; 264; 265.
NASA 137; 138
Natyasastra 17.
Nicolescu, Basarab 312; 315.
Nietzsche, Friedrich 57; 258; 307.
Nychthemeron (Nictémero) 99-108; 131.

Old Vic, The 51; 60-1; 88; 365.
Olmeca 1 227; 235-6.
Opera (Tibetan) 12-21; 25.
O'Toole, Peter 60-1.
Otto, Rudolf 195; 198.

Ouspenskaya, Maria 62.
Ouspensky, P.D., 99.

Padmasambhava 11; 22.
Paratheatre 4; 156.
Participatory 3-5; 7-8; 25; 44-6; 51; 114-20; 126; 129-34; 137-138; 149; 154; 173; 177; 191; 223-225; 251; 265-7; 273; 284; 286; 289; 321; 359; 361-64; 366; 370; 377.
Pastorale 38; 44
Paz, Octavio 9; 50-1; 118; 209; 219n; 269; 287; 312; 313; 318; 319; 328; 358; 372-3.
Plá, Daniel 170n; 241-2
Pradier, Jean 99; 114.
Prieto Stambaugh, Antonio 192; 193; 211
Psychophysical 4; 86; 89; 137; 138; 140; 141; 143; 149; 155-60; 163-4; 166-7; 170-172; 176-8; 189-208; 212; 224-5; 227-8; 232; 236; 238; 243; 251; 267; 271; 297; 311; 358; 359;
Puentes Invisibles 321-33

Queztalcóatl 227; 265.
Quilici, Cassiano Sydow 187-8; 234-5.

Rancière, Jacques 150; 256; 258-9.

Rascón Banda, Victor Hugo 173-6
Relaxation 35; 64; 72; 118; 158; 201; 227; 237-8; 242.
Rhythm 12; 15; 42; 49; 53; 55; 56; 71; 78; 87; 104; 105; 109; 118; 123; 132; 133; 135; 136; 137; 144; 158; 162; 163; 164; 165; 170; 174; 193; 194; 201; 205; 211; 223; 225; 227; 228; 229; 237-8; 241; 247; 257; 264; 265; 271; 276; 282; 312; 318; 327; 339; 343; 362; 370.
Rickwood, Lee 204; 211.
Rite 5; 7; 24; 25; 33-59; 73; 81; 91; 134; 153; 156; 159; 170; 174-76; 178; 209; 228; 230; 269-284; 298; 304; 306; 339; 357; 360; 365; 366-71.
Eleusinian 228; 269; 279; 294.
Ritual 3; 4; 7; 9; 15; 23; 24n; 25; 35; 37; 44; 45n; 47-8; 54; 74; 77; 78; 89; 110; 132-34; 149; 153-179; 183; 189-212; 226; 231; 238; 239; 251; 253; 257; 263; 265; 276-7; 279; 280; 304; 315; 323n; 325; 332; 357; 369.
Roerich, George 16.
Roerich, Nicholas 16.
Rolmoe Tenchoe 16-7.
Roth, Gabrielle 219.

Sandström, Karoliina 6; 203; 210; 234; 241; 243-5; 289-92; 293n.
Sartre, Jean-Paul 113
Schechner, Richard 53; 99; 110; 114; 159; 180; 209; 273; 315; 316.
Sensitization 226; 308; 325.
Shakespeare 53; 129-31; 144; 174; 289; 299; 300; 310; 312; 338; 362.
Shaman 11-12; 48; 50; 84; 131; 134; 156; 157; 189; 191; 197; 201; 219; 273; 326; 332.
Shambhala 135;180; 209; 277.
Shell dance See Dance.
Snail shell 27; 41-2; 100; 102; 106-8; 109-10; 116; 118; 119; 124; 128; 131; 164; 355; 362.
Solís Gil, Ana Luisa 26; 109-10; 132; 192n; 226n; 325-6; 355
Sologub, Fyodor 150; 257-8.
Stanislavski, Konstantin 8; 53-6; 61; 62; 64; 67; 70; 86; 88; 91; 98; 114; 153; 159; 168; 217; 231; 239; 251; 253-5; 335; 353; 365; 366.
Strasberg, Lee 61-5; 72; 88; 99; 153; 365.

Tai Chi 4; 343-4;
Tempest, The 129-31; 278; 362.

Templeton, Deborah 321
Tezcatlipoca 37; 227; 231; 291; 318.
Thangton Gyalpo 12; 18.
Theatre: Laboratory 51; 73-5; 87; 120; 146; 253-4; 357-8.
Mexican 3; 33-52; 84; 86; 134-5; 355; 358;
Nahuatlan 4; 7; 8; 24; 33-52; 84n; 99; 132.
Tibetan 12-21; 25.
Tibetan Institute of Performing Arts 7; 11-25; 51; 153.
Tloque Nahuaque 108; 211; 223; 227.
Tonatiuh 114; 116-119; 123; 131; 149; 158; 163; 164-9; 223; 225; 227; 234; 361; 366.
Transdisciplinarity 302; 315.
Transformation 8; 75; 161; 163; 175-179; 187; 189; 209; 211; 216; 229; 230; 234-5; 236; 243; 247; 253; 255; 256; 258; 282; 302; 305; 308; 316; 332; 354.
Tsering, Tashi 16.
Turner, Victor 155; 160-2; 169; 178; 273; 277; 303.

Valencia, Rodolfo 43.
Velasco Piña, Antonio 29; 150; 192-3; 365; 373
Verticality 234-5; 312; 315; 319.

Vibration 15; 22; 24; 25; 27; 48; 50; 119; 131; 137; 164; 223; 225; 295; 323; 328; 338; 360; 365; 373.
Voice 17; 22; 24; 25; 29; 34; 36; 43; 44; 48; 50; 101; 115; 118; 120; 128; 137; 140; 299; 313; 317; 323; 344; 357; 362; 363; 365.

Weisz, Gabriel 33.
Wilber, Ken 206-7.
Wilson, Tray 234; 247-9.
Worley, Lee 312.

Yoga 4; 80; 163; 224.

Zarrilli, Phillip 167.
Zen 80; 167; 339.
Zorrilla, Oscar 33; 84; 374.